Di
Lo
Shrink ...
the Wash?

BOOKS BY KRISTEN BAILEY

Has Anyone Seen My Sex Life?
Can I Give My Husband Back?

KRISTEN BAILEY

Did My Love Life Shrink in the Wash?

bookouture

Published by Bookouture in 2021

An imprint of Storyfire Ltd.
Carmelite House
50 Victoria Embankment
London EC4Y 0DZ

www.bookouture.com

ISBN: 978-1-83888-973-9
eBook ISBN: 978-1-83888-972-2

This book is a work of fiction. Names, characters, businesses,
organizations, places and events other than those clearly in the
public domain, are either the product of the author's imagination
or are used fictitiously. Any resemblance to actual persons, living or
dead, events or locales is entirely coincidental.

This book is for my babies.
And for Joe. I finally named a character after you.

Prologue

'Babies' – Pulp (1992)

The first time I had sex, all I could think about was getting pregnant. There I was lying quite naked under the duvet of one Christian Riley (seventeen years old, blue eyes, loved The Cure, now fixes fridges) and the only thing that went through my head was how scared I was of bringing this boy's kid into the world and becoming a teenage single mother. All I could see were the ruddy faces of middle-aged biology teachers, the righteous tones of my mother echoing in my ears. *I don't want to be a mother. I can't be a mother.*

Needless to say, the sex was a bit of a non-event. I spent most of the time asking him if the condom was on, never came and watched in bewilderment as his bulging eyeballs informed me that he had. Any momentary joy was only experienced some fifteen days later, after my period made her appearance and I squealed with delight in a toilet cubicle, so loudly that a rumour started that someone was masturbating in the college loos.

My sexual adventures soon progressed at university where, admittedly, I thought less about the possibility of babies, and more about personal fulfilment, exploring the potential joys of a penis around my person. There were episodes of morning-after shocks, morning-after pills, sex in cars, great sex, stoned sex, stranger sex, bad sex, your best mate's crush sex, on a countertop fridge to get revenge on Paul who dumped me the night before my first-year exams sex. A fair bit of sex. As university should be, I was party to an educational experience that enhanced my interpersonal relations and allowed me to build a credible and applicable skills base.

Then I left university, and I started having real-world sex which is like university sex except the rent is higher. On a teaching placement, I shagged the head of PE (decent cock; made hamster noises throughout). I went out *a lot* and hooked up with postgrads who ran marathons but lived in house shares with bad Wi-Fi and rotting bathrooms. One time I half had sex with my sister's brother-in-law (non-penetrative dry humping in the back of a black cab; they bring that story up to shame me at most family meals). I had a couple of flings that never really went the distance, a couple of relationships that ended in heartbreak (I'm talking to you, Tom Edwards; he who shagged his ex-girlfriend the night he broke up with me).

Until along came a young man called Will Cooper and with him, sex in a long-term relationship. Being on the pill gave me licence to envisage babies as part of our sketchy, future life plan of suburbs, family motors and possible rings on fingers. For now, there was just spontaneous sex, condom-less sex, comfortable sex, know-how-to-make-me-come sex, unshaven legs sex, make-up sex, sex in the shower, sex on an IKEA coffee table that couldn't take our collective weight (ending with plywood splinters in my arse cheeks). Sex because we loved each other.

Then one birthday weekend in October, we ended up at one of those electronic music festivals in a London park where we consumed far too much alcohol, painted our faces dayglo and had drunk sofa sex when we got home. I awoke the next morning worse for wear and forgot to take my pill. Or I may have thrown it up. That bit I don't remember. And now, I'm lying in a hospital bed, having trouble looking over my bump as a midwife called Maggie wears me like a hand puppet.

And believe it or not, as I lie here, it's young Christian Riley who jumps into my head: scuffling about in his bedside drawer, pretending that those weren't the first condoms he'd ever bought in his life. I think back to that atypically responsible teenager who understood the biological realities of the situation. I lie here revelling in the irony that I have become such a rubbish adult. For as soon as I had pushed babies out of mind, into some realm of contraceptive impossibility... well, here I am. I seriously think that Maggie has her whole hand in there.

It's a Wednesday night. I'm fourteen days overdue so I'm being induced, having just experienced another sweep, though I might need to get Trading Standards in on that debacle. A 'sweep' is a light, feathery motion favoured by orchestral conductors and autumnal leaves. I would have defined what I just experienced as a looter's ransacking of my undercarriage. In the neighbouring bed, another pregnant woman called Kate is giving explicit instructions to her husband, Rob, as to the whereabouts of her forgotten paper knickers. According to my sister I won't need those. 'Imagine knickers made from kitchen roll,' she tells me. I don't suppose to tell Kate. She has brought the baby car seat along and everything. Ours is in the boot of the Suzuki Swift. I hope.

Will's holding one of my hands, looking though a names website on his phone. 'What about Rex?'

'Like the dinosaur? The musical band? Or Harrison?'

'Who's Rex Harrison?' he enquires.

Lordy, you think you know people. I'm about to have his child.

Maggie the Midwife interrupts. 'Looks like you're only one centimetre dilated, my dear.'

Maybe she's joking.

'He's just too happy in there.'

She's not. She continues to lecture us with some authority about drips and possible two-day labours while my eyes glaze over. Maybe I'll be like an elephant and gestate for three years and they'll make a Channel 4 documentary about me. 'The baby was "too happy" in there so grew and emerged as a feral toddler beast with long mullet hair, suckling until he was ten. The mother grew to the size of a house and survived the gestational period in a series of kaftans made of old curtains.'

Maggie looks unamused by me, like I won't provide any good midwifing excitement for a couple of days, so she gathers her gloves and giant tube of lube, abandoning us. Will still mumbles about baby names like Ace and Gandalf. I think it's to hide the fact that he's nervous as balls about what's going to happen in the next day or so. That's if this baby ever comes out. I huff with boredom and realise the only way to better my disappointment is with babies of the jelly variety.

'Why don't you eat the green ones?' asks Will, his fingers raking through the sweets.

'They look like bogeys?'

He doesn't question it. We're strangely silent. He then directs an impromptu jelly baby play on the bed sheets. I am red and he is green. It starts innocently enough – the jelly babies slow dance for a while to a porno soundtrack which makes me giggle. However, they end up quite quickly in a 69 position.

'Why is my jelly baby so easy?' I ask.

He pops them in his mouth. 'She wore red, the hussy. What did the midwife put inside you?'

'Some sort of hormone gel.'

'How does it feel?'

'Like my vagina just ate an oyster.'

'I love you.'

'I love you too.'

A kiss. He always kisses me on the forehead. I like to think of it as a tender gesture of love but he often jokes it's because I talk a lot. I tend to ramble, so he can never get near enough to my lips. A smooch on the forehead allows him to display love but also calm me down like an off switch.

'How about Spike?' he asks.

'Dog's name.'

'Ted?'

'Bundy.'

'Noah?'

'Too biblical.'

'Henry?'

'Too… royal.'

Will puts his head on my pillow and looks up at me like a forlorn cat.

'Adolf?'

'Wanker.'

'That's a terrible name. You can't call a baby Wanker.'

I laugh. He puts his hands in mine and pulls me up in the same way you see whales being released back into the sea.

'C'mon. Midwife's orders. Let's go for a shuffle.'

I decided to have this baby in a hospital because I just wanted to go down the easiest route possible. At my NCT groups, there was a mix of women who touted around birthing pools, home births and hypnobirthing but I always took a more practical approach: I don't want fuss, I don't want a baby in a bath, if I ask for drugs then give them to me, let's get this baby out. Zero expectation would mean that no one would end up disappointed if it all went wrong. My sisters birthed babies in a variety of ways: Meg had the emergency C-section as her little Eve was upside down, Emma had her girls in posh hospitals with birthing centres where they gave away free pyjamas. I opted for my local hospital that provide extras like birthing exercise balls, free hot drinks and dimmer switches but you have to bring your own slippers and snacks. I bought said slippers from Primark. As for the snacks, Emma told me to bring glucose tablets for energy in case I have one of those eight-hour inductions but I haven't eaten those since I did cross-country running when I was eleven.

I look down now and the slippers are the wrong size. My feet look like bricks they're so swollen. I toddle along next to Will, who looks like he's taken his pregnant girlfriend on a walk. The walk is supposed to push things in the right direction, downwards I suppose, so we're doing as we've been told. I spy a rainbow of vending machines and stop. Ice cream. It's been nine long months of Will getting to know and understand how pregnant ladies must be fed so he rustles around in his pockets.

'Are there any fancy ones?' I ask. Now is not the time to fob me off with a crappy fruit-based lolly.

He looks at me, bemused. 'They've got Magnums: white, normal or nuts?'

'Nuts. Get three. One for the baby.'

'The baby might like white chocolate.'

'I know the baby likes nuts.'

'Do we get a sense of which football team he might support?' he asks.

I smile. 'He's a Gunner. I feel it. Can we call him Thierry? Bergkamp? Tony? A combination of all the Arsenal legends, perhaps.'

'It's like you want me to leave you to birth on your own.'

We find a window bay to perch ourselves on. It's silent, bar the crack of chocolate, mainly due to nerves about all that unknown territory we are throwing ourselves into. When they say a baby isn't planned then you start to realise what that really means. It means the sketchy blueprint that was once life is being totally rewritten, with all control and free will lost. When I got pregnant it was scary as crap, but all Will and I knew was that we liked each other enough to bring a baby into the world. I drop a bit of chocolate on my bump and am grateful it's there to catch it. See how useful the baby is already? I retrieve the chocolate and pop it in my mouth. Will looks over and laughs. I wasn't going to waste that. He then hugs me, the only way you can hug a pregnant woman: with your body arched out to the side.

Wait. I think Will may have squeezed so hard a little bit of pee came out. I pause for a moment. Something definitely just happened. Like someone's fired a water pistol up me. Have my waters broken? I stare at my feet. Not the tsunami I expected but I clutch Will's hand and he instinctively knows it's time; there's a look in his eyes like a rollercoaster is just setting off. We're having a baby.

'It's just a show, my dear. You've got a while to go yet. Any pain and you can have a paracetamol.'

I glare at Maggie the Midwife. Surely stuff leaking out of you is a warning that the baby is on his way? The curtain closes. I was told that the drugs would be stronger, like stuff I wouldn't be able to get in Boots. A period-like pain stabs at me and I bend over the bed.

Will gets his phone out and sets it to timer mode. 'What exactly am I timing?'

Neither of us know. Will abandons the phone and starts massaging my back. I inspect my knickers again. Blood.

'Is that supposed to be there?' Will asks. I'm not entirely certain myself. Surely all that's supposed to emerge from there is water and babies? Will roots around in my bag and finds my marrow-sized sanitary towels. Whatever boundaries we may have had between us are gone as he sees me attach it to my knickers and lunge to adjust how it sits in my gusset. I don't need to say anything; he can read that emotion in my eyes. What the hell are we doing? We press our call button and I fall into a squat position. Pain. Bad period pains. Will's massage turns into a baker's kneading.

'Siri, WhatsApp call Emma Callaghan,' I hear Will instruct his phone.

I look over my shoulder curiously as he puts the phone on speaker, calling my sister, the doctor.

'Hello, Will? Has she popped yet? I'm adding in the other sisters. Put her on.'

I shake my head. Now is not the time for a phone conference. The screen splits into five different views and all of their faces appear: Meg, Emma, Grace and Lucy. The first two are mothers, the others are not. They all strain their necks, trying to work out if there's a baby in the room.

'We didn't do this for Meg, or you, Ems?' I inform them.

'That was because the technology wasn't available. What's happening? Are we in a position to livestream?' Meg says, laughing.

'I DON'T WANT TO SEE UP HER VAG!' Lucy shrieks. Will turns the volume down.

'Can we get the midwife to GoPro it?' Grace adds, her screen going fuzzy, in and out of focus. I wave at her. I miss my Grace. What time is it in Japan? Is she in a karaoke room? They all talk amongst each other, someone commenting on the weather and someone asking why Lucy is sitting just in her pants. *Hello? Woman in labour here, you bitches.* They're all laughing at my discomfort. None of them are getting birthday presents.

'Ems, the midwife thinks I had a show. Am I supposed to be bleeding?'

'How bad? Give it to me in egg cups,' she replies.

'Who measures blood in egg cups? I feel like I've got my period.'

'Standard. How many pads have you filled? Waters?'

Ems is like this, efficient. I imagine she coaxed her babies out with an encouraging tone at the precise time of her choosing. The sisters all listen in, Lucy's face a tight grimace.

'I think they're still there,' I reply.

'You think? Mine burst like the banks of the Seine,' Meg tells me. 'All over the kitchen floor. The dog licked them up.' Will retches off screen.

Emma studies my face. 'If you were in real labour then you wouldn't be able to talk, let alone stand.'

'It hurts though.'

'Squat, open up the passages.' Meg had her third five months ago. In her front room. I think they literally walk out of her now.

'Should my back hurt?' I ask.

'Didn't you read those books I gave you?' Emma replied.

I didn't. I read magazines and I binge watched *Friends*. I thought if I saw Rachel and Phoebe give birth enough times then I'd just absorb the knowhow through the screen. The two younger sisters look ashen but also know when they're out of their depth.

'Ems,' Grace pipes in. 'Go easy on her, we love you, B.'

'Yeah, can we go? I don't need to see the pushing and fluids bit. I just want to see the little baby,' admits Lucy. The elder sisters relieve them but then switch their glares in my direction. Guess it could be worse. Our mother could be here. *Beth, we're Callaghan women, we birth things. In the olden days, I am sure we birthed them in fields and went back to work within hours. Pull yourself together.* I wince out loud at another stabbing pain in my back. Meg jumps into action.

'Will, get her to breathe. Long exhalations.' I hand the phone back to my boyfriend and hear the group talk amongst themselves. He nods, his face white, as the two sisters give him instructions. Is she telling him how to check my dilation?

He hangs up and takes a breath. 'Are you sure you're in labour?'

'What?' I know what Meg and Emma would have said. She was always a nightmare on her period, this may be her hypochondriac tendencies coming into play.

'Emma said that it's early to be…'

'Seriously, you can all piss off.'

'OK. Emma told me to get a midwife. I'm going to leave you for just a second. Do you want music?'

I nod. That much I know. We devoted evenings to preparing this playlist in preparation: 'Labour of Love'. Music is a shared love of Will's and mine that the baby needs to inherit or else we will disown him. We have played him everything in our indie lockers; we explained that trance and house are two very different genres; we experimented with classical and rock and punk because we want a child who has edge too. I've even decided to birth him in a Kings of Leon T-shirt. If we play our cards right, this child will end up being an international hit-producing DJ or the next John Lennon. Will sets up my phone and carefully inserts two AirPods into my ears. It's some jazz. Jazz is calming. 'Jaaaaazzzz,' I say in a lilting voice. It'll do. He does some curtain twitching while I feign impending death.

'Go, find someone.'

I climb into the bed and curl into a ball. It's like someone's throwing weights at my stomach, like fire enveloping my nerves. I whimper and suck air through my teeth. Right, let's put those NCT classes to some use: a house on a beach, palm trees and warm summer breezes, the sun shining, waves lilting on the sand – and deep, gut-wrenching spasms pounding my stomach and punching into me like a double-decker bus. I try to gain perspective: this is surely not the worst of it – the midwife said with inductions it could be a wait of up to two days. Two days of this? *Breathe.* Pain means the baby is coming and he will be with us soon.

Crapping mother of tits, that stings. My beach house has been enveloped by an upsurge of liquid magma. Jazz can piss off. Next up on the playlist, Boney M., 'Daddy Cool'. That's some bassline. I hum it out loud but assume a position on the bed on all fours, rocking to that beat like I'm a small bucking donkey. Christ alive, this is horrific. So horrific I yell. Kate and Rob next door stop chattering to eavesdrop. The curtain opens and Will stands there a little confused to see me in the table-top position. I pull him close, retch repeatedly and throw up on him. He looks down at his new trainers, trying not to care. My knuckles turn a lighter shade of pale clutching my metal bedstead. A girl stands there who looks like she's here to wash my hair and sweep the clippings off the floor.

'The midwife will be with you in a minute,' she whispers. 'What's the matter?'

I glare at Will. Is this girl medically trained? How old is she? I want ID.

'I think, I think I'm in labour…'

She shakes her head and reassures me that it will probably be a while yet. I glance at her badge: *Maternity labour assistant trainee breastfeeding clinic girl.* I nod and smile, shooing her away like a pigeon.

'When I die, can you make sure our baby learns to be kind? Make sure he appreciates the outdoors. And Stevie Wonder, play him Stevie.'

I hope Will heard that. Maybe he needs to write it down. He mops my brow and tries to kiss me but I can't even feel it. A dentist could be pulling out my molars now and I wouldn't feel it compared to the volcano that is my abdomen.

'Don't give the baby a stupid name either. Everyone will think he's a tosser.' I wince. Will furrows his brow at me. I am jibber jabbering away which is my default setting when angry or stressed. Usually he solves this with chocolate and leaves the room. I can see the thoughts whirring around his head. *I am pretty sure this is not death.*

'I'll make sure our baby isn't a tosser.'

The curtain moves again and this time it's Maggie, who twitches her eyebrows at the sight of the blood. She hoists my legs up in the air and examines my nether regions.

'Daddy, can you just push the button to the left of the bed, please?'

The button? That's the emergency button. Aren't you supposed to push that if my heart's stopped? Will does as he's told and looks at me, panicked. Another wave of pain strikes me and I bellow out some feral crescendo through the ward. Wolves in London Zoo howl back in reply.

'Yup, Mummy. Looks like that gel worked quicker than we thought. We're about seven centimetres dilated at the minute. Let's get you moved into a room on the labour ward,' she says, trying to contain her concern.

'I can't be. It hasn't been two days yet.'

'Babies don't work to schedules, love.'

Baby. Now? I look into Will's glassy eyes, tears on standby, trying to keep up as he skids around in a puddle of my vomit. Shit, it really is time. I feel Will's hand in mine, fingers squeezed down to the bone. I squeeze back. It's a flurry of activity as they adjust the bed and start to wheel me out of here. Kate and Rob look over at us, ashen. *I'm sure your birth will be much different. There will be candles and stuff. Not like this visceral slanging match I'm having with my own body.*

We stop at a lift. All fours worked before, so I take off the sheets covering my nether regions and try to rearrange myself, baying like a wounded deer, my bulbous arse and much more staring at the face of the porter. This is how farm animals birth and they always look fairly unaffected by the process, I tell myself. Will and the midwife wrangle me down.

'Let's leave that move for upstairs, Mummy.'

Who is Mummy? Oh, that's me. I'm a mummy? Everything is a bustle of strip light, a metal-clad service elevator, nosy onlookers, orange curtains. We suddenly stop. I see Crocs and retch again.

A man with blond hair smiles at me. 'Hi! I'm—'

But the pain charges through me and I arch my back, trying to get off the bed to better position myself.

'Whoa! Careful. If you break your arm, how are you going to hold your new baby?'

At this moment, I'd wear him on my back like a monkey for all I care. Blondie can see my reticence for polite chit-chat, spreads my legs and gloves up, chatting to Maddie from downstairs. Will, who would normally be more protective about who looks at his lady's private areas, has a look too and they all rub their chins like they're figuring out the best way to tackle a blocked drain. Blondie looks up.

'Alright, this baby wants out.'

'DRUGS!' I say with some force.

I'm handed a mouthpiece. I bite down on it and I inhale. Not even inhale, I suck that stuff in like crack. Man, this is good shit. It numbs everything for a small moment and takes my focus elsewhere. I love Will. I really do. I love Blondie here too. I take a couple more hits, wondering why this isn't sold in supermarkets. They need to sell this part of labour far more.

'OK, so I can see the head and I need you to concentrate on pushing. No more gas and air.'

I pout. Will laughs as he tries to prise the mouthpiece from my hands.

'Mine!' I bark back at him. 'I'm not sharing this shit. Get your own.'

'Beth, do what the nice man asked…'

'No.'

Will is forced to wrestle me, which is excellent preparation for fathering a toddler. He releases my fingers from the mouthpiece and transfers them to his hand.

'You can do this, B.'

I suddenly feel pressure. I push and grunt against the flood of pain with every ounce of reason, sweat and gumption I have, waiting for my body to respond. We're doing this, aren't we? Just summon something up and push like a motherfucker, right?

I push.

And push.

And push.

And is that the baby?

No. I think that was an actual poo. Was it? To be fair, I couldn't give a flying fajita right now. I'm just glad I'm not in a bath. Will keeps whispering clichés about pride and love. I inhale some Will instead. He smells fruity. Like jelly babies.

'You need to push down,' Blondie informs me.

I give him an incredulous look, wondering how else I could have indeed been pushing. Up? Sideways? Wait. What in the living daylight of fuck is that? Stinging. What exactly am I giving birth to? A traffic bollard? A watermelon?

Puuuuuuuuuush. A head. The head is out. Blondie asks if I want to touch it but I'm a little scared. And it's crying. I have a crying head hanging out of my foof. I close my eyes and pretend I'm tired and in a deep state of concentration because I'm too ashamed to admit that I don't want to acknowledge my own baby's head. All I can hear is ritualistic chanting about pushing. Part of me wants to tell them to piss off, part of me just wants to meet this baby. I opt for the latter. I bear all my energy through the lower half of my body, ready to propel myself off the bed, my teeth gritted so tightly I feel they might pop out like broken tiles. Where are my legs? I didn't know they could stretch that far apart? My stomach contorts and I feel a strange fish-like presence gliding out of me.

'Congratulations. And we have a boy.'

I don't look down. I lie back, hearing a full-bellied scream as his little lungs fill with air.

Relief. We're OK. He's here. They push him up on top of me and perch him on my chest, gift-wrapped in a yellow NHS blanket.

'Hello,' I whisper.

He doesn't reply. It's a really, really little person. Tiny. He has eyes and ears and toes and everything. I do a swift digit check, because that's what they do on the television. All accounted for. He nestles into my T-shirt which I take as approval for guitar music. Good lad. He stuffs his whole hand in his mouth and stares straight into my eyes. *Hello.*

I await the love to overwhelm me, my world to change. Yet all I feel is slightly confused. Blondie is clambering about with injections, placentas and cutting cords. 'Well done. Now there's a tear that I'll have to fix up. Can you hoist your legs open or do you need stirrups?'

I've pushed a baby out; I can take on the world. Without stirrups. I swing my legs up in the air like a showgirl. The little one still stares at me like he wants me to claim ownership. I'm knackered. The anaesthetic stings. I keep saying 'hello,' not really knowing how to follow that up.

Then I look over at the corner of the delivery room where Will has been taking cover. Eyes glazed over, cheeks moist, both hands on top of his head. I reach out a hand and he comes over to inspect his son. He nestles into me and kisses the baby's head, grimacing as he realises our son is still covered in baby goo. We're both maniacally speechless.

'I'm your midwife,' says Blondie. 'I'm sorry I didn't introduce myself.'

'I'm Beth and this is Will. I'm sorry I shouted.'

'I've had worse. And what about bubba here?'

'Just Baby Cooper for now.'

'Well, I'm Joe.'

Midhusband Joe continues to talk from in between my arched legs. His face and the giant lamp down there are slightly disconcerting, like he's mining for something.

'You did well there, Beth. Some inductions can be brutal like that but A-class pushing if ever I saw it. This is quite a tear but we will sort you out.'

I don't want to envisage what that looks like and frankly, I don't care. The relief that the pain is gone is everything. Instead, I beam. I did that.

Will perches on the bed beside his family.

Family. We are family. I should sing. I don't.

The screaming has subsided. Perfect silence. A bizarre concoction of feelings overcome me: I can feel the adrenalin thrusting through my veins, pride at the marvels of my female biology, disbelief at the speed of everything. Pure shock. I can't quite believe my little body-popping foetus is here in my arms. Someone call my sisters. *Hello. Again.* However, I can't help wanting to ask if this is what he should look like. Is this normal? He has a cone-shaped head, wrinkles and masses of encrusted, flaky skin, lots of colours shining through like a fresh bruise. He even has nails, like tiny claws. He looks annoyed. Not necessarily happy to see me. *This is Will, he's Dad. I'm your mum.* I try and stare him out.

'So, I am done,' whispers Joe. He takes off his gloves and gives his work a look like one would a freshly plastered wall. 'Tea?' Will and I eye him curiously. Tea is, strangely, the answer here. We nod. Joe looks at this tableau of new family and smiles. I am sure he has many an icebreaker for situations like these. *Congratulations. How does it feel? He's beautiful. You had a baby! Nice one!* He looks down at our baby and then back to me.

'He looks just like you.'

Track One

'Always Like This' – Bombay Bicycle Club (2009)

'Joey, Joe-Joe, Joooooeee. Go to sleep. Sleepy sleep sleep. Pleeeease. I'm so tirrrred. So tired my eyeballs may actually explooooode. I don't want you to see thaaaaat.'

My baby looks up at me like I have finally lost the plot. *Those were song lyrics? Those were terrible. They didn't even rhyme. The melody was shocking.* Baby Joe. We lie here together, my face buried in a baby playmat. 4.11 a.m. says my phone. I think the only time I've ever been up this early pre-motherhood was after an all-night bender or to catch a cheap flight. I let Joe nestle into my body, hoping my body odour won't suffocate him. Why is this playmat damp? I've either drooled or Joe has pissed himself. Or maybe I've pissed myself. I'm so tired I'm not even sure if urine has left my body.

For everything they say about motherhood, nothing can prepare you for the mind-bending, dizzying energy drain that is the exhaustion you feel in those twilight moments when your baby has their midnight feed and they won't go back to sleep. This is not mentioned on the websites, the manuals, the podcasts. Sleep when they sleep? BUT THE BABY NEVER SLEEPS, no matter what you do. You feed it some more, you clean its tiny bum, you sway and jiggle and rock and sing. Badly. Odd nonsensical songs. You'll even run a bath and consider going to sit on a night bus or starting a clothes wash so you have something nearby that might, just might vibrate the wee thing into a slumber. Instead, your child looks at you, all wide-eyed: *It's not sleep time. I'm awake. I'm ready for life, entertain me, lady. Isn't this nice, just you and me? Tell me everything you know. EVERYTHING.*

Except he doesn't say this because he can't talk. He'll just stare at you and you have no idea what's going on in his little head. And no one tells you how there'll be a point where you cry out, exasperated, frustrated into a room, drowned of light, 'Please just fricking sleep.' They don't tell you about the guilt that then comes from saying those words out loud. You believe you're a truly terrible parent, so you hold the baby closer and apologise softly. I wish someone had told me about those times.

And I wish someone had told me about the endless nights and days, all merging into one. I've stared at a hanging cuddly donkey, a wall, a screen, a sliver of sky, not really processing whether it's three in the afternoon or the morning. Am I asleep? Am I tired? Am I conscious? What time is it? I had a baby? When did I order this coffee? Why is there food in my mouth? The television is on? That's nice. Time ticks on. This lethargic catatonia is both curious and alien but somehow, you get through every day.

The baby cries, he grows, he drinks, he poos, you clean him, you comb his soft baby hair into a comb-over, he sleeps, he wakes. You live in a universe of messy buns, nursing bras and stained trackies, of moisturising your nipples instead of your face. A universe littered with trips to the supermarket, the health centre, the park, where you both sit in the fresh air and the little one looks in wonder at this big blue stuff above him and you sit there doing bad baby maths. *When did he last eat? When did I last eat? Is it Tuesday?*

I smell the dampness. It's wee. I sit up and pull the changing mat out from beside the sofa. He is soaked through – I didn't tuck his willy in when I last changed him so it's sprayed in some upward motion and drenched his clothes. This is why girls are better than boys. There's no way we can pee upwards unless you attach a hose to us. He smiles as I change him. I always smile back. He looks like a tiny comedy bear, with hazel eyes that turn overcast and grey when he's sad. Does he understand that he's a miniature time lord who has me questioning my whole existence? By the way he's studying my boobs, I'm thinking not.

He's less comedy, more grizzly bear tonight as he emits a noise that's not quite a cry, not quite a moan. I mimic the noise and he stops momentarily as if he knows I'm mocking him. Maybe it's wind. People don't talk enough about wind. I used to see babies being given milk and then delicately being laid down to sleep. No, wind is the enemy, Meg tells me. You feed your baby but if he closes his eyes, you wake that little bugger up. You force him to take another boob so you're not too lopsided but you sit him up and pat him on the back like you're performing some sort of first aid manoeuvre on him. I do that but all it does is add another level of sound to his grizzle, like a helicopter is coming in to land.

'I bought an experimental dance record that sounded like that once. On vinyl.' Will stands in the doorway to our bedroom, wearing just his spotty boxer shorts. It's late summer so his brown mass of hair is unkempt and sweaty, sticking to his forehead.

'I'm sorry,' I say. 'You've got work, just get back to sleep.'

He looks at me. The muggy summer night air has made me abandon all sense of fashion and self-respect so I'm just in a large pair of knickers, a vest top and my maternity bra, into which I've tied a muslin that smells vaguely of sour milk and body odour. I tie the muslins to me now like some rosette of motherhood so I know they're always near. Will comes over and puts a hand to my cheek.

'You look a state,' he mumbles.

'Charmer. You're supposed to say I look radiant and mother-like.'

'Like Madonna?'

'The religious icon or the pop star legend?'

'Well, you don't look like either.'

I shake my head and allow him to take Joe while I collapse onto the sofa.

'Hey, little man? What's going on here then?' he says.

There is a look of recognition from Joe but still the grizzle. I can't fall asleep now. We have to do this together as a show of commitment and support. This sofa has never been more comfortable though. I wish it would swallow my face.

'Sometimes I think we used to party so hard that it became part of Joe's genes? Maybe it's part of his constitution to be able to stay up so late?' Will whispers.

I smile. 'You mean he's a born raver? It's in his blood?'

'He is our child. I only hope he's inherited the best parts of us.'

'But we have to home this child for at least sixteen years. I can't have sixteen years of no sleep.'

'When he gets to his teens, it may be more fun. We could have all-night raves as a family?'

'I imagine our teenage son would love that. Us old folk joining in with our whistles, bucket hats and nineties dance moves.'

Will goes quiet. 'I'll be forty-six when he's sixteen. Shit. That is ancient.'

He looks a bit perturbed by the fact and runs his hand through his hair. One thing's for sure, he'll still have hair at that age. He likes to think his huge, uncontrollable mop makes him look like the lead singer of an indie band but really, it's starting to look a bit eighties bouffant.

Will starts pacing the room. 'What have you tried tonight?'

'Everything. Bit of white noise, wrapping him up like a spring roll, I tried to feed him asleep too.'

'Obviously all worked then.'

I grab my phone. 'Siri, list me all the ways to help a baby get to sleep.'

'This is what I found,' Siri suggests.

'Try lying him down and brushing his eyelids gently in a downward motion,' I read off some parenting website.

Will does as he's told. Joe seems annoyed that we're touching his eyes. *Don't touch the eyes.* His grizzle gets louder. I hear footsteps upstairs from the flat above. Mrs Siddiqui has never openly complained before but she always gives me curious if well-meaning looks on the stairwell as to why I haven't quite got the hang of motherhood just yet. Sometimes we hear loud footsteps above in the middle of the night as if to inform us we've woken her, and make us feel all the guilt.

'Pick him up.'

Will bundles our baby boy up into his arms and places his head next to his chest. Joe rubs his face against the chest hair wondering if we've acquired a new rug.

'OK. There's also a method where you cradle him and then swing him from side to side in big sweeping motions,' I say.

'Like I'm swinging a golf club?'

'Yeah but don't let him go.'

Will twists his body around, trying to achieve the desired effect. Less golfer, more swinging Jolly Roger pirate ship ride. Joe giggles. I do like that sound. Just not now. Will laughs quietly and holds the baby's face to his. He comes to sit down next to me and balances Joe on his jiggling knee.

'You don't have to be up. Get back to sleep,' I tell him.

'I'm up now.' He glances over at the television. 'What was this?'

'*The Crown.*'

'Any good?'

I shrug. It is most likely very good but I've mainly kept the queen on in the background for company. I'm glad she's found the depth of character and strength to lead our good country, but I bet she never suffered with cracked nipples.

Will scrolls through Netflix looking for something else to gaze at. I revert back to my phone, where he notices Facebook open.

'What news befalls social media land?' he asks.

This was your post from one year ago, Facebook informs me. *Would you like to share?*

I show Will my phone. 'Christ, how was that a year ago?'

I can see the cogs whirring in Will's brain trying to do the bad maths. That was from a whole other life. The post was from a music festival. I'm wearing denim cut-offs that I'd struggle to now get past my knees, a white vest top and a straw trilby decorated with daisies. I am drunk – and revelling in that drunkenness. My arms are slung over Will's shoulders and I am jumping in time to Bombay Bicycle Club's music without a bloody care in the world, without having to worry whether the contents of my pelvis are going to combust and displace themselves. And I am singing into the late summer sky with a bottle of beer held aloft, getting overly excited about HOW MUCH I LOVE THIS SONG, slightly sweaty and pink but oh so happy and carefree. And braless. Just my B-cup wonders bouncing around, unaware, joyous. We did that exactly three hundred and sixty-five days ago. Why does it feel like time has moved at glacial speed this year, and yet also at a rate I've not been able to fathom? I take my phone back and start to scroll up.

'Apparently, your brother's closest celebrity soulmate is Elon Musk,' I say to Will, filling him in on what else is happening on Facebook. 'I really needed to know that.'

Will laughs.

'A bloke I went to college with is angry about dairy farming, funny meme about Trump, promo, things for sale, Lucy posting selfies and wow, remember that girl I went to school with… Karina? She's having twins – man, that's four kids under five. How does she look so shiny?'

I show Will their family picture. There's a strong theme to her portraiture. She likes a sunset and everyone is wearing white linen. I compare it to a photo Will and I have on our bookshelf that's a selfie of us in Ibiza. Will's mouth is open so wide you can see his tonsils.

Will stares at the picture for a moment. It's so far from our reality and I can't even mock it because I'm so tired.

'Don't ever make me pose for a picture like that.'

'I see you in white linen. Backstreet Boy style.'

He chuckles. 'I'd look like a cult leader. Look at her husband. What is he? Finance, I bet.'

'Hedge fund manager.'

Will has a pained look to his face. It always intrigues him how other people get and keep their money. We try. We save and scrimp but have never been quite able to amass the millions that I suspect Will thinks we should have in our bank accounts now we're both thirty.

'Move on,' Will says.

Joe's gaze turns to both of us like he's disappointed in the quality of the conversation. I'm not sure what he wants here. It's nearly daybreak. He's not going to get highbrow and interesting with us at this hour. I study his face. He's all Will, with my eyes. In his moments of cuteness, I *think* we get each other. *I am your mother. You are Joe, my child.* But that still feels like a strange thing to say out loud.

'Have we tried any music yet? Some sort of sound bath, meditative shit that could help Joe nod off?' Will asks.

'I've tried whale music. He wasn't sure about that.'

'What about some nineties chill out? Morcheeba? Air? Groove Armada? Something with a melody at least.'

I scroll through my phone. Deciding on Groove Armada's 'At the River'. A soft beat lulls out of my phone. This was the song that

Will and I used to get stoned to. Joe looks at us strangely. *These are not nursery rhymes.*

'Are his eyes going?' I ask.

'I think he's just studying the beat.'

We sing along in time and he watches us like the saddos we are. We know a lot of lyrics. If nothing, kid, that is our special superpower that we hope to bequeath to you. I mean we don't harmonise but we know exactly when a bass will drop and all the extra ad libs. Will goes as far as to mimic a trumpet. The song ends and then another suddenly comes up – 'I See You Baby'. Joe smiles. He likes this one despite the borderline inappropriate lyrics about ass shaking. Will and I resent having to move that bit quicker. But is it working? He suddenly nestles into his dad's chest. Will's eyes widen, and he urges me to recline slowly with him onto the sofa. We still continue to mumble the lyrics, laughing that our baby would think this a lullaby. I turn my phone to a different angle and take a picture of the three of us, to capture this moment where, for once, it all seems worth it, it all makes sense. I inspect the photo. Thank God for Joe because Will and I are seriously letting the side down. I am half blinking and Will has a big sleepy grin on him.

'I like that one,' he says. 'I look like I'm about to eat him.'

I laugh in my delirium. 'Nope, delete. I look drunk.'

'I wish. Maybe we should put him down,' Will whispers. We both sink into the sofa.

'Sssshhh, just hold your position,' I say.

'I love this song.'

'New favourite.'

'I think he smells of wee.'

'That might be me.'

'I love you.'

'Yeah.'

Track Two

'Taper Jean Girl' – Kings of Leon (2004)

XS
S
M
L

I've often debated why sizes are labelled to reflect *actual* size. I know I'm large. I've just had a baby and we've stretched my body to its capacity *and* tripled my boob size. But large is a word you use to describe houses, elephants, the biggest thing on the fast-food menu. So my suggestion is that why don't we describe all sizes by standardised superlative adjectives instead? I'm not Small, I'm Fantastic. And I'm not Large. I'm Fabulous. And when I'm Extra Large, I'm Extra Fabulous. And why do they put the bigger sizes on the lowest shelves? Why am I on all fours like a sweaty dog scouring shelves and trying to work out which one of these black T-shirts will fit across my gargantuan bosoms? I think I might fit one of my boobs into a Small. Stretch is good but it will be reveal-ing. It'll cling to my many guts. I move across to a 'slouchy' style, except it's a vest with a strange crochet back which will show off my mammoth nursing bra. I look across the rails, at a bigger one which is practically a dress. Yes. I take it off the rails but then see it has a giant Mickey Mouse on the front. I can't get away with that anymore, can I? So maybe I go for the original stretch T-shirt in XL. Though if I wear these T-shirts with black leggings then with my pale face and lack of ability to make conversation, I'll look like a mime artist.

I keep strolling along to the knicker section. My beloved minis have not been my friend recently so I look at what's available. Do I go full support pants that kind of look like cycling shorts? It's the summer – that will be sweaty crack territory. I opt for a multipack of boyfriend shorts. Are these sexy? No. How big do I go? I don't want a baggy knicker but then I don't want the elastic to cut off my circulation either or for them to leave grid line indentations across my butt cheeks. I laugh out loud at the thongs, thinking about a piece of string devoured by a couple of sizeable burger buns.

I'm supposed to be here to buy some babygros for Joe, who seems to be getting bigger at the rate of knots. However, my quick in and out has caught me being sucked into trying to also sort my dire clothes situation. I am at that in between stage where none of my old skinny jeans go past my thighs, and I can't really wear maternity clothes anymore, which is a shame because an added stretchy waistband to a jean is what the world is missing. I also thought it might cheer me up. Obviously, it hasn't. To feel better, I throw some socks into my bag. At least I haven't got fat feet. I also throw in a cotton tote bag, a two-pack of leggings and a multipack of stud earrings. Joe looks worried for me. He wriggles in his pram. This store always seems to be warm, no matter the season. I pick him up, his back and head all matted and sweaty, and throw the basket into his seat, doing the impossible move of trying to push, steer and pacify at the same time. I watch as the sales assistant notices me knocking a row of bargain flip flops from their rack. I'm not even going on holiday this year but I throw some of those in. And a hairbrush.

'What else shall we get?' I ask Joe.

Nothing? his eyes tell me. *A ticket out of here?* I suddenly hear my phone ring. I search for it in my cavernous bag, jiggling with Joe on the spot. Lord. Does she really have to call now?

'Mum. How are you?'

'You sound tired.'

'I am tired.'

'Are you out?'

'I'm just grabbing some shopping and a tea.'

'Not caffeine. That's why Joe's not sleeping because he's essentially just drinking tea.'

I also ate half a packet of Bourbon biscuits before I came out. That would be a perfect cocktail-flavoured drink.

'Try that camomile stuff I gave you.'

'I will, Mum.' I won't.

'And when are you next coming round? I want hugs. I could come to you?'

'No! Don't do that…'

There's a toss-up here of what's the lesser of two evils. Do I haul my arse all the way over to hers on two buses or do I let her come to my place and judge my lack of tidiness? Usually the first thing she does is locate a hoover. I'd also have to clean the toilet and clear the fridge of septic vegetables. There is a pause where I can tell she's wondering whether to be offended.

'I'll try and pop by next week? Maybe?' I say, trying to be as vague as possible.

'Good. Your father will be happy. Won't you?' she says to Dad.

I smile because he's most likely sitting in his armchair nodding along but not processing the conversation.

'How is Dad?'

'He's marking. He's also tired, he taught this morning.'

I would doubt he's as hellishly tired as myself, but depends on the year group. This is the one thing I have in common with my folks. I was the only sister who followed both parents into their chosen profession of teaching. I've never been quite sure why. It didn't feel like a calling, more like a career I stumbled into.

'Ask for help too. I can look after Joe any time, you know that. Except Mondays because that's when I'm in full time,' Mum carries on. 'They started another psychology A-level group.'

'That's good.'

'Classic case of dossers using my subject to fill a gap. That's why they give them to me so I'll snap them into shape.'

She is the sort of teacher people will talk about in years to come as part of the horror story that was their secondary education. She likes kids to *maximise* their potential. It's what she's been wishing for her daughters for years.

Joe starts to grizzle; shuffling on the spot is clearly starting to lose its appeal.

'What's wrong with him? Is he hungry?' she asks. 'Make sure you use us, Beth, we can help out whenever you need. And use your sisters. Use Lucy, keep her occupied. If she's not occupied, she finds mischief. You never heard this from me but she's very good with children.'

She should hear that from you, I think.

'I will.'

'Please remember to hydrate or Joe will have nothing to drink.'

She makes it sound like my jugs will turn to rock and the world will run out of fluids for this baby of mine.

'I have to go. I'm doing the rounds. I'm calling Meg now,' she says. It won't be a call. It will be a battle of wills. 'Take care of my grandson.'

She hangs up and I exhale softly. *I'm trying, Mum.* The phone rings again. Why does everyone always call me when I'm out? I stay at home all the bloody time and none of these bastards call me then. This time it's Will.

'Beth?'

I respond with a strangled growling sound that a waking sloth might make.

'That bad?'

'Mum just rang.'

'Ouch. Was she awful?'

'Just her being Mum.'

'How's Joe?'

'We're in Primark. He hates Primark.'

'I taught him that,' he says, laughing.

'I'm sorry we got you up so late,' I say. 'Or is it early? I don't know anymore.'

'I just think it's part of my constitution now.'

Will slipped out of our house at six thirty this morning. I'm not sure what stage of consciousness I was in, but I mumbled something about loving him and he mumbled something about him changing Joe. I wonder if I should get up when he does. We'd sit around a kitchen with freshly brewed coffee, the baby would laugh and we'd wave Will off like he was going to war. Instead, I lay face down on the sofa and heard the door click closed. I fed Joe again and then passed out, awaking two hours later to find the baby still at my nipple and that I'd missed yet more of *The Crown*. Had Joe been drinking the whole time? Could I have drowned him with my milk?

'Siri? Can you drown a baby when you breastfeed them?'

'I'm sorry, I didn't understand your question.'

'What did you have for lunch?' I ask Will.

'Food.'

'What sort of food?'

'Tasty food. We have these vegan, ethical living sorts who pass through the office once a week. Today they came with tiffin lunch tins. I think I ate jackfruit?'

'And liked it?'

'Stranger things have happened. Bloody East London. I also sat opposite a girl on the Tube today who was wearing head to toe acid-wash denim. She was reading Dickens and ate a whole apple. Like even the core.'

'Then an apple tree will grow in her stomach,' I reply.

'That's what I told her.'

'Is double denim back then?'

'Who knows? There's a girl in the creative media office opposite who wears a tiara,' he says.

'What shoes?'

'Metallic brogues. She's also a known pen thief.'

'Bitch.'

There's a pause. We do this every day at lunch, our own ritual of trying to stay connected.

'When is it a good time to tell you I'm going to be late again?' he asks.

I don't know how to react to this anymore. It's been this way since Joe was about a month old; Will took on a new job with an architecture firm in Shoreditch that apparently pays more money but the commute and sheer volume of work means we see him less. I can't be angry about it but it compounds on my loneliness.

'Will you need dinner?' I ask.

'I'll grab something at Waterloo. I'm sorry.'

'It's cool. Love you.'

'Yes, lemons.'

I smile. Will didn't want to be to the uncool person in the office saying 'I love you' out loud so we've come up with a code word. 'Lemons' is an acceptable alternative that can be repeated within the confines of his ultra-trendy hot desking office where it seems everyone stands up and just hangs around in communal spaces talking about *Fleabag* and non-dairy alternatives.

'Idiot.'

'And don't forget your dinner date,' he tells me.

I freeze on the spot. *Shit.* 'That's tonight?'

'Yes.'

'Balls. Big giant balls.'

That shop assistant who was tutting before gives me an evil look, I guess because I'm holding an infant. I could be talking about any balls: tennis balls, beach balls, disco balls. I'll have to get on a bus. What are the queues at the tills like? Seriously, *balls*.

'Good luck,' Will whispers before hanging up.

By the time I get home, I am bang on time but sweaty and the colour of beetroot from fighting my way onto a bus with the pram, shopping stuffed into the lower basket. I clamber into our block of flats and struggle to navigate the buggy through the corridor. The front door opposite ours opens, and our neighbour emerges looking slightly perturbed at my levels of sweatiness.

'Was your marathon today then?'

Paddy. I would laugh if I had the breath. He opens his door fully, and I see he's standing there in a blazer with a buttonhole. I smile. Oh my. He's dressed up and I'm wearing cut-offs and a yellow stripy T-shirt. I feel awful but he smiles broadly. I don't suppose he's too surprised. Paddy is our garden flat floor neighbour and we share a corridor in our block, home to his wonderful ferns, our buggy, an old Christmas tree base and a few pairs of really old stinky trainers. Every day since Joe was about a month old, he knocks on our door so we can have a cup of tea. I won't lie, it's become a highlight. He's even sometimes done the washing up and helps me fold clothes. It gives me some routine in an otherwise unstructured day – and company. I also feel indebted to him as some of the noise Joe has created over the past months or so will have travelled, no doubt. However, today is different. No tea. We are out to dinner and

I am super grateful for Will's reminder. Paddy fiddles with the handkerchief in his top pocket.

'You forgot, didn't you? You're such a dopey mare.'

This is also why I keep Paddy in our lives. For all his gallantry, he also is good comedy value.

'I didn't forget. I'm just running behind.' I forgot.

He shakes his head at me and rolls his eyes mockingly. 'Come on, you go sort yourself and I'll take the young 'un.' He holds his hands out and Joe goes over willingly, as Joe does. The lad isn't picky which makes me worry he's the sort who's likely to be kidnapped easily. He likes a cuddle and the variety of a new face that isn't mine. I try and feign enthusiasm with Paddy, hoping it may mask my guilt. You see, today would have been Paddy's fiftieth wedding anniversary. His wife, Betty passed a few years ago and he's been on his own ever since. I've never heard a man speak so affectionately of a woman. So affectionately that every time her name is mentioned or he shares an anecdote with me, I usually burst into tears (that'll be the hormones and lack of sleep). Once he told me about the time he proposed outside a bookshop, the one where their eyes first met over their shared love of Graham Greene, and I actually lactated. I didn't want him to be alone on today of all days so I suggested we go out for dinner. Nothing fancy (Betty would have hated that) but she liked fish and chips and a half of shandy to wash it down. So the pub it is – and we'll raise a toast to his love. Except I'm a dopey mare and I bloody forgot.

'Come on through.'

He wears a light slack and a smart navy blazer. I want to hug him but I don't given I'm slightly balmy. I may need to have a quick refresh with the baby wipes.

'Excuse the mess as always.'

I do a quick scan as he enters. Paddy has seen all sorts lying around, from bags of nappies to bras drying on the radiator but he always seems to turn a blind eye, once telling me he'd seen worse in the war which made me feel marginally better.

'And how are you? How's little man?' he asks.

I kick a box of pantyliners behind a sofa.

'As usual. Sleep is kind of getting better, I think.' My haggard face probably tells a different story.

'Well, you're doing a sterling job,' he says, eyes glancing over at the kitchen where last night's chicken pie sits there on the counter, a fork in the dish where I've been picking away at its cold carcass over the course of lunchtime. Paddy always says this without even a hint of sarcasm. We all know different but it's like he's telling me to keep on keeping on.

'How was that new bridge thing? Did you go this morning?' I ask.

'I did. They were a bunch of old arse hats though. It's the same faces you see all the time; allotments, woodcraft, all those classes they put on in the community centre. I'm just sick of seeing the same mugs. And turns out the bridge is all recreational too, no playing for money. Not sure why you'd bother? I can play poker online.'

'But it's the social side of things, no?' I ask.

'Maybe. But that's why I have tea with you.' He puts a hand to my shoulder. 'How long do you think you'll be?'

He scans the puffy outline of my mousey blonde hair. I try to think if I own any hats.

'Ten minutes. I promise.'

He gives me a look. What stands before him would take a makeover show at least three days and some industrial threading action. But I've done it in less. That time I forgot a health visitor was coming round, I managed to brush my teeth, put on a hoodie and deodorant myself in a single thirty second action. I smile as he makes Joe laugh by turning his hand into a bird. I spy a wedding ring and smile broadly.

'You look really nice by the way,' I tell him.

'You hitting on me? Is Will not doing it for you these days?'

'It's the blazer, I'm a sucker for a blazer.'

'If I'd known, I would've worn it more often. Did my house slippers not give you the fanny flutters?'

I laugh, loudly. 'It's the tartan, makes you look well old.'

He turns to my infant son. 'Joe, your mum's a bloody cow, did I ever tell you that?'

My son seems to laugh in agreement and I shake my head at the two of them.

'Well, Joe and I will make ourselves useful while you get ready,' he says. 'It's recycling day tomorrow.' He gestures over to my recycling bin which is a Jenga-style configuration of tins, card and junk mail that we pile in the corner. I shuffle over in my shame to assist.

'Did you see that new muppet in flat five?' Paddy asks. 'He keeps putting takeaway boxes in the recycling. No foil, I told him, and he called me an old nosey git.'

I wince. 'Really? Is it worth the fight?'

'It is. More like that and next time, I'll steal his sweet and sour pork balls.'

'Paddy!'

'We're a family in this block, we look out for each other. You play by the rules. Have you seen his cat too? Miserable looking sod, just like his owner.'

As I tie a bin liner full, Paddy looks around the mismatched cupboards and counters that line my messy galley kitchen.

'I'm sorry about—'

'— the mess, I know,' he replies, laughing cheekily. 'Come on, little lad, let's do a quick sweep in here for your mum. You looking forward to your first pint in a bit?' he says to Joe.

He opens all my cupboards to put dry washing up away and looks confused by all the mismatched mugs and biscuits. Many biscuits. He chats to Joe like some old mucker he's met down the pub and I smile. Is it terrible that I think Paddy may be my current best friend? Aren't I supposed to have a mum friend whom I meet at baby tai chi lessons once a week? Her name should be Laura and she should wear Joules. Instead I have a septuagenarian standing in my kitchen, wondering why someone would use their oven to store their entire collection of saucepans. He turns to me.

'I love you, Beth, Joe does too. But we're not going to the pub with you looking like a fricking tramp. Get a wriggle on.'

'Harsh.'

'But true.'

Track Three

'Too Young' – Phoenix (2000)

I can't quite remember why we moved to Surbiton. Will and I both knew we wanted to stay in South London to be near family but that we also needed somewhere commutable and within budget. This suburb is the place where people come to shed the skins of their young selves and grow up. Before here, we'd been in Brixton which was once up-and-coming and trendy but through the eyes of parents-to-be suddenly looked unsafe and polluted. So we begged, borrowed and ploughed our minimal finances into our flat in this leafy commuter belt and we got it at a bargain price given it hadn't been renovated since the seventies. This didn't faze us. It was retro, a style statement. We could peel back the shag pile and do some of the work ourselves. Except we didn't have any money left. So the shag pile and the avocado bathroom suite stayed. And instead of cool cafés and bars that served trance with their cocktails, we now drink at sensible pubs that play Adele and give you crayons so you can help your little ones colour in their menus.

'Bitter shandy, a lemonade for the lady and two fish and chips,' Paddy tells the barman. We've opted for one of the pubs on the high street. It's not one of those newfangled wine bars that serves sweet potato substitutes. Paddy is in the mood for chunky chips which is another reason he's an ally.

'What are you having, Joe?' he asks.

'Vodka tonic?' I suggest.

The barman is a serious sort so doesn't take too kindly to the joke. He glares at Joe almost as a warning that he's not allowed to cry in here or he'll bar him. Paddy smiles as he goes to retrieve our drinks.

'Ignore this fool, go get us a table, pet,' he mumbles.

I smile. I do love a pub but they are alien places to me these days. Now I come equipped with a buggy, bags and a small human who may at any given moment explode with poo, cry or demand food. Leaving the house, therefore, always puts me slightly on edge.

Negotiating the pub, I find us a table by the window (hitting a row of bar stools as I do) and park the buggy next to us. Joe looks around. *Where are we now? This is new? It's not the supermarket or our front room.* I've made an effort with him in his best baby jeans but see that he's lost a sock somewhere. I spot my reflection in a nearby window. Christ on a bike, who's that bird? I looked vaguely presentable in my bathroom mirror. I put in some dry shampoo, slicked my hair back into a bun, threw on some mascara and found a maxi dress that covered my bumpy, misshapen body. I thought I had a sleek minimalist mother look to me. I don't. Why does this dress suddenly look like a holiday kaftan? Why am I so sweaty? I try and blot the worst of it off with Joe's muslin.

There's a strange clientele in here today: the people sitting around us seem to be single, older men drinking away their sorrows. One table away are a group of people in some sort of meeting; they're well heeled and engage in animated chat over a sharing platter that involves cured meats and calamari. Why does this feel so strange? Maybe because I won't be drinking. Or maybe it's because I just want to curl up on this bench and have a nap. Paddy approaches and puts our drinks down.

'Love, I ordered you some mushy peas too.'

I smile. The truth is I don't like mushy peas but now I breastfeed, I eat everything. My appetite knows no bounds. No one told me this was a side effect of breastfeeding to the point where I can smell the calamari on the other table and am thinking about ways I can brush past the table and steal a piece.

'Is the pub OK? I didn't know. I think it's nice. The murals are a bit wanky but I can look past them,' he says.

'It's fine. So tell me, what else have you done today?'

'Apart from bridge, I went up to Betty's grave. That was nice.' *Don't cry, Beth.* 'And spoke to my boys on the phone but you know how it is, they're working and I didn't want to trouble them.'

I put my hand on his. 'I'm sure they know today means a lot. You're wearing your wedding ring, I've never noticed that before.'

'I've always worn it. Never taken it off.'

I tear up slightly.

'Just shows how observant you are,' Paddy jokes.

'I miss most things. I've just had a baby.'

'Crap excuse.'

Before I can retort, a flurry of women exit what looks like a function room to the side of the bar. I recognise two of them and they clock me immediately, looking a little embarrassed.

'Caroline, Nas… Hi!' I say reluctantly.

'Oh, Beth…'

Both Caroline and Nas were in my NCT group, another bizarre ritual of early parenthood, where I was expected to be the best version of me and attach myself to others with babies, while in reality I was at my physical and mental worst. *Hi, I'm Beth and this is Joe. He is a baby. You also have a baby. Let's be friends forever.* NCT was supposed to be the perfect way to make fellow parental friends. Let's sit in this community hall, our chairs in a circle, set up like we're about to either chat addiction issues, pray or play musical chairs. And let's get our bumps out and discuss the impending excitement of parenthood. Except our group never really gelled. Will and I knew why. After years of IVF, Caroline didn't take too lightly to the fact our pregnancy wasn't planned. That said, we also didn't quite take to her husband, who spent most of those classes buttering up Will to do free architectural consultation work on their converted rectory house. Also, when Nas hosted a coffee morning in her five-bedroom detached house with a kitchen bigger than our whole actual flat, we knew they were out of our league. *Could you imagine them coming to ours?* Will said. *People would have to spread out and sit on our bed.*

The rest of the parents were just a strange mix of individuals: a really young mum who was nineteen, who came with her mum and Snapchatted constantly through the sessions, and then there was Alison who was fifty-five. She already had three kids, the youngest of which was fifteen. She was going through the menopause so had been attending some acupuncture sessions, the side effects of which were increased fertility and thus she got knocked up. Alison knew more than the NCT tutor but I especially liked how her and her husband would sit there mumbling about how they'd thought they were done with this shit. *You wait until the baby's teething, and it then starts throwing tantrums, won't eat anything and will speak more to people on YouTube than it will to you.* And you used to see half of the mums clutch their bumps protectively like it'd never happen to them. Will and I thought all these people were nothing like us: too old, too organised, too highly strung, too young, too boring. We used to stride in there thinking we were the cool cats. The baby would just follow us around like a trendy accessory. He wouldn't even cry because we'd be that laidback. It's just parenthood, chill out. Yet seeing Caroline and Nas now only reinforces how different our approaches to parenthood really are. They appear so effortless and preened, whereas this is something that doesn't come to me naturally. Both of them have their babies swathed in slings and are dressed head to toe in exercise wear. Joe eyes them curiously. He is not familiar with this style of dress.

'You're both looking really well.'

'So do you?'

I'm sure there was a question in that. 'How are Valencia and Leonard?' I ask.

Paddy chokes a little on his lager.

'Thriving. We were actually in a baby yoga class. It's so good for the babies,' says Caroline.

'We would have invited you but we didn't know your number,' mumbles Nas.

They do know my number. I smile while their eyes scan my thrown-together kaftan dress look. Nothing's changed with them. I've been to all-girls' schools so I know the score – for all the ways we convince ourselves that putting women together can form some sense of sisterhood, it can also summon up the worst sorts of bitchery. I am wise enough to understand these dynamics to not be hurt – yet I'm also relieved. I lent off the bed the other day to get my phone and I think I displaced my spleen. Yoga would break me.

'Oh, it's fine,' I reply. 'Not really my bag anyway.'

Little Valencia pops her head from over the sling and glares at me, the scrunched-up face of a young cub. Paddy looks perturbed by the aggression in her stare.

'Joe looks well,' Caroline says, trying to drum up some civility.

'He is. I wish he'd sleep but he's doing great.'

Next to us, Leonard kicks his legs out, his face starting to curl into a cry. His mother placates him with a dummy.

'Oh, Leonard and Valencia have slept through since week six. Didn't you follow the links to the sleep schedule that Lolly put on the WhatsApp group?'

Paddy looks confused. Did someone pick all these names out of a hat? Lolly was our fearless NCT leader who had convinced us all that motherhood was something that could be run with a combination of hypnosis, timetables and letting them cry. It's all about the babies letting you know how they feel, apparently.

'I guess Joe's a little different.'

Their smiles and silence say it all: *We came to this pub for well-meaning baby activity, glowing and fit and handling this like pros. You're here to eat chips with your baby in a supermarket clothes range.*

'Are you the proud pop-pops then?' Caroline says, turning to Paddy.

'You what, love?'

'She thinks you're Granddad,' I tell him.

Paddy laughs. 'Oh no, Will's not in the picture anymore so this is a date. We met on Tinder.'

I close my eyes and try to hold in the laughter. They both look ashen at the scandal. They didn't get that, did they?

'This is Paddy. He's my neighbour.'

'I'm her bestie.'

'Oh… that's lovely,' says Nas, still getting to grips with our humour and the fact I have an old man as a best friend. 'Well, we must be going. It's nearly feeding time here.'

'It was good to see you both.' It wasn't but I am loath to carry this conversation on any further. 'Take care and say hi to Pete and Greg too.'

They nod. 'And to your husband, of course.'

He isn't my husband and his name is Will. He definitely won't be going anywhere near your extension now. They stride away speedily and I take a long sip of my lemonade.

'Crumbs, where are those two bitches from?' Paddy announces, possibly still within earshot.

'Mother–baby group thing. We didn't quite click.'

'You think? Are they all like that then?'

'Mostly. I've done that circuit of classes and groups. I went to the local community centre, some music thing. It was—'

'Shit?'

'Strangely competitive. Look how well my baby can keep rhythm and pick things up! And Joe just really wasn't bothered.'

'Of course. Because Joe is super smart and knows what's worth his time.' My son seems to smile in agreement. 'And did you see their babies? Joe is bloody handsome. I've not seen a better-looking baby and that's before my own grandkids. And who calls a baby Leonard? That's just cruel.'

I laugh under my breath. 'Fanny would have been cruel. I think Leonard is verging on trendy.'

'And he wasn't good-looking. Face like a cabbage. She's just inviting that kid to be beaten up when he's older.'

'You can't say that about a baby, Paddy.'

'I'll say what I like when people are obviously not very nice.' He returns a hand on top of mine. I don't need him to slag off innocent babies to make me feel better but I'm grateful for it nonetheless.

'You do have other friends though, yes? Mum friends?' he asks, concern on his face.

I nod but it's not really the truth. I mean Facebook and Instagram tell me I have about four hundred friends, really. I'm also members of forums and groups where my friends are random people who swap advice over cheap nappies and start conversation threads that voice their anger over people nicking parent–child parking spots. They're avatar pictures and emoji friends who I engage with so I can just watch them have heated debates that devolve into raging online fights. I have university friends but they live miles away so they've become 'social media likes and comments' kinda mates. I guess I have my sisters? I have Will? It's one of those close-knit circle things.

Platters of fish and chips suddenly make an appearance next to us and I sit back from the table as a bosomy waitress puts them down. The scents of salt, vinegar and deep-fried battered goodness fill my nostrils and my body relents. Feed me this, immediately.

'Isn't he a gem? What's his name?' The waitress holds on to my baby's fingers and he gazes up at her.

'This is Joe.'

'You're making my ovaries hurt. Treasure them when they're like this. They grow up so quickly.'

I never get the meaning of that sentence. At 3.a.m. when he's howling the place down, I feel no need to treasure that moment. I want to put him on eBay but I don't say that out loud. She waves at Joe as she walks away and I pick up his hand to wave back. Paddy's eyes light up at the 'fat' chips he so desired and he goes crazy with the condiments. I hope Betty is looking down at this fried feast and smiling. I pick up my glass in front of me.

'To Betty?'

He nods but doesn't reply. It should be her sitting here seeing in their fifty years of marriage. The smile, the eyes, tell me how much he misses her. We clink glasses and Joe gurgles in approval. I'm going to have to balance him on my lap now, ensure he doesn't grab at things and I don't use him like a napkin. This is the true, delicate balancing act of motherhood.

'Hello, there little man,' say a voice, popping up behind me.

It's a gentleman who was sitting at that meeting a few tables down. He's dressed in black skinny jeans and a brightly patterned shirt, his black and white peppered hair well styled.

'I am so sorry to disturb your dinner. I really am. I'm Giles.'

I tentatively go to shake his hand. Paddy looks cautious that he may be another parental acquaintance come to say more awful things to my face.

'We were just having a meal over there, that's my team and we just saw your baby and… Is he always like this?'

I am slightly confused by the question. He doesn't change into Batman in the evenings if that's what he means?

'I mean, he's very good,' he continues. 'Very receptive to people.'

As if on cue, Joe reaches up to stroke the man's beard and inspect if this stranger is to his liking. Giles laughs.

'He's generally very good with people. I have a large family so he's used to it,' I say.

'He's got gorgeous eyes. Is there any Mediterranean in him? I'm assuming you're Mum?'

I nod. 'I'm Beth and this is Paddy and the baby is Joe. There's no Mediterranean there. He's more chihuahua mixed with koala.' He laughs in reply. However, the fact he had to question my relationship to Joe makes me think he doesn't hold my face in the same esteem.

'He has a very symmetrical face,' Giles replied. 'I'm not sure if anyone's told you that before.'

I now narrow my eyes at him. Paddy grasps his knife and fork tightly in case he needs to intervene.

'I'm sorry, I'm being weird. I should have just opened with who I am. I'm a creative director – I do commercials, ads, photography. I mean I know that we've just met but could you do me and my team the biggest favour, if you're up for it?'

'Up for what, exactly?' I enquire.

I grip onto Joe tightly.

'So, that young lady over there is Special K,' says Giles.

Paddy looks at me like he can't quite believe the comedy value the pub is giving him tonight for names. The girl in question is wearing denim that's pretty much ripped from all angles like she's been caught in a shredder, shards of her brown skin shining through. She's undeniably pretty, edgy too, and waves in our direction. Paddy waves back.

'We were supposed to shoot her album cover today. It was very high concept, there was supposed to be a baby involved but the baby wasn't playing ball and so we were just wondering if we could use Joe here?'

'She's a musician?' I ask.

'A rapper.'

'But named after a breakfast cereal?' Paddy asks. I laugh.

'I just shoot the pictures,' Giles says, waving back at the table. 'We're shooting in a studio down the road. Come on over when you're finished, it'd take moments. Your son is a beautiful baby and you'd be digging me out of a massive hole.' He places a glossy business card on the table, that says *Twinkle Twinkle*. 'We're eating too; finish up and maybe think about it? Look me up or give the head office a call if you're worried.'

Paddy nods while I scan Giles' team trying to work them out. It's all very trendy, definitely not in keeping with the early bird special vibe of the pub.

'I am so sorry to interrupt your family meal,' he says.

'It's fine, thank you.'

I'm not sure what else there is to say. Paddy's not family. And Joe could be a model? All at once, I find that quite hilarious. The kid can't even crawl; how will he manage a catwalk? He also eats a fair bit for a baby. I believe that's not what models do. I sit here for a moment as Joe's eyes follow Giles back to his table, mesmerised by the patterns on his shirt.

'Told you Joe was beautiful,' Paddy says proudly.

'All babies are beautiful,' I reply.

'Nope, he wasn't chasing that mum whose baby looked like a cabbage.'

I stuff some chips in my mouth, all golden and crispy. 'Wasn't that a bit weird? Scouting a baby in a pub?' I say through mouthfuls of potato.

'Maybe. He's also got a beard. Just tread carefully.'

He studies their table from behind me.

'What's wrong with beards?'

'They're unhygienic. That bloke in flat five has one and I saw half a meatball fall out of his beard once.'

'That never happened.'

'Yes, it did. Now eat up. All things considered, I quite like the idea of Joe being on an album cover. Betty would love that.' I smile back broadly. The business card shimmers on the table, and Joe promptly puts in his mouth and starts eating it.

Will gets back at nine thirty that evening. By this point, I'm filled to the brim with pub grub. I'm sitting in bed, changed out of my dress and back in the safety of my trackies and T-shirt, chowing down on some Maltesers. Joe is sprawled out next to me and has that look about him, like he's wasted on milk. I wonder if it tasted like fish and chips. I'm binge watching some crime drama that makes me never want to go on a night bus again.

Will comes straight through to the bedroom. Whereas I've lost control of my wardrobe and all concept of what is fashionable these days, Will has battled hard not to be a white-collar suit man, wearing his standard uniform of checked shirt, jeans and Converse. He was dressed in the exact same thing when I first met him. It was at a Fun Lovin' Criminals gig at the Brixton Academy where we struck up a conversation in the cloakroom queue. *I'm Will. Beth.* We joked how these queues were always super long and how we shouldn't have brought a coat. But then we'd never have met, Will said. We both laughed when we were handed our khaki parka jackets at the same time. And let's face it, we were both pretty smashed so were snogging by the time we got outside the venue. He accessorises today with giant wireless earphones and a cool Scandinavian-branded satchel. In the winter, the look features a duffel coat and a beanie. It's indie chic that's been dragged into our thirties.

'You eaten?' I ask him.

'I had a Burger King. I went large. I feel filthy.'

He comes over to kiss my forehead. I immediately pick up on a strong scent of beer.

'You've been drinking?'

'I had a few pints with Jason. Killer day. Sam was down my neck, the stress was unreal. I had to unwind.'

Jason was his single Londoner mate who always held Will's hand and led him down the wrong path. I had assumed Will was late because of work but I don't want to question it. Scrap that, I don't have the energy. I can't work out whether the emotion is jealousy or anger so I let it slide.

'I made it to dinner with Paddy,' I say.

'Oh, the anniversary thing. How is he?'

'He was fine. Quick question, remember that couple from the NCT group, the one who asked you to help draw up that extension? What came of that?'

'He emails me once a week to remind me.'

'I saw his wife today. They did end up calling their baby Valencia.'

'That's a very good football team. And you were upset that I wanted to call the baby Gascoigne. I ignore the emails. He's a posh twat. Get rich, stay rich by grabbing freebies and not treating people very well.'

'Good,' I reply. 'Also, something strange happened in the pub... We got approached by a guy who was a creative media type and he asked if he could borrow Joe for some shoot he's doing for a rapper's album cover. It was mental.'

Will perks up for a moment. You can tell he's thinking his son may be as famous as the Nirvana *Nevermind* baby.

'I Instagrammed her already. Her name is Special K. Up and coming British rap,' I carry on.

'Special K as in ketamine or the cereal?'

'Neither. Her real name is Kimmie, it was her dad's nickname for her growing up.'

I meet a lot of teens through my line of work as a teacher but I liked this one. She was polite and engaging and for a seventeen-year-old had a confidence that was way beyond her years, way beyond even someone like me.

'So yeah, we did it,' I say.

It was a crazy half an hour. After we agreed to be involved, we got led out to a studio across the road. They changed Joe into a new T-shirt, putting miniature earphones around his neck while a couple of people dragged some oil drums and rusty BMX bikes into view. I handed Joe over to Special K and he was entranced by her braids and big statement earrings. Why have a baby on a rap album cover? I was told it was a nod to youth, birth and innocence except I knew from Joe's face that he was peeing in his nappy as she cradled him, so not so innocent at all. I then watched as he smiled, they got the photos Giles wanted and he offered us payment.

'You didn't take payment?' asks Will.

'It felt a bit wrong. Like I'd pimped him out.'

Will has his phone out to examine what this girl is all about and finds a video of her music. I've already had a listen. A touch of nineties garage with a strong bass and a meaningful rap vocal.

'You're in her Instagram stories already,' he says. 'She refers to someone called JoJo, is that our son?'

'I guess. The director bloke also invited us in for other work. Baby modelling.'

Wills laughs, taking off his bag and earphones and lying next to his infant son. He does this every night when he's not been here to wish him good night, putting his head next to our baby's chest and watching it rise and fall.

'Well, people keep telling me he's cute. Magnus at work brought in pictures of his new baby. It's sweet and all but it looks very shocked in all the photos,' says Will.

'I think it's a bit awful judging a baby on its looks.'

'I was an ugly baby. I had a giant head like a marshmallow. It was very square.'

'And yet look how you blossomed,' I reply.

''Tis a mystery.'

Will smiles at me and starts to disrobe, heading to the bathroom to relieve himself. Inside, he splashes his face with water like he's trying to bring it back to life and jumps in the shower. He left at 6.30 this morning – it's clearly been a day. And it'll start all over again tomorrow. Will returns to the room, a towel around his midriff, drying himself in the way that you do when you've been with someone for nearly a decade, casual, knowing I won't care that he stands there for a moment to give his balls a good scratch.

'What you watching?' he says, nodding at my laptop.

'Crime thing. Those detectives are shagging but he's married. They're chasing a serial killer who likes to collect eyes.'

'Who goes on the top deck of an empty night bus? That's just asking for trouble.'

'Right?'

I leave the bed as he gets cosy and go to brush my teeth. Lying down has refrizzed my hair so I look like I'm about to build a city on rock and roll. Where did Joe get it from, eh? Not from this blob. I stretch out my sallow cheeks and examine the bags under my eyes. With Will's focus on the television, I also lift up my shirt to examine the damage. I always knew motherhood was going to change me physically. I know why. I have an appetite and I'm hardly the sort who was going to run to the gym as soon as a baby popped out. But as we left today's pub photoshoot, one of the set dressers in bang-on-trend denim culottes gave me a look. And her eyes shuttled between me and Joe, questioning whether we matched or not. Paddy saw it too and nipped her in the ankles with the buggy, but I knew exactly what she meant. I can't be angry. I am not at my physical peak. I've birthed a baby. I'm breastfeeding and it's not like I'm dieting and nothing is changing. It's just not on my agenda. This is my body now. I turn off the bathroom light and find Will set to pass out next to Joe, both looking like puppies who've been running in circles all day long.

'What would your rap name be?' I ask him.

'Coop Doggy Dogg,' he whispers. 'Or W.C. My first album would be *This is the Shit*.' I laugh before finding a corner of the bed and passing out next to them.

Track Four

'She Moves In Her Own Way' – The Kooks (2006)

'Yeah, I know them. They do big commercials for Pampers and that. What were you doing in a pub?' Meg asks.

'Having dinner with her old neighbour lover,' Lucy informs the group.

'Is he handsome?' Emma asks.

'You're shagging an old man?' Meg looks confused.

I glance over at my sisters, sitting in Emma's kitchen, mocking me as per usual. Meg the eldest, who normally lives up North, is here given it's the end of the summer holidays, so she's come for a bank holiday visit and to remember what it feels like to be in the warm embrace of the South. Meg was my partner-in-crime when she lived in London. She worked in magazine publishing and I was a newly qualified teacher so we had a brilliant couple of years pissing our salaries away on alcohol and rent in dire house shares. I was there when she first met her husband, Danny, on a night out. I say I was there. I was so drunk that all I remember is that he had rubbish shoes. Her youngest kid, Polly, is a few months older than mine but as tired as Meg looks, it's as if she's just absorbed that chaos into her soul.

'I've told you this before, plates to the left and then the bowls on the next layer, facing out.'

Emma and Lucy stand by a countertop, bickering over a poorly loaded dishwasher. Emma is the second eldest, the deputy, while Lucy is the youngest, who loads the cutlery the wrong way up because she's a rebel and enjoys the danger. On the order of my mother, Lucy moved into this place after Emma's divorce. I did put my hand up and say that was the worst idea I'd ever heard given they are complete character opposites, but Lucy does seem to be helping in her own way, even if that translates into helping Emma stand up to her cheating ex-husband and not cleaning her house. I hear girls thunder up and down the stairs asking if they can have crisps. The shouts of their mothers tell them to wait for dinner or to eat a piece of fruit. *I don't like fruit. Then you can't be that hungry.* I love the clamour. This is what our childhood was like, it was busy, frantic and loud voices filled the room like music. The one sister missing is Grace, who's on her travels having been through a horrific year after losing her husband. She is the one we all miss, the one who holds it altogether because when all the sisters are in the same room, there's a kind of strange mystical magic that overcomes the place. Stars align; it's a lot for the universe to deal with.

'So, he's legit?' I ask Meg, drawing the conversation back to the baby modelling. Her eldest daughter, Tess, swoops in to hug her from behind. She was my first ever niece, the first Callaghan baby. I remember the day she was born, it felt like an heir to the throne had arrived.

'Yeah, look them up. They're big potatoes. I'm not surprised you were approached though. Joe does have a very symmetrical face.'

'Giles said that too. Is that a thing?'

'Aren't all faces symmetrical?' asks Emma. She hears a buzzer from her utility room and goes in to stop the tumble dryer. To my shame, I sometimes bring laundry here so I don't have to hang wet sheets from my dining room chairs in the living room.

'No, my face isn't,' says Meg. To prove a point she gurns at me. 'Babies are strange things. Like when we did family shoots at my old job, they never wanted a skinny baby, they wanted something with chub. And as a magazine, we never went with ones with too much hair.'

'Babies can have too much hair?' asks Lucy. Her attention has moved to a pot of hummus that she spoons out with her fingers. Emma looks thrilled.

'God, yes. But then it becomes distracting. Instead of looking at the baby's outfit which they're modelling, you're looking at this insane amount of hair. Remember Tess, she looked like she came out wearing a toupee.'

Tess doesn't look too impressed so jumps off her mother's lap to find her cousins.

'Plus Joe has the temperament, I know he doesn't sleep but he's a good baby. Like Eve would be an awful model,' Meg adds.

'But she's gorgeous.'

'With a complete mind of her own. She doesn't do as she's told. She'd be the set diva. She'd throw coat hangers at people.'

'And Polly?'

'She's a drooler, snot city,' Meg says, kissing the top of her sleeping head in the carrycot next to us.

Emma is busy folding some pillowcases for me. 'My two hated the camera, far too shy.'

'I'd say do it, B,' Meg continues. 'The money is decent for child modelling if you wanted to go down that route? Maybe go and find an agent first and get him on their books.'

'Maybe…' As glad as I am for the sisterly advice, Will and I haven't really thought much more about it. It was a moment of fun but not really our scene.

Lucy comes over, picking Joe up and throwing him in the air.

'Well, I look forward to seeing you in *Vogue*, little Joe,' she says in a sing-song voice.

She struts up and down the kitchen with him in her arms, throwing her best Blue Steel expression and arching her hips when she gets to the end of the room. Joe does not look convinced but Lucy gets her phone out for some selfies.

'Didn't you model once, Luce?' Meg asks her.

Lucy is our entertainer sister who's done every job going alongside studying. She went to dance school, spent six months on a cruise ship, has been an extra and once did a two-month stint in *Les Misérables* but currently earns her bread and butter from performing at children's parties which means she owns a lot of wigs and always has glitter in her bra.

'It was hardly modelling. It was promo work for an Audi garage. I had to do the splits on a car bonnet to get the punters in.'

'Lovely,' says Emma.

'Degrading. I was in my actual pants on the A316. Though that is how I met Gordon, the one with the big—'

'You are holding my infant son,' I say.

'He can't process things. He's only interested in milk. If I tell you' – she glances around for nieces then proceeds in her best Disney

fairy-tale voice – 'that I had sex for three months with a man called Gordon who had a knob as thick as a beer can then he will have no idea what that means.'

'LUCY!' screams Emma.

I keep Lucy close because as much as I love the older two sisters, the youngest has been good entertainment in these early days of motherhood. She occasionally comes to hang out or we meet here and dine off Emma's better internet speed and satellite TV packages. I can also live vicariously through her tales of going to gigs and clubs and hear how she's not slept and got her boobs out for reasons of fun and frivolity.

'So, plans for the next few days?' I ask Meg.

'Oh, nothing much. Eat the contents of Ems' fridge. I'll have to hang out with Mum and Dad, museums and shite for the kids.'

'And no Danny?' I ask, referring to her husband.

'No, he's working and doing boring Lakeland stuff. He's really got quite dull in his old age. It's all walking sticks and mint cake. He's bought a flat cap, you know?'

Lucy interrupts. 'Flat caps are cool.'

'He doesn't do it as a style statement, he looks like the old farmer off *Babe*. Also, big news – his brother is coming home soon.'

'Stuart?' I ask.

Lucy cackles unattractively. Stuart was the brother I once had a drunken dry hump with, though Lucy also had her way with him, years later, at Meg's wedding. His name is now used to taunt and ridicule me. I've never told anyone this but I actually threw up on his knob the evening we met.

'Give him our best, won't you?' Lucy says, putting an arm around me. I hate them all. Meg reaches over to take her nephew from her, her face lighting up to play aunty.

'God, he's a gem. Is he sleeping much?' asks Meg.

'I have no idea. He just doesn't keep to normal hours.'

'They do that. You look rough.'

'Meg, seriously?' Emma signals from across the kitchen.

'I've looked rough for years,' Meg replies. 'It's what kids do, they drain all the good humour and youth out of you.'

'I HEARD THAT!' screams her other daughter, Eve, as she enters the room, and bundles herself into her mother's lap for a giggle.

'We made Mummy fun. She was boring before she met us,' Eve says.

Meg shakes her head and looks into the distance, as if trying to wind her memory back that far. She wasn't boring. But love, and her family, mellowed her out. It changed something in her for the good. Eve disappears and I hear the clatter of all my nieces' footsteps on the stairs again.

'And is it normal for Joe's brain to be throbbing?' I ask.

Emma rolls her eyes at me. 'Explain throbbing.'

'Like there's a hole in his skull and you can see his brain beating,' I reply.

'That's his soft spot,' Emma explains. 'From where his skull hasn't fused together yet. It allows for growth. Don't touch it.'

'Do I have to cover it? Like with a hat?'

'No,' says Emma.

'But it creeps me out. And the poo, is it still supposed to look like korma?'

'Yes. Way to spoil our curry night later though,' Meg adds.

Emma goes over to examine Joe. It's what she does – she's like a living medical Wikipedia page. She knows why his eyes are changing colour and why he stuffs his fist in his mouth. She takes him off Meg and I notice how easily he sits on her hip. How does Emma handle him like that? Meg is different though. She's practical, hardy. Her intuition is more finely tuned, especially when it comes to her sisters. She studies my face like she's counting every new wrinkle and worry line I've obtained over the last year.

'Hang on in there, B. And I know what you're like, don't google everything,' Meg says.

'I don't do that.'

Lucy interrupts. 'You do. You were here last week and you asked Siri if babies can see things on screens because you were worried he'd be cross-eyed.'

Meg laughs and looks at me.

'He's not a dog. He can see in 3D.'

'Well, I didn't know that,' I reply.

'So, you were also saying before about heading out to some company party?' Meg asks.

'Yeah, on Saturday. Will's boss is organising some social to celebrate a contract so if Emma could take Joe… well, that would be awesome. I may need thirty Red Bulls before I leave the house though.'

'A date with my favourite nephew. That I can do,' Emma replies.

This social was Will's big chance to make an impression at work but in truth the sheer idea was exhausting and terrifying. When he'd been headhunted by the avant-garde, boutique architectural firm he now works at, it was such a huge move for him professionally that

I urged him to take it. But I do worry about the extra stress, time and pressure it's adding to his life. I'm also worried about being by his side at this event when I'm finding it hard enough to string simple sentences together. Me. Beth. Will. Boyfriend.

'You'll love it. You need to let your hair down, have a date night,' adds Meg.

'You know what I need? A night in a Premier Inn on my own with a bath and a takeaway.'

Emma looks at me strangely, wondering when my standards changed.

'Wow, your bar is low. We could do that here. We could role play. I can be on reception?' Lucy jokes.

I laugh but truly, a good night's sleep, some grown-up crisps and a Netflix binge would be the ultimate dream.

'And what are you wearing to this thing?' asks Meg.

'Whatever fits and whatever I can squeeze my bosom into. Seriously, did your norks get as big as this?'

Meg glances down and reaches across to give them a feel. I don't flinch as this is not new. Lucy comes over to join in the grope fest, as Joe's curious eyes wonder what this conversation may be about.

'Bloody hell, girl, is that all milk? You haven't got your refill under control,' Meg says.

'I'm a 38G.'

'I never went bigger than an E,' says Meg.

'I was a D,' Emma chips in.

'Those are porn boobs. I reckon you could balance things on them,' Lucy says. 'There's a club I worked at once that had a lady who did that. She served champagne off her rack. Girl got TIPS.'

We all look at Lucy curiously.

'It's not natural. I feel very off-centre,' I add.

I scan down as Meg reaches over to hold my hand. Having both recently had babies, we're both suffering from our bodies being in some sort of postpartum limbo but she doesn't seem to care. Maybe she's just had the time and experience of her other pregnancies to channel any despondency she has about the situation.

'Flash me, your bra must be huge,' says Meg.

I lift up my top, tentatively.

Lucy laughs. 'That could fit on my head.'

Meg, however, notices my arm clutching my stomach and rolls her eyes at my hesitancy. 'Oh, give over.' She lifts her shirt up to reveal rolls of flesh, stretch marks scattered across them like silver waves.

'Do the stretch marks ever fade?' I ask. 'Mine are dark red, I look like a tiger.'

'Own them. They're your new warrior stripes. We've just produced life. Give yourself a break.'

We sit here with our guts out in our sister's kitchen. Emma and Lucy don't even baulk, but also don't join in for which I'm glad as I know they both indulge in weekly exercise.

'It's just how it is for the while. It gets better,' Meg says.

'So this is the status quo, knackered and flabby?' I say.

'Well, yeah. Just get some high-waisted jeans that suck it all in. And big floaty dresses are good. The wrap dress is our friend. You can hide all of that.'

I look down. I'm wearing a giant T-shirt with extremely elasticated leggings. It's all about the comfort, less the look.

'I'm just worried I'll look crap at the weekend. I don't want to let Will down.'

'You won't. You're fun. People like you. You're the nice sister.'

'What does that make you?' I ask Meg.

'I was thinking about this the other day when I was watching *The Walking Dead*. I'm the ringleader spokeswoman, then you have Ems and Gracie who are the "sensible" ones telling us our plans are stupid. *Don't go there, that's insane, safety first.*' Emma doesn't disagree with this appraisal. 'Then Lucy is the fun one keeping spirits up with sarcasm and joy and you're the heart, the one we all come to for hugs and empathy.'

'That's nice. That person always gets eaten though.'

'And turns into a zombie.'

Meg pulls a face, rolling her eyes back, tongue hanging out. Joe laughs only because he's so familiar with it but he gives me a look. *How come everyone's allowed near the boobies but me? Surely they're mine?* I smile back at him.

'Give him over, Ems, he's due a feed,' I say.

I adjust myself and prop some cushions up behind me. I have yet to master the slick magician style manner that most have when feeding their kids without being noticed so I just plonk my tit out in the middle of the kitchen. Lucy's eyes read like an asteroid has just hit the room. Emma hands Joe over and he suckles for his life, like this might be his last meal. This part, at least, always feels useful, though it does have a milking cow element to it. The older sisters watch intently and I wonder whether they're assessing the technique.

'I bet Will's loving the bigger bangers though, eh?' says Lucy, casually.

I smile awkwardly. 'He's a bit scared of them. They're unpredictable. And you never told me the milk comes out like that, through lots of different holes,' I say, pointing at the older sisters.

Lucy looks horrified, staring down at her own boobs.

'Like a sprinkler,' I tell her as she tries to work that out. 'And the pressure when they're full is immense. No one told me about that either.'

'It's fun though, eh?' says Meg.

'Like how?' I ask.

'Like on a good day' – she gestures to a glass by the sink – 'I could hit that.'

Lucy's eyes light up but Emma shakes her head indicating that I won't be doing a demonstration in her shaker kitchen. Meg is reading my face though. Given my revelation that Will doesn't know what to make of my boobs, she clocks what this may mean.

'You've not done it, have you? Since…' she says.

'Meg, we've not done it since I was too big to get off the floor without help.'

My sister shrugs and I sense it may be the same with her.

'I don't think my bits are ready,' I say.

'How so?' asks the doctor sister.

'I'm scared he'll put it in me and everything will fall out.'

'I don't think that's how it works,' replies Meg.

'It can. I read about it on the internet,' I say. 'You can have a prolapse. All sorts can fall out.'

Emma shakes her head at my Google Medical School factoids.

'Yeah, that can happen if you're old and had multiple babies, lost all your tightness and not done your pelvic floors. You are doing your pelvic floors, right?' says Emma.

I nod. I do five in a row to make up for it.

'But Ems, the first wee I had after giving birth was an emotional event.'

'That is a universal thing,' she says with some gravitas.

'Neither of you kept me informed. You didn't tell me my nipples would grow to the size of brazil nuts. You just kept telling me to buy muslins.'

'Which was also useful advice,' says Meg. 'Like how bad was that tear?'

'Second degree,' says Emma. I never really understood what that meant but Lucy's grimace and crossed legs is what we're all feeling.

'Like I never looked, I didn't want to scare myself but he was a ten-pound baby so you can imagine the damage.'

'Crap, so did it look like a dropped lasagne afterwards?' Lucy chirps in.

Meg cackles in laughter but Emma stares at the youngest in wonder.

'I hate you all.' I carry on. 'But you know, Will and I are both knackered and I just don't feel hugely sexual at the moment. Will's also not about as much.'

'Work?' asks Meg.

'Kinda. He still likes a drink after office hours too.'

'While you stay at home with the baby?'

My sister doesn't seem too impressed but that seems to be her raison d'être. As the eldest, she enjoys holding our collective spouses and boyfriends to task when they misbehave.

'He's allowed a social life, to decompress.'

Ems pipes in. 'But what about moral support? Next time he does that, please ring me or Luce and we can come over with a takeaway or something.' Lucy nods and drapes herself off my shoulder, kissing the top of her nephew's head. I pout at the sincerity of the gesture.

'You're still hot, Beth. Just got more cushion for the pushing, you know?' says Lucy.

'Nice.'

Meg and Emma study me intently. They fell into motherhood so easily, like it was simply the next step in their womanhood. Their babies came and they clutched them to their bosoms and knew what every burp, cry and gurgle meant. It's their true superpower. It arrived the days their babies were conceived. I feel like I'm still waiting for my powers to come in the post.

'Maybe we can have a dinner party for your birthday?' Emma suggests, trying to cheer me up. It's about a month away but the thought alone is exhausting. Thirty-one. It's such a nothing age. It's miles away from forty but marks some depressing ascent into being an adult. Dinner would be very grown up, even civilised, but dull. I know Emma. There'd be matching placemats, a bread basket, and she'd whack on some Norah Jones.

'YES!' cries Lucy.

'Maybe?'

'Just nothing like your thirtieth,' Meg says, nostrils flared from recalling the horror. Even Emma stares into the distance like she's still not over the shock. Lucy and I just look at each other smugly. It was my last fling with youth and it *was* epic. There was a sensible element – afternoon tea with my parents – but after that it was a frigging free-for-all. Gracie was here. But so was her husband, Tom, who's since passed away. It was just before his diagnosis so we went out like some motley crew without a care in the world. We wreaked havoc in a Mexican restaurant where Will drank tequila shots and licked salt off my cleavage. We got Emma so drunk that we lost her and Meg found her passed out in front of a betting shop sleeping next to a tramp, using his Labrador as a blanket. Meg and Ems flaked on us after that but us young 'uns and a group of my friends went on to an electronic music festival in Victoria Park. Yes, *that* festival. I think about scattered flashes of pastel light across my sister's faces as we jumped in time to the beat of the music. We danced so hard. Will was abnormally sweaty as he came in to hug me.

'You're old now,' he said.

'Piss off. You're thirty in seven months.'

'I love you so much. I really want to have sex with you,' he yelled over the throb of the music.

And I knocked my head back and kept on dancing. Well, not really dancing. Just this wild prancing around with dancey spaghetti arms and Will did that move he does where he looks like he's repeatedly tossing pancakes. We had sex back at our house share in Brixton. On the sofa. Our housemate, Georgia, caught us at it and shamed us all the next day by leaving a note on the communal fridge and asking us to sanitise the area. I look down at the little baby staring up at me, his chin moving up and down as he squeezes more milk out of me. *That's how you happened. I'll save that story for when you're eighteen. You were quite the birthday present, little one.* He looks up, smiles for a moment and milk pours out the sides of his mouth.

Track Five

'Daddy Cool' – Boney M. (1976)

One of my favourite memories of Will is when we were sitting on the steps of the monument at Seven Dials in Covent Garden on one of our first dates. The weather was just starting to warm up so he bought me a drink and we sat outside and got to know each other. He liked that I drank beer, I liked how he took his parka off and draped it over my shoulders when the weather got a bit cooler. That would teach me to go out in just a denim jacket. The conversation was mainly peppered with musical references. We spoke about bands and festivals and I hit him hard with all my music trivia in an attempt to impress him. Like how Finland has more metal bands per capita than anywhere else in the world and how Lucy once went out very briefly (briefly equates to a day) with the drummer from The 1975. I loved the way he rubbed the back of his head when he was nervous, how he had dark brown eyes like chocolate buttons and how he gave me an architecture lesson about how the streets converged around that point in Central London, by taking out an old receipt in his satchel to draw the angles out. The drawing made me kiss him. He kissed back. It led to three men next to us telling us to 'get a room' jokingly. One of them shook Will's hand and then told him he was 'punching', the other asked when the wedding was. It was date three. We both blushed and laughed. Will then took me for chips. We ate them outside, clouds of grease shining through the paper, licking the salt and vinegar off the nooks and crannies of our fingers. We talked about foods that one can batter. We agreed battered cheese should be a thing. He also told me he had recently come up with a litmus test when it came to dating women. He had started asking them what their favourite Stevie Wonder songs were. If they didn't know who Stevie was then they were out on their ear. If any of them said 'I Just Called to Say I Love You' then he never called them back. He hadn't asked me yet because he'd pinned quite a lot of hope on my answer so he didn't want to be disappointed. 'Golden Lady' off the *Innervisions* album, was my response. He smiled. I was allowed to stay. Of course, I slept with him afterwards. I brought him back to the flat share I lived in. It was a hole. I remember the letter box was held together by gaffer tape and my curtains were old batik wraps. We had sex. Sex so loud that a housemate knocked on my bedroom door and said I was an awful human being as I was reminding him that it had been four months since he'd last slept with anyone. That was eight years ago.

Everything I liked about Will was dictated by how easy it was to be with him. Pre-baby, we'd be watching television and then one of us would suggest what was for dinner, the other would say takeaway and forty-three minutes later, one would be at the door, usually delivered by Sanj, who we'd come to know by name, which is why Will thought we always got free naan. We'd then open an extra couple of beers and pass out together on the sofa, only waking to switch off the telly. We both worked, we socialised, we travelled and we partied and we had moments where we'd fall out of gigs with his arms around my side, and we'd roam the streets of London searching for chips and things in batter.

Tonight feels different, however. The usual ease I feel to be by Will's side is gone. I am his plus one at his company night out and I feel like an imposter. I stand outside this organic pub in Angel, looking through the window. Will is surrounded by about ten people and they're immersed in conversation, looking earnest. Oh, architecture: gables and architraves and buildings and… stuff. He's a different Will, one that doesn't quite look like himself. He's buttoned his shirt up to the top and just looks so serious, not the laidback kid who I'm used to. If the conversation is earnest then so is the pub. It's all organic, sustainable, and uber woke, confirmed by the sprightly folk soundtrack and the high level of punters in hats. I could play hat bingo and get a house in seconds: beret, trilby, newsboy, flat cap and I think that might be a loser in a bowler hat trying to be ironic or possibly trying to get me into his circus. Lucy would have a field day with him.

But I am trying. I am. I panic bought a floral wrap maxi dress and I'm wearing it with trainers and a row of gold chains Lucy lent me so I look like I vaguely used to be trendy. Does it flatter my figure? Who knows? But it contains me and that's a start. I just need to remember to hold on to it on the Tube as it is floaty in every sense of the word and I almost took off like a parachute when a train pulled into the platform. Still, I came to support Will. I am here. But my mind is with Joe, my bed, the fact I don't know who half of these people are. I also am very suspicious of Sam. Sam is the head director person whom Will has spoken about plenty but who I always assumed to be a man, probably because in between babies and sleeplessness, I don't really process things with too much clarity. But no, Sam is a woman. And she's the sort of woman I want to be when I grow up. She's assured and confident, wearing a kimono-cut dress with gold shoes and she has that sort of natural minimalist make-up look that you know is really achieved with three products that cost the same as our monthly heating bill. She also calls me B which makes me wonder if she just initialises everyone to be super-efficient, or just because she's the boss so she can get away with it. Will sees me outside and waves through the window. I excused myself to take a call and check in on Joe so I dive in my shoulder bag to find my phone and pretend to push some buttons, talking into it. Why has Sam got her hand on Will's shoulder? Is she wearing a bra with that dress?

'Hello? Hello?' Oh flaps, I've actually dialled someone.

I look down at my phone and smile. I'm glad I fake dialled you.

'Callaghan? To what do I owe the pleasure?'

'Maccers.'

Sean McGill. In modern terms, my work husband. We both went to university in Warwick and bonded as we were South Londoners studying education because we weren't sure what else there was to do in life. We always stayed close to each other through placements and work, we shared houses at one point, and as luck would have it, we ended up applying to Griffin Road Comprehensive at the same time. He's a friend, we share mugs, we cover each other's playground patrols. We had a drunken fondle at university once but that's as far as it went. I love him like a brother and I also know far too much about him. He's a bit geeky and a religious football fan. He now lives at home with his mother, who makes him a cheese sandwich every day for lunch and he kicks off when she tries to give him brown bread. Back when I was at work and I'd call him of an evening to check about school stuff, it was common to hear him marking but also playing *Call of Duty*, asking his mum if his chicken nuggets were ready.

'I butt dialled you, mate. Sorry.'

'No worries. How's tricks? Are you out? You sound out? Why aren't I there?'

It dawns on me that this is the first communication we've had since Joe was born. Sean has kept his distance. I get why. Every time he saw my pregnant bump in the staff room, he'd look at it like a strange growth, an alarming sign of the times that we were now proper adults. He didn't even send a card; his mum did and signed his name in it.

'I am. Will's work thing. First time since Joe was born. Currently outside the pub trying to figure out how to make conversation again.'

'How's the little one? How's motherhood treating you?'

Like its bitch, but I don't say that out loud.

'It's all good. How are things at Griffin Road?'

'Same old. It was parents' evening last week and I had at least five kids I have no recollection of ever teaching. Jane Kelsted is preggers.'

'That's good.' Since joining this school three years ago, Jane had been obsessed with getting pregnant to the point where most of the staff room knew her fertile days.

'But it's dull without you. I have no one to make me tea. Please come back. Bring the baby. We'll give him to the ladies in the library and he can ride the book trolleys all day.'

I laugh but feel immediate pangs of sadness. I do miss Sean. I miss the anecdotes about his failed attempts at finding love and how he's fallen asleep teaching kids about tectonic plates. Once upon a time, I'd share moments on pub pavements with him, someone I actually liked. Instead, I'm surrounded by strangers.

'You are coming back, right?' he asks.

'Of course.'

I'm supposed to return in the new year but the thought alone is exhausting. There's so much to prepare. I need to find a decent breast pump, finalise childcare and remember how to spell my name.

'You alright, mate?' he asks, hearing my low spirits.

'Tell me I'm fun and interesting.'

'You're fun and interesting. Go knock 'em dead. Do you need any jokes to break the room?'

'Your jokes? No thanks.'

He laughs. 'Enjoy, I'll catch you laters. My dinner's ready. COMING, MUM! Love you, Callaghan.'

The line goes dead and returns to a screensaver of Joe. My little boy looks up at me. Speaking to Sean brings all my thoughts and guilt-laced emotions about returning to work to the forefront. I could bring Joe into school and feed him in between lessons, keep him in a drawer. If we passed him through every department for a five-minute cuddle session, that would see me through most of the days. A tap on my shoulder gets my attention. It's an impossibly tall blond man with a very severe haircut but excellent taste in Japanese graphic T-shirts.

'Do you want a smoke?'

I was introduced to this man half an hour ago. Balls. My mind is like a sieve. Oh, he's Magnus with the shocked-looking baby.

'I don't. I just came to check on my baby,' I say, waving my phone in the air.

'Oh, the adorable Joe.'

'You have a baby, yes?'

'Agnes. She's two months.'

'Is she sleeping much? Ours doesn't sleep.'

'No, she reminds me of my teenage self. Party all night, sleep all day, eat everything,' he says.

'Did you poo all over the sofa too at that age?'

He laughs but sees my gaze caught by Sam and Will through the window. She's incredibly tactile with him and my boyfriend doesn't seem to mind.

'Don't worry about Sam, she's like that,' Magnus says. 'She likes to pet her newcomers. That was me once.'

'What is she like, as a boss?' I ask.

'Oh, she's an architectural genius. I've known her for years but her genius comes with sharp edges. She likes to wield her power, work us hard. She hasn't got to where she's got by playing nice, if that makes sense?'

I am not sure what to make of that statement so nod politely. I was never very sure what an architect did when I first met Will. I just thought they built stuff, thought maybe he could build us a house out of shipping containers like on *Grand Designs*. He was passionate about it; he would get angry at poor design and work his arse off to reach deadlines. We always had nice pens in our house, too.

Magnus puffs hard on his cigarette. I gave up smoking three years ago but man, sometimes I just like to hang around the smell. The scent of a youth filled with cheeky cigs on the pavement, trying to look cool and feel better about the world.

'What's rillettes?' he asks me.

'I have no idea.'

'I'm eating one. Can I sit next to you in case it's something weird like the French word for a tongue or a kidney or something?'

'Only if I use your shoulder for a nap?'

He shakes my hand. 'This also saves me from having to sit next to Philip.'

'I'm sorry, who?'

'He's the one with the thin moustache like a lost pube and the slacks and vest.'

We both glimpse him through the window. I think that's a monocle attached to him. Will he get that out to inspect the food?

'Oh, and I need to tell you something. This is awkward but I am going to touch you. Is that OK?'

He says his words hesitantly. I mean, we've just met. Does he want a hug? We're both exhausted new parents and I'm up for some bonding if he wants. I put my arms out to tell him I'm ready. He looks at me curiously, reaches up for my armpit and quickly tugs down, handing me the price tag in his hand. I hug him anyway.

It turns out rillettes is a chunky pâté. Magnus was happy. I had a homemade Scotch egg that was locally sourced, fed on grain and coated in more than just breadcrumbs – maybe some sort of extremely healthy seed. In any case, I was so hungry by the point it arrived that I picked it up and ate it like an apple. And I thought what an idea it'd be to batter a Scotch egg and serve it with chips. Naturally, I'd tell Will but he's sitting at the opposite end of the table while I'm with Magnus to my left and Joyce, the office manager, to the right. Joyce likes a velveteen moccasin, she has a cat called Chunk and played it safe with the soup of the day which was green and cold and not what she expected.

'I remember when my two were babies. Seems like yesterday,' she says. Except they're nineteen and twenty-two respectively, moved out and are living in Kent, but I don't argue with her about the concept of time.

'Will is so proud to be a dad, you can see it at work. He's got pictures up of Joe all over the place. He really is a sweetheart.'

Joe or Will? I want to ask without sounding needy if there are any pictures of me but I like the idea that photos of Joe stare at Will all day, that he gets to spend some time in his son's company. It's been an odd evening. I haven't minded being with Magnus and Joyce but this has not been the evening sold to me. I wanted some quality time with Will. I wanted to feel relaxed. But I only managed a few sips of wine before I really felt it go to my head and I am clock watching thinking about Joe. I dropped him off at 6.30 p.m. and filled him to the brim with milk at Emma's but ideally, we need to leave here at 10 p.m. for me to be able to feed him. It's 9.57.

'Excuse me, I just need to absent myself to the loos.' I try and locate Will but his end of the table is empty. I find my way to a quiet corner of the pub and text Ems.

How is he?

He's fine. He just took a bottle.

He never takes a bottle.

Usually because you're nearby and he can smell your boobs. He's had another feed and then I'll get him down for another nap.

My shoulders slump. Joe was going to be my excuse for us leaving.

Should my boobs hurt? They're getting quite hard, almost painful.

Express?

Where?

Anywhere? Meg once expressed into a Fanta can at a Take That gig. I used to do it at work. I even expressed into a paper cup once in the staff room. It's that or clogged milk ducts and abscesses and then you will know real pain.

You're both feral.

This is your life now. Just get on with it. And Joe is fine. Take your time.

I stare down at my phone. The pub hums around me. I want to go home. The gents door opens and Will emerges, followed by Philip, who pats him on the back and carries on through to the restaurant.

'You OK?' Will asks, coming over to put a hand around me.

'I think? I was worried about Joe.'

His expression changes immediately. 'Do we need to leave? Is he alright?'

'He's fine. Ems, as usual, has it all under control. She's just told me to decant my tits in the sink though so they don't go humungo.'

He chuckles but sighs with relief. 'What a night. Thank you for being here, for humouring everyone. I do bloody love you.' He stumbles as he makes that declaration.

'How drunk are you?' I ask him.

'Drunk enough so I'm fun and breezy and don't punch Philip in the monocle.'

I bring him in for a hug and he clasps me tightly. This is what I miss: long hugs in dark corners where he whispers funny snippets of nothing into my ear. The ladies bathroom door is behind me, and he puts his head through tentatively and pulls me inside. Oh. We're doing that? I'm so not prepared for us to have public-space sex. Not to mention it's the first time we've had sex in forever too.

'Dude. Now?'

'Hell, no. But if you're squeezing your boobs in a sink then I'm not missing out on that.'

I laugh. Needs must. I push the fabric of my dress to one side and unclasp my bra as he locks the door then comes to stand next to me, smiling at me through the mirror. I hand him my bag.

This is a perfect date night activity. It's what all new parents do. I can do this. I can milk my tits into a sink. I have to lean forward slightly, angling the nipple over the basin and squeeze. As is the case with my milk supply, the first squeezes are a relief and shoot out across the porcelain before they peter out into a dribble. This must sound like I have an extraordinarily unpredictable bladder to anyone outside. Will can't stop laughing.

'If you get your phone out, I will smother you with these things,' I say.

'Can I have a go?' he asks, half drunk but half trying to help me preserve some sense of dignity. I shrug. These boobs don't belong to me anymore. Have a squeeze. I place my hand over his to provide instruction.

'Like, fingers there and there and squeeze.'

A stream of milk trickles over his fingers.

He giggles. 'It's warm.'

'It's not come out of a fridge,' I tell him.

We're both in hysterics. This is the first time he's been near r breast for a while, so there's relief he's not completely fearful of the It feels like he's dipping his toe in the waters again to check it's s

'You want me to milk you next?' I ask.

He raises his eyebrows at me but we both keel over laug I remember a time when I gave him a blowie at a concert. so far removed from that point. I poke at my breast, now so the touch and grab his hand, kissing the fingers. It's not re sexual in any way but it's a comfort. I wouldn't want to be by anyone else. I want to ask if we can just stay in this cu the rest of the evening, away from the rest of the world.

'That better?' Will asks.

'I mean it'd be better if someone attached their mouth to it a. drained it properly.'

'That's kinky. Are we ready for that?'

I laugh a little too loudly and Will hushes me as we hear the shuffle of feet waiting by the door. He pushes some hair away from my face as I re-adjust myself in the mirror. I smooth down the hair frizz and reapply Vaseline to my lips and the dry patch of skin that has formed on my chin like some hormonal soul patch. As I do so, Will opens the door and as joy and luck would dictate it, Sam stands there, beaming like she's had too much of the organic wine. That doesn't look suspicious, us hogging the loos together and me re-applying my lip balm. I wonder how much she may have heard of our conversation too.

'Oh.' I can't tell if she's disgusted or impressed. 'How are you both enjoying the evening?'

'It's a really lovely pub. The food is great,' I say, my face rising to an ever deeper blush.

'What did you have? she asks.

'I had the chicken,' Will mumbles.

'I had the burrata and the risotto, it was all a delight,' she replies. 'So fresh.'

I pause. Burrata is a food trend I've not caught up with in the past year. I think it's cheese. It's not a burrito. But I can't look uncultured and ask. She grabs my hand which takes me by surprise.

'It's so nice to finally meet you. I'm totally in love with your boy.'

With Joe? Oh. Will? Like literally? If she is then we need to have a fight in these loos, right now.

'We're headed on to another bar, you are coming... yes? You must, you must.'

I smile. Make your excuses, William. We have a twelve-pound baby at your sister's house, he's the best excuse we've ever had to get out of things. But then if we stay and laugh at his boss's jokes and compliment her then will this help him be part of the gang? Might she give my boy a bit more money and shoo him out of the office at a reasonable hour to see his infant son?

'Sure thing, sounds fun,' I say.

Will looks mildly shocked at my acceptance of the invitation. She squeals and links arms with me like she's known me forever. 'I'm going to do some lines now and then I'll be good to go. You two want any?'

We both shake our heads in firm unison. She closes the door as Will and I stand there, his hand reaching down to grab mine.

Track Six

'Scooby Snacks' – Fun Lovin' Criminals (1996)

Will is drunk. Properly drunk. I know Will is drunk because he's standing in the middle of a Tesco Metro stroking the biscuits.

'There are so many biscuits!' he says, in wonder.

I am not drunk. Nowhere near. Ever since my mother and sister told me Joe ingests everything that goes in my breast milk, I've been paranoid as hell. I'm staring at energy drinks, craving them but knowing I had a double espresso in the restaurant which means if I take in any more caffeine, next time I feed, it'll be like giving Joe jet fuel. He might take off and shoot into space. I should drink a shedload of water and wash that coffee out of me. I'm also hungry. Why am I always so effing hungry? Will comes in for a hug. I've always liked that about him, that my boyfriend is a hugger. Though he really chooses his moments.

'I'm drunk.'

'I know.' While I did espresso, Will did more wine at the restaurant before we left. I cup his face. His eyes are swirling in different directions.

'Thank you for coming tonight. I don't know what I'm doing. I'm trying to keep her onside.'

'By showing her how well you can handle your alcohol?'

'I thought the alcohol would give me a second wind. I am now completely wired. Why are we doing this?' he asks me, knowing I accepted this invite.

'Maybe we stay for the one drink then slink away? It'd get you in her good books. They'll be so drunk and coked up by that point they might not notice we're gone?' I suggest.

Will's eyes light up and he clicks both fingers into shooting signs in my direction. 'This is why we're together. I've done so much sucking up tonight. I feel sullied.'

'Is it working?' I ask.

'Who knows? But Philip and I are apparently both up for associate and she's playing us off against each other. It's borderline evil.'

'You never told me that?'

'Extra three grand a year. It'd be awesome.'

He goes quiet for a moment to think about that. I always fear he focuses too much on the financials of his career now, but I hope he's not selling his soul in the process. I hope he still enjoys and loves what he does. It's not the time to question this though as he's stroking a packet of Oreos.

'Do you want to get some Oreos?' I ask in maternal tones.

He nods and hugs me. This is what happens when Will gets drunk, he regresses and I have to mother him and make sure he feels safe. Many an evening has been spent feeding him a kebab on a bus or making sure he doesn't jump off things under the illusion that alcohol has given him the power to morph into Spider-Man. Tonight, he flits in and out of being super distracted and then dancing on the spot, grinding his hips like he's listening to reggae.

'I want to dance, shall we dance?' This is a mystery to me given that they're playing Celine Dion through the speakers.

'Or not?' I say, laughing.

'But this is great as well, you and me being out and feeling like us again?'

I pause when he says this. When it was him and me versus the world, it was all so simple and fun. I remember night-time visits to corner shops, leaving with armfuls of chocolate-covered pretzels, Peperami, bottles of Beck's and a few random scratch cards, and we didn't even baulk at handing over our debit cards. But the word 'us' involves someone else now and there's guilt at leaving Joe out of the picture. I am not the same girl anymore. I see her in this aisle bulk-buying Snickers. She's thinner, full of joy and believes sleep is for the weak. I'm not sure that I actually like her much.

Will wraps his arms around me, again. 'Let's have sex later!'

I love how he announced that to the lady picking up a multipack of baked beans.

'You really must be drunk.'

He embraces me tightly and looks me in the eye.

'I've milked your boobies, that was all the foreplay I needed.'

I think the lady with the baked beans heard that too.

'I always want to have sex with you. I love having sex with you, it's just we don't do it so much anymore because you're…'

Please don't be so wasted that you're going to say the next bit out loud.

'A mum now. We're old.'

I laugh. 'I believe you can still have sex after you have children.'

'But it won't be like before…'

I widen me eyes. 'Because I've had a baby come through my lady parts?'

'Because we have a baby… Oh my God, we're parents. I'm a father. We need to have really crazy sex, like upside down and hanging off a wardrobe, hairy pits and everything."

I laugh and hold him close to my chest. I mean sex would be nice, I guess. If I wasn't so tired and if he follows through on the promise that I won't have to do anything to my body hair, and we could keep the lights off and the covers on.

I study Will as he still stands there dancing. He's broken out into some strange body-popping move but I am distracted by his eyes: wide like I've just hit him around the head with a saucepan. 'Have you taken something…?'

He stares at me with big eyes, dilated pupils. I grab at his cheeks and look at him intently.

'No…? I'm just drunk. I…' He pauses for a moment then goes slightly pale. 'Crap. But when I was in the loos, I told Philip I had a mild headache and he gave me a pill.'

'A pill?' I ask, my eyebrows raised high.

Both of us look at each other. Philip is not the sort of organised first-aid person to be carrying around painkillers, plasters and a pack of handy tissues.

'Oh my Goddy God. He said this would do the trick… Has he drugged me?' he says in a paranoid panic.

'You didn't question the fact he was offering you a tablet in a public toilet?'

'No? That was a nice respectable establishment. They're fully organic. I wasn't at a rave. I didn't even see if it was marked. What if it was ecstasy or Molly or LSD?'

Words trip out of him now as he stares maniacally at the biscuits that he was once in love with just moments ago, rubbing his temples like he's trying to keep his brain inside his skin.

Will and I weren't angels in our youth but I'm unsure how his thirty-year-old constitution can handle this. For now, he feels like a child who's had too much sugar; this is not a *Pulp Fiction* moment. But on the tip of my tongue, what I really want to say is we're parents now. We should know better. Don't pass out on me either. At least I'm sober and carrying a bit more weight on my bones so it should be easier to carry him into an Uber. The CCTV will record the moment a woman with a giant rack and voluminous dress gave a grown man a piggyback and sent a display of Pilsner flying.

'Philip didn't give you any clue what the tablet was?' I ask.

'No. Isn't that a funny name too, Philip. Philip.' He repeats it in regal tones.

'Yes, when said like that. He's a bit try-hard.'

'He's very cool. I don't think I've ever been that cool.'

'Have you seen what he's wearing? That's an old man vest. My dad wears those vests. I hardly think he's a barometer of what's cool. He's wearing a fucking monocle.'

'I just wish I had that bravery to wear what I want, make a statement, be effortless and confident.'

I cup his sad face. Don't we all? *If you started wearing vests like that though, your nipples and chest hair would make you look like an Italian gangster.* He stands there in his jeans and Converse, eyes glazed and doleful. 'But you're a beautiful butterfly, you don't need to be like the others,' I tell him.

He laughs and hugs me again.

'What are we doing here?' I ask.

'Oreos and one drink at this trendy bar and then home, I promise.'

'Promise?'

But before he has a chance to answer, he sprints towards the till in the style of an overexcited toddler.

'BETH, THEY HAVE TIC TACS! CAN WE GET TIC TACS?!'

When we get to the bar, and are queuing up, the group has shrunk considerably. Magnus has had the good sense to return to his wife and child, and Joyce has also absconded so we are left with Sam, Philip, Will, myself and Kiki and Shu, who are originally from Hong Kong but work as designers. They smile a lot and have a quirky kawaii thing going on with their clothes that is both cute, cool and which makes me insanely jealous as I'd never be able to carry off cat ears unless it was Halloween. In the queue now, I'm standing next to Philip who is as much of a wanker as I anticipated. He's standing there with a rollie and a hand on his hip harping on to the group about Grayson Perry. I'm almost disappointed that Will thought this douche had any positive qualities at all; he's a million times better than Philip.

'I mean the expression is either too graphic or too understated. There's no happy medium. No one does diptychs anymore either. There's no point,' he says, posturing through his cigarette as he talks about the artist. I pause to hear the word diptych. You're the diptych, Philip. The girls nod in agreement out of sheer manners. Will is finding it hard to focus; he keeps shifting his eyes side to side like he's just working out how far his field of vision can stretch. *Oh please, don't, Philip.*

'I like Grayson Perry. I like the courage and the mixed media,' I say.

Philip gives me a look that I can't read. Was I not part of this discussion or were his opinions only meant for the architects? Will squeezes my hand. He looks more energised than me but we'll blame the possibility that Philip may have spiked him. Do I ask Philip about the drugs? It would sound like I'm telling him off which would not be cool yet possibly quite parently. I wish Will would control his face a bit more as he's showing us that he has Oreo crumbs lining his teeth like he's been eating soil. Don't smile too much, Will. Philip starts jabbering on at Kiki and Shu about Hockney. Sam is on her phone and seems to be inviting the world along to this bar.

'Babes, it will be incredible. Jacques can get us in on the guest list. I have him on the other line too.'

Even from outside, the bass pulsates under my feet. Oh my geez, it's going to be loud in there. Sam had better be buying the drinks too because this doesn't look like the sort of joint that has 2-4-1 deals on the cocktails or dry-roasted nuts behind the bar. I actually used to queue outside these sorts of places; the queuing was the foreplay to the main event. We'd be chanting and dancing, half cut, dying to get inside, arguing with everyone that we should have got here sooner but using that time to catch up and take selfies before the bad lighting became the enemy. Philip suddenly turns to us, looking a bit panic stricken.

'Shit. They're checking people on the door.'

I arch my head around the queue of about ten people to see three burly security guards at the entrance. I glare at Philip, who is patting down the pockets of the baseball jacket that makes up his ensemble. Surely if you're packing illegal substances then the best thing to do here is to just go home, Philip. I can lift up this barrier for him if it makes things easier.

'Sam, babes. They're checking bags.' I look over. She's complicit in this? I look to Will, imagining his office to look like something out of *Breaking Bad*.

'It's OK. I know these guys.'

Philip doesn't look certain and I see him tuck something down the back of his waistband. In his pants? Definitely don't be doing any more drugs from this one, Will. He then whacks out a small plastic bag of weed. He is a veritable pick 'n' mix pharmacy tonight. Please don't attempt to shove that up your bum in front of me. He looks at all of us. Will sets eyes on that bag like it's a bomb. Damn it. I grab it. The queue before us creeps forward. I'm holding drugs. What if they tackle me to the ground, call the cops and I get arrested for possession? I have a baby. I can't even put this in my bag because they'll search it. I hate you all. I slip the plastic bag into my bra behind a breast pad. I will have to disinfect my tits before I give them to my infant son. I really hate you all.

'Evening.'

The security guard is the sort with no neck who you feel has a poster of Jean-Claude Van Damme on his wall at home. I give him my bag and smile, gripping on to Will to help him stand a bit more upright. He removes half a packet of Oreos that I've twisted shut with an old hairband.

'For if you get hungry later?'

I laugh unconvincingly. He digs through my handbag in the same way I look for my keys. I know my bag is cavernous and receipts line the bottom like bedding material. I also carry an assortment of pens, none of which would work. He then pulls out some small plastic-wrapped items. *Please. Don't.*

'What are these, madam?'

'They're breast pads.'

'Like to pad your bra out?'

I feel the judgemental collective breath of the queue behind me.

'I'm breastfeeding. It's so my breasts don't leak.'

'Milk?'

I don't know how to respond to that. We all wish they leaked gin but no one's figured out how to do that yet.

'Never heard of them.'

'Oh.' I just hope he doesn't ask for a demonstration as an eighth of weed will fall out of my cleavage.

'So you're saying they're like sanitary pads for your boobs?'

'Kind of.'

'Then why aren't you wearing them?'

'They're spares.'

I can't tell if he thinks I'm lying. He puts them back. He then pulls out two double A batteries, some old hand cream I've never used and a charger cable. Mary Poppins ain't got nothing on me. He gives me the look my mother has given me for years. *You need to have a good clean-out, love.* After scanning down to my shoes, he then looks at Will.

'We don't normally allow for trainers.' Will and I watch as the others get ushered in. Sam waves to the bouncers like she's their old friend but still caterwauls down her phone, not really bothered about us. Do I fight the trainer thing? I have in the past but inside me tonight there is also mild excitement brewing at knowing that Will's battered Converse and my old Adidas Superstars may have saved us from this night out. 'But I'll let you in.' Seriously? My shoulders slump. He scans us both again. I know Will looks completely wired but what else is he looking at? Do we not match this place? Does he really think those breast pads are hiding drugs? 'Go on in, have fun.'

He says that last part like he's allowed us to have our fun tonight, he's enjoyed wielding that power. I grab Will's arm and we proceed. His arm is hard like he's tensing every muscle in his body. *Chill, Will.* Inside, it's as I imagined: dim lighting, neon menus and searing drum and bass blasts out the speakers, so loudly it's really just people standing around sipping drinks made by their 'mixologists' and nodding at others because conversation is near impossible. There's a small dancefloor to the rear, queues to the bar, queues to the toilets and exposed light bulbs hanging from the ceilings. Will's wide eyes now look like they've been caught in headlights so I back him into a quiet corner.

'How's it going? Do I need to book you into rehab yet?'

'I'm too old for this. I bet Philip did that to make me look bad. Drugging the competition. What if it was cut with something dodgy?'

'I knew a girl at university who got hospitalised for snorting Shake n' Vac once.'

He laughs but there's a scared, almost paranoid look to his face. So we're at that stage now. I embrace him.

'I'm sorry I didn't back you up with the bouncer. I was trying to stop my face from twitching uncontrollably.'

'I noticed. How do we get you down again? Water?'

'Weed. I think. I believe there's some of that in your bra.'

'And he's not getting it back. I'm selling it to pay for our Uber home.'

He kisses me on the forehead. We suddenly hear a sharp whistle and turn to see Philip standing on a table of a booth, urging us over.

'One drink?'

'One drink.' He interlocks his fingers into mine and we weave through the crowd of revellers. At least I have somewhere to sit tonight.

'Oh my God, did the 5-0 do a strip search?' Philip asks when we get there.

'I don't think they were the actual police,' I tell him. He glares at me like I just ruined his bad joke.

'What are we drinking?' asks Will.

I glance at Will. We need to scrape him off the ceiling. Are we seriously adding more alcohol to the mix?

'Oh, Sammy's got us bottles of Lanson for the table?' Philip says, swigging from a glass. Kiki is kind enough to push two glasses in our direction and I take a polite sip. Geez, that is the good stuff. It tastes like money. Will drinks his a little too enthusiastically. Pace yourself. I suddenly feel an arm drape itself around my waist.

'Darlings, you made it in!' says Sam. 'I was worried. I was on the phone to Terry and Giselle. You will *love* them, Will. They own an agency in Prague and are here for the week. Such intense ideas about urban regeneration. Jacques is also coming.' I have no idea who Jacques is but nod. 'And we just *have* to dance. Come on, gang, a celebratory boogie because we got that Lambeth gig.' She swipes a glass from the table and holds it aloft, grabbing at Will and grinding at him in a time that doesn't quite fit the music. You have to applaud the gall of a woman who does that right in front of his girlfriend. Is she just so drunk that she's blissfully unaware? Or is this some sort of boss privilege that she's playing out here? Do I play along so I don't get Will in trouble? Or do I pretend to sling my handbag over my shoulder and take her out? I have to laugh, don't I? I have to push down all my feelings of jealousy and judgement and self-worth and let her do this. Kiki and Shu place their handbags on the table and shift out of the booth while Philip removes his jacket, ready to launch himself onto the dancefloor. I am not a part of the team who got the Lambeth gig so I understand my role here. I'm saving our seats and looking after the belongings. It's one down in ranking from the designated driver. Go. Dance. At *least* dance the drugs out of your system. As Will follows them, he looks back at me, apologetically. It's cool. I don't like this song anyway.

'Excuse me... excuse me... is anyone sitting here?'

I jolt myself awake and sit up to see a group of girls looking over me. God, they're so young. I want to see ID. How long was I asleep?

'Yeah, sorry… they're on the dancefloor.' I point over to the little crowd of people I assume to be Sam, Will and the others. They seem to have been joined by a few more. There's a neon aura of merriment around them. The girls don't look too impressed with me. Do I allow them to perch for the meanwhile? Or is it because I nodded off and used this nook like a tramp? They skulk away and I sit up, taking a sip of this expensive champagne to refresh myself. My milk will be posh now, Joe. I hope you appreciate it.

Along the sides of the banquette seating, I've arranged coats and bags to protect our space. I refold Sam's coat. It's Balmain. It's so chic. I stroke at the suede fabric. I don't buy suede because it bobbles when it gets wet but it's so nice to touch. I can't believe I fell asleep. Actually, I can. Realistically, all that's getting me through this evening is momentum but the fact I've stopped and taken pause on a seat with cushions has meant my body has taken over. This is more exercise and excitement than I've had in months. To be fair, is anyone actually looking? I could have another ten-minute power nap and I don't think anyone would care. But a figure suddenly appears at the table.

'Breast pads.'

It's the bouncer from before. Is that my new name now? But he points over to my dress. My nap has meant a breast pad has shifted out of position and sticks out my cleavage. I'm half grateful it's not the eighth of weed. I adjust my tits and look at up him.

'I was told there was someone asleep in the booths.' I look over his shoulder to see the same group of girls standing a distance away, glaring at me. Is that a reportable offence now? I glare back at them. *I hope one of you drops your phone in a loo tonight and you lose all your pictures.*

'I'm not asleep. As you can very well see.' I smooth down my hair and unconvincingly wipe at the corners of my mouth where I may have been drooling. Please don't throw me out and put the nail in this evening's coffin. I'm not sure why but I then reach for Sam's coat and drape it on my shoulders. To make myself look richer, more powerful perhaps, so he may think I'm important. Instead, he comes to sit next to me. I am slightly unnerved so put my handbag in between us. Crap, this is when I'm supposed to slip him a fifty-pound note to bribe him, isn't it?

'Can I say something?' he asks.

'Only if it's nice?'

'You look very tired. Are you alright?'

I laugh at his honesty. I thought I'd used enough concealer to hide the worst bits. I suspect cheap product, summer heat and the nap has melted it all off.

'Honestly? I have a new baby. I'm not the best version of myself this evening.'

He smiles. 'How old?'

'Ten weeks.'

He scans my face trying to work out what I looked like before this. I didn't look as bloated for a start. And I'd have taken greater care with my eye make-up and hair.

'My wife is eight months pregnant with our first.'

I smile at the fact he wants to share this with me though I'm pretty sure I act as some sort of advisory warning.

'When I met you in the queue I realised I didn't know what a breast pad was. This baby is going to be here in a month and I don't know half of what I need to,' he tells me, panicked. 'And I'm

standing in the queue searching down punters and thinking are
Lil's boobs going to leak milk the whole time? Like, how does she
switch them off?'

'They're not taps.'

'Yeah, I googled that on my break and found that out. Did you
know men can lactate too? If you stimulate their nipples enough?'

'Will hasn't got round to that yet.'

He laughs. 'Will, is he your husband?'

'Boyfriend. We've never sealed the deal, as it were.'

'And the baby's name?'

'Joe.'

'Do you have a picture?'

I reach down in my bag for my phone, scrolling through my
photo roll. It's all Joe. I have no other recent pictures except one I
sent Will of a double sausage and egg McMuffin I bought about a
fortnight ago, and a few dozen memes that I seem to collect to try
and spice up my social media.

The bouncer's face softens to see Joe on my screen. It's a shot
where he's just woken up and his bedhead is whipped up like a
mass of fur.

'Wow, he's very cute.'

'Thank you.'

He scrolls through a few more photos, smiling at them all. That's
the thing about baby pictures. We take them when the baby is cute,
when he's smiling and just woken up or covered in food and mess,
revelling in the adorability. We don't have photos of them crying,
crimson with wind and discomfort and covered in barf. I'm selling

him the cute side of parenting, though maybe that's what he needs instead of worrying about how he can try and milk himself.

'So this is your first night out since having the baby?' he asks.

'That's why you let us in, isn't it?'

'You both look like you needed it. How's your evening going?'

'I fell asleep.'

He smiles. He scans across to Will, almost angry with him. But Will needed this as much as me. He needed to relax and let loose. I don't want him babysitting me or holding my hand. And maybe one of us needs to get something out of this evening. I wish our first night out together was more fun, easier, with not so douchey people but it's just one night. I see him jumping about, joyous, happy.

'Can I get you anything? A hot drink? A cushion?' the bouncer asks.

'You make me sound like your grandmother.'

He laughs again.

'Just tell that group of girls to do one.'

'I'll them you're famous. You look like Keira Knightley.'

I look at him like he's been the one drinking. 'If she'd eaten all the pies.'

He gives me a look, almost angry at my need to self-deprecate, then hands my phone back to me. A message from Emma flashes up. It's a picture of a very sleepy Joe, his hand tucked under his face. It makes my heart hurt. Or maybe that was my boobs.

'I'm Beth, by the way.' I put my hand out to shake his.

'Eric.'

'You're going to be a great dad, Eric.'

He beams. I mean, I don't really know him but sometimes you just need to hear those words said out loud. He salutes me and returns to the girls. I hear one of them laugh loudly as he tries to fob them off with the Keira Knightley lie. Will and Sam suddenly pop up at the table.

'Problem, babes?' asks Sam. 'This table is booked out.'

'It's fine. He was just doing the rounds.'

She spies her jacket draped around my shoulders. Now she thinks I'm being far too familiar or that I'm a coat thief. I try to casually remove it to Will's amusement.

'I'm going to order a few more bottles for the table,' she tells Will, the intimacy of her body language still jarring with me. She takes her Louis Vuitton tote and Will comes to sit next to me.

'One drink, Will Cooper.'

'I'm sorry.' He takes my hands and kisses them.

We hear a song in the background. It's a remix of Joe's favourite Groove Armada song and we smile, swaying together in our seats, shoulders moving in time. It's what we did, everywhere. We know the lyrics or we have a story about how we have this song on vinyl, have heard that band live. We bop in our seats, the music gluing us together. I like this. I miss this. But then I see Sam ushering Will over to the bar. He lets go of my hand.

'You're being summoned,' I say.

He puffs out his cheeks.

'I'm going to go,' I say. 'I'll get an Uber to Emma's and stay there.'

He doesn't reply. I see his mind whirring.

'Stay. You're having fun,' I tell him.

'You're not?'

I shake my head. 'I love you. I'll see you tomorrow.'

He embraces me tightly. *Come with me*, I want to say. You're better than this, Will. But he hears Sam calling his name from the bar and he shuffles out of the booth.

'When you get to Emma's, just message me to let me know you're safe, yeah?'

I nod. He disappears into the crowd and I grab my bag, seeing Philip's baseball jacket there in the pile. I bet you've never played baseball in your life, Philip. I pat down the pockets and find a bag of pills. Twat. I take them all and stuff them in my bag, reminding myself to find a bin on my way home.

Track Seven

'Waking Up' – Elastica (1995)

'B… My nephew is hungry again…'

I wake up on a sofa that isn't mine. I know because mine is second-hand and has always smelt mildly of damp dog. I jolt up. Am I still in that bar? Or maybe I'm in an Uber. I fell asleep in that too. All I remember was a very lovely conversation with a man called Jamal from South Norwood who liked a bit of Smooth FM and had rosary beads hanging from his rear-view mirror. But then I must have fallen asleep because before I knew it, he and Emma were trying to wake me up in the back seat. I then received a telling off from my big sister that I should never fall asleep in the back of taxis. That's how people end up in ditches without their organs, apparently. She got me inside the house, made me drink a pint of water because she assumed I was drunk and then attached a baby to one of my boobs before I fell asleep. Again.

Now I'm awake on this sofa and everything smells fresh and new, unlike my flat which is normally filled with the scent of stale milk and nappy sacks. My eyes spy a hot cup of coffee and a plate of toast on the table in front of me. I'm wearing a giant nightshirt

and my make-up has been removed. This is why we keep Emma.
I sit up and she's sitting next to me. A freshly groomed Joe in his
panda sleepsuit looks over and beams. *It's you. I know you. I think I
missed you*, he seems to say. *This one is great but the boobs are useless.*
I smile back.

'Thanks, Ems. Where's Lucy?'

'Like a cat, she crawled back as the sun came up. So it was just
me and Joe having a date night. We got through half a season of
Downton and ate giant couscous. Didn't we? How was your evening?'

I shrug. I'm disoriented and without caffeine so it's hard to know
how to communicate. The key word is disappointment.

'I'm not impressed that Will just put you in a cab and abandoned
you,' she informs me.

'He didn't. I left of my own accord.'

'Still. He should have gone with you, no?'

I don't know how to reply to that. Do I wish he'd sacked off his
dance party and accompanied me home? Yes. But I knew why Will
had to stay. It was a work thing, a potential for promotion thing.
We also don't have the sort of relationship where we tell each other
what to do. Of course, we scrap over chores and things around the
house, like how he leaves his wet towels hanging off the wardrobe
doors, but I am also me. I leave empty mugs everywhere, and little
molehills of my clothes lie around the floor of the flat.

'I'm fine. Your sofa is dead comfy.' I look at the clock on her
mantelpiece. 'And that's the longest I've slept in forever.'

She rubs my shoulder reassuringly and I'm relieved as it removes
the judgement from her face. She hands Joe over to me and I realise
that to feed him, I will have to hike up this shirt and sit here with

my knickers and overhang. Emma's a doctor so I suppose she's seen worse but I try and hide everything with the fleece blanket she draped over me. She watches as I unhook my bra and remove my breast pad to see an eighth of marijuana drop on my thighs. Her eyes may as well fall out of their sockets. This is the wrong woman to see that. Meg would have been fine, Lucy still smokes on occasion, but Emma, who has dedicated house slippers for her visitors and Marie Kondos the shit out of her knicker drawer? No.

'What on earth, Beth?'

I want to say, *That's oregano. I like to self-season in restaurants.* But she's not that stupid and I'm sure she knows what it looks like after Mum found some on Lucy once and reacted by chasing her down the street with a dustpan.

'Are you smoking weed? Do you know how harmful that is to Joe?'

'Of course I'm not smoking weed. I haven't in years.'

She rifles around on the coffee table, trying to find some baby wipes.

'Wipe your boobs down immediately before you put that anywhere near my nephew's mouth! There could be traces of anything on that packet.'

Her panic is warranted, to be fair, but Joe looks upset that there are delays to his breakfast. She runs to get a bottle of bleach and sprays it at me.

'Disinfect?' I look at her strangely but do as I'm told. 'For my life, are you dealing?'

'Out of my bosom? No! One of the group had drugs and they were searching bags and pockets so I hid it there. It's all sealed, there's no risk to Joe, right?'

I finish wiping and she runs to the kitchen to dispose of the offending wipe. Joe smiles at me before latching on. Emma returns, cradling her coffee. The plastic packet still sits on her sofa and she eyes it curiously before picking it up with two fingers and flinging it in my nearby handbag. 'You're not even curious to keep it and have a puff?' I ask.

'No. In medical school, I saw a man fling himself off a roof once completely razzled on acid. So, I just say no.'

'Goody two shoes.'

She pretends to polish an imaginary halo. 'And how was it? Did you have a nice time at least?'

'Do you know what rillettes is?'

'It's another word for pâté.'

'Oh. Anyway, I just wasn't in the mood.'

She scans my face.

'Did you two have a fight?'

'No. Not even that. He's got some flamboyant new boss and I think he was trying to keep up with her and his colleagues to prove a point. It was painful to see and I was just seriously lagging by the end. Not being able to get drunk didn't help.'

'So Will was drunk?'

And possibly off his bollocks on an unknown substance. But I stay quiet. Given her reaction to the weed in my bra that may be too much for her to digest at this time.

'*He's* not breastfeeding. He was allowed.'

'But did he at least check you got home safely or ask about Joe?'

I grab at my phone and show her my last text to him which he replied to with a row of lemon emojis. She doesn't quite get it.

Emma's not usually so judgy but her recent divorce has made her hold people to different standards these days. She's more guarded, more closed off.

'This is great coffee,' I say, trying to change the subject, reaching for my toast. 'Thank you for letting me stay.'

'To be fair I liked Joe's company. Saved me from sitting here on my own like a loser.'

'You could have gone out with Lucy.'

'To a trance night in Hoxton? I don't think so.'

She looks over at my face and studies my fatigue in the same way that Meg did the other day.

'But seriously, are you really OK, B? After you were here the other day, it got me thinking. I know what motherhood is like. It's totally displacing. You know I'm here if you need me, yes?'

I smile and nod. Displacing isn't even the word. Beth Callaghan is gone. She's a mother now. I used to have a name, be an actual person but I don't even know who she is anymore. I keep my thoughts to myself. Emma never appeared like this as a mother to me. She was completely zen and it felt like motherhood fit. It was a crown that never slipped, that never sat too tight. My crown is bloody huge, and heavy. And I can't see anything as it covers my eyes.

'You know what would make me happy?' I say.

'Shoot.'

'Can I have a shower? A long one. And wash my hair and dry it properly. And maybe have another micro nap on your stupidly comfortable sofa.'

I'm skirting around the issue. It's very me but I don't want to conduct a comparative life exercise here with my sister. I love her completely but I am under no doubt she is a much better mother than me and that doesn't make me feel too great. She wants me to pour this all out to her but now's not the time. I need much more white toast and sugar in my system for that to happen.

'Deal. I washed your dress. I'll make sure it's dry and bring it up to you,' she replied.

'Of course you did.'

My phone ringing breaks up the conversation and I lean over to answer it. It's Peter, Will's brother.

'Peter? Hey.'

'Thank God. Are you OK, Beth?'

'Yes? Why do you ask?' I'm a bit alarmed by the tension in his voice.

'Because I literally opened my front door this morning and found Will sleeping on my porch?'

'You what?'

'Drunk as a fricking skunk too. It's a wonder Kat let me bring him into the house. She thought it was a homeless man. Have you two had a fight?'

'No, we went out and I left early because of Joe. Is he OK?'

He comes off the line to speak to someone in the background.

'He's safe. I think you had the house keys and then he realised you weren't there and— When are you going to grow up?' I can hear Peter and Will having a brief exchange of the sorts of insults you can only share with siblings. 'I am going to drive him back to yours now. Can he meet you there?'

'Sure, give me half an hour?'

I hang up and Emma eyeballs me from her armchair.

'He could have brought him here?' she says.

'Don't.'

'I'm just saying, at least let your son finish his meal. And I am going to put on some more toast.'

'But I said half—'

'There will be traffic. They can wait.'

We hear a sudden clatter of running down the stairs like a wounded wildebeest. Lucy appears in just her knickers and a vest, blonde hair bundled into a bun.

'I thought you might still be here,' she says, clutching her phone.

'Are you OK?' I ask.

'The rapper. You said Joe did some album cover thing for a rapper. Is this her? Because that's Joe. That's definitely Joe.'

She turns her phone towards me and sure enough, it's the album cover Joe posed for.

'"Best debut British rap album I've heard in years" says Jay Z,' Lucy quotes.

'Who?' Emma asks. We ignore her as Lucy comes to sit next to me and we read the article together. Special K is duetting with Stormzy, has festivals lined up and she's the new face of Missoni. And in all her pictures, there's Joe just sitting there keeping it casual. Lucy and I stare down at him happily suckling away on my breast. He looks up at us. *I'm just having my breakfast, ladies. Nothing to see here.*

By the time we get back to our flat, it's been almost an hour and I find Will sitting in the communal corridor having a cup of tea with

Paddy. He looks relieved to see me but the fatigue and hangover sit heavy in his face. Hardly surprising given he slept like a stray dog outside his brother's house. He takes Joe and pulls faces at him while I dig around for my keys.

'Look at you in a dress,' says Paddy.

I twirl for him. 'I let the legs out once a year, it's a blink and you'll miss it kind of event,' I say jokingly. He takes Will's mug and winks at me.

'Did you lock him out again?' he says.

'I think we're just ill-rehearsed at this going out lark,' Will replies.

'Well, a relaxed Sunday is what you both need. Give us a shout if you need anything.'

I nod and we both struggle getting the car seat through the front door. Inside, the air is flat and stagnant. There's none of Emma's fresh linen smell. The sofa is lined with a pile of dry but unpressed baby clothes and remnants of me getting ready for a night out: hairbrush, make-up and random coins and crap that didn't make it into my handbag. I put Joe down on the floor as Will embraces me from behind.

'God, I am so sorry. I'm such an idiot.'

I pat his hand. Joe looks up at us curiously. *Who are you two people? What happened to you? You look like a scarecrow.* I pick at some bits of grass from Will's hair.

'I should have waited,' I say.

'I should have left,' he replies.

He parts our embrace to smile at me and then sorts through a plastic bag in his hands. 'I asked Pete to drop me on the high street. I wandered around the supermarket like a tramp just putting random things you like in a basket to say sorry.'

He pulls out an assortment of things: an actual lemon, a Kinder Egg, a Twix, a family-sized trifle, a trashy magazine, a bottle of fizzy water and half a baguette that he's already had a munch on. I smile at his desperate attempts to make peace when in truth, I'm not angry. I just think it was an ill-planned evening that neither of us were feeling. Will escapes into the kitchen to switch on the kettle.

'Kat hates me because I threw up on the pavement near their house. She made me clean it with a bucket,' he tells me.

'Yikes. What time did you get there?'

'Four? I just remembered you had the keys and I didn't want to go to Emma's, and Pete's house was closer but then I didn't want to wake him.'

'A drunk's logic then. How was it after I left? How was Sam?'

Will's voice weaves in from the kitchen.

'A nightmare. We got through so much drink. Philip was trying to get in her pants but I think she left with that other bloke, Jacques. And it turns out Terry and Giselle are stuck-up twats.'

I want to say I could have told him that. But I hope he did what he needed to help with his work situation and blow off the cobwebs.

'What about Kiki and Shu, they seemed nice?'

He doesn't reply as I collapse on to the sofa.

'Also, Philip lost a whole load of pills in the bar,' he says. 'He went mental which confirmed to me that he didn't give me a paracetamol in the pub.'

'I may have had something to do with that...' I shout out towards the kitchen.

Will's head appears at the doorway and he eyes me suspiciously. 'You dark horse.'

'I'm an expert drug smuggler it would seem. The pills are in a bin in Islington. I also gave that weed to Lucy as an early Christmas present.'

There is the familiar clink of teaspoons against mugs and the clatter of them landing in the bottom of the sink as he returns to sit next to me. I halve the Twix and give him one of the fingers. I bite into one and crumbs line my cleavage and dress. I am a messy eater; it means when we give Joe solids, he'll have an ally. Will wipes a slug-like trail of caramel from the side of my mouth, and looks me in the eye, almost like he wants to tell me something.

'This… The whole night, all I thought was, I just want to be on our sofa with you,' he says.

It's a romantic declaration. I'd rather it was Emma's sofa but it does feel nice to be back in our nest, somewhere that's familiar and not vibrating with noise and energy. We were out in the world like two scared kittens; it was possibly too much, too soon. I go to unstrap Joe from his car seat and bring him into the huddle. My head finds Will's chest and we lie there for a moment, taking it all in. Joe still looks very confused, like he's waiting for a party to start. Will circles a finger in his palm and he grasps it tightly.

'Funny story. Do you remember those photos Joe took outside the pub with that rapper girl? I think they've become a thing?'

I get out my phone to show him. He laughs and studies the pictures in detail. I also notice Lucy has copied them and tagged them into her Instagram stories and my inbox seems to be pinging. Will cups Joe's face.

'Well, something fun to tell him when he's older I guess.'

I scroll through the messages on my phone, one of them from Giles, the creative director.

'Wow. Giles has asked if we want to be in a music video too.'

'You want to be in a music video, Joe?' Will jokes.

Is he asking Joe? I don't think our son would mind as long as the milk kept coming.

'We could be on MTV. Is that still a thing?' I mutter. My attention is drawn to the details in the message. 'It's next week and not too far from here. We could take the train.' But when I turn back, Will is looking down at his own phone, worried.

'Problems?' I ask.

'Work. Sam loves this. She got us all drunk last night and now she's sending us stuff to do on Sunday, making us feel guilty if we don't pitch in. I'll need to fire up the laptop.'

He cradles his head in his hands.

'Maybe have a power nap, a coffee?'

'I'm sorry about this, B.'

I glance over at her emails. She likes her FULL CAPS and the tone is slightly blunt and unappreciative. I don't say a word, but in my mind, that's the workings of a pretty shitty boss. Will mutters under his breath about deadlines and drawings. He paces the room going through his satchel, Joe's eyes following him as the stress radiates from his face. He disappears into our bedroom to take a call.

I look down at Joe. 'Is it time for a nap yet?' I ask him.

Joe giggles back at me. *Errr, it's mid-morning, lady. I got baby things to do. We've got videos to be in and I have nappies to get through.*

It's going to be one of those lost days, isn't it? Tired and sleepy and running chores like laundry and washing any traces of weed off my tits. It may involve hamburgers later. It will certainly involve being Will's tea bitch. I hear him discussing architecty things through the door. My eyelids feel heavy and my head drops but then a gurgling noise wakes me up, bright bear eyes gazing at my sorry face.

Just you and me then, milk lady.

I guess it is.

Track Eight

'You Got the Style' – Athlete (2002)

Are you there? Is it posh? texts Lucy.

Uber posh. There was a receptionist with eighties shoulder pads and there's a lot of glass. I keep walking into it.

LOL. You idiot. How's Joe? Is he nervous? Did you put him in red? He looks good in red.

I put him in head-to-toe black as I was told that's slimming.

You did?

I didn't.

I want pictures later. I'm telling everyone.

I smile and put my phone away. I'm in a warehouse studio after replying to the messages from Giles about the music video. Am I little worried about entering into something superficial and self-important? Yes. But am I desperate for company and entertainment beyond the confines of my flat? Also, yes. There's also payment involved and I thought it might be a way to earn some pocket money.

I wish Will was here. He'd love the stylings of this place, the white and exposed concrete floor. He'd raid the table of free refreshments and take extra condiments to put in his pockets because he thinks they are useful but they always end up in the door of the fridge or the glove compartment to be forgotten.

Joe's not the only baby here today. Special K will be surrounded by babies and children for a few shots of the video so we wait to be called in. I look across at the rows of parents and children. They are all different, all beautiful in their own way, but I am transfixed by a few whom I'm not too convinced by. There's a baby opposite that might be wearing make-up. There's a bit of blusher and I think they've done something to her lashes. Lordy. Who puts make-up on a baby? There's another one in a hair band, in a desperate move by the mother to prove it's a girl, I guess. There's also a baby in braces, trousers and the tiniest of flat caps. Hipster baby. I have no idea what they're asking for here. Was I supposed to tart Joe up? He looks up at me. I've put him in dungarees that were a gift and ran a comb through his hair. Do you moisturise babies? I haven't really felt the need; he has really good skin, the sort of soft child skin I envy as it's the very opposite to my greasy, hormonal breakout face. Joe looks up at me and grabs onto my thumb. *This is new, eh?* I am also wearing more than just leggings and trainers. I'm in that maxi wrap dress again to get as many wears out of it as possible and I like that I haven't had to shave my legs. I may just wear this forever.

Hearing a bassline pound through the walls, one baby looks at it strangely like Godzilla might be gatecrashing this event. I look down at Joe. *I hope you're OK in all of this. Have fun. Smile plenty.* I'm not sure to what extent he takes instructions.

'Is this seat taken? May I?' The voice comes from a gentleman next to me carrying a little baby girl.

I clear my bags and coat to the floor. 'Sure thing. Hi.'

He's classically handsome like Jude Law in his prime, and his hair is extraordinary. It makes me smile awkwardly; I may also blush. I'm too used to only seeing my sisters, Paddy and characters on the television to know how to interact with new people. His daughter is in a car seat and has bundles of blonde corkscrew curls. She scrunches up her face sweetly, smiling at me. I smile back.

'I'm Harry. This is Delilah.'

Crap, he's speaking to me. I need to reply.

'Beth and Joe.' I bend down and shake Delilah's hand. 'That's awesome hair, young lady.'

She giggles.

'Nothing to do with me, all my wife. He's also a handsome little sod, eh?'

I want to reply, *So are you.* I don't.

'He has his moments. He has good light today.'

He smiles and studies my face. Don't look at the light on my face, it's not so great.

'You're the baby. The album cover one?' He talks to Joe, though I'm pretty sure he won't answer.

'I guess?' People in the room turn to listen.

'That was a huge gig. Who's your agent?'

'We don't have one.'

'So a street cast, interesting. He has awesome eyebrows.'

Joe smiles. *I know, mate, I grew them myself.*

Harry studies both of us for a moment, his gaze quite intense. He's doing that thing where he's checking if we match. But before he has time to scrutinise us further, a door opens and Giles stands there with a clipboard.

'It's the pub baby. Yay! I'm glad you're here. I need you all to sit tight. We just need Joe for this first bit.'

A woman opposite me rolls her eyes. I can't tell if it's because she has to wait or whether it's because I took Joe to the pub. I bet you drank through these early months so don't judge me.

'Come through when you're ready.'

I scurry about trying to stuff jackets and muslins into bags.

As I head through the door, Giles' enthusiasm shines through. 'Hello. I'm so glad you agreed to do more of this. That is a really good dress on you by the way. I like the colours.'

The compliment is sincere and lifting and I smile back. *It's super comfy too and has pockets*, but he doesn't need to know that. I turn the corner to a huge empty set lined with lights, white walls and lines of dancers in unitards and heels rehearsing some pretty complex balletic moves.

'We didn't warm up,' I whisper to Giles, who luckily finds that especially funny. My senses are overwhelmed by all the activity, but Joe seems to take it all in his stride. I'll credit that to manic days sitting around Emma's kitchen.

Special K sees us and runs over, excited. I still have a soft spot for this girl's energy and excitement. I've also heard some of her lyrics and they seem to be more focused on her experience as a youth, her struggles, as opposed to being about sex and sex and more sex. Today, the theme still focuses on shredded denim – but I will admit to coveting her yellow Nike Blazers and voluminous hair. As soon as she sees Joe, she puts her arms out to carry him.

'I can't believe you're here. Hello, Mummy. Hello, little man.'

I hand him over and watch as she engages with him. I like the lack of divaness, the grace of her manners, which I'm under no illusion makes me sound ancient.

'He is so beautiful. I am glad we tracked you down again.' I follow as she walks over to hair and make-up and sits down, balancing Joe in her lap.

'It's our pleasure. And congratulations, things have gone a bit mad for you, eh?'

She widens her eyes like that might be a complete understatement but smiles broadly too. A wardrobe person comes over and presents her with a different top; it's shiny and revealing and she looks at it briefly and shakes her head.

'Talk to Giles. I don't want my breasts spilling out as part of this video. He knows this.'

Giles signals from across the room. I pick up on a bit of tension, as does Joe, so try to divert, noticing a book on the dressing table in front of her. It's Sylvia Plath's *The Bell Jar*.

'This yours?' I ask her.

'Yeah, have you read it?' she asks.

'I have. I recommend it to my A-level students. I have an alter ego as an English teacher.'

Her eyes seem to light up at this point. 'Don't you love how it doesn't conform, how it's got this amazing feminist streak running through it that women don't have to be defined by traditional roles?'

I laugh mainly because literature-wise I haven't been able to focus on anything more than a takeaway menu for months. Joe looks up at her animated face.

'I love the way it parallels her real life too,' I tell her. 'What else are you into?'

'I like Zadie Smith.'

'Who doesn't? *On Beauty* is brilliant, have you read it?'

'It's on my TBR list,' she says, rocking Joe. 'Isn't it Joe Joe?'

A person behind Kimmie starts adding product to her hair and Joe watches in wonder. That is not the bird nest bun that I am used to seeing in the mirror. I sit and watch as a make-up artist puts finishing touches to her face and rubs a brush on Joe's nose to make him giggle.

'And Beth, this is Zahra, she's our baby wrangler,' says Giles, appearing next to us. I laugh a bit too heartily until I realise that's a thing.

'Oh yeah, sure. Lovely to meet you.' I shake her hand wondering if that's what she writes down in the occupation box on forms. She's basically a sheepdog for little people. I hope she has a crook and a whistle that only my baby boy can hear.

'And this is Yasmin, who's going to be heavily involved. There's quite a cool narrative where she's an Amazonian street warrior handing over the baby. Like Beyoncé meets Wonder Woman. There are all these symbols for youth, innocence and female empowerment

in the room. We are birthing Special K into the music industry,'
Giles says.

I would like to say that I am trying to take all of that in. But I
am stunned into silence. Blah, blah, youth, innocence, blah… For
me, the most important part of that sentence was at the beginning.
Yasmin? She stands there looking like Tina Turner in a gold head-
dress, legs up to her armpits. There is a moment of hesitancy as she
looks at me. Then comes the moment we realise who the other is.

'Yasmin, this is—'

She cuts him off before he can draw breath. 'We went to school
together, didn't we?'

Shit.

I say shit. No fucking way is more appropriate here. You see, this is
Yasmin King. Of all the people in the world, bloody Yasmin King?
There's a lot I can tell you about Yasmin. She's the same age as me
and for the past ten years has made her career out of modelling. She
was never a catwalk model but open your Next catalogue around
New Year's when all the sales come to the fore and she'll be there
in a lavender fleece or caressing a leather sofa. Occasionally, her
face adorns something slightly more highbrow such as cosmetics
or high-street fashion but that's as much as I've ever seen her in. I
know this because Yasmin King has been a model all her teenage and
adult life and the reason I know this is that she started modelling
when we were at school. Together.

You're here? Now? And how have you not aged? Or changed? She
has the same mint-green eyes, mahogany-coloured hair, honey-

toned complexion, non-existent waist. It's like she's been set in formaldehyde since our teens. She was one of those girls who was in all my lessons and for some reason, they always sat me next to her in an attempt to separate her from her bitchy troublemaker mates, and thereby flatten any notions of self-esteem I had about my looks. We did English literature together. I'm having flashbacks of her copying an essay I wrote for our coursework. *I owe you*, she said afterwards, and stole my best biro. She got a A- for that essay. I got a B+. Go figure.

I haven't seen you since our final year ball. You were dressed in Lipsy. I think I wore something that was a tenner in the H&M sale. I got so drunk I went around telling everyone how cheap my dress was. You were horrific at that ball. I know because I caught you shagging some lad in a stairwell and was so drunk I went back into the hall and told everyone about that too. I wonder if she remembers that. This is not a happy reunion or a chance to reminisce. However, she certainly piques my curiosity. She was one of those girls at school who were an urban myth, a source of speculation and gossip in the corridors. I'd heard all the rumours: she'd got into porn; shagged Mr Baker, the design tech teacher; nearly burnt down the PE sheds.

And now you're here, standing right in front of me.

'You know each other?' Kimmie says, clearly confused. I know, it wouldn't seem we match in terms of our potential social circles.

'Yeah, we went to the same school,' I reply.

'King Charlie's,' she mutters. Yasmin looks down her nose at me slightly. Man, it's like we're still sixteen. You don't have to imagine how much being told in your teens that your beauty supersedes that of your peers, shapes your ego and transforms you into a queen bitch. She's still on that pedestal, looking me up and down. Well, only down, as she feels about a foot taller than me.

'You had a baby?' she mutters.

'You're still a model,' I retort.

I'm not sure what else there is to say to her. Did you go to the school reunion? I did. They served wine out of a box. Could I have my best biro back? This is something to tell the sisters at least; how all my worlds have collided in one day. I just feel glad that I am wearing support knickers.

'So you give Joe to Yasmin and you just watch from here, is that OK?' says Zahra.

I nod. I'm not going to demand I be in this video too. I don't have the footwear or the dance moves. But this feels bizarre to hand over my most precious thing to someone I didn't really rate at school. I guess this is what we signed up for though. I hand Joe over and Yasmin cradles him in her arms. He looks up at her and gurgles. I won't lie, this makes me slightly resentful, but I didn't give him any warning of our history. Standing back, I watch as they carry Joe to set, strip him down to his nappy and swathe him in white. Like baby Jesus? Oh dear God, there's also a lioness over there. I literally thought that was real. It isn't. Obviously. But please don't put my son on the back of the stuffed lioness. I really want to get my phone out, but I signed an NDA when I came in here. They've put a giant crown on Special K now and the dancers take position. The sound gets turned up and Joe sits in Yasmin's arms. I panic for a moment at the dry ice, thinking it's smoke. I wave at my son. I'm sure he would wave back if he could. Then a bass kicks in. Except

I'm standing right in front of the speaker so I jump and scream in fright. The whole set turn to look at me.

'Stop the music. Who are you?' asks a director in a baseball cap. Those are some piercing glares.

'No one, sorry. I'm no one…' I reply. 'I'll just…' I point a finger to the left of me as I sidestep awkwardly away, disappearing into the shadows, clutching a slightly damp muslin.

Track Nine

'The Less I Know the Better' – Tame Impala (2015)

'No fucking way.'

'It's exactly what I thought. Look her up on Insta immediately,' I tell Lucy on the phone.

'Where are you?'

'We've finished but there's some strange wrap-party thing. I'm waiting on Will and breastfeeding Joe in a corridor, it's all glamour.'

I didn't want to feed Joe in the bright lights and noise of the studio or get my boobs out in front of all the skinny model types so I escaped into the quiet of a corridor and perched myself on some stairs. It's not glamorous but it means Joe has a chance to breathe and drink without distraction. He now has a mouth full of breast and looks up at me. *That's Aunty Lucy, isn't it? Tell her I say hi.* Naturally, Lucy was the first person I thought to call when my baby got handed back to me by the one and only Yasmin King. Lucy and I are of close enough age that she would know exactly who I meant.

'Seriously, I can jump in an Uber and be there in like half an hour. I'll pretend to be Joe's agent or something. This is too good.'

'Stay. Away.' I can't imagine what adding Lucy to this party would bring.

'That bloody school casting its web again. I once met someone on the Metro in Paris who went there.'

We both sigh deeply. Us Callaghans all passed through the doors of King Charles Girls' Grammar School. They were tolerable days; five Callaghan girls meant we were renowned throughout the corridors, more for our multiplicity than anything else. But we had each other – we never got bullied, we always had someone to run to if we forgot our lunch money. A few of us broke the mould: Ems was Miss Brainiac so won the awards, and was the only Callaghan to be head girl. Lucy was our resident rebel. The skirt was short, the tights had holes in them like cheese. I was the run of the mill, slap bang in the middle, Beth Callaghan. I went to school, I got Bs to match my name and I played the clarinet. Badly. The most rebellious I ever got was to wear a bit of eyeliner and some Doc Martens. University, independence and maturity changed things later on. But school was never a place I shone. I kept my head down and just never dared to look up.

'Found her,' says Lucy. 'Urgh, Yasmin has got a whole Insta influencer thing going on. She's Ayurvedic.'

'What is that? Like an allergy to something?' I ask.

'No, you donkey. It's yoga, Hindi, veggie bollocks. She also only wears ethical clothes, hand-sewn and eco-friendly too,' she says, mocking it with her tones.

'So no supermarket brand three for a tenner T-shirts in sight?'

This makes Lucy snort with laughter.

'She also has a sideline in organic hand creams. I know those hand creams. I bought them for Meg. She told me it was like rubbing jizz into her hands,' she continues. 'She has a quarter of a million followers. Her boyfriend is in some indie rock group. There's a dog that looks like a giant rat too. B, it's literally posey pose pose, deep filter action, sponsored posts of her in a bikini telling us how ethical it is but it's got a five-hundred-pound price tag.'

'You can buy a bikini for five hundred quid?'

'Sis, for that money I want it hand-sewn by monks and it has to swim *for* me.'

I giggle. It's been such a random afternoon. Joe was captivated by Yasmin, hanging on to her every move. Her teeth came out, the posture straightened out. If you saw that music video, you'd watch it multiple times on YouTube and share it with all your friends. Did it hurt to see Joe with all these perfect people? It did. But these were the images that were going to sell things. No one wanted to see me standing there, bopping away out of time around my baby-changing bag.

'Is she still a mega bitch?' Lucy asks. 'She was awful at school. She was part of that gang who stuck sanitary pads on that girl's locker when she came on in PE. That girl never recovered from that.'

I remember the horror of that day, the brutal laughter, the nastiness. 'Nothing damaging like that,' I reply. 'But she's snooty, up her own arse. I met a dad called Harry earlier in the waiting room and she was all over him, mad flirting.'

I cringe to even think about it. As I left the room, everyone air-kissing and supping on their low-cal drinks, she stood there basking in his compliments, exposing her neck. He was literally peacocking, lunging in front of her to mask the tenting in his trouser area. I was brought back to many an eighteen-year-old birthday party where she'd done the same.

'Not surprised. And the others? How's it been?' Lucy asks.

'I like the rapper girl. She hugs me a lot. That Giles director man is kind but the dancers, the make-up people, it's a very stagey vibe.'

'Look, I've worked with creatives for years and it gets a little like this. These people are not your tribe, B. How's my Joe?' she asks.

'He's immense. He loves it. He's so vain.'

'He gets that from me.'

I suddenly hear a door bang in the corridor and peer around the wall to see Will wandering about with his satchel. I wave him over.

'Will's here, got to dash,' I say.

'Laters, ho.'

I laugh and hang up. Joe still looks up at me, drinking away. Will saunters through the halls looking a tad confused.

'You told me there was a party,' he says, giving me the customary kiss on the forehead, smoothing down the frizz of my hair.

'It's all in there. The rapper, the dancers. There was even fire at some point and two men stood there with extinguishers in case the copious amounts of hairspray caught alight.'

It was how I imagined these things would be. None of the glamour but all of the posturing. It's so divorced from my everyday, from sitting in front of daytime TV stacking biscuits on our coffee table.

'And have I ever told you about someone I went to school with who was a model?'

'No, was she the girl who lost a tooth trying to give a boy a blowie on a swing? I tell everyone that story.'

That was Carly Evans. She had to tell her mum that she tripped on the pavement and her parents tried to sue the council.

'No,' I reply. 'She was just some queen bee who ended up in a few magazines and she's here today. Of all the people…'

'Yikes. Did you two have beef at school?'

'We had small beef. She copied my essays, looked down her nose at me. She had bigger beef with another girl called Hannah. I think Yasmin had sex with her boyfriend and Hannah and her had a full-on scrap on the hockey pitches. People lost hair.'

Hannah had to have a side parting after that fight. I remember watching it from a crowd of baying girls. There was cheering, there was ripping of tights. I'd never heard shrieky swearing like it and I have Lucy as a sister.

'Just a shock to see her after all this time.'

'So what's the deal? Are they all snorting lines of coke and drinking Cristal in there?'

'God, no. Kimmie's only seventeen so it's soft drinks and Krispy Kremes. Not even the interesting ones with toppings, all glazed.'

'Boo.' Will comes over to sit next to us on the steps.

'And it went OK?'

'It was weird. I'll drag you in when the little man is done and introduce you to people. He's a bit of a superstar, this one, though.'

We both look at Joe. He's clueless, isn't he? He's so unbelievably chilled. I have no idea where he gets that from. Will's quiet, staring at a spot on the floor.

'You alright?' I ask.

'Tough day at the office, that's all. I am beat.'

'Do you want to talk about it?'

He pauses for a moment. See, I do try and be the good girlfriend and ask him about his day. He always used to do the same for me after a particularly bad school day. He'd make me tea and remind me they were just children. Their awful judgement and inability to listen was more about bad parenting than me. He hardly speaks to me about his architecture woes though. He once told me it was because the dramas were usually down to printers not working, or someone had laid the wrong sort of concrete.

'Then maybe we can bail on this. Grab some food elsewhere, go home?' I say.

He grabs my hand. 'I need to tell you…'

But before he can tell me, one of the doors swings open again and we crane our heads around trying to work out who's joined us. It's Yasmin texting on her phone.

'That's the one I went to school with,' I whisper to Will, pointing in her general direction. He goes in for the second glance. I try not to act offended but with her looks she warrants it. I join him. How have her legs just got longer as she got older? Mine look like they are turning into rhino stumps. I should probably try to moisturise mine better, try and do something to smooth out my knees.

'Is your house free? I could try and get there later tonight,' a voice pipes in from the other side of the corridor. Oh, that's Harry, the dad she was flirting with.

'I can't. We could try a hotel?' Yasmin replies to him.

My eyes widen. Hotel? Will looks at me. 'Not her boyfriend. Massive flirting,' I mouth, trying to pull a weird seductive face. He puts a thumb up at me. We sit here in silence trying to work out their story. Joe still attached to me, I realise we need to stay put, don't we? To suddenly emerge from this little nook will look a little strange. Ta-dah! Carry on, don't mind us!

'Come here…'

There's silence. Should we poke our heads around again? I don't think he's told her to come and look at a funny meme on his phone, has he? Will pops his head around the corner and retracts it back in again, making smoochy faces at me. My hand goes straight to my mouth trying to stifle my laughter. How has this girl not changed since school? I heard she was at a party once and charged boys to kiss her. Lucy just told me she has a boyfriend as well. And I am pretty sure that man told me he has a wife. That's not right. It's bordering on scandalous. OK, now that's a proper snog. We can hear it. Urgh. Will's eyes widen and I know exactly what he's thinking. Don't have some hot, spontaneous sex session now because if we can hear the snog, the sound levels of anything else will be horrific. A door suddenly opens. We guess they're not kissing anymore.

'You looking for someone?' Yasmin asks.

'Have you seen that mum with the baby? Kimmie is leaving, she wanted to say goodbye,' someone replies.

'There were lots of babies.'

'You know, the one with the chubby mum?'

Neither of them reply. I won't lie. The words stake through deep into my psyche. But I see Will's face and he immediately looks angry. He stands up. What are you doing? We're hiding in the shadows. Yasmin and her snogging partner will know we were round the corner, listening. We'll look like pervs. I try to pull at his sleeve.

'Hi, we're here,' Will says, waving. He stands in the middle of the corridor eyeing them up, looking annoyed at the choice of words that that person, whoever they are, used to describe me. I am less bothered by the random words of a stranger. They will always sting a little bit but it's part and parcel of how people talk, no? I am rounder, curvier, fuller than the norm. I'm not bloody Yasmin King, that's for sure. I am also mid-feed though. Crap. I pull Joe off my boob and rearrange myself clumsily, standing to attention. Yasmin and Harry do not look impressed. Well, don't kiss people in corridors, right?

'Yes, sorry. We just needed a quiet corner to feed the baby. We'll be there in a minute.'

'I think you owe my girlfriend an apology,' Will blurts out. I look at him curiously and shake my head.

'It's fine,' I reply.

'It wasn't. That was rude. She's a person, with feelings.'

The assistant who was sent to find me can hardly look at me and mumbles some half-audible apology before scuttling through the door. I bow my head, mortified. Yasmin and Harry continue to glare at us.

'Who are you?' Yasmin asks Will, casually.

'This is Will Cooper, he's my boyfriend. Joe's dad,' I reply.

'Oh…' she says, almost disappointed for one of us. There's a pregnant silence, like some sort of stand-off where she obviously thought we were spying, and we know that both of them have got up to no good.

'Will, I went to school with Yasmin. We were in the same year.'

'I thought I was in the same year as the other one? Emily?'

'Emma?'

'Yeah, that one.'

'No, still me. We sat together in English?'

'Oh, you.' Again, this disappoints her. Will can't quite work her out and Harry looks like he wants the ground to swallow him up. He gestures to Yasmin that they should go, leaving Will and I alone. She eyeballs me as she escapes back into the studio.

'Wow, she's got the charisma of a boiled potato.'

I, however, don't respond. I cling to Joe, who looks at me strangely. *Can we finish feeding now? I wasn't quite done.*

'You didn't have to do that...' I mutter.

'Do what?'

'When that girl said I was chubby. You should have just left it.'

Will looks at me sadly, like I am telling him off for defending my honour.

'She shouldn't talk like that. Now she knows to think before she opens her mouth.'

'Or I can just ignore crap like that. Be me. Not kowtow to people's idiocy? You drew attention to it. You made it a thing. I already know I look different.'

'Beth, you look fine...'

It's a compliment but it's not. I know my body has and is still doing amazing things but it has changed, as has my perception of it. It's a reality that's slowly dawning on me, that I'm learning to accept. But for every day I look at a stretch mark and see it as a mark of growth and womanhood, when I spend a day in a room with a group of dancers in unitards, staring at some gazelle-like creature I used to go to school with, I just feel like the dumpy bloater in the corner. Sometimes, I'll strut around my kitchen and shake what my mother gave me to something on the radio. But sometimes, someone says something, or looks right through you, and it's like a barb to the side. It's a dichotomy of emotions Will doesn't seem to quite understand.

'You're such a lemon,' he tells me.

'Is that your way of telling me you love me?'

'I'd rather shag you than her. Just thought I'd add that in. No one snogs that loud unless they're a dolphin.'

'You've seen dolphins have sex?'

'No, but she was slurping away at him like a bowl of ramen. I bet that's how dolphins snog.'

I smile broadly. He looks me in the eye and kisses me on the forehead again, like it may take away any bad feelings that are whirring around in there.

'You've got me thinking of ramen now,' I say, dreaming of tea-stained eggs and char siu.

'I know a place. We could get gyoza.'

'I swear you just said gyoza and I felt something deep inside of me.'

He raises an eyebrow.

'You said you needed to say something to me before?'

His expression suddenly drops, and he looks at me almost blankly.

'It was nothing.' His phone starts to ring in his pocket and he goes to answer it, turning his back to me for a moment. 'I'm halfway home, why? What do you mean those documents didn't go through? Well, I can't send them from here. They're on my hard drive. OK… OK… I'll head back. I'm so sorry, I really am.'

Sensing trouble, I step back, dreams of crispy pan-fried dumplings diminishing. Will hangs up and looks back at me, a pained expression on his face. He slaps his hand against a wall in rage and I step back from him.

'I hate this. She's angry like it's my fault but I told her to check the files before sending it.' His voice is raised and pained.

'Sam? Then why doesn't she do it?' I say.

'Because I'm new. I've got to make a good impression and get that promotion. I've been in that office since eight this morning. I can't believe she's doing this.' He carries the frustration, the anger in his tired eyes.

'You should tell her that, you should communicate this to her.'

'Or not. It'd be like poking the beehive. Look, I'm sorry.'

We're both silent as we process what this means. At best, a supermarket sandwich for me. Maybe Joe and I could go with him to keep him company? We have time, we could see where he works? I want to help and take away that stress. But I see his fingers scan for an Uber.

'I guess I'll see you at home,' he says.

And something strikes through my chest. I don't know what that feeling is. It might be my heart, a sharp feeling of sadness, or most likely my never-ending hunger. Will strolls ahead in front of me and I look down at Joe, gazing back up at my confused face. I know, mate. Ramen-flavoured milk would have been frigging awesome.

Track Ten

'Slight Return' – The Bluetones (1995)

'OhMyGodMissCallaghanYouHadABABY!'

It's a Friday down at Griffin Road Comprehensive and I'm surrounded by a group of my Year Nine form girls who crowd around Joe. He looks up wondering how and why it's possible to have that much eyeliner and stretchy skirt fabric in one place. I was worried this was the wrong decision. Sometimes you like your students to think you're untouchable, that you live in this very school and you are simply here to teach, guide and be a provider of information. Even though I'm not that cool teacher who's going to teach them poetry through the power of rap, I always like them to think of me as human, as one of them, so they won't turn me into a meme (this happens a lot to Mr Willett in physics).

Griffin Road only allow teacher parents to come back in with their babies on a Friday so it doesn't make the children too excitable. Room C2 was my old form room. It also homes modern languages, so it's always felt like a very small version of the UN with all the flags, photos and declarations of *OÙ EST LA BIBLIOTHEQUE?* plastered across the walls.

'He's very cute, Miss C,' a student called Kelly informs me. I'm fond of Kelly in that I know she has a plan – you can tell from the way her pencil case is labelled with her name. She's a teacher's dream, even though sometimes you want her to go up to the line, have a look over it. Experiment with your hair, Kel. Read a book that makes you question the system. That makes me think of Special K for some reason and I realise I may have an ace card in my pack here.

'Actually, he's a little bit famous, old Joe.'

They all look at me curiously while I get my phone out and show them the album cover.

'No way, Miss – that's your baby? That's unreal! That's totally lit.'

I think lit is good. All the boys who had been congregating at the back of the classroom come and have a peek, except the ones who really are too cool for school.

'And do you know her? Have you met her?'

'Yes, at shoots at stuff. Joe's in her new video too. She's really nice.'

It feels strange to brag but with kids of this age, I need all the help I can get in persuading them that teachers aren't the enemy. They all crowd around and congratulate Joe for being so much cooler than his own mother.

'Is Joe short for anything?' asks Becca with the braces (excellent at long jump; slightly obsessed with Bieber).

'Just Joe.'

'Like Jonas?'

Not what Will and I had in mind but yes. Joe smiles and the students coo and entertain him further. I feel I need to have a proper conversation with these girls about motherhood though. Yes, babies are cute but please wait until you're old and mature enough to consider this life choice. This, however, does make me sound a tad hypocritical. I leave them be and I make my way over to the lads at the back of the classroom; both are in white socks, black trousers that are way too short, and non-regulation shoes.

'Harvey, Aaron – how are things?'

Aaron leans back on his chair and shrugs, which is standard.

'Nice to see you again, Miss,' Harvey replies. Harvey's a more interesting kid to me. Beneath the hard man exterior he exudes with Aaron, there's a sensitivity there, a desire to work hard and do more with his life. These are the pupils that become a mission because you just want to steer them in the right direction.

'You coming back?' he asks.

'After Christmas.'

'Nice one.'

'Did you go for art in the end with your options?'

'I did, Miss. That and graphics.'

I nod. It was the one time he'd ever spoken to me in this classroom bar from telling me he was present each morning. He thought it'd be all 'painting and stuff' and I explained differently. He may have even smiled at me. Those were the tiny moments that kept me in teaching, the ones where I thought I was being useful. Do I miss it? I think I do. I miss a job where I feel proactive and the kids actually speak back to me.

I try to imagine Joe in this scenario and it feels so far away, part of some distant future where I'm middle aged and have taken to gardening and sensible loafers. Is he going to be a chair loller at the back? The gobby one who we suspect deals drugs out of his rucksack? The sports star all the girls fawn over? The organised school council member? Who's the Yasmin King here? None of these lot, I hope. She'll make an appearance no doubt and I hope they all are wiser to her game.

I always laugh as these characters never change, not even from when I was at school. I was Tamara, who stands away from Joe but observes from the back of the group. She has in-between hair that she's not sure whether she wants to grow out or keep short and a fringe which she may trim herself with kitchen scissors. She excels in some but not all subjects, her tights are bobbly but she always has gum. That was me. She sees me looking at her and smiles. I like seeing myself in all these kids. I also like how every day in this job is different. How you'd walk into the form room one day and there'd be two girls scrapping in the corner over Leon with the good hair; or the next day, they'd all be gathered over someone's phone watching something ridiculously unfunny involving a famous TikTok star whose name is a series of initials.

'Did it hurt, Miss? When the baby comes out? My cousin had a baby and she said she like had two epidurals and the second one meant she couldn't feel her bits for days and she like wet herself like all the time.'

And just like that, when I was going to launch into a speech about the beauty of childbirth and my experiences, Leena does that for me. We applaud how Leena wears a sensible coat to school but she needs to take breaths in between sentences.

'Well, it hurt. That bit is true.'

'Like a really bad toothache?'

Yes, but in your vagina? It's not a pain I dare to bring to mind and not one I need to share. I want them to see me as human but not to have intimate knowledge of my undercarriage.

'Is it true you can grow teeth down there?' she continues.

'I think that was just a horror film, no?' I reply.

'Nope, it can happen.'

'Something to ask Mr Fields in the science department, maybe?'

She nods enthusiastically. How can I ask her to film that conversation?

Joe grabs on to one of the onlookers' fingers and there's a collective coo.

'We always thought you weren't married?' asks Imogen. Imogen is a sweet girl but we have to tell her off far too much about the length of her skirt. It's a glorified belt. A handbag is also not a school bag.

'I have a boyfriend. His name is Will.'

'Really?' she replies. I'm not sure whether to act offended that she thinks it's not possible.

'But the Year Elevens said they always see you down the pub with Mr McGill from geography.'

I laugh. 'Sean? I mean, Mr McGill?' They all laugh. I think they like finding out that we have actual first names too.

'We have juice on our lunch breaks, I'll just clear that up.'

'Yeah, whatever, Miss,' Imogen replies, cackling.

'Sean is just a mate.'

A voice pipes up from behind us.

'I didn't realise you knew him?' asks Connie Wharton, the PE teacher covering my class.

'We did teacher training together.' His mum still irons his underwear.

Connie nods and looks over at the baby. As with the majority of PE teachers, she is lithe and eighty per cent Lycra. You'd imagine she'd be the sort with a very neat baby bump and who snaps back into shape when the baby leaves her body. I don't know her all too well but I know she is big on hydration and reusable cups.

'And the bell will be going soon so let's say our goodbyes to Miss Callaghan and, boys, I need this room back how we found it. Chairs and tables, please.'

She claps her hands which is something I would never do and I collect our belongings. I feel I need to say something but I won't. I'll be back. I'll teach some of you. I'll see some of you in the corridors. Stay awesome and make good choices. Don't do drugs. But I don't. I wait for the bell to ring and see them all file out of the classroom with smiles and waves. I follow them as far as the stairwell to the staff room.

'CALLAGHAN!'

I hear the voice boom from behind me. Sean, you idiot. He comes up to hug me from behind which is probably what fuelled the rumour that this baby is his. I remember these hugs. This is what got us through our degrees, break-ups and awful teaching placements. This and alcohol. He still smells of Lynx Africa and whatever floral fabric softener his mum uses.

'What are you like?' I say. I turn and he looks exactly how I left him, without a tie and the same dodgy haircut he's had since he was eighteen.

'You've brought the rugrat in?' He gives him a glance and waves.

'Yup, the grand showing and then a chat with Alicia about after Christmas.'

He studies my face and looks over at what I'm wearing. I went very neutral with leggings and a shift dress but I can tell he's scanning the extra baggage I'm also carrying.

'They gave me a Year Seven group for form,' he says. 'Two months in, still looking completely petrified. I have one with a camping rucksack.'

'Like with a tent?'

'I should check.'

I laugh. He leads me through to the staff room where people buzz around trying to get to their first lessons. The place hasn't changed much. A mural of a Michelle Obama quote still sits centre stage across the back wall. Jack Lindsay still has a pile of paperwork that blocks out the light in one corner of the room and no one is washing the mugs and wiping down the sink despite the best laminated signs printed out by Betty in the office that come with giant smiley faces.

'I have a free period. Wanna cup of Maxwell House's finest?'

'Naturally.'

He heads over to the kitchenette while I set up base for us. Tony Kirby gives me a wave. He's the sort who's been a teacher since the dawn of creation. There is tweed in his wardrobe, pain in his eyes and possibly brandy in his flask. Jane Kelsted, now also with child and carrying her pregnancy far better than I ever did, comes over to coo.

'I can't believe you're a mum!' Ditto, Jane. 'I have to run; come back because I want cuddles.' I put a thumbs up at her. Joe looks less amused. *Is it one of those days where I'm going to be passed around like a doobie? They get their baby hit and pass me on to the next person?*

Pretty much, kid.

'Someone has brought in shortbread,' Sean says animatedly, appearing behind us. The joys of staff-room living.

'Result,' I say, grabbing a few biscuits. 'So? I haven't seen you in a bloody age. How are you?' I tell him.

'Surviving. This place is shit without you,' he mutters in hushed tones.

'Stating the bleeding obvious really.'

He takes a big sip of his coffee and watches as I get Joe out of his car seat and sit him on my lap. Joe takes a moment to look around. *We really go to the least interesting places in the world, Mum, eh? Who is this now? He's not my father. But that's a nice crew neck jumper that looks like it may have merino wool in it. I might throw up on that later.* Sean studies Joe's face like he's thinking about an answer to a really hard question.

'Did you want to…' I say, handing him over.

Sean acts like his mug is weighing him down. 'Oh no, I'll just look at him. Hello, mate.'

I examine Sean closely. 'Have you been around many babies?'

'That would be a no. He's alright, eh?'

'He's OK.'

Joe looks unimpressed that we're not speaking about him in superlatives.

'I can't believe you've got a baby.' He studies me, almost with disbelief. 'That's so bloody grown up.'

'We were always grown up, no? We commandeer all these children on the basis of our maturity?'

'Speak for yourself,' he says, laughing.

'Is that why I haven't heard from you in a bit?'

He smiles but looks slightly ashamed which wasn't my intention.

'I sent you that meme about teaching the other day. I tagged you in it. Mate, I just don't do babies. I thought I'd give you some space.' He shrugs. People do this. They forget babies are quite small though, they don't take up that much room. A simple hello would have sufficed.

'That rapper thing was cool. I saw that on your Insta.'

'Bit surreal.'

'Seems like Will's got into the swing of things too, eh?'

'He has?'

'He was out the other night with that friend of his I met once, Jason?'

My mind goes blank. He never mentioned it? I've seen less and less of Will since that video shoot. He's had long hours at the office and he creeps home past midnight; the only way I can tell is by feeling his weight balancing out the mattress.

'Are you sure it was him?'

Sean gets out his phone and scrolls through Instagram, finding a picture of Will in a bar. It's half his face but that is him. It was the day he went back to the office after the video shoot. The day I was promised noodles. Seriously? Sean reads my shock immediately.

'You two OK?' Sean asks.

'Just… he probably said something and I forgot. Classic baby brain.' I'm unsure why I feel the need to cover for Will but the staff room doesn't feel like the place to air my worries.

'That or the fact that we're old now,' Sean says, almost in disgust. For him, the ascent into our thirties meant we needed to start booking cruises and taking up relaxing pastimes like lawn bowls.

'We're not old. Thirty isn't old anymore. Look at Tony. He's like in his fifties,' I say.

'Fifty-seven; there was a cake in the summer term.'

'I missed cake?'

'Baked by Jackie in Drama so you didn't miss much. You're OK, though? Yeah?'

I don't know how to answer this. He doesn't need to hear about my sore boobs, fatigue, feelings of severe imposter syndrome – and Will possibly lying to me about nights out. He just wants his mate back. He wants someone to sit and have coffee and staff room gossip with. We used to sit on this sofa and have a moan about teenagers, quote lines from films and plan big nights out. He even countersigned my passport.

'Getting there. So how's your love life?' I ask.

Sean's love life is the stuff of legend and I miss his dating tales most of all. Living at home with his parents (and having no shame about that) means he pulls girls in clubs, brings them home and has no problem when the next morning his mum emerges at their bedside with a cooked breakfast.

'I went on Tinder. Didn't know what to write about myself. *Sean, 30, likes food and films and cats. The animals, not the musical.*'

'And I bet you got… zero swipes?' He puts a thumbs up at me. 'What about Connie from PE, she seems nice?' I say.

'She uses a lot of highlighters. Very well organised. I'm not sure we'd be the best match. She only eats meat on Tuesdays and Thursdays so you know what that would mean.'

I laugh. I do miss him but I don't know how to tell him that.

'We should go out soon?' I tell him.

'God yes… like I want to get totally bladdered. What are you up to at the weekend?'

'I mean… lunch? Coffee? I don't drink too much these days or survive nights out.'

'Oh yeah, sure.' I can't tell if he's disappointed.

'Oh, and I'm having a party in a few weeks. Lucy and Emma wanted to throw something for my birthday. It was supposed to be some civil dinner party but you know Lucy, it's evolved into something bigger. Come along, bring some people? It's fancy dress.'

'I'm so there, mate,' he says, animatedly giving me some strange fist bump. Joe still keeps looking over at him. *I don't think I know who you are. So here, have a hand that I've been sucking on and let me cover your sleeve with drool.* Sean wipes awkwardly at the snail-like trails.

'Yikes. Here, hold him for a second while I get some muslins out.'

I hand Joe over and Sean holds him aloft like a cartoon monkey would a lion cub over the savannah. Joe seems to enjoy the aerial view. However, if Sean doesn't know how he feels about babies, the next noise to come out of Joe is not going to help matters. That sound is part of my everyday now. It's like a drain emptying its contents. Sean's eyes open widely. *That was a human sound?* I stare at Joe.

I've been saving that for the right time, Mum.

Sean returns him to me in haste while that wonderful sweet smell of baby crap permeates the nostrils. You choose your moments, little man.

'Mate, did I do something wrong? Did I break him?' Sean asks, panicked.

I laugh. 'No, he just crapped himself, like babies do.'

Sean's face reads shock and confusion. 'Oh. Well, that's beyond my pay scale. Go forth and do your mum thing.'

'Will do. Go be a teacher. And, Maccers, don't be a stranger.' We then share a look I can't quite describe. A baby has come between us, hasn't it? 'Come to that party.'

'Try to stop me, Miss C.'

He salutes me as I gather my belongings hurriedly before anyone else in the staff room can shame my infant son for the smell. Right, where does one change a baby in a school? Do I go out to the car? The sports field? I'm pretty sure there are no change tables in this place so I duck into a girls' toilet, trying to work out the logistics before I meet with the headteacher. I hear hushed voices go quiet as I enter but hey, I'm not in teacher mode. Not yet. You kids should be in your first lessons. I pretend to ignore them and find a space on the floor to change Joe, unfolding my change mat and laying him down with all the grace associated with my lack of co-ordination.

You rascal of a baby, this is not good. I see the dark yellow shadow of something against his jeans and try awkwardly to remove his clothes. I'll have to burn them. I don't know if I even have enough wipes. Maybe I can dangle his little baby butt in the sink and rinse him down. I tussle with bags and nappies, struggling to find a change of clothes for him. Did I recharge this bag with new clothes? I bloody hope I did, or Joe will be presented to the head of my school swathed in a scarf like Gandhi.

Finding some wipes, I clean the worst off my hands. Loo roll, that will help. I hook Joe over my arm and grab a whole roll, throwing the used wipes in the loo, and flush. No. That was a bad move. A really bad move. They're not flushing, are they? I look down the toilet. Please don't. I close the lid and pray silently to the toilet gods as I return to Joe. Now is the perfectly perfect time for a stream of urine to arch over me and my clothes.

'Aaaaargggh…' I half mumble, looking up at him as he smiles at me. *But such fun, Mum. Look how high I can whizz, it's like a fountain.* 'Why can't you do this at home? You little…'

But before I can possibly swear at my baby, a hand appears behind me offering a stack of paper towels. Looking up, it's Imogen from my form room.

'You alright, Miss?' Her expression reads both horrified and scarred. I use one of the towels to protect Joe's modesty.

'Thank you, Imogen.' I glance over but see the shape of the other shoes hiding in the cubicle. They're boys' shoes. She notices me looking.

'I can see you. You can come out.' The lad shuffles out quietly. 'Harvey.'

'Are you going to tell on us, Miss?'

Both of them look down at me as I try to be an adult, change my infant son, all while hiding the piss patch that's appeared on my dress.

'I need more paper towels, Imogen. Like, just hand me the whole stack.'

Imogen looks at me curiously.

'I'm going to assume you two weren't in there discussing *Macbeth*?' I tell them.

Harvey giggles nervously.

'Are you dating?' I ask.

'We are,' Harvey replies. I like how he says that so definitively. For a boy who's normally so quiet, of this much he was sure. I like the way it makes Imogen smile too. Joe starts kicking his legs about and I try and wrap him up in paper towels like a mummy to absorb the worst of the mess.

'Well, that is cute but time and place, kids. Nicer venues to court a lady than the school toilets too.'

I think back to a time when not so long ago, my boyfriend milked me in a public loo. My boyfriend. Such thoughts lead me to think of that nugget of information I learned about Will from Sean and it fills me with a deep sadness. Did he lie to me? Harvey and Imogen still stand there awaiting their punishment, watching as Joe puts his hands all over the messy nappy by his side.

'Joooooooeeeeee…'

Harvey bends down and starts to help me wipe the floor and walls down. How can someone so tiny make such mess?

'Go to your first lesson. Never speak of this – especially to the caretakers because I may have blocked a toilet. If I hear some rumour circulating on Snapchat that Miss Callaghan's baby shat like Etna all over the girls' loos in the east wing then I'll tell your heads of year. Deal?'

They both smile.

'And before you go…' I think of Will again. What advice to give two young people who want to spend every minute of every day with each other? Who are still bathing in the warm bask of first love? I want to tell them to enjoy it, have fun, absorb all those cheeky texts and messages. Be present, be grateful, be spontaneous.

'Use a sheath.'

Holy balls. I just said that, right? They both try to hold in their giggles. That was an adulting fail on all accounts.

'We will,' mutters Harvey, confused but still surveying the carnage.

'We'll see you after Christmas, Miss,' says Imogen.

They both nod and scamper out of the bathroom as Joe lies there looking at me. *Don't worry, Mum. What they've just seen here was contraception enough.*

Track Eleven

'Shallow' – Lady Gaga and Bradley Cooper (2018)

What is an awful thing to do in a relationship? Like the pinnacle is probably violence, murder and abuse, but something like bigamy would rank up there too, wouldn't it? Some serial affair that went on for decades that spouted extra children and layers of deceit. Maybe a different sort of lie? Gamblers, addicts, perverse political opinion. I know someone who dumped their boyfriend because she discovered months down the line that he was a flat earther. He was so adamant that this was a truth that she threw a mug at his head because of his stupidity. We all have our deal-breakers. I once dumped someone at university who referred to his penis as a meat Calippo. These thoughts go through my head on the train as I think about what I did this morning. I had a sneak peek on Will's phone. We can call it a moment of hormone-addled lunacy but the truth is I was worried. I haven't been able to confront him about the fact he'd met up with Jason that night and why he didn't tell me. The day of my school visit, he came home. We had pasta for dinner and I did the typical Beth thing of not grating enough cheese. We spoke about school, I described how Joe exploded like a dirty bomb, and went through details of my meeting with my head, Alicia, who patted Joe like a farm animal and made my molars hurt with boredom as she described the new prospectus to me and the different fonts she'd chosen.

But I couldn't ask him about that night. It was an easy enough question but in the back of my mind, I knew he'd kept it from me for a reason and I wasn't sure if I was ready to hear what that was just yet. So, we shared a family bar of Dairy Milk for dessert and we watched a few episodes of *Ozark* in silence. The moment he fell asleep, I looked through old WhatsApp messages and texts. I then put the phone back on the dresser and lay there staring at the ceiling thinking about the infinite bad possibilities of what could be happening. On the train now, I look down at Joe, whose eyes dart in time with the golden autumnal scenery dashing past the window. I don't think your father is a bigamist. I don't think he thinks the world is flat. But there's a feeling that makes me wonder if he hung out with Jason so he didn't have to hang out with us – and that is the worst feeling of all.

We're on a train today on our way to see Giles, who wants to discuss our future in baby modelling. I haven't thought as far as Tuesday to be fair, Giles. But it felt like a good excuse to get out of the house and delve a bit further into what this could entail. The video was fun if absurd and there was money at the end of it, so it feels good to invest in Joe's future and save up for trainers and tertiary education. We're meeting for brunch which is probably the main reason I accepted this invitation as well. Brunch is my favourite meal of all the meals simply because it's an excuse to eat breakfast without having to wake up too early. It was a stock meal for Will and I as people with weekend social lives. We used to pour out of bed, have eggs and Bloody Marys, swap sections of the *Observer*, and friends would join us and we'd compare the size and horror of our hangovers. I ask myself where those friends are now and I realise they're far away enjoying their boozy brunches alone, without the risk of a baby spoiling things. No one needs a hangover *and* the extra work of having to a find a highchair.

As we pull into Wimbledon station, I scan my phone and a text sits there from Will. I open it and it's a picture of someone on the Tube wearing a dress with a giant owl sweeping down the front. I think there are feathers to the arms. *You knew that would make me smile.* I send an owl emoji back. He replies with a lemon. I kiss the top of Joe's head and put my phone away. To doubt you, to think you'd lie to me or do anything to hurt me is just stupid. Almost as stupid as me thinking that I could carry Joe on the train in a carrier. Why did I think a carrier was a good option today? I had visions of Joe swaddled against my bosom, all secure, bonding skin-on-skin. I was fooled. You know what happens when you have to get off a train and are carrying a baby bag and a baby and are trying to remember what pocket your wallet is in? You sweat like balls. I am going to look like I've jogged here. I traverse the commuters and make our way through the barriers to find Giles waiting for us on the other side: the epitome of cool in a peacoat and turn-up jeans, a style that I think Will has been trying to emulate for years.

'Yay! Baby Joe and his Mama Bear Beth!'

This is a new nickname. Is this a reference to my body hair or my size? I'm not sure how to respond. Should I growl? He's going to notice that I'm wearing that maxi dress again, isn't he? This is my version of ethical fashion, wear something to death until it's falling apart.

'Hey! It's Giles!' I can't think on my feet to come up with a suitable nickname in return.

'Is he always so cute? It hurts my eyes.'

He reaches over and strokes one of my son's cheeks. Joe, who seems to know when compliments come his way now, looks over and smiles. This is part of your power now, eh?

'How are you? I am so glad you could make it,' Giles continues.

'It was kind to be asked. And to be fair, I'm a sucker for brunch,' I tell him, though conscious that it sounds like I'm here just for bacon.

'Aren't we all, lovely? So, a slight change of plan – we were initially meant to be meeting in a café but the other person here today offered her home. It's literally around the corner, and I thought it'd be more comfortable for Joe?'

'Oh, yeah sure.' That person had better brew coffee strong enough to strip paint. I smile politely. Giles is right though, this may mean less baby juggling and I appreciate the gesture.

'She literally lives down here. I've never been to her house before but…' He studies the maps app on his phone. We've turned away from the main busy high street on to a residential road where the houses start to stretch into the sky and the frontages are sleeker and more contemporary. I am going to assume we're going to see a director or possibly someone famous. I hope it's someone cool like Phoebe Waller-Bridge. Maybe she wants to cast Joe in a film or give him a long-running role in a sitcom. He'd be a sitcom baby. Like the baby in *The Hangover*.

'And here we are.'

I glance at the modern font of the house number and the ivy hanging over the custard yellow door. Whoever lives in a house like this definitely gets their milk delivered too as they have a wooden holder for the bottles. I buy my milk from the petrol station on the corner of our street. This is all lifestyle goals on steroids. Giles rings the bell and the door swings open. Oh, bollocks. Seriously?

'Yasmin, hey!' Giles says politely.

'Hi, guys, come in!' She gives me a smile. If you can call it that; she has that stony resting bitch face thing going on that makes me question the sincerity. I guess the last time we saw each other was in that corridor where she was going full tongues snog with someone who wasn't her boyfriend. She's in a slouchy cashmere jumper, showing off the straps of her vest, cropped leggings and bare feet. I suddenly feel overdressed. A chihuahua runs up to my feet and starts barking.

'Down, Dicky.'

Dicky? Small dogs like this scare me. My worry is that I'm going to trip over or tread on them. He scurries around my feet and gets lost underneath my maxi skirt. I have visions of him climbing my leg like a tree. I am lucky she bends down to retrieve him and picks him up, cradling him in the nook of her arm. Look at us with our respective babies. I glance around the hallway. Sleek concrete floor, check. Cylindrical copper light fittings, check. Full nude photo of her by the door, crossed leg and a bended knee blocking her foof, check.

'Do you want to leave your coats here?'

I nod as she slides a door back. It's an actual cloakroom that houses at least thirty different pairs of shoes, baskets full of maps, sunglasses and keys. This is the difference between the rich and the poor, they have space to put everything. I keep all my trainers under my bed and my sunglasses at the bottom of handbags.

'This is a beautiful home,' Giles mentions.

'Thank you,' she replies. She may as well have said, 'I know.'

When do I mention that I live in a garden flat with woodchip walls and dodgy plumbing? I turn to see another picture of her and her boyfriend in a field, looking all intensely loved up; he's standing behind her, his hands acting as a bra. Will would need *much* bigger hands if we were going to pose like that. She leads us through a door and into a kitchen/diner space punctuated by steel girders and a glass roof. I stare up like some tourist admiring the ceiling of the Sistine Chapel.

'There's so much light…' I mumble.

'What was that?' Giles asks.

'Just the light. My boyfriend would love this. He's an architect.'

'Then your house must be amazing,' Yasmin says in a slightly competitive tone.

'You'd think…' I mutter under my breath.

'What was his name, Bill?'

'Will.'

'And what's your boyfriend's name?'

She eyeballs me as I say that. It wasn't supposed to sound so adversarial, but I guess it would always have that tone given I caught her noisily sticking her tongue down someone else's throat.

'Jethro. He's in a band, The Chateaux?'

I have heard of them; Will calls it happy music for people who cry after sex but I don't say that out loud. Instead, I try to avert

Yasmin's gaze by glancing over at the kitchen where she's set out bowls and platters for this brunch we're supposed to be having. Oh dear. My shoulders slump to see a fair bit of fruit and yoghurt. It's *that* sort of brunch. I bet there's granola and not a trace of heavily fried meat or white buttered toast anywhere.

'Thanks for letting us have this meeting here,' Giles says, touching her arm. For all of Yasmin's social aloofness, I still applaud his attempts to be friendly with her.

'It's no big thing. I find most restaurants don't cater for my food ethics these days anyway. You can set up base on that sofa if you want? Just don't get anything on it with the baby. It's vintage and suede.' The baby has a name, I want to say. Plus, that's almost like an open invitation for Joe to barf on it, isn't it? I line it with muslins just in case.

'Do you want a tea?' she asks me.

'Yes, please. White, one sugar.'

'Oh,' she replies. Christ, there's not even caffeine today. 'I've brewed some kombucha fruit tea?'

'I'll give it a go then,' I reply weakly.

Giles goes to help her in the kitchen and I look down at Joe. In the corner of my eye, Dicky still looks at me strangely, like I'm not the sort of person who usually frequents his abode. *Usually we welcome artists and cool people.* I start to unwrap Joe from the carrier. It's like unwrapping a fajita, trying to make sure the contents don't fall out on the floor. My clumsiness is not made for this contraption, it has swathes of material wrapped around me like bandages that when left hanging make me look like I'm going to do an aerial acrobatic act. Joe never looks totally convinced at my lack of co-ordination either. Have more faith, kid. I haven't dropped you. Yet. As I dump the material in a ball, I literally peel my son off me. Balls, he's left a head print on my front. I look like I have a third boob made out of sweat, like I've come out of a bath that's too hot. I pull frantically at my dress to air it out and try and blow down the front. Both Yasmin and Giles return watching me curiously. They're armed with trays of crockery that all match and bowls filled with exotic fruits that I'd normally just stare at on supermarket shelves because I wouldn't know where to start.

'Have you had physalis before?' Yasmin asks me.

Once. I got a cream for it though, I want to say. That joke would sail over the room.

'I haven't,' I reply. I lay Joe on the sofa and he looks up at me. *Tell the room that you usually have a bowl of Rice Krispies for breakfast and drown them in sugar. Go on, Mum.*

'So we have quinoa and buckwheat pancakes with coconut yoghurt. This is a homemade lemon and passionfruit curd and a chia seed sprinkle.' A tiny part of my heart cries inside me, shedding a tear for the bacon that isn't here. The kombucha tea is the same colour as dark urine. It will all be good for me, I tell myself. This is why Yasmin looks like the way she does, isn't it? Maybe it's best to take a leaf out of that book.

'You look hot,' she says, plating something up for me. I don't suppose she's referring to my levels of attractiveness.

'I'm not too good at carrying Joe around. It's like cardio.'

Giles laughs. 'This all looks great, Yasmin, thank you.'

Yasmin hands me my plate and looks over at Joe. 'What do babies eat? Does he want anything?'

Giles and I both look over, confused. Kid doesn't even have teeth yet.

'He's cool,' I reply. 'He'll get his brunch out of here.' And for some reason, I grope one of my boobs. That was not classy. I stick my fork into a pancake and take a mouthful with the fruit and yoghurt. It's not terrible but it's what health tastes like.

'So, the reason I got you ladies together was I've been offered a gig and I think both of you would work well together in it. I have some visuals…'

Yasmin and I? Like some Laurel and Hardy comedy duo thing? Oh, he means the baby. Giles gets a file out of his bag with pictures for some sort of organic yoghurt brand.

'They're looking for new family images to promote their brand and Joe and Yasmin would be such a good fit.'

His words are going in but I am also trying to work out how to spit out the lychee seed in my mouth. Do I remove by hand? It feels safer to try and swallow it in an attempt to hide any potential embarrassment.

'So, I would be cast as Joe's mum?' Yasmin asks.

I don't know what's the worst insult – that she's serving me pancakes without syrup or that she's telling me that Joe's mum should look like her, not like me.

'Yes,' Giles says, looking pleased with himself for matchmaking them. I look Yasmin up and down. She's hardly mother material. For a start, she's wearing cashmere. A real mother would never wear cashmere, it'd be at the bottom of the washing pile for months. And she no way has the hip and arse flesh on her to have sustained life in her loins; it's mostly bone and gristle.

'I also think it's hilarious that you two used to be friends at school, so serendipitous.'

Giles seems to have missed the mark slightly on this one. We used to sit in the same classroom. She'd steal my work and my pens and more than often would scan down and judge my school coat because I didn't have a shiny Schott bomber jacket like her. At a push, we may have been at a few eighteenth birthday parties together. Friends is a loose concept in our circumstances.

'I'll look at my schedule, Giles. It could work. I have some shoots in Croatia in two weeks' time and we're thinking about diversifying my food brand but I could squeeze it in.'

I am not quite sure how to respond. I will be spending the next few weeks in my pyjamas drinking tea with my elderly neighbour, having emotional quandaries about the state of my relationship and loading stuff into my TV planner.

'If you think Joe and Yasmin would be a good duo then that's fine with me. I guess?'

Giles looks ecstatic. Yasmin takes to her phone and starts taking pictures of the table, obviously for some Instagram content, while I wonder if it's rude to get my un-manicured hand in the picture and just help myself to more pancakes. I spy Joe making an attempt to roll off the sofa and put an arm out to stop him. Yasmin watches, comes over and picks him up. I will Joe to voice some contempt but he smiles broadly at Yasmin. *Traitor.* She sits him in her lap and sips at her tea concoction. This is the image that will sell things, not me sitting here trying to pick chia seeds out of my teeth with my tongue.

'So, who's your agent?' Yasmin asks me.

'Oh, Joe was a street cast,' Giles informs her.

'Weren't you spotted like that?' I ask Yasmin, trying feebly to make conversation.

'How did you know that?' she asks.

'All-girls' school. News got round.'

'I was. In Waterloo.'

That's a great tale, Yasmin. So much detail. Do you have any more stories?

'You have any more babies?' Yasmin asks.

I don't know if Giles can sense the conversation here is like pulling teeth while having an intimate wax. He's my only one. I mean this one's literally only just come out too. I clench when I have a wee because my vagina is still traumatised.

'Joe's the only baby in my life.'

She smiles without showing her teeth, clearly not amused by me at all. I feel she views me like some nightmare alternative life where the focus would be away from her and on someone else. Share my spotlight, are you insane? I'm also trying to work out how she achieved all of this since we left school. Is this all funded from the modelling? Or is it boyfriend money? Everything matches in here. She even has a DJ booth in the corner, and also looks like she spends money on her skin too. I have post-pregnancy acne that rates up there with when I was fourteen and my face looked like a dot-to-dot puzzle.

'So, it's a done deal. This is brilliant. I am really looking forward to working with you both. I will get my office to send over schedules and contracts and I'll inform the client. I will share your contacts and maybe start a WhatsApp group so we can keep in touch,' Giles says, excitedly.

Yasmin puts her hand to the air and Joe looks like he's possibly high-fiving it. They're both in hysterics while I look over, not really knowing how to feel. This is the next step in our adventures in modelling. I hope it means we get paid in yoghurts for life. Suddenly, I feel a Dicky brush against my ankles. Hello again, rat dog. Do I pick him up? Is that what you do with dogs? I've never had a pet. He's under my skirt, sniffing at my trainers and I sneak him a bit of pancake. Please don't be allergic to it. He stares up at me, looking a little cross-eyed. I have obviously brought another sentient being into his home and he's not impressed. He disappears under my skirt again and I scramble about trying to extricate him as he weaves in and around my ankles, then cocks a leg and pees all over my feet.

Standing in Yasmin's downstairs bathroom, I study myself in the mirror. I think I've got a zit growing right between my eyes that punctuates my worry lines. I've been sent in here with a kitchen sponge and antibacterial spray but I'm pretty certain I may have to bin these Superga trainers or leave them in our communal corridor for a while until the smell dissipates. The door flies open and Yasmin comes in, Dicky under her arm.

'Giles has Joe. I am so sorry. You're a bad Dicky.'

Dicky is actually grinning. He doesn't care.

'I found these,' she says, holding up a pair of trainers. 'They're a bit old but luckily, we're the same size.'

Bit old? They're Stella McCartney for Adidas and they're easily two hundred pounds. Is she gifting these to me? If so, I've forgiven her rat dog and his tiny weak bladder.

'Saves you having to walk home in wet shoes.'

'Thanks.'

She hands me a Chloé shopping bag for my wet trainers and notices the bottom of my dress is wet from where I had to wring that out too. Please do not embarrass me by offering to lend me clothes.

'I'll get a hairdryer out and we can sort that too.'

'I have a baby. I am used to these things now. It's why I don't own anything nice.'

She half-smiles. She then does something very strange, putting her dog down and going over to the toilet, pulling down her trousers and proceeding to have a wee herself. I am still in the room, woman. Do I leave? I turn, falling to a squat position to put on the trainers. I can hear her wee. Don't do anything more, pretty please. Is that what this means, now that you're playing my son's mum, we need to develop some sort of familiar bond?

'This is a tad awkward…' she says, unravelling loo roll. You think? We're conversing through this too? 'But what happened the other day, what you saw with Harry. Have you told anyone?'

'I have no one to tell,' I reply. That is a lie. I told the sisters.

'It's not what you think.'

'I don't know you well enough to think anything.'

'Well, you probably remember me as some complete bitch from school. I mean, I practically invented the rumour mill.' It's a bold assumption to make but not far from the truth. 'But whatever pre-conceived notion you have based on our school days, you should know I'm not a homewrecker.'

I don't respond. I feel like I'm being told off by her.

'And I do remember you now. I think I only passed English literature because of you.'

I pause for a moment over my laces. She remembers that?

'You passed because you stole my work. You plagiarised a whole essay off me.'

'Yeah, it's pretty much how I got through secondary education. You're not the one I paid to do my coursework, are you?'

'No. I actually got nothing in return. Not even a thank you.'

She shrugs back at me. I mean, I leant on Emma and Meg a fair bit but yes, she was renowned for being a blagger, a slag, a bitch, for getting away with murder mainly because of how she looked. I'm glad she has that much insight into herself to know how it would have garnered her a reputation. But does this mean she's changed? I still don't want to turn and see her on the loo so am grateful to hear my phone ping in my bag and go to find it to escape the awkwardness. It's a message from Will.

I'll be late again tonight. These deadlines can fuck off. Lemons xx

Oh. Again? All that suspicion and bad feeling is brought to the surface once more. I hear the toilet flush and turn to see Yasmin reading the expression in my face immediately.

'You OK?'

'Just a text from my boyfriend.' I wish I'd said that with less worry in my tone.

'Phil?'

'Will.'

'Oh yeah.'

We look at each other. It's a strange look. There are stories here, and information to share but I'm not sure I want to share it with you, of all people. Something's up with Will. You were snogging a married man. You just peed in front of me and are going to be my son's new mother. I don't like you much. She comes over to wash her hands.

'Keep those trainers,' she tells me.

'Really?'

'They're *so* last season. I'd have given them to the charity shop otherwise. I'll hit Stella up for some more.'

Here, have my charity, Beth. It looks like you need it.

She opens the door and scoops up her pissing dog. I wait until her back is turned, and stick my middle finger up at her.

Track Twelve

'Red Alert' – Basement Jaxx (1999)

'Where did Lucy get this dress from again?' asks Will.

'A mate at work. Hers was too small, I needed the plus-size version. I'll breathe in. Just tie up the corsetry bit.'

As if the plus-size thing wasn't insult enough, Will puts a foot to my back and levers my backside into this dress as I breathe in and he pulls tighter. This is the sound you hear when rugby players fall into a scrum. Flesh pushes its way up and over my cleavage while some of my bodily organs seem to shift into other positions. This is what is needed on my birthday, a complete re-organisation of my insides. Will looks down at some nest of hair beside us.

'You're not wearing the wig?'

'No. It makes me look some madam who ran a brothel through the French Revolution,' I say.

We're both dubious about what's going to happen this evening. A chilled dinner turned into Lucy and Emma increasing the scale of the event beyond the quiet soirée which I had hoped for. So now, we have a sound system, a two-tiered cake and everyone dressing up as something beginning with B. I am not sure whose benefit this is all for but tonight, I am Belle from *Beauty and the Beast*. I hope people get this otherwise I am just going to look vaguely regal and full of self-importance. Maybe Will should have gone as the Beast. He's dressed as a builder instead. It's a lazy costume option that he literally fetched out of the boot of our car but I won't lie, it's slightly arousing. If I could remember what it's like to feel aroused, that is.

I still can't quite navigate what's happening with us at the moment. Last week, when I was at Yasmin's and he told me he was working late, it became a theme. For most of the week, he'd crawl in through the door past ten and we continued our lives in the same vein. Work, baby, work, box set, takeaway, looking at the baby and wondering why it's not sleeping, tired as fuck, work, baby. I left him be to stew in his work stress; he did the same as I wondered why Joe had a touch of nappy rash and only wanted to drink from my right boob. This isn't a tag team situation. We need to deal with our own fires accordingly.

I look at myself in the mirror. I don't look like royalty. I look like a Ferrero Rocher. It's very gold. Will steps back to look at me.

'How awful is it?'

'It doesn't look safe. It looks highly flammable. Don't stand next to any open flames.'

'Lovely, I have staff at my school coming to this. I'm going to look like an idiot.'

'You won't. There's always some clown at fancy dress who'll take it next level and everyone can stare at them. Lucy, maybe?'

He's not wrong. We've just left Lucy and Emma in her bedroom next door and I can still hear them laughing in anticipation for the night's events. Lucy has gone for pink Barbie vinyl while Emma is

Bo Peep in a bonnet. It's *Little Women* vs. *Pretty Woman* (for which we all blame Lucy).

'Did I pick up on something before?' Will asks. He's been around me and the sisters long enough to know when a fight is brewing and he may be right this evening.

'Stuart Morton.'

'Meg's brother-in-law? The one you…'

'I didn't sleep with him. But it turns out Emma now has. He's working his way around the sisters.'

'Yikes. Isn't that incest?'

It happened after Emma visited Meg up North recently but it just makes no sense to me. It went against her straight sister persona and she's since started a relationship with a new bloke, who is going to be at the party tonight.

So, between that bomb and the general locking of horns she always has with Lucy, I can't quite focus. When is it a good time to say I don't want to be here? I should have dropped that in a week ago before they hired speakers and bought one hundred red cups and a pillow-sized bag of sausage rolls from Costco. Looking up at us now dressed as a little bear is Joe, in a travel cot. The idea (wishful thinking) is that he may sleep through all of this. I wish I could crawl in that cot and nap with him.

'You look thrilled, B. It is your birthday, you know? You could just leave,' he says.

'But they've gone to all this effort. There's bunting with my face on.'

'There is? I mean, you look knackered.'

'Thanks.'

'We're both knackered. Bloody crisis at work too.'

'How so?'

'We lost a client. Sam is pointing the finger at everyone except herself. I've been taking phone calls all evening. She's not been pleasant.'

'I'm sorry... I mean, it's thirty-one. It's such a nothing age.'

'You'd have been happy with a takeaway and a film.'

'You know me too well. I reckon I'm just going to get pissed. Sod the consequences to my milk supply.'

'It's a plan. I got you a present, by the way. I mean, I got the cake and this. It's from both of us.'

Will reaches into his back pocket and gets out a small envelope. I open it tentatively. It's an M&S gift card for twenty pounds. I stare at it in my hands; my shoulders drop.

'I dunno...' he says with a shrug. 'Didn't know what to get you?'

Oh. Gift cards can be good. They're super practical, aren't they? But I'm drawn back to all the gifts I usually get from Will. The homemade CDs, the nostalgic postcards, books with handwritten messages and themed stationery. He also had a habit of buying me retro band button badges that I'd wear on my satchels. But maybe this is a sign that we need to be older and more sensible. I am making him take part in this ridiculous charade after all. I can buy myself some new slippers. He comes in to give me a hug.

'Happy birthday, B.'

'Thanks.'

The baby looks up, his gaze expecting more.

*

'And so we were wondering about the Ofsted requirements and we thought it'd be an excellent way to comply.'

It turns out when you're throwing a party, your friend and sister conspire so that half of the teaching staff rock up. That's Nick from the maths department chatting to Emma and that's Mr Forbes from history grinding against Lucy. It's a collision of worlds that sits uneasily with me. I feel like some sort of social glue. Every time I see a form of interaction, I run over to intervene. Hello, this is Jack, he teaches history; this is someone off my sister's course at university hence the strong smell of youth and the dirty vest. Oh, he's come as Bruce Willis. I knew that. I hope you save Nakatomi Plaza, don't trust anyone who looks like Alan Rickman. People inundate me with gifts and greetings and ask me where to put their coats and I point them towards the stairs. Lucy turns the music up, Emma turns it down. I think I've had about four shots of sambuca so the strong scent of liquorice fills my nostrils. In front of me is Alicia, my head teacher, who apparently also got the invitation but has turned up just wearing blue. Like a blueberry? She clutches a drink which is an interesting punch concoction that I think Lucy mixed. I have no idea what's in it but with every increasing sip, Alicia seems to lean further to her right like a tower in Pisa.

'That's brilliant. All good for the kids, really. Have you met…' I tap a person next to me on the shoulder. 'Bruce Lee, here?'

Bruce turns around. I am surrounded by Bruces: there's also a Springsteen behind me supping on a beer and I think that's a Forsyth. Nope, that's just Nigel from design technology. Oh. Bruce Lee is *actually* Jason. What is *he* doing here? Will's friend instantly sees my disdain for him but tries to hug it out.

'Yo, B-Box.' That's his nickname for me. It makes no sense. I can't beat box unless he's hinting at the shape of my face or my genitalia which then is really quite offensive. I never really understood Jason. He works in some sort of social media and marketing gig and is completely and resolutely single. I don't think it's because he doesn't want a relationship but because he's in love with himself. I like how he loves Will and I am in awe of his banana yellow tracksuit today but I blame him for the times where he's made Will drink so much that he comes back home throwing up out of his nose. Maybe I need to ask him? Why has Will been hanging out with you and not telling me?

'We match too,' he says, alluding to the colour of our outfits. Alicia finds this hilarious.

'Jason, this is Alicia, my boss. Jason is a friend.' Of sorts. She's polite but waves at a member of the school office behind me and is distracted. Jason stands there while I glare at him.

'How's things? How's the tiddler?'

'Joe? He's well.'

'That's good. Parenthood suits you and Will.'

'Except when you've been leading Will astray.'

He studies my face, wondering how much to divulge and how hard I am going to fish for information. The bro code is strong with this one.

'He told you? I told him not to tell you.'

This is why Jason and I have never got on. He makes me feel like I keep Will under my thumb. We stand here in a strange showdown situation where I wait for him to at least wish me a happy birthday but he doesn't. I'm loath to carry on speaking to him so smile and pat him on the back (hard) and try to traverse through the crowd. A person appears in front of me in a burger costume. Sean.

'Oh my God, what have you come as? Are you wearing tights?' I ask him, laughing.

'My mum's. They're light tan. Happy birthday, matey.'

I throw my arms around him. He hugs back.

'You look a state, never mind me…'

'You're such a knob. Have you seen Will?' I look around the room.

'Nope, here, have my punch, you don't even have a drink…'

I down at least half of it nervously and he smiles; that's the Beth he remembers. But shit on a stick, that is strong. The fumes coming off that feel like they may dissolve my corneas.

'Are you OK?' he asks, trying to catch my eye.

'Yeah… Or not. I just don't know half the people here. Like that Batman.' Batman walks past us swaying slightly, letting me know he's had his fair share of the booze. 'Is he a new teacher?'

'Or maybe he's *actual* Batman. Taken a few minutes off crime fighting to wish you well…'

'…And have a cocktail sausage?'

'Exactly.' I grimace at him pacifying me but I'm quiet because this should be Will's job too. He helped with the initial melee of people when the doors opened and they filed through but since then I've been having conversations and mentioning him, and then swinging my head around to let people know who he is. Except he's gone.

'Connie from the PE department came as Beyoncé. Did you see? She kinda looks hot.'

I see her leaning against Emma's mantelpiece. If I took care of my body and had legs up to my armpits then I'd probably don a one-armed leotard too.

'You alright?' he asks casually.

I want my bed. I want to change into some leggings.

'Yep. Go have some fun. I'm just going to look for Will.'

I move through the crowd of people, trying to navigate the room. John from IT is here. John is into medieval re-enactments at the weekends. His wife sews his outfits and he's here today as someone historical. Lordy, is that a real sword that he's wearing? He waves and I wave back, remembering to shout at Sean later. I bet he made an invite on Word and put it on the staff room noticeboard. He probably used really naff clip art too, a jazzy font and all in my name.

'Hi, are you Beth?' A man stops me in my tracks.

'I am.' I look at him carefully. Sharp suit, lovely skin, he carries a Barack Obama mask. I like him already. He's not a teacher and he looks far too old to be a student.

'I'm Jag.'

'Emma's man?'

'Is that what she said?' he enquires.

I laugh and shake my head. He hands me a gift bag.

'Wow, you bought me a present?'

'It's your birthday, right?'

'Yeah, but you shouldn't have.'

'Don't get too excited.'

I open the bag and see it's a yellow mug with a giant B on it.

'Emma said you liked yellow and you can fill it with coffee, wine, gin. Whatever beverage is getting you through these first few months of being a mum.'

I tear up and he looks absolutely horrified. This was not the impression he wanted to make. But it's thoughtful. It's not a gift card. And I'm angry with Will and I'm angry with my sister because I've just found out she slept with someone else who isn't Jag. And I want her to appreciate someone like him, to grab him by both hands and drink in all that love and respect that she deserves. I mean, I don't even know him but I like you better than that Spanish teacher over there who came as Boris Johnson.

'Have you got a drink?' I ask. He holds up a beer and we clink drinking receptacles. Well done for steering away from the punch. 'Thank you for coming today. Last I saw Emma she was in the front room chatting to Brian May.' I reach over and give him a kiss on the cheek and he's slightly taken aback.

Will? Must find Will. I need a hand, someone to lean on and make sure no one steps on this skirt. I head to the hallway. The kitchen is a hive of noise so I head upstairs to check in on Joe asleep in the girls' bedroom. He lies asleep in his cot and I stare at him, relieved for a moment of quiet. I down the rest of my drink looking like the classiest Belle I've ever seen and sit down on my niece's bed, her yellow bedcovers decorated in stars and polka dots. Iris always has a lot of cuddly toys. I pick up the closest one which is a panda with large sparkly eyes and look at him. *You look as wasted as me, mate.* I am wasted, I realise. If I fell asleep now, no one would notice really, would they? I bet the party could just go on without me, they could sing and Lucy could have a dance-off with Beyoncé and everyone could have a slice of cake and boogie until they passed out and/or decided it was time to leave. I get out the mug again. It's like sunshine. It really is. I dig through my bag and look for my phone.

I can't find you! This is mad! Jason is here, so is Alicia.

I send the message to Will.

Delivered.

Read: 22.04.

But no reply? Will? I leave the room and head downstairs. I haven't been in the kitchen yet. As soon as I open the door, Emma seems to be standing there inspecting a man dressed as Britney Spears from a strange angle. Emma? Your boyfriend or whoever he is, is in my living room and he's been super nice to me. In the centre of the kitchen sits a cake that Will contributed to the party. It's large and chocolatey but my immediate thought is I want to eat it all. Upstairs. On my own. Just give me a fork. That's where we've got to in this party and we're not even two hours in. Where is Will?

I can't focus as Emma starts blethering on about Lucy's punch and trying to make this party nice for me. She then opens her utility room to find Lucy in a clinch with one of the Batmans. I am not surprised but Emma is furious. Lucy starts accusing her of hypocrisy. Emma is being melodramatic about living her own life on her own terms. I try to calm these two with small platitudes but it's Emma and Lucy. They're opposite ends of the spectrum. Emma suddenly points her fingers at me.

'Your boyfriend isn't even here. He left…'

I let her words wash over me. Will left? I tear up at the thought of that, my sister shouting at me. Both of their voices get louder, their inner bitches emerge but I can't even hear them. When these two fight, it's a literal shitstorm which is why I was the one who suggested they don't live together. I mean I said it out loud and no one listened. No one is listening. And before I know it, Lucy has picked up my cake and slung it at Emma.

This is when you need a Meg. A Grace. I'm half tempted to call our mother. Because here are my sisters being complete bitches to each other and I've seen this fight over mascara, over cassette tapes, over space on the sofa. My work colleagues are all eavesdropping in the rooms next door, my boyfriend is missing and there's a baby upstairs. Lucy picks up a bottle, throws it and I leave the room.

Will left? I make my way upstairs. He wouldn't have left. I bet he just fell asleep in a room. I head up there. Joe is still asleep in the girls' room. The irony – he hardly sleeps any other time but can do so soundly through a raging party. I look in Lucy's room and then open the door to Emma's bedroom. Oh. Crapping crap. I did not need to see that. That was Sean taking Alicia, our headteacher, from behind. On Emma's bed. You idiot. I shut the door. Screeching and panic still ringing out downstairs, I locate my phone and check it again, then go to ring Will.

'Will?'

'B.'

'Where are you? Ems said you left? Is everything OK?'

He's silent. I can hear him standing on a train platform, the distant sound of an announcement and train doors closing.

'I just needed a breather.'

'But… It's my birthday. Joe is here. The sisters are at each other's throats tonight. It's a mess. Please come back.'

'It was just all a bit much. I've had Sam in my ear all night with work stuff, telling me I should be in the office. I'm exhausted, completely. I couldn't put on a face with all those people there.'

'So you've gone back to work?' I ask him, completely confused.

'No. I was…'

An emotion suddenly rises up in me. 'Funny how when work is stressful, you still manage nights out with Jason though?'

He goes quiet. As soon as the words leave my mouth, they feel bitter and resentful. This has never been what our relationship is about but the last few months have been exhausting. I need him more than ever. I can't do this on my own.

'What did Jason tell you?'

'That he told you not to tell me. I can't believe you, Will. We've never had secrets from one another.'

His voice suddenly warbles with panic. 'I can't believe Jase. It was one kiss. Just one… I wanted to be upfront with you but Jason said…'

And that's when it feels like someone has punched me in the guts. I stumble back into a wall, the air thick in my throat.

'What?' I whisper.

'This is what this is about, isn't it?'

'No. Sean showed me a picture of you on a night out with Jason. You never mentioned it. I thought…'

'Oh, Beth. No, not like this. Oh fuck fuck fuck…'

I struggle to talk, to breathe. 'Who did you kiss?'

'When we went out that night together and I stayed on. I kissed Shu from work. Like, I was off my face. I didn't know what I was doing. We were in an Uber together, she invited me up to hers. I didn't go up. I didn't…'

He scrambles for words but they just dig that hole that much deeper. Not even a snog on a dance floor; it progressed, it saw them get in a car together, the initiation of something that could have ended up being sex. It's unfathomable.

'Will… I…' Tears race down my cheeks.

'Nothing is happening there, nothing. I wanted to tell you the next day, I really did, but I didn't want to hurt you. I met up with Jason that night for advice and he said to just hold on to it. You've just had a baby…'

'*We've* just had a baby.'

I look down at Joe in his crib and the tears fall faster and harder, like rain.

'Oh, Beth. You weren't supposed to find out like this.'

'I just wasn't supposed to find out. You didn't even come home that night, you went to your brother's?'

'I was so ashamed. I couldn't face you. I knew I'd done something awful…'

The alcohol in my system makes me unsteady but now I feel nauseous. I can't throw up in a child's bedroom so I run to the bathroom and lock the door. I can feel the pulse in my neck quicken, like someone's come with a wrecking ball and ploughed into me, completely unannounced. I hold my phone to my ear and hear him breathing on the other end.

'Beth? Are you alright?'

'No. I'm not. You came back that morning with a trifle. A fucking trifle. I'm so sad, Will.'

'I'm so sorry…'

'And I don't know what I'm sadder about? The lies or the fact you're not here. Why are you not here? Why aren't you running back to me, right now, right this moment knowing what you've just told me?'

'I left because I need to clear my head, all of it is so overwhelming.'

'Overwhelming? *You* are overwhelmed?' This is my birthday. You're not here. You've just told me, on my birthday, that you've kissed someone else.' I want to staple that gift card into his face. I wish I could run from all of this. But I'm here and he's there. The bitterness that has been stewing in me rises to a simmer. 'What's happened to us? This isn't us. This is you running away from me. Where are you going? Kisses with other girls aside, I've lost you in the past months, to work, to something else. Why do I feel abandoned?'

'You don't understand the work stress I'm under…'

'Then leave that, not me.'

'And where do we live? Who pays the bills? What do we eat?'

I perch myself on the edge of the bath now and I look at my reflection in Emma's bathroom mirror. The tears roll freely. Deep down, what breaks me is that he's not confided any of this to me. All those times we sat together on our sofa, gawping at nothing on the television, sipping mugs of tea; the opportunity was there and he never said anything. And we're now having this conversation in my sister's bathroom. On the phone. Dressed in Disney.

'I am sorry, Beth. I didn't know how to talk about any of this. I was ashamed I'd let you down.'

'So you went to Jason? Before me?'

'He's my best friend.'

I thought I was your best friend.

'Do you want me to come back?' he asks. I can hear the tremor of emotion in his voice. I want to stab him. But I also need him. I need a Will hug. A kiss on the forehead to take everything away. To hear him say 'lemons'. I nod without saying a word.

'I think maybe we just need some space to digest,' he says. 'Everything's got so stressful: work, new house, Joe. And now you know what I've done and I feel awful. Maybe I'll go stay at my brother's for a few days to work some things out? I'm really hurting here.'

You're hurting? Oh, Will. No. This is eight years of a relationship. There's a baby in the picture. We can work this out together, not apart. Space from me? From Joe?

'Is that what you want?' I whisper.

'Please don't hate me.'

But I can't answer him. I hang up the phone. My fingers hover over who to call, who to message. I don't know what I'm doing anymore. Do I want to throw up? I want to sleep. Why can't I stop crying? I'll sleep in the bath. I swing a leg over to climb in and bottles from the bathroom shelf go flying. Grabbing at some towels, I curl up next to them, desperately clutching at anything to hold. He's gone. My phone glows.

Well, that was fucked up.

It's from Sean.

Yeah, it was.

Track Thirteen

'Keep Your Head Up' – Ben Howard (2011)

Do you know what I had this morning? I had a really long shower. The one I'd been hoping to have about a month ago. I stood there under Emma's multi-jet showerhead and let the water rain over me, washing away everything. I'd have shed some tears if I had any left but it felt good to wash my hair and not be hopping about listening for Joe wailing. Emma also buys the expensive shampoo that has extracts of natural crap that will make me look like I'm worth it.

I don't know how I feel this morning. I'm pretty numb. I drunk dialled Mum last night so she came to intervene and shout at Emma and fish me out of my bath bed. I have no idea what Will's doing or what last night meant. It feels better to try and sort this out in proper clothes though, without Lucy's punch concoction, in the quiet of a new day. We were drunk and we need to have proper conversations to put us right. He's probably at home now with a cup of tea watching Saturday morning football rubbish. I look at myself in the mirror, back in my normal uniform of T-shirt, hoodie and leggings. This feels more like me. Hold it together, Beth. For Joe. For us. Downstairs, there's an awkward sense of quiet. I gave the sisters and my mother a limited version of events. If they'd heard that Will had kissed someone else then they'd have gone after him with pitchforks and chucked his body on a pyre. Lucy and what looks like some of her university friends are tidying up. She looks like she's been dragged through a bush and is collecting up bits of old canapés that people left in pots and on windowsills. I can see Emma through the kitchen clutching Joe, and Mum standing by the sink. The once proud bunting that had my face on now lies on the floor, a punch-coloured footprint on one of my faces like there was an assassination attempt on my life during a parade in my honour. Lucy comes up and hugs me immediately. She knows.

'I'm going to kill Will,' she whispers to me. I'm glad I withheld the truth now.

This is not beyond Lucy's remit. If all the sisters were standing over a dead body then you'd hedge your bets on her.

'You are not.'

'I am. I will let you choose how we kill him if that makes you feel better.'

I hug her tightly while her friends make themselves scarce and start collecting bottles, taking them out to the recycling. That one looks like Britney Spears from last night but I can't tell without the wig.

'You didn't say anything. Was it building up to this?' she asks, confused.

'We've had a hard time. He's just been stressed. And he was working late in the office with this new boss and she's a bit of a slave driver.'

'SHE? A woman? Is he shagging his boss? EMMA! WILL IS SHAGGING HIS BOSS!'

Emma pops her head around the door, followed by Mum. All their faces read concern but they also carry those pointed looks, like they're poised to go on the attack. I know these looks. I remember them from a few Christmases ago when Lucy found Emma's ex-husband sexting in an upstairs bedroom of our family home and Mum went ballistic and broke his nose. I know where all that collective, protective emotion comes from, but don't hurt Will. Not yet.

'He's not. He has a horrible new boss and he's also been lying about going out with Jason.' It feels awful lying to the sisters but I don't want to reveal the ugly truths just yet.

'I've never liked Jason,' adds Lucy. Emma doesn't like where this story is going at all. She suffered years of cheating and lying so looks upset for me more than anything.

'So this is about that? Or what about that time you guys went out and he let you go home on your own?' she asks.

'He did what now?' asks Lucy, baring teeth. This is why we don't always tell Lucy everything.

'That company dinner, I came home early.'

'On her own,' adds Emma.

Mum doesn't need to say anything; her nostrils say it all.

'It's just been a difficult time. Joe, a new flat and new job. It's taken its toll. He's not taken his foot off the pedal, I can't see I'm so tired, I just… I guess it just came to a head last night.'

'So more of a row?' Mum tries to confirm.

I nod.

'What exactly did he say?' my mum enquires.

'Just that he needed a break, he's overwhelmed.' I know my mum won't respond well to this sort of statement. She likes her men wilful and strong. This sounds far too wishy-washy to her.

'Do you want me to talk to him?' Lucy asks.

I know what that will mean. It will be a lecture loaded with sarcasm. I shake my head.

'Or can I go on social media and post something a bit cryptic and passive-aggressive?'

'Just don't scare him off until I know the real score, OK?'

'You know we're all here for you, right? You should come round here more?' Lucy says. 'Hang out with me. Let me look after Joe. Give you a break.' Emma sits there, nodding. 'We can go to KFC because Ems refuses to eat there.'

Lucy cuddles into me, knowing hot wings, mash and gravy are things which soothe my soul.

'It's because I don't believe it's chicken. And it's greasy and nasty,' says Emma.

'Which is why you have no joy in your life,' replies Lucy.

'You should be coming to my house more often too. Dad and I can help with Joe,' my mum adds. She studies my face. When she came round last night, she held me quietly and with not a single trace of judgement which was strange for her. She then tasked Emma to look after me while she tended to Joe, and we both lay on little girls' beds as she watched me like a hawk all night, literally sleeping with one eye open. She used to do this when she was fifteen to ensure none of us touched her Boyzone posters.

'Your sisters also have something they would like to say to you…' Mum adds, glaring at both of them. I know I'm going to like this part because I know they will have got a bollocking. They both look down to the floor.

'We're also very sorry we ruined your birthday,' Emma says. 'We were not very mature last night and we made everything about us and I said some awful things.'

She elbows Lucy.

'Yes, I did too.'

'Who was Batman in the utility room?' I ask her.

'A school run dad.'

My mum shakes her head. I laugh which is very much needed. 'Sean shagged our headteacher in Emma's bed,' I mention to her.

Lucy tries hard to keep in the giggles.

'I know. My sheets are on a hot wash as we speak,' Emma replies, less than impressed.

'Sean was here? I haven't seen him for ages!' my mum adds.

'The world was here,' I tell my mum. 'There must have been at least forty people. They were sitting all the way up the stairs.'

Lucy acts like this wasn't a problem. You can imagine Emma's reminding herself to check the contents of all of her drawers.

'It wasn't all awful. A man dressed like Bart Simpson said it was a really good party. He liked the vibe,' Lucy says.

'Punch-drunk madness?' Emma says, glaring. Lucy widens her eyes back at her. Don't, girls, please. Behind us, a person knocking on the living room door gets our attention. They seem to have let themselves in. I stand up in shock.

'Yasmin.'

'Hi.'

My sisters and mother look at her, confused.

'You are here. In my sister's house?' I say, my mind playing catch-up.

'I am?'

Lucy stands up and points at her. 'You're Yasmin King from school?'

'You went to King Charles?' asks my mum.

'I did.'

'Why are you here?' I ask.

'I was at your party. You sent me an invite via text?' she tells me.

She waves at Joe, who gestures back coolly to his surrogate mother.

Lucy realises what she may have done. 'I may have nicked your phone and sent an invite to all your contacts.'

I give Lucy a highly confused face. All sorts of people are on my contacts. My doctor's surgery, my hairdresser, our aunty Melanie. Was she there too? She's seventy-eight. Maybe she was the one who came in the banana suit.

'I'm sorry I didn't know you were here,' I say.

'It's fine. I had fun. It's not a party without a raging fight in my opinion. I'm just here because I dropped some keys here last night. I swear I put them down on a coffee table. Sorry to bother you.'

Emma stands up with Joe and goes to a dresser where she retrieves them from a drawer. I peer over and it also contains a wig, a mask and what looks like a Doc Martens boot.

'Yes, I have those,' Emma says, handing her the keys.

'Thanks. Gemma?'

'Emma.'

She surveys the house and I am immediately glad we had the party here instead of my garden flat. 'I guess I'll see you at that shoot,' she says.

I nod. She waves to everyone in the room and makes her escape. I throw a cushion at Lucy.

'I can't believe you. What must she have thought when she got that text? She must think I'm a loon.'

'I think she was the one in the mask. And if my mate is right, she and someone dressed as Boba Fett possibly did the fandango in Ems' downstairs bathroom.'

Ems' face curls up knowing she'll have to do an extra-deep clean on every surface later.

'And who's Todd?'

My face reads horror.

'Todd Michaels? He's my mechanic. He services our Suzuki.'

'Well, he was here and he can service me whenever he wants.'

My mother play slaps Lucy while Emma puts protective earmuffs over Joe's ears.

'How are you so awful?' my mother asks her. 'It's like I raised you in a barn. Where are your standards?'

'So you're saying shagging a mechanic is beneath me? How terribly classist of you, Mother,' Lucy retorts.

'That is not what I meant. I mean at least get to know his last name before you spread your legs for him.'

'MUM!' shouts Emma, who looks like she may need to disinfect her ears.

Lordy, they're still at it. What will they throw at each other now? Please don't use the baby. I stand up and start to put things into Joe's changing bag. My mother stops to look at me.

'What are you doing?' she asks.

'I'm going home. I need to find out where Will is.'

'Then let us come with you?' Emma says.

'You were throwing stuff at each other last night. If either of you come with me, you'll lash out all your anger on Will and I don't need you scaring him off.'

'Then what about me?' my mum asks despondently.

'Mum, two Christmases ago, you broke Simon's nose.'

Oh, how we cheered. Still.

'What if I get there and it turns out Will has another woman or wants to leave?'

'Then I'd scalp him,' she says calmly.

'Exactly,' I reply. I think about how she'd do that. With a butter knife?

'We thought we could get some food in?' Lucy asks. I pause for a moment. As lovely as that would be and as much as I crave a pizza right now, it would feel like hanging around the scene of a crime and I don't fancy the continued interrogation.

'Or not?' Emma says, reading my expression.

'But you'll have no one with you?' my mother says.

'I'll have Joe.' We all look down at him. He glances up, strains his face and I think fills his nappy.

*

I end up getting an Uber back to mine and it's not a graceful re-entry to the flat as I balance Joe and bags of birthday gifts and cards but I'm grateful for the familiar space. Dumping everything on the sofa, I pull the curtains back to let in some light. I look down at the coffee table, seeing the hard hat that Will was wearing last night. Then I hear noises in the bedroom. My heart skips a beat and I unravel Joe from his car seat. He's here. I open the bedroom door. Oh no. You're not Will. I take on a strange ninja stance as the person in the bedroom turns around.

'Peter?'

'Beth.'

I have no reason to dislike Will's brother, he's amiable enough but he's the straight man, the serious brother. He runs a neat line in chinos and sports jackets and he likes golf. Privately, Will mocks him as mature, old, and dull. In our bedroom, he has one of Will's old sports holdalls and is putting some pants and socks in there. His actions mute me for a moment.

'I thought you might be with your sisters for the rest of the day.'

'Well, I do live here. What are you doing?' I ask.

He studies my face, realising he's the messenger. In medieval times, I would shoot him after he'd delivered the bad news.

'I just thought I'd come here and pack some of Will's things, given he's staying with us for a while.'

'A while?'

'He was pretty cut up when he got to mine last night. He's low, not himself.'

Does Peter know the full story? What he did? What was said?

'Oh. How long do you think he'll stay with you?'

'A week, maybe?'

Last night, it was a few days. I stand there with Joe, who looks at me strangely. *That is not the other human that I'm used to. My human doesn't wear old man moccasins with sports socks.* I watch as he takes Will's pants out of his drawer. Don't take those, there's a huge hole in the back seam that will expose his arse. Kat will hate that. Kat is Pete's wife. She's an adult who still eats ketchup with everything and can't eat her food if it's all mixed together. I smile thinking of a time when Will and I were in the middle of a supermarket and he said we should get her one of those kid's sectioned plates for Christmas. We stood in the aisle pissing ourselves over how hysterical she'd get over her peas touching her meat and I suddenly ache. Peter also takes T-shirts. That one's too small, not that hoodie either. He's had that since university. He only wears it around the house. He'll need work shirts. I sit on our unmade bed, with old unwashed mugs and dozens of my hairbands dotted about the place. Lines of battered trainers sticking out from under the bed, tongues hanging out and laces all double knotted and frayed. He might also need a pair of those. But I say nothing.

'Did you get our birthday present?' he says casually.

'I haven't checked.'

'It's just an M&S gift card, nothing special.'

I stop for a moment to digest that. Well, if I wasn't flat out on the floor before, I am now lying here with someone's foot on my chest. A tentative knock on my front door gets my attention and I peer my head into the living room to see Paddy standing there with a potted lily and a card.

'Paddy, hey.'

'You alright, love? I'm so sorry to intrude. Door was open. I just… I have a birthday present for you.'

I smile warmly 'Oh, you didn't have to do that. And how did you know it was my birthday?'

'Well, I got a strange text last week inviting me to a party, telling me I had to dress as something beginning with B, so I assumed…'

Bloody Lucy. 'I am so sorry – it seems she sent that text to everyone I know.'

'You'll understand why it may not have been my scene though?'

'No, I'm glad. The party was a bit of a disaster, anyway,' I say, trying to mask my pained expression.

'How come?'

'Stuff.'

I start to tear up and he puts an arm to mine. His eyes shift to the bedroom, hearing Peter emptying drawers and cupboards, and then back to my face.

'Is that Will?'

I shake my head as Peter emerges from the room, his face scrunched up trying to work out who Paddy is.

'Peter, this is my neighbour, Paddy. Peter is Will's brother.'

Paddy sees the bag in Peter's hand.

'Is Will OK? He's not poorly, is he?'

I smile at Paddy assuming this. He thinks Peter is here packing a hospital bag for Will who's broken a leg or burst an appendix. I wish I could burst that appendix on his behalf.

'No, Will is moving out for a bit. He's just having a time out.'

Peter saying those words out loud feels like a jab to the ribs. Paddy's gaze shuttles in shock between me and Peter.

'A time out? What is he? Five years old?' he says.

I laugh as Paddy says this. Peter shifts on the spot awkwardly, carrying a pillow like he's going on a sleepover with a mate. Will is very fussy when it comes to pillows, like a fairy-tale princess: not too soft, not too hard.

'Look, I don't know who you are but Will's really struggled trying to keep this family afloat. He's working long hours and you're not giving him much support,' Peter says, turning to me.

'Peter, I've just had a baby. This is hard on both of us.'

'Are you looking after him? No. That's your job too. As his girlfriend…'

'OI! No…' Paddy suddenly says, stepping in. Peter looks taken aback.

'And aren't you his brother? Why is this the first time I'm seeing your mug around these parts?'

'I work too…'

'And? So you think it's a good idea to come here and turn your guilt on this poor girl?'

Peter turns to me, looking for me to defend him. Not today, Pete.

'Will will call you.'

'She might pick up…' Paddy says, shrugging.

I don't watch as Peter exits the flat. I take a seat on my battered sofa, staring deeply into space. I feel an arm go around my shoulder.

'Oh, love, can I get you anything?'

I think I'm still processing it all. Last night felt cruel, barbed words spoken when we were drunk and angry and all the emotion flooded out of us. You kissed someone who wasn't me. I hate how that feels, how I imagine that in my own mind. Now I just feel lost, like I'm wandering through a street that's unfamiliar and I've forgotten where I live. I can tell that Paddy knows I'm at a loss for words.

'Pete's a bit of a titgibbon, eh?'

I laugh and cover my mouth, tears clouding my eyes.

'You didn't have to do that. Thank you.'

'Yeah, I did. I don't get it. Did Will tell you this was happening? Seems a cruel move for him to send his brother over to get his things?'

'We had words last night. It's a bit of a blur.'

'But I thought you two were alright?'

I thought that too, Paddy. I thought we were going through what everyone does when a baby comes on the scene: sleepless nights and absorbing the shock of having another human in the house, your old life together a distant memory. I didn't think it had got to this point.

'He doesn't have another bird?' he asks.

I shake my head. I am too ashamed to speak of the kiss. But what if it's more? Who is this girl?

'Then a time out. Is that what we're calling it?'

'Apparently.'

'If you wanted a time out from the baby in my day, you'd just go down the pub. Out in the garden and smoke in the shed.'

'You smoke?'

'I did, that's what parenthood did to me.'

He sees the sadness in my eyes and places his hand in mine, trying to find the words.

'You know watching you two and little Joe here brought it all back to me – when Betty had Jack, our firstborn. And you know how I feel when I see you?'

I hope he's not wincing at how awful I look, wanting to back away in horror.

'I see someone who does an amazing job, who's trying her best. That first year of having a baby, it's the biggest test to any relationship, any human. I never bonded with my second when he was born, did I tell you that?'

'No.'

'He was a whiny baby, everything set him off. I'd get so angry with him. And then I'd realise I was getting angry with a baby. That's when I went up to twenty a day.'

I sit there quietly taking it all in, Joe looking up at me. *I'm not that whiny.* And he's not at all. I kiss the top of his head.

'For all the times I speak about Betty, we had our moments. She once threw an iron at my head. And I'd say the majority of those moments were when we had young children.'

'So you think this is just part and parcel of having a newborn? Other fathers don't just walk out…'

'No, I don't like that he's left you here, holding the baby. But I like you two. I also think he'll come back. Some people are full-on wanker dads and I don't believe he's one of them…'

'You know wanker dads?'

'We all know wanker dads. The sperm donors who can't be arsed or don't see their kids. I knew a bigamist called Alan once. He had hair plugs and wore sweater vests. If I thought Will was like that then I'd barricade those doors before I let him near you and Joe again. Give him that time he needs. I'm here. Literally across the corridor until he comes back.'

He laughs and brings me in for a hug. He smells of tinned soup and ginger nut biscuits but I needed to hear those words. To hear that this is just a blip, that all we need is time and patience. Joe reaches up and pats him on the face. *I'm glad you're here, Paddy. I can't look after Mum on my own.*

Track Fourteen

'Golden Lady' – Stevie Wonder (1973)

'And next it's *Ninja Warrior*,' blasts the television. Joe seems to gurgle in response. Paddy stayed for tea, giving me sage advice and anecdotes, but then left me and Joe to nap. Joe has been my saving grace. He demanded my milk, my attention and saved me from staring at my phone, trying to compose ridiculously long text messages outpouring all my emotions to the man I thought I loved – and I thought loved me. How long has the television been on? Joe seems to be entranced by an ad promoting TENA Lady pads. All the ladies are jumping are about with wild abandon letting me know they're pissing themselves but it's OK, they're protected. Joe giggles at one of the women, who thinks it both acceptable and safe to wear white jeans. Suddenly, loud competitive tones fill the TV screen and excitable audience members scream in their seats. There's a man in a neon pink shirt in the front row who looks far too excited to be sitting there. It's just a game show, love. I don't think I could ever be that excited about anything, ever again. The sound goes in one ear and out the other; I remember putting it on so I could hear something else that wasn't the creak of the central heating system or the whirling void of my own emotions. 'And who is going to beat that wall?' Not me. Never. Ever. Not even if you got three people to push me up there by forming a human chain. Joe looks up at me from a playmat. Does he sense something's different? Or is he just wondering baby things? *Do I need to have a bath tonight or are we having one of those wet flannel, quick wipe-down nights? Have your boobs refilled?* I suddenly think about what this means now if Will's not here. It'll just be me and this television in this front room. Who will I eat dinner with? Who will leave a cup of tea on my dresser that I will never drink? I look down and Joe is sucking on one of our four remote controls.

'Don't do that, Joe…'

He sticks a bottom lip out at me.

Don't cry, don't cry, don't cry. I don't think I can deal with that now. I give it back to him. He presses all the buttons leaving a contrast/colour menu up that I don't know how to remove. What is he trying to tell me? That he needs the remote control? That the batteries need changing? Maybe he's telling me doesn't like Saturday night TV.

I lie down again next to him. He switches remotes to suck the remnants of milk out of an old muslin. That's just rank. Have the remote control again. Let's stay here until we both fall asleep, eh? Will I ever sleep again though? What is my next move? Sit here until Will comes back?

Reliving our conversation from last night makes tears run down my temples. He's not called or messaged. Has he spoken to anyone? Jason. Maybe I should call Jason to find out what's going on. I log on to social media. Lucy and I have expert-level stalking skills and it's not too hard for me to find Shu, Will's kissing partner. I shouldn't do this – it's not healthy – but what else is there to do? She's skinny and pretty, slightly preoccupied with bubble tea, and now all I can see in my head is her and Will kissing. With such imagined passion that it makes me want to retch. I cannot stomach the fact that, every day, he would have returned to that office where she was. Did they kiss again? Was she good at kissing? Does she like him? Does he like her? I stare at her profile for too long when my phone suddenly vibrates in my hand. It's not Will but I inhale deeply to see a foreign number appear on the screen.

'B? Can you hear me? See me?'

'Gracie?'

'Wait, I'm going to sit on the roof.'

The roof? I imagine her scaling roof tiles to get better reception. Suddenly, her picture comes into view and I smile to see her face. Grace is our traveller, the sister lost in space and time who decided she couldn't sit still after the death of her husband but had to keep moving. Am I allowed to say that out of all of us sisters, I miss her the most? I think I'm allowed.

'I can see you. Where the hell are you?'

'Somewhere on the coast here in Vietnam.'

Behind her a night sky shines brighter than I've ever seen it here, untainted by pollution and clouds. She looks tanned and relaxed in a white vest top and her brown hair is sun-kissed, streaked with blonde. I scrunch up my face.

'Girl, is that a tattoo?'

She pulls a face at me. 'Yes?'

'Is that a shark?'

'I panicked in the shop. We wanted a fish but now I have this monstrosity on me. And the red bits look like it's demonic. I'll have to get it covered up when I get back.'

'Can I screen grab that for the sisters?'

'No, you can't. I was ringing to wish you a happy birthday. Sorry I'm late…'

'God, even Lucy got in before you.'

'I hear she put on a party. Was it as good as my eighteenth when she punched the DJ and Dad and Meg had to carry her home?'

'Better.'

She smiles through the screen. It's so silent where she is, just the sea breeze, the night air… even to see it feels soothing. I angle the camera at Joe.

'Little pudding! Oh, B! Hello, hello…'

She waves at the screen and smiles while Joe looks at it blankly. He seems more entranced by the fact someone's just fallen off a rotating log on the television.

The doorbell suddenly goes.

'Hold up, I just need to get the door.'

Resting the phone on a coffee table, I pick up Joe and shuffle to the hallway. Standing behind my front door is a man with a pizza box in a red baseball cap and beaten-up trainers.

'Beth Callaghan?'

'Yes?' He hands me the box. 'I didn't order this.'

He holds a piece of paper up and reads the order. 'Someone did.'

My mind goes through what's happened here. Stolen credit card, prank, maybe I am stealing someone else's meal.

'Happy birthday, by the way.'

He gives me a weak salute and then walks away. I take the box inside, confused and rest it on the coffee table.

'Well, are you going to open it then?' asks a voice. I turn to Grace and then the box. Inside: a ham and pineapple pizza, the toppings spelling out the greeting 'HAPPY BIRTHDAY B' along with some interestingly placed olives. I let out a small yelp of excitement.

'The man in the shop thought I was mad. *Yes, I'm ringing from Vietnam and yes, I'll give you an extra fiver if you can spell out "Happy Birthday" with toppings and stick a candle in the box. And no, her name isn't Bev.'*

It sits there in all its cheese-topped glory. It's perfect. She knew. It's so perfect that the tears start to roll down my cheeks. Joe watches and sticks his bottom lip out.

'Oh, love, don't… is this about Will? Please stop crying or I'll cry too.'

'Who told you?' I ask her.

'Luce. She told me to call, that I was far away enough to be reasonable.'

'That's true. The others are on the verge of warpath.'

'Standard?' she replies. She tries to study my face through the pixels. 'This is very strange Will behaviour though, right? This doesn't feel like him.'

Grace, Tom, Will and I were quite the double couple situation back in the day so possibly out of all the sisters, she knows him best.

'He kissed someone. Someone else,' I say, my voice cracking. Grace's eyes widen. Lucy was right. Her being there mitigates any risk of harming him in the flesh. 'Don't tell the others, promise me you won't. I'm telling you because I need to tell someone.'

'Because Lucy would cut off his bollocks and turn them into earrings,' Grace tells me.

'Which is why I don't need her anger making things worse. He says it was a one-time thing. I'm just trying to work out what it means.'

'It means he's a dick.'

'Or that he's made a mistake?'

'Saying two plus two equals five is a mistake. Who is she?'

'Someone he works with. I've been checking out her profile, she's really pretty and smart.'

'Stop that. And what else is going on there?' she asks knowingly.

'We've just drifted apart. He needs space. He's stressed at work.'

'Please don't make excuses for him.'

'I'm not. Do you know what he got me for my birthday? A gift card. Except I think it might have been a present his brother gave him that he repurposed.'

'Oh,' she says, sharing in my disappointment. 'For how much?'

'Twenty pounds. M&S.'

'That's a meal deal and a decent bra. No knickers though.'

I laugh, using my sleeve to wipe away at the snot.

'He's really hurt me, Grace.' She looks heartbroken that she can't be here to hold me, embrace me. 'And I can't believe he's not here.'

'Except he is. I mean, it could be worse, he could be dead.'

She chuckles but closes her eyes and turns to the sky to breathe in the night air. It seems like we're at the point of her grief where she can try and joke about it now. That's progress, I guess. Studying her face, I know she's right, but I don't know how to reply. Tom's death always felt like this huge catastrophic event and no words or action from me would be of any worth in piecing her heart back together.

'He's really hurt you. He's betrayed your trust. Process that first. Be angry with him. Get all that emotion out, all the tears, all the sadness. Then work out the other stuff,' she tells me.

'All the other stuff is so muddled though. We're both exhausted. Things are just not how they used to be…'

'Well, it was never going to be the same. You're both pretty terrible with change.'

'We are not.'

'I've seen you both kick off when bands replace their drummers. When McDonald's stopped doing the Big Breakfast. You wrote me a whole email on that.'

I can't help laughing that she thinks this is comparable.

'So you're just going to sit there until he comes back?' she asks me.

'Maybe. Can we come and see you?'

'I wish.'

I couldn't even afford the flights right now, but I ache to hold her again and sit next to her, share a slice of pizza even though she'd pick off all the pineapple.

'B, if we're going to learn anything from me, it's that life is too bloody short. I know we hear that all the time like the clichéd trite mantra that it is but it's the truth.' As she says it, she turns her gaze to the sea. She looks beautiful, serene, like she's found some peace. I tear up to think of her healing at least. 'Just get up. One foot in front of the other for now. Don't sit in your crap flat and wallow about this.'

'My flat is homely, not crap.'

'It's crap. Change that carpet.'

She cranes her head to see it in all its swirling brown wonder.

'Whatever that bellend wants to go away and think about, remember you have that gorgeous boy and just embrace that.'

'Will is not a bellend.'

'He is today. If you sit and wallow then I will tell Lucy where Will's brother lives and how Will kissed someone else.'

'Fine, I won't wallow.'

She smiles again to see Joe kicking his legs on the floor. She wouldn't be smiling if these calls came with smell.

'I bloody love that you're a mum now, B. I wish I could have been there when Joe was born. It still sucks that I've not cuddled him yet.'

'He's very cuddly. You'd like him.'

'I bet. Now, light that candle on that pizza before it gets cold. I need to sing.'

'Do I have to hear it?'

I grab a lighter from a drawer in the coffee table, wedging it into an olive. Grace starts singing. She's not known for her tune but the enthusiasm makes Joe giggle. I remember her and Lucy in my car blasting out Alanis Morissette in my back seat, downing cans of apple Tango, Lucy shouting at her inability to harmonise. I look down at the candle. This is when I make a wish, isn't it? I close my eyes and blow. Will. I wish for Will. And abs. And to win the lottery. I hear clapping on the other end of the phone.

'Did I get you the best present this year? Did I? Did I?'

'You win, hands down.' She does a fist pump from her rooftop veranda then takes a little bow.

'What else did you get?'

'Haven't checked.'

'Well, let me have a look,' she says, her head craning. 'It's gone midnight here, everyone's asleep. You can entertain me.'

I hang a slice of pizza from my mouth and dig through the crate of gifts on the living room floor. There's so much wine. And so many cards. Oh, a card from someone who thought it was my thirtieth. They can come again.

'Emma's new bloke got me a pretty new mug,' I say, holding it up.

'Very nice. Also useful.'

'More gift cards, a cotton tote book bag and some organic candle melts with hints of ginger and tangerine.'

'A veritable treasure trove.'

I hold everything up for her approval. She pulls a face to see the sunflower suncatcher that may be homemade. She mocks the old lady scarf, though maybe that's someone hinting I need to hide my aged turkey neck. I gorge on this pizza. Man, it's everything I need: crisp base, soft gooey cheese and tangy pineapple. She even called a fancy restaurant to order it. I'm the only one in the family who says pineapple belongs on pizza and even though the sisters tease me for it, it's also become my trademark. Even if I have nothing else to look forward to, tonight me and this pizza are having a torrid one-night stand.

'You really love pineapple, eh?' Grace says.

'It's the king of fruits. It even has its own crown. It belongs on everything.'

'Just not pizza.'

I stick my tongue out at her.

'I miss you, Gracie.'

'I miss you, too. Can we just hang out tonight? Until my reception decides it's going to give up? I could keep you company?'

And for a brief moment, my heart glows. That could be the acid from having eaten three pieces of pizza in quick succession, but I prop the phone up next to me to let her watch the telly. *This* is birthday goals. She holds up a bottle of beer to the screen to toast me and sits back in a striped folding chair, faded and worn.

'Is this show basically a modern-day *Gladiators*?' she asks. 'At least back then there were fit blokes to look at in leotards…'

'Exactly.' We watch someone fall in after slipping off a Tarzan rope. 'Amateur. I would have made that,' I say.

Grace giggles. That sound is everything. And we sit here not saying a word to each other, me with my pineapple pizza, watching the glow and excitement on the TV, listening to the waves lap onto some foreign distant shore.

Track Fifteen

'Figure It Out' – Royal Blood (2014)

Joe is sitting on a changing table before me, dressed like a banana. He's a sodding cute banana but even my amicable and lovely baby can sense that he looks like a fool and this is being done for the amusement of others and to the detriment of his baby street cred. *I usually only do high-end music video work now, Mum. I'm on iTunes.* He was even sewn into the outfit to make it fit. There's a tailor here who seems to deal in bulldog clips and safety pins. *Breathe in*, I told Joe. The tailor didn't smile. I put a hand to Joe's cheek, apologising to this son of mine. But we like bananas. They're great, they have their own packaging. And yellow is a brilliant colour on him too. If he did one of his giant poos in this, I don't think we'd be able to tell so it's basically like camo.

Today, we're in a South London studio for our first yoghurt ad with Yasmin. And because according to Grace's advice, I needed to get out and do something that isn't worrying about Will. Have I seen Will in the last fortnight? No. A couple of days at his brother's turned into ten days. Not that I feel days anymore. We've spoken by text. He's not so callous as to not want to know about his son, so I send him pictures but when I ask him how he is, he shuts off and the conversation ends and I sit there wondering what I've done wrong. Then I get angry, sad, and stalk everyone he knows on social media, unable to stop thinking about that bloody kiss. I've had daily teas with Paddy to keep me sane, and Lucy came round one evening with a bucket of fried chicken. In fact, all the sisters have checked in regularly. Mum as well, but we agreed not to tell Dad. Dad wouldn't have got angry, but he'd have worried. At the heart of it, I don't want to worry people. So instead of staring at the same four walls, contemplating my life, I'm here with yoghurts. These yoghurts are all fruit apparently, organic and yummy because kids are what they eat, hence the banana costume which is a nice idea but if I was three years old and I saw this ad of all these kids morphing into giant pieces of fruit, I'd probably give them a miss. We got here early today because Joe has been up since 5 a.m. I woke up and turned to the empty space in the bed next to me, muttering, *You should get up, jump in the shower.* Then I realised I was speaking to nothing.

The studio is heavy industrial chic: lots of exposed brick, steel girders and massive glazed walls. We're a chiffon curtain away from an eighties music video. As soon as Giles see us, he scuttles over and hugs me. It's a good hug. Good grasp, little pat on the back. He bends down to grab Joe's finger and perform some type of celebratory jig for him. Joe giggles, his eyes growing and sparkling.

'Good morning! How are we today? So the yoghurt people love you. And when I say love…'

He shows me photos of Joe but the images seem to be scattered with other pictures of babies whose faces are crossed out. Slightly cruel but I do smile to see Joe's face. He seems very excited about life.

'So the costume looks bloody fab, we'll do some initial shots. We're waiting on Yasmin but help yourself to coffee and snacks, whatever you like. And yoghurts, geez…you're in luck if you like bloody yoghurt. Joe's isn't intolerant in any way, is he?'

'He actually doesn't do many solids yet…'

'They won't care. It's just for the visual. No one wants an ad of a kid with a full gob of food.'

Giles starts walking which I take as a lead to follow. His enthusiasm for the day seems infectious to Joe, who waves his arms to Giles' ramblings. I'm slightly bewildered by the quantity of information coming thick and fast, yet am glad to be in the company of someone who distracts. It's the reason we're here. Let's have fun today. This had better be fun. As we arrive at a line of make-up chairs, Giles hands over a gift bag.

'Also, happy birthday.'

I look at Giles, silently.

'Let me guess, you were invited to the party too?'

'I did get a text.'

'It was my interfering sister. I am glad you didn't come actually. It was a car crash.'

'Those are the best parties.'

I smile knowing the real truth, and make a mental note to give Lucy a good sisterly kicking next time I see her. 'You shouldn't have got me a present.'

'Rubbish. Anyway, the good thing about me is that I get a lot of free clothes. That maxi wrap you wear so well, it also comes in other prints. I think these two would suit you really well.'

I look down at two dresses, wrapped in ribbon. I am stunned into silence, almost tearful at how sweet this is. 'Thank you.'

'It's the only reason we work for him really. He gets me free jeans,' a girl pipes in with make-up brushes attached to her waist in a holster. 'I'm Natalie.'

She bends down to smile at Joe.

'I'm Beth and this is Joe, who likes a light foundation, a bit of contouring,' I joke.

Giles bursts into laughter. 'Oh, this little button doesn't need it…' he says, bopping him on the nose. 'But Nat may fly on and off the set so we'll let Joe get used to her. This is Zahra. You know her already…'

The baby wrangler. She stands there with a box of toys on sticks.

'Nat is one of my best.'

She smiles but something suddenly makes her expression drop. Is it my hair? I know I don't always have the time to condition. I realise she isn't looking at me though. Her eyes point towards someone behind me. The expression on Zahra's face falls too. Do I turn? I won't turn, that'll speak volumes.

'Crikey, she looks rough as toast,' Zahra says, tutting loudly.

'Urgh, it's an industrial concealer kinda day then,' Natalie adds, digging through her make-up toolbox.

Giles turns, grimacing slightly but also showing concern. I turn slowly and notice they're talking about someone who's just walked in the room. Yasmin? At first, I don't even recognise her. She looks peaky and pale, with heavy eyebags, which seems to be my main styling forte these days, but she doesn't look like herself at all. I'm wondering to what extent I'm rubbing off on her. She strolls over, oversized glasses in hand and proceeds to air-kiss Giles. She sees me and smiles, faintly.

'Yasmin, morning,' greets Giles.

'Is it? I am hanging, Giles.'

Natalie rolls her eyes behind her.

'Well, let Nat work her magic. What can I get you? Tea?'

'Green if you have it. Make sure the water is filtered too.'

'Beth, what about you?'

'Coffee, milk, two sugars?'

Yasmin eyeballs me. It's early and I'm not in this photo shoot but I have every intention of trying every wrap and finger sandwich on the catering table and topping up on caffeine and highly processed sugar. One of Giles' assistants trots off to make the drinks while I am sitting here with Yasmin beside me. She spies Joe through the mirror and waves at him, her gaze studying him intently. I guess it's time for one of our legendary conversations again.

'Morning. I'm sorry I missed you at my party…' I start. 'There were so many people there, it got a bit out of hand.'

'You have a shitload of sisters, don't you? Lucy's a riot. I like her.'

Lucy will be glad that she has notoriety and that Yasmin got her name right.

'Four sisters. What did you dress as?' I ask.

'Fancy dress is for children. I got bullied into wearing a butterfly mask though.'

'Probably why I didn't recognise you?' I say.

'Your costume was hilarious. Did you lose a bet?'

'No.'

'Oh.'

Natalie is starting to make work of Yasmin's face with a foundation brush but looks between us wondering why she'd have been
at any social gathering of mine when we obviously have such a
tight bond. I am not sure what else there is to talk to her about.
Weather's turned, eh? Did you buy the school bi-centennial aqua
polo shirt a few years back? My mum bought five and made us pose
for a picture in her garden. Did you really sleep with Mr Baker,
the design tech teacher, so he'd give you better grades in graphics?
That rumour went around for months.

'You're wearing the trainers I gave you,' she mentions.

'I did. They're a good fit,' I mutter, glancing down at my feet.
They are without doubt the most stylish and comfortable shoes I've
ever worn though there's no chance I'd say as much out loud. 'And
how is Dicky? Still peeing on the house guests?'

For some reason, she seems highly offended by this. 'He's an
old dog, he's ten.'

I don't quite know how to reply. My sister has an old dog and
he just sleeps and they have to carry him into the car. He doesn't
pee all over people.

'He's usually a really good dog.'

Is she inferring that he peed on me because it was my fault? Do
my legs look like fire hydrants?

That assistant suddenly appears from behind us with trays of
drinks and I grab at my coffee, inhaling it for the escape and the

extra hit. She also has a tray of pastries and fruit, placing it on the table in front of both of us. Yasmin turns to the assistant.

'I'm gluten-free?'

I'm not, so I take a pain au chocolat and stick it in my gob. The assistant stands there not knowing what to do. Does this mean she can't even look at the pastries in case she absorbs the gluten through her eyes? Natalie purses her lips and I can see she's trying hard to bite her tongue.

'Are you allergic?' I ask. I once had a housemate called Rich who couldn't even sit next to bread or we'd have to get the epi pen out.

'No. I just find my digestion is better without it.'

I continue to eat. This hazelnut chocolate is the fancy good shit, sandwiched in butter-laminated pastry. This is a reason to be alive.

'Then leave them there, I'll find a way to make them disappear,' I say, trying to make the assistant feel marginally better. Yasmin watches, in disgust, as I lick chocolate from my fingers.

Meanwhile, Natalie is doing some concealer work on her eyes but Yasmin suddenly bats her hand away.

'Don't touch me! Tell me if I'm doing something wrong,' Natalie replies in harsh tones. Giles, who was chatting to the photographers, wanders over to see what the fuss is about.

'Are we OK here, ladies?'

I can't read the expression on Yasmin's face. Why is she so pale? She gets up from her chair, grabs her handbag and puts a hand to her mouth.

'I just need the bathroom. I can't deal with the smell.'

Of Joe? Of me? The gluten? She trots off and Giles emits a long deep exhalation. Was the way I was eating that pastry making her nauseated? I did wolf that baby down to be fair.

'Party girl Yazz is back then, G,' Natalie says.

'I know. I thought she was over all of that though.'

My ears prickle with curiosity. Giles fills me in. 'She was a big party girl in the day. All the drugs and the drink. I thought all this clean-eating nonsense meant she turned a corner but maybe not. Crap, the client gets here in an hour. Nat, go check on her.'

'I don't do vomit,' she says, wandering off. Giles looks around frantically for his assistant, the stress and panic making him twitchy. Joe looks up at me. *You mean I'll be wearing this banana for another sodding hour?*

'Shall I go and check on her?' I ask. 'If you take Joe perhaps?'

I don't know exactly why I say this. What if she's in the bathroom smoking a crack pipe?

'I can take Joe,' Giles says. 'If you don't mind. You can report back if it's really bad. There's Voss water on the table; it's all she drinks.'

Joe goes over to Giles while I grab some bottles and my satchel and drape it over my shoulders. Inside the ladies' loo, one of the cubicles is shut and I hear a glorious retching sound. At least it looks like a sanitary place to be on all fours hurling into a loo.

'Yasmin, are you alright?' I ask in sing-song tones.

'Hmmm…' she moans in reply.

What would I normally do in these circumstances? I'd be in that cubicle patting a back or holding back hair. Is she crying? Is she that sort of hungover person? Meg used to cry through a bad hangover, disowning me for not having controlled her alcohol intake. The door slowly opens and she stands there, all that good foundation work possibly ruined. I rummage about in my handbag to offer her a muslin but she refuses and heads straight to the sink to wash her hands.

'Are you alright?' I ask.

She breaks into tears. 'Yeah, perfect,' she replies sarcastically.

'Look, I'm just trying to be nice.'

She scans my face. 'Where's Joe?'

'With Giles.'

She can't seem to keep the emotion in. The tears well up as quickly as they roll down her cheeks. Hugging her would be weird right now, especially as I am so much shorter than her that I'll come up to her breasts. She puts two hands on the sink, hangs her head down and makes a low humming noise.

'Seriously, are you—'

And then like some mountain geyser comes more puke. From a place deep within her soul. There is splashback but Joe has given me enough experience to know when to jump backwards really really quickly. She takes the muslin this time and I hope she knows she can keep that.

'Big night?'

She gives me a look that seems vaguely annoyed. Is this drug or alcohol related? Or is this a lurgy thing? Eating disorder? She tries to stand up but struggles and sways.

'I've got a dodgy tummy.'

'Then we should cancel today, right? Prevent people catching stuff?'

'I don't cancel,' she says firmly, holding the muslin to her mouth. 'Did you have this when—' She stops before she finishes her sentence.

'When, what?' I ask.

'With Joe?'

It's early and I'm trying to piece these thoughts together. Do I get sick like that? We've all puked like that at some point in our lives. I went Euro-railing at sixteen and once yacked in a wellington boot after ten shots of Jägermeister. How does this involve Joe? Have I ever thrown up when I was with Joe? Yes, when I was—

'Oh, holy shit. You're pregnant?' I exclaim.

She looks sheepish that I've just said those words into the air, like she's worried they may escape elsewhere. She awaits my reaction but I appear to react quite flatly. There are many questions and statements that encircle me. Which to ask? How far along are you? Have you eaten today? Your baby will be *really* tall. What about that dad you were snogging at the video shoot? I opt for the congratulatory route.

'Wow, that's good news though? A baby?'

'Is it?'

'Usually. You should tell everyone out there too because they think you've been on a bender.'

'You can't!' she snaps, horrified.

I hold my hands up as she does. It's not like I was going to broadcast it with a megaphone.

'I… I need to get used to this myself. Decide what to do…'

Those words make me pause for a moment. I remembered when I first found out I was pregnant. It was a decision. Do I take this moment to turn my life down a different path? But I think about if Joe wasn't here. For all the change he's brought to my life, he has added colour, adventure. I can't imagine being without him now. This could be a good thing, Yasmin. At least allow yourself to extract some joy from the situation.

'They can think what they want out there, I don't care. Please keep this to yourself for now. I should never have told you. You're not good at keeping your mouth shut.'

'Excuse me?' I reply.

'You've obviously told Giles about Harry?'

'I haven't actually.'

'Well, you told all those people at school that I shagged Diego Paz in a stairwell at the sixth-form ball.'

Crap, she remembers that?

'I was drunk and that was over ten years ago.'

'Well, that was all people did at that school, spread news that I was a slapper. Little's changed. People like you just keep that rumour mill turning, don't you?'

I step back on hearing her affront. 'Hold up. People like me? You don't even know me! You trampled all over people like me at school. You didn't do anything to stop us thinking any different. You stole essays, you belittled people and you took advantage of them.'

She is silent as she takes in those words, wondering whether to be insulted or ashamed. She created a lot of that drama and reputation for herself. Plus, school was a very long time ago. I'd like to think we've all progressed since then in terms of our maturity. I'm not sure she's allowed to make face judgements about me. Not anymore.

'Look, think what you like of me. Get yourself together because everyone's waiting outside,' I say abruptly.

As I turn to leave, she attempts to compose herself and rifles through her handbag, swearing under her breath. From the corner of my eye I see her take out a small bottle of which she takes some long inhalations. I don't know why I'm still here.

'Let me guess, peppermint?' I ask.

She seems surprised that I would know what that is.

'About as useful as a bag of dicks,' I mutter.

For some reason, she laughs at this reference.

'Trust me, I've tried it all. You have to eat. Nibble on a cracker. Gluten-free if you must, otherwise it's just hormones swimming around in your stomach.'

'Where did you read that?' she asks, like she might not trust my sources.

'From one of my "shitload" of sisters; Meg and Emma have five between them.'

She arches her eyebrows at the sheer number of babies in that sentence.

'What about these ginger chewy sweets?' she says, holding up a box from her handbag.

I wince, remembering how I tried those too and spat them out, thinking Will was trying to poison me. *Will*. At least when I found out I was pregnant, I had a Will. My satchel by my hip, I open it up and pull out a bag of Tangfastics.

'These. Any sour fizzy sweets you can get your hands on. These got me through my first trimester. I used to keep mini bags in my desk at school. I could have been sponsored by Haribo.' I place them on the counter next to the sink with the Voss water.

'And you just carry them around with you now?' she asks.

'I took the train here. I like a travel sweet.' Haribo makes me happy. I like keeping it around me.

'Are they organic?'

'They're gluten-free?'

She stares out my snarky reply. I can't quite read her. Is she sad? Behind all those tears, what is the emotion there?

'Look, do you need anything else?' I don't know why I ask this. Fifteen years ago is when you should have got to know me and realised, despite my duff haircut and my hand-me-down rucksack, I had good taste in music and I would have probably still looked after you in a toilet if you'd needed me. She grabs onto my hand and looks me in the eye. The girl's got grip. What are you asking from me?

'I'm sorry I stole your essay at school. That was shitty.'

I don't know how to respond to that. You're welcome? Feel better?

'I am sorry I told everyone you shagged Diego Paz in a stairwell.'

'We didn't shag. He couldn't get it up. He spent half an hour rubbing himself against my inner thigh, ripped my four-hundred-pound dress and told everyone in great detail about a vagina that certainly wasn't mine. He had a cock like a hairless mole.'

'Oh.' I pause. 'You should have told Diego. He might still be having sex like that. He might technically still be a virgin.'

I think she might laugh in return. 'I'm sorry I thought you had blabbed anything to Giles. And for what it's worth, half of what you heard about me at school wasn't true. I'm not the same girl I was back then,' she tells me.

'Is anyone? There's a chunk of something in your hair,' I say. 'You might want to wash that out before it gets stuck in Natalie's curling tongs.'

She rakes her fingers through the strands. 'You weren't Bethany at school, were you?'

'No, that was someone else. She was the religious one with the thick tights who was good at the cello. God, you are really bad with names, aren't you?'

'I know some names. Your baby, he's called Bo, right?'

'Joe.'

'I was trying to make a joke.'

I do a very fake, uncertain laugh.

She stands there and doesn't reply, just clutches the bag of Haribo to her chest.

Track Sixteen

'Sparks' – Coldplay (2000)

'And that's a wrap.'

People start clapping and cheering and I don't really know why. I clap along and see Joe's eyes scan the room for me. Still here, mate. Don't worry. The official baby wrangler picks him up and hands him to me and he snuggles into my chest. You are awesome, little Joe. I hold him tightly to let him know. It's been a strange day. Yasmin is the consummate professional. She strode back onto set like she'd never been ill; they used the really good concealer; and she smiled and posed, all while entertaining my banana baby. The clients showed up and she charmed them too. I don't want to blow my own trumpet here, but one can never underestimate the power of a packet of Tangfastics. Zahra comes over with Joe, now stripped of his suit, and places him in my arms. Hey, kiddo. I hope this isn't confusing, little one. Remember: I'm Mum. She's Fake Mum. I have the good cushioning to rest your little head on. Let's get you home.

At least today we had a distraction. We didn't look at the same four walls and we didn't think about Will. Joe looks tired. Mate, tell me about it. Nando's is calling. A whole chicken for one. That feels obscene but it's all protein, no?

We navigate the corridors out and get outside to late autumn rain and a chill in the air. The weather has turned and I'm not wearing my big coat. I work out how to put the plastic rain cover on Joe's pram and think about how I'm going to do this. I'll have to light jog, stop by trees for cover and not give two hoots about my hair. I have a small, weak umbrella but I can't hold that and push a pram; my co-ordination is not that well developed.

'Are you guys walking?' A voice suddenly calls out from behind me. Giles.

'Yeah, we took the train, it's fine.'

'Love, you'll get soaked through. Where do you live?'

'Surbiton?'

He studies my pram and its attachments. 'I know Surbiton. Jump in, let me give you a lift.'

'Are you sure?'

'Very. I don't want you both getting drenched and ill on my conscience.' He points over to a very normal-looking Ford Mondeo parked right outside the doors. He clicks Joe's seat into place while I fumble at the buggy, trying to fold it up, shove all the accompanying bells and whistles away and put them in his boot. I watch as he straps Joe in with ease. How does he make it look so simple? I'm usually left huffing and puffing like when I have to change a duvet cover. When I get in the car, I see a few juice boxes scattered on the floor, a toy car, along with the normal crumb trails you see in a parental vehicle.

'You have a kid?'

'I do. Is it obvious? Sorry, the car is his dumping ground. He's the ultimate mess monster.'

'No, it's fine. Ours looks similar.'

He starts the engine and the rain starts to get torrential.

'Joe did so well today by the way. I usually have a hunch about these things but I'm so glad we found you.'

'No, it was nice to be involved. Thank you. The whole music video thing too with Special K, it's been quite an adventure.'

He reaches over, sincerely patting me on the arm. 'How was Yasmin in the loos? I am glad she turned that around. My team say a lot of stuff about her but she's a true professional. Never let me down.'

I know to keep my lips sealed but I am not sure how to reply. 'I think she was genuinely quite ill today. She told me she had some oysters last night. I'm terrible with oysters, they go right through me,' I fumble. Perhaps a bit too much information there, Beth?

'You also came in the nick of time. We were close to giving this gig to another baby but I really am not fond of the family,' Giles says, changing the subject.

'How so?'

'Have you ever met Harry? He was at the video shoot with his little girl.'

I nod, hoping my face doesn't give too much away.

'He's a horrific pushy parent. Him and his wife love having their girl in the spotlight. They're competitive and obnoxious, they weasel their way into jobs. He's a washed-up has-been, trying to relive his youth. He was shagging Yasmin at one point, too.'

'You know about that?' I say, trying to act surprised.

'You did?'

'I saw them having a bit of a moment in a corridor at the video shoot.'

'It's what he does. I thought Yasmin had better sense than that.'

His phone suddenly rings. 'Excuse me, while I take this…'

'G? You on your way back? We need milk,' a male voice pipes up.

'Sure, about half an hour? How was Kai's assembly? What was the certificate for?'

'For flawless commitment to his maths and always setting himself challenges.'

'That's all me.'

The voice on the other end laughs and I hear a child shouting in the background.

'See you in a bit.'

'Sorry, that was Oliver, my husband. Kai's other dad.'

I smile but feel strangely sad. Those were the phone calls I used to make to Will – those little fragments of conversation that used to piece the day together.

'How old is Kai?' I ask.

'Six, he's this little ball of dynamite. You thought babies were hard? You wait until they can answer back. My phone is just there, look at the screensaver. That's us last year on holiday.'

A little boy with a mop of sandy hair looks up at me, with two grinning faces either side. It's sun-drenched and perfect. His husband has a smattering of stubble and warm grey eyes.

'And while you have my phone. Open my last WhatsApp message and follow that link. I think you'll like it…'

I do as I'm told and open a Vevo link to Special K's new video. The thumbnail image is her holding Joe, along with that lioness who is now real down to some CGI. The video is very slick and choreographed and Joe sits there in the middle of it all and just takes it all in. I smile. Hang on. One million views. My face gives it away.

'It's blown up, right? That was released like an hour ago. And look at Joe, he's a little superstar. He's a credit to you.'

I take in the compliment but I'm not sure how much I've taught him in the way of sitting still and not getting too disturbed by bright lights.

'I mean, if you want to stick with this then I can introduce you to plenty of people. You're very easy to work with.'

I hear Joe from the back almost gurgling in agreement.

'Would we be working with Yasmin?' I ask.

'I'm now working out that even though you two went to school together, you weren't friends, were you?'

'Were you friends with everyone you went to school with?'

'No, I was gay. I got beaten up most days.'

I furrow my brow. Secondary education was like that, anywhere. It was 'eat or be eaten', or do what I did, which was hide behind sisters so no one could touch me. Power in numbers.

'What can I say? We moved in different circles. She's always been pretty and willowy. Even now, we are polar opposites.'

I try to laugh that last comment off but Giles studies my face.

'Her looks, it's all smoke and mirrors, you know that, right?'

'I do. I guess I'll always use someone like Yasmin as some sort of benchmark of what my body should look like though.'

This feels like quite an open thing to say to someone I don't know particularly well but he smiles.

'It's just one side of beauty we're selling. It's very superficial.'

'Yeah, but those ads always show me people who look like Yasmin. I don't exactly feel well-represented anywhere.'

He nods, almost grateful to open up that line of conversation.

'It's changing. It is. I am always pushing for more representation, diversity, not to sell people lies but it's a slow-moving machine. I don't see many gay couples represented, for example…' he says, resentfully. 'I am trying though.'

I smile, thankful that he at least understands that much.

'Why do you not think you're beautiful?' he asks me, quite directly.

'I'm OK…?' I reply, my eyes shifting awkwardly.

'You don't sound convinced.'

'A woman's sense of their own beauty is always a little warped. Let's say I fall in and out of love with my looks, my body.'

He pauses to reflect on my words.

'But you have kindness. I see it in how you helped Yasmin, how you are with your baby, that man Paddy at the pub. I see something that exudes from your eyes that pictures don't capture.'

I blush. He doesn't know me that well but to pick up on those small things makes me realise he's been looking at much more than my penchant for maxi dresses. 'That's really nice of you to say.'

'I mean it. I like you, Beth. I like your boy. Don't take this world to heart. It's all veneer. All models who survive on water and celery, and competitive parents trying to milk their kids for money. There's not much beyond the pictures.'

'Just celery? But all that chewing?'

'Right?' he says, laughing.

I'm grateful in more ways than one that I got that lift. Giles' normality and conversation were a tonic, a relief, and I liked the way he hummed along to the radio and sang along to jingles. However, as we pull into my block of flats' communal car park, my heart quickens to see our rusty Suzuki Swift in its usual spot. I remember when we first bought it second-hand and we thought we'd taken huge steps in our relationship. It was as big a moment as when we started finishing each other's sentences or when I first allowed him to kiss me with a mouth full of morning breath. Giles pulls up to a spot and senses my pensive look.

'Are you OK?'

'Yes. I think.' Will emerges from the front doors. Crap. I hunch down in the seat but he clocks me immediately and walks over to the car. I undo my seatbelt and take a huge breath. Giles watches curiously. As I exit the car, I see Will's wearing his khaki parka and a sweatshirt that I bought him for Christmas. His facial hair has grown out slightly but he carries a hoodie in his hands that I know was in the airing cupboard. I know because I used to smell it on occasion. Like some sad case.

'Hey.'

'Hey.'

Giles emerges from the other side of the car to make his introductions. 'I'm Giles. You must be Will?'

Will's eyes shift between us.

'Giles was just giving us a lift home. We went on our first commercial shoot today,' I tell him. Giles looks confused. Shouldn't he
have known that already as he's Joe's dad? Will hovers and Giles
helps me get my stuff out of the car. Before he closes the boot, he
whispers, 'Do I need to stay?'

I shake my head and he hugs me. It's welcome and I have a
moment where I don't want to let go.

'Thank you for the lift, for everything today. Seriously, I'm fine.'

I lift Joe – who is sleeping soundly – out of the car, and then
Giles gives me one last look. Will hovers beside us. This is the
first time I've seen him in the flesh since he confessed about the
kiss. I was unsure how I'd react, but at least I now know I'm not
capable of launching myself at him and banging his head against
the tarmac.

'You want to come in for a cup of tea?' I ask him.

'I guess.'

He guesses? 'Why are you here? You came for a hoodie?'

'I came to see you guys but you weren't in.'

'You should have called.'

'Maybe.'

'Well, come in?'

I don't know what he expects here. Does he want me to be
angry and give him reason to not be here? *I don't want to fight you.
I want to know why you're not here. I miss you but I don't want to
say those words out loud.* He helps gather all our belongings and we
do that strange dance of getting ourselves through the front door.
There are no words, no eye contact. I can't tell if he feels happy to
see us or guilty. As we get through to the flat, he looks around as

if to check if anything's changed. Putting Joe down on the floor, I turn around. Will stands there and throws his arms around me.

'I'm so sorry, B.'

I want to tense up and push him away but it's impossible. It's Will. I hug him back, wrapping my arms around him tight. We break free to look at each other. When did we start to look so tired? So old? So far away from our former selves? It feels like we're living in some different dimension where it's just about getting by, surviving, day by day.

'How's Peter? The family?'

'Kat's driving me up the wall but it's nice to spend time with the girls.'

Peter has two daughters. I love that Will is spending time with his nieces, but surely it's his own son he should be with? I still don't have the bile to find those words.

'I miss you guys though.'

'You do?'

'Yes.'

'Then why aren't you here?'

He goes quiet for a moment and sits down on our sofa. 'It's kind of hard to explain…'

'Have you been sleeping with Shu?' I ask. My tone is direct. 'If that's the big secret then I'd rather know so I can work out what to do next.'

'No, it was definitely a one-time thing. I was so wasted I could have snogged Philip that night.'

I don't quite get the joke. 'But you see her every day at work. That must be awkward.'

'It is, but I deal with it and I've drawn that line in the sand.'

I have to believe him, don't I? For as much as I am haunted by the image, as much as what happened and could have happened that evening makes me physically sick, I have to try and find a way to wipe it from memory. 'So the space, this confusion you feel... Tell me about that.'

'I didn't get that promotion at work. I worked my arse off – you saw the hours I was doing, but she gave it to Philip.'

'I'm sorry, Will.' I sit down next to him and put my hand on his knee.

'And I felt stupid, humiliated. All that time I'd spent away from you guys, the kiss, everything was muddy. I just... I can't remember how and when we ended up... like this?'

'Like what?'

'This flat, this life. I sit on the Tube sometimes just frantic thinking about our finances, counting the hours Joe was up, trying to work out how to get out of here...'

We examine the peeling paint of this place, this godawful carpet, all our furniture which we either inherited or are random, cheap pieces from Ikea.

'Out of here? What, like away from us?'

'Like trying to work out where this goes? Affording somewhere bigger? I don't want to live in this flat forever.'

I am silent. We've only technically been here for a matter of months. Moving when I was heavily pregnant was difficult enough but we've always known it's a temporary measure. However, deep down I worry his words mean more than that. Is this what he's doing then? Has he gone away to sketch up a new plan?

'Why are you being so hard on yourself? On us?' I ask him.

'Because look at people. Look at Peter, Jason, they're so sorted in life. Meg, Emma… I just feel like we could be living like this for years, no one giving us a break. You and Joe deserve more.'

'You want to be single like Jason? Divorced like Emma?' It sounds like he's craving their material lives – townhouses and rampant social lives. Is that what he wants? Not us? Are we stopping him from having those things? I also can't work out if this is a really convoluted way of dumping me. It's not you, it's me. You deserve better. I can't give you what I want. If he goes down some route of cowardice and dishonesty, then it'll break me. Mainly because I never thought Will was that gutless.

'Do you want to get married?' he asks me.

The question sits in the air for a while. Was that a proposal he just put out there? Surely that's the next step in this equation: babies, marriage… something of permanence. But at least get a bag of Hula Hoops out of the cupboard and do it right.

'Well, no. Did you?'

The lack of romance here is heartbreaking – that we may be deciding on marriage as a way to glue this all back together. I can't think of anything I want less at the moment than to wear a white dress and vacuum away our finances on a wedding. This has always been something we joked about, something we would possibly do when we were grown up but we never spoke about it seriously. We spoke about the playlists, the canapés and the quality of the party. We wanted a walking brass band playing funk. That would not be the answer now.

'No…'

We sit here together contemplating what that means.

'I do love you though,' he says.

I don't say it back. Those words mean nothing to me without him here. I don't need him here with limp words. I need him here in this flat, despite all his misgivings and fatigue and showing up. He looks over at Joe.

'I just thought parenthood would be easier. People made it look easier.'

I know. But that's part of how we live, no? We spy people through their social media, through glossy magazines – people who seem to have their lives sorted, sewn up. Jeans. How do people find jeans that fit? How do people afford half-a-million-pound houses? How do they slip into being parents without even batting an eyelid?

'It's not easy,' I reply. 'I know... it's fucking hard. I've never known fatigue like this and it's the hardest thing we've had to do as a couple. But all Joe really needs is a dad. We need you here. It felt like this got hard and the first thing you did when that happened was to walk out.'

I start to tear up at my words. I care about this man so much, I've lived and loved and been by his side for the best part of eight years but the now deserves his full attention, his presence.

'I'm sorry...' he says.

I reach over and hold him close to me. I think about all the things that used to be us. How he'd come in from work and we'd sit here and absorb the details of each other's day. We'd argue over who would make the tea. It was always enough for me; I didn't need more. He starts stroking my arm and then brings me in tighter. *I've missed you more than you know, you idiot.* I reach up to kiss him, unable to remember the last time we actually achieved this simple level of intimacy. His face meets mine and he gives in, his lips meeting mine. I lean him into the sofa. Please come back to us. And then out of nowhere, I do a very strange cumbersome move where I try and straddle him. It's anything but spontaneous. Crap, I think I am trying to seduce him. In a nursing bra. How am I going to do this? The baby is right there. Maybe I should turn Joe away? Will this scar him? We should go to the bedroom. I climb off him and lead him there by my hand. I haven't shaved anything but the curtains are closed so he might not be able to see. It's not even passion driving this but pure panic. I can try and sex him into staying. I start to take off my clothes and he does the same, getting his top stuck on his arms. He smiles at me. OK then, let's have some sex.

'Do you have a condom?' I ask.

'I don't.'

'Then I don't think you can cum in me?'

'I can't?'

'You were going to?' I go to kiss him again to cover up the awkwardness. 'We'll make it up as we go along.' I push him into the bed and he bumps his head on something hard. My laptop. I move the laptop to the floor and attempt to climb astride him. This bra is bloody hideous. I can also feel my many stomachs hanging. Like udders. I haven't moisturised my legs. I don't even know if I'm aroused; I've not even had the courage to look down there in six months. We used to be decent at this. But, it all feels alien to me, foreign. Those bits have a different purpose now. They make babies. Can I do this? I must. Will pulls his boxers down and I take off my knickers. Please don't be completely horrified by my muff. I won't release the boobs. I then reach down to touch him.

'Is that alright?' I ask.

He nods. I kiss him again. But it's not alright, is it? There's nothing happening. He doesn't want this one bit. Oh. Oh dear. I retract my hand, heart sinking, and lie next to him quietly. That sealed that deal then. Wow. I felt as seductive as a beached walrus anyway, but now I feel utterly stupid. A tear escapes, because all I can think about is that girl he kissed at work. I think about how they kissed, how those lips were not mine. However drunk you are, you kiss someone because there is an attraction, a spark. This feels like someone throwing a match in a puddle.

'Could you leave?' I whisper.

'I… I…' I don't know who this is embarrassing more but I don't really want him here, watching me as I try and shift my body weight out of this bed, covering my body and putting my clothes back on awkwardly. I put a pillow over me.

'Beth… it's not…'

'Seriously, shut up now.'

'I don't want to fight…'

'Then it's simple. Decide if you want to be here or not. Decide if you love me or not. But this? This is humiliating trying to work out what you're thinking, trying to work out if I can handle the fact you kissed someone else, sitting here with our son trying to work out if you've abandoned us.'

'I haven't…'

My loud voice has obviously travelled into the other room and I hear Joe stirring in his car seat.

'You're not here. You're debating this life we've made, you're kissing other women and sitting in your brother's house while you have some crisis over everything. You've shut me out. You're making me feel like shit when I deserve better. I deserve to be wanted. Enough. Get out...'

'Are you breaking up with me?'

'I'm telling you to fuck off.'

This is not me. This is Lucy, this is Meg, this is – Christ – my mother. Will sits on the edge of the bed, struggling to put his clothes and shoes on.

Joe's crying grows to a sharp crescendo.

'Do you want me to check on...'

'I'll deal with him. Just go.'

'But...'

'GO!'

He skulks out the room and I hear the click of the front door. Sitting here in my knickers and bra, I glance at the ripples of my stomach in the mirror, the light hitting my skin so every crease, stretch mark and fold across my thighs, breasts and arms are magnified. Who am I? Why do I feel like this version of me is failing? Joe keeps crying and I hear loud footsteps, then a knocking on the ceiling above that falls in time with my own tears.

Track Seventeen

'L.I.F.E.G.O.E.S.O.N.' – Noah and the Whale (2011)

'I've been with men who can't get it up. Was he drunk?' Lucy asks me, a little too loudly. A pigeon looks at us strangely then flies away.

'No.'

'I've had some who were just plain tired?'

'No.'

'Well, I know what you're thinking and that's complete bull. I'm not even going to say that out loud…'

'You're allowed to say it. My body's changed. Maybe he's just not attracted to me anymore.'

Lucy looks over at me from the park bench on which we're sitting and pushes me over, my stomach almost bouncing off the seat. For all the moments I'm proud of my body, of what it's achieved, where I know this is just a natural evolution of my female form, it doesn't mean I won't have moments where I'm struggling to come to terms with this change, with who I am, which is why the other afternoon haunts me.

'You've had a baby,' Lucy informs me, like this is news to me.

'Giselle had a baby and she slimmed down in weeks.' I make a gesture with my hands like she could fit through prison bars.

'Giselle the model? Yes, because she has nutritionists, a personal trainer, and it's her job to be a skinny cow,' Lucy replies. 'Did Will actually say that to you?"

'Not in so many words.' I look down at my hands and Lucy goes in for a hug.

'Please. Sex isn't about looking at people and getting hard. It's energy, words, conversation, connection. It sounds like you were trying to glue it back together with sex.'

'Is that not a good idea then?' I ask.

'No. You're both in such different headspaces at the moment. Sex should be very low down on the agenda.'

'I just can't read him anymore, Luce. Not like I used to. I got so angry with him.'

'For good reason. He's messing with your head, your emotions.'

'I guess he's confused, hurting.'

'And you're not?' Did Grace tell her about the kiss? 'You're the one who pushed this little bugger out. He was ten pounds – that is next-level cooch trauma.'

Joe is facing us in his buggy and looks over at me. *I am sorry about that, Mum.*

Last week's bad, non-existent sex debacle has left our relationship status even more confused and muddled. I was angry about that kiss. We both needed space to digest that. There was also some thread there about work, changes and understanding new roles and our ability to cope. But the conversation left me frustrated and angry.

And now, when I think of Will, I don't think of someone I know and love; I think of someone who's decided last minute that they're not getting on the rollercoaster, abandoning me on this crazy ride all by myself. *I don't think I can do it, I'll just sit this one out.* So I'm some sad single rider, hanging upside down, my body tossed in all directions, I can't feel my face half the time, and I am well and truly on my own.

'Are you getting out? Distracting yourself?'

'I did the model thing which was random, and we went to a baby-friendly screening of some romcom.'

'Some romcom?'

'I fell asleep. So did Joe.' It turns out that all Joe needs to break into some deep sleep is some Dolby Surround Sound, the muted crunch of overpriced popcorn, complete darkness and the aircon cranked up to icy.

'I've been getting more involved in school stuff. Chatting to Sean again,' I say, trying to persuade Lucy I'm not a complete social saddo.

'In the flesh?'

'On WhatsApp?'

It's mostly been conversations where we send each other memes and laughing out loud emojis.

'So you think this is the answer?' she asks, referring to what we're about to do.

'Yes. Maybe I need to up my game. Get some endorphins flowing and it might help me get into better shape.'

'I'm not exercising with you if you think you need to be skinny to win back Will.'

'It's not that.'

She studies my face.

'I also need to just be a better human. I'm in terrible shape. I thought I was having a heart attack the other day walking up the stairs in the Tube. Joe deserves a mother who's looking after herself at least.'

'So this is all self-care?'

I salute her and nod. I need to work on me; my brain is like porridge so I need to fix the sum of the parts so that the whole can function again. This body, this life, this role is one I need to embrace wholeheartedly and throw myself into. So today is phase one of bucking up my ideas: time to tone and sculpt and get me all Botticellian/Rubenesque goddess as opposed to the head-all-over-the-place Dalí-esque mother I am.

And it starts with a healthier frame of mind, by regaining my fitness. I say regain – I'm not always sure I had fitness. I had luck. I walked to places and had a twentysomething metabolism. I ate badly thinking it was important not to shut out the major food groups, like alcohol and sugar, but now age and post-partum biology is anything but forgiving. It's time to be one of those mums who run around parks with their buggies and convene in a circle to lift tyres and skip. Yes, apparently this is a thing in this park we're in. I've even sat on this bench and watched as some ex-military man shouted at the mothers while they all bench-pressed their babies and I ate crisps and laughed. Except that sort of fitness costs money, a lot of money. So do gyms. I don't have the energy or confidence to exercise in front of others anyway, so that's why Lucy is here instead, decked out in tight Lycra to lead me in some exercise regime. I have no idea what she has planned, but I am very much not in Lycra.

I am in cropped threadbare cotton leggings, a giant hoodie and Reebok Classics. I feel like I should be wearing a sweat band at least.

'Is this because you're hanging around them models too?' Lucy asks suspiciously.

I don't doubt that having Yasmin in my line of sight may subliminally have had some effect on what I'm feeling. But turning me into Yasmin King might take major surgical intervention as opposed to a few jumping jacks in the park. I reach down to my phone and reveal a picture on my camera roll that Giles messaged over yesterday. It's Joe and Yasmin in the yoghurt ad, looking completely perfect. Banana Joe looks up at Yasmin adoringly (he's not really, he's looking up at a toy being jingled on a stick) while Yasmin is keeping it casual, leaning against a kitchen counter, not a hair or an eyelash out of place. It's not reality, I know it isn't, but that doesn't mean it doesn't hurt to look at Joe with some other perfect mother.

'Maybe…' I tell Lucy.

'I can write you a list as long as the Nile of the ways you are better than her. I've met models in my game. Half of them live off Cup-A-Soup and air to keep them that skinny. And drugs too, they take all sorts of laxatives.'

'Speaking of laxatives…'

'You didn't…?'

'No, I went on Yasmin's page and tried some of that Ayurvedic shit.'

'Yoga?'

'Lentils. I made a curry like on one of her Insta stories. It was yummy.'

'That's a start.'

'But the spice gave me the squits and the most phenomenal wind. I thought I was going to explode.'

'You idiot.'

We sit there laughing. Maybe that's all I need – a diet of dried fruit, lentils and extremely hot spices.

'But if you want to take it seriously,' Lucy says, 'then let's do something now. I can do a HIIT routine with you?'

'What does that mean? Is it a fighting thing? Will I get to actually hit you?'

'No, numpty. It's high intensity interval training.'

'Will it hurt?'

'If it's not hurting, it means it's not working. Pain before gain.' She says this in a booming man's voice like I'm about to go in an actual ring. I was more thinking something light and dance-based?

Lucy walks over to a patch of grass, setting up a small wireless speaker. Some energetic dance music plays out of it and she starts jogging on the spot. Self-conscious, I look over my shoulder to ensure no one thinks we're just a group of errant youths.

'This will be good. It may limber you up.'

'If it doesn't kill me.'

'So I'll play a series of bleeps at time intervals and I'll tell you what to do in each one. For the first minute, we're going to do some prisoner squats.'

She puts her hands to her head and squats like she's sitting down. I can do that. I follow.

'Really deep, like you're sitting on a chair. Feel the burn in your thighs.'

My thighs seem to quiver like this is the first time they've been asked to operate beyond supporting my body weight. I feel a burn but the bleep hasn't gone yet so I keep going.

'It burns.'

'Keep going.'

Bleep. Thank crap for that.

'Good and now fast feet.'

Oh shit, we're running on the spot. I can feel myself jiggling. Like every part of me, even my eyeballs. I should have done something with my hair. She looks at my face curled up in pain.

'You really don't do any sort of exercise, eh?'

'Oh, piss off.'

She can actually breathe. She has full working capacity of her lungs. How? I've run on the spot for literally just thirty seconds. I can feel my underboobs sweating.

'Now, thirty seconds off. Take in some water.'

I glug at my bottle nearby and watch Joe as he looks over, concerned. *Be good to this one, Aunty Lucy, she's all I have at the minute.*

'And we're back into some jumping jacks.'

'With my norks? I'll take an eye out.'

'Then slowly, less jumping. Legs out, hold on to your core.'

I do as I'm told but can feel the elastic on my bra begging me to stop. How do I hold on to my core? Isn't that my spine? Or is that my stomach? Whatever it is, it's begging me to stop.

'It hurts, Luce.'

'That's your fat cells dying.'

'It's *me* dying. Maybe we should have gone for a spirited walk instead?'

'You could have done that with your old man BFF neighbour. I bought a bus ticket to get here. Now, walk outs.'

I drop to the floor. My arms take on slow pounding motions like you'd expect the legs of a brontosaurus to make on the ground. This is not dignified. I am not doing anything in time to the music either because I can't hear it; just my heartbeat and my cells crying out for mercy.

'Use the rhythm of the—'

'Seriously, piss off…'

'You're a moody bitch when you're exercising, eh?'

I pick up my water bottle and throw it at her. She dodges it which is something she's learnt from many years' experience as the youngest sister. I see some dog walkers mooch past watching, talking in whispers. Bleep. Thank almighty crap for that. I collapse to the floor and curl up into the foetal position. The coolness of the hard autumn ground is my only friend here. I don't even know if I'm sweating or crying.

'And now flutter kick squats. These are different to the squats we did before.' She does the normal squatting thing but then some strange scissor action with her legs. This takes co-ordination beyond my remit. I do one and she giggles.

'Some of us aren't born dancers,' I bark in between breaths.

I look like an awkward human pretzel, my arms moving to a different rhythm. These squats are also not good for my bottom half. I am not toned down there so I think I can feel my kidneys jump up and down too. Are those my kidneys? Or my uterus? I imagine it empty and vacant now there's no baby in there. Or maybe it's my… flaps. Yep, that was pleasant. I think I may have just pissed myself just a little bit. But who knows these days, I have so little connection with my nether regions that may have been a flood. I look down quite pathetically.

'Don't stop.'

'I think I just wet myself.'

Lucy looks at me and keels over in laughter.

'Don't you dare.'

'Oh my God, you *are* old.'

I have nothing else to throw at her. I am thankful for dark leggings and large tops at this present moment. Collapsing to my knees, I lie in a star shape on the floor. You know how most people post-exercise perspire and glow and look healthy? I look like I've been in a fight with myself. My face is burning with colour. Lucy comes to lie next to me, her head propped on my shoulder. We look up into the bright blue sky, framed by clouds, squeals of children nearby on the playground arguing about turns on swings.

'You can have a break,' she says.

'Well, you and your routines officially suck. I'm still fat,' I say, patting my belly.

She punches me in the arm. I am silent. Joe peers over at me, disappointed.

'Am I supposed to hurt?'

'B, you did seven minutes. We haven't even started planking.'

'I don't want to plank. I'd just be holding that position and looking down at my stomach hanging like an old sofa cushion. It would be too demoralising.'

She curls herself into me. 'You were never like this, Beth. You never cared about these things?'

'Maybe that was part of the problem?'

'If Will has left you because you've put on a couple of pounds post-pregnancy then that says more about him; you know that, right?'

'Maybe…'

'Well, I think we should sign you up for fitness that's more fun. Swimming?'

'Then I'd have to do my bikini line.'

'No, you don't. I swim at the lido near Emma's and there's a lady who goes out with full pits and fanny. It sprouts out like alfalfa.'

'I'd die of the shame.'

'But that's the point. She doesn't care. I quite admire her for it.'

I look over at Lucy. For all her faults, she has this inner shield, she never lets the outside affect her, and she frankly couldn't give a flying fudge what people think. I wish she could just hand me a portion of that.

'You need to fall in love with yourself again, B. Are you masturbating?'

'Luce!'

'I'll take that as a no. Like where do you get any joy then? You're starving your body of pleasure.'

'Food, obviously. Carbs mostly.'

She narrows her eyes at me. 'Your body did something brilliant and gave us Joe, you now need to connect back with it, learn to love it. How can you let anyone else poke it if you can't poke it yourself?'

Crude, if true. 'But it's different down there.'

'Gaping?'

I punch her on the arm.

'Just remember, you're fab,' she continues. 'I love you and that's really all that should matter.'

It does, more than she knows.

'This is fun though. Coming here, watching you whizz yourself. I know I'm focusing all my time on Ems at the minute but I can come round any time. We can hang out in the park like this. I don't have to shout at you.'

'Can you bring crisps?' I ask.

'Obviously. And my music and a few tinnies. We can smoke that eighth of weed you gave me and heckle boys.'

'With a baby? Classy.'

'Oooh, I know!' She reaches for her phone and the song turns to 'Juice' by Lizzo. She starts to sing along to the lyrics, smiles at me, then drags me to my feet.

'Dance!' she orders.

'I'm not a performing monkey.'

She turns the music up.

'We'll get thrown out of the park,' I tell her.

'And?'

I sense this happens to her a lot. I sidestep awkwardly.

'This is not how my Beth dances. Come on. We used to do gigs and festivals in parks all the time.'

Lucy's movements get cruder. 'You can't twerk in a public park, Lucy. There are rules.'

'There are no rules when it comes to dance,' she says in accentuated dance-teacher tones. 'Come on. Tell me you're the baddest bitch alive.'

'I am the baddest bitch alive,' I say in a monotone.

Lucy shakes her head at me. It is a very catchy song though. Lizzo is good like that, the beats are very persuasive. My hips start to swing.

'She's getting there,' Lucy says.

Oh fuck it. I may do something that resembles freestyle swimming arms and a shimmy, singing along with Lucy. The dog walkers who are circuiting this park look supremely confused at how this exercise class has devolved. I didn't even dance at my own party. I haven't since Will left and definitely not in public for the longest time. My face falls into a pout, my pelvic floor isn't pleased but there is certainly something freeing about the movement.

'People are looking,' I sing.

'Because they're jealous,' she sings back.

I laugh as Joe looks over at us, confused but somewhat entertained. *You look fine to me, Mum. I like your juice.* Maybe *that's* all that really matters. Lucy comes over and mimics slapping my ass. We may have overstepped levels of decency here. But I laugh, a laugh I feel penetrate right through me. And yes, my gusset is really damp but it's wonderful to feel my chest opening up to find something for my heart to smile about again.

'How have you still got this manky carpet?' Lucy asks, as she walks around my flat. 'This place looks like it belongs in a seventies sitcom. Hey, that could be a project? We could do this place up?'

'How? With what money?'

'I watch *Queer Eye*. Bobby has taught me everything I know.'

She walks through my flat as I breastfeed Joe. We came to change out of wee-sodden clothes (Joe's and mine). Later, to repay the favour of her humiliation in a public park, I've told Lucy we'll get Emma's girls on the school run in my battered Suzuki Swift. Will left me the car, possibly the worst parting gift he could have imagined. *I couldn't shag you but have our old car instead.* I may as well put it to use and save Lucy a trip on the buses. It's also a perfect excuse to go for a drive-thru McDonald's. The doorbell sounds and Lucy goes to answer it.

'Who? Oh, I know you. You're her old man afternoon love interest. I'm Lucy, the cheeky one,' I hear echoing through the corridor. I look at the time. Paddy. It's tea o'clock. At least I have some routine in my life.

'She's a crap shag your sister though.' I hear cackling in return. Bastards, both of them. They filter through the corridor, Paddy appearing with a packet of biscuits and my mail.

'Afternoon,' he says, winking at me. 'Tea?'

'Always. Make one for trouble, too.'

'You never told me he was funny, B,' Lucy says.

'She doesn't tell anyone about me. I'm her dirty little secret.' Paddy heads to the kitchen to switch on the kettle. He leaves the mail on my coffee table and Lucy sifts through it.

'Oooooh, you have a new kebab van opening soon that does delivery and twenty per cent off orders for the first week.'

'You're supposed to help me be healthy?'

'No chips, no mayo. It's basically a healthy sandwich.'

'Don't you worry about where the meat's come from?' I ask.

'Do I look like I query the quality of my meat?'

I retch a bit in my mouth.

'Do you need new windows or a conservatory? I guess not...' she says, scrunching up flyers.

'How do you take it, Lucy?'

'Oo-er, Paddy. That's a question and a half. Milk and one sugar today though.'

Don't flirt with the old man, his heart won't take it. Through the crack in the kitchen door I see Paddy smelling the milk.

'Ooooh, what's this?' Lucy holds up a padded enveloped to me and I recognise the writing immediately. She reads my reaction. 'Is this from Will?' she asks. I nod. Whereas I am filled with uncertainty, Lucy is less so and goes to rip the envelope open. I'm pinned to this sofa with Joe attached to me so have no way to tackle her.

'It's addressed to me,' I say.

'And…?'

'That's mail fraud.'

She doesn't seem to care, pulling out a CD and a letter and starts reading. As her eyes look across the words though, her expression changes. I can't tell if it's sadness or anger. Paddy re-enters the room, holding the tea, and picks up on the tension.

'Oh, B. He made you a mix CD,' she says, holding it up in her hands.

'William?' he asks.

I nod.

'He says this was the birthday present he should have got you and he's sorry and he still…'

'No!' I stand up, Joe still on my breast, and reach over, grabbing the letter from her hands, tearing it into quarters. The process itself is cathartic. Paddy looks horrified at my reaction.

'B, you should listen to him. He's trying to make amends…'

'He wants to make amends? Then be here with me. Why send me CDs like some cheap token of his affection?'

Lucy's face is all scrunched up. 'It might be decent. You don't know what he's laid down here.'

'And I'll listen to it and run back into his arms, will I?'

Lucy looks over at me sadly. I know why. I have never been the cynical sister; that was her role. Paddy puts the tea down slowly on the table, his eyes urging me to sit down, cover up and calm down as Joe is still attached to my nipple.

'Music can be a powerful aphrodisiac. I once slept with someone at a Halloween night because he knew all the words to the *Ghostbusters* song,' Lucy informs me.

'Everyone knows the words to that song.'

'He knew the dance from the cartoon too.'

'You should have locked that down.'

'Well, technically I did. For one night. Shame he had a chipolata for a wanger.'

Paddy chokes on his tea to hear her frankness. I am sure that was me once. Pre-Will, I saw my fair share of sausage too. It feels like a different lifetime, though. Would anyone approach me with their sausage ever again? Of course they would. I'm the baddest bitch alive.

Paddy comes to sit next to me. 'Betty and I had music, songs – don't we all? They're all part of your story.'

Lucy looks sad to hear him talk about Betty in the past tense.

'Was Betty into hip hop?' she tries to joke.

'She had a hip replacement?' he replies.

Bless them both for trying to make me laugh. Lucy collapses onto the sofa and she comes to put her arms around me and rest her head on my shoulder, stroking Joe's tiny arm. *Thank you both for being here.* I look at the CD in her hands. The title of the CD is 'PLEASE PUT ME BACK IN THE RIGHT CASE' and it's decorated with his expert doodles. I smile. Briefly. Will and I came together with an amassed collection of about five hundred CDs. No one ever got it, but for us it was an achievement of sorts. Except he hated my filing system. He loathed that I sorted them by colour and that they were never in the right cases. Paddy has picked up that letter and is trying to piece it together and read it.

'I've seen you and Will from the beginning,' Lucy intervenes. 'I want this to have a better ending.' That she has. Lucy was eighteen and in the first year of university when I was navigating teaching college. She was at the gig and watched as I drunkenly pulled that charming indie kid.

'You were going to kill him a few weeks ago?' I reply.

'Yeah. I still would if you wanted me to. But maybe listen to this mix CD first? If it's truly shite then at least we can have a laugh before you dump him properly?'

I smile but try to process the words. *Dump him.* I've thought about that to some degree over the past week. You don't walk out on the mother of your son. He's left me alone for my heart to become shrivelled and desiccated.

'His spelling is shockingly bad too. I'd dump him over the spelling,' Paddy adds, still scanning over the ripped quarters of the letter.

I like the bad spelling. Teasing him about it, hearing him call through from the next room asking for advice with tricky words. And I miss it: the soundtrack of conversation that was our relationship. Then I remember all the things he said on the sofa, all the hurt and upset. Everything is so fractured. A little face looks up at me. Joe. He's mesmerised by the CD in Lucy's hands and he watches the reflections shine off her face, trying to catch them with his hands. *What do you think, Joe?*

'Bring it in the car. If there's any eighties soft rock on there, then the deal is off.'

Track Eighteen

'Something Good Can Work' –
Two Door Cinema Club (2009)

'How do I feel for teeth?' I ask frantically on the phone.

'Well, you don't ask him to open wide… just put a clean finger in and feel around the gums. Maybe use a muslin.'

Meg is on the phone taking my emergency call as Emma is working and Google is being as useful as nipples on a man.

Siri, why does a baby grizzle?

Here is what I found for grizzly bears.

Joe grizzles away in my arms, that low-grade sound he's so fond of emitting.

'Hot bananas, there's something hard under there. That's a tooth?'

'Or a fang. Teething is the enemy,' Meg lets me know.

'You told me the enemy was wind.'

'It comes in stages. New teeth will change everything. Does he have nappy rash?'

'Yeah?'

'Sudocrem. Spread that thick like butter too. Like how Lucy used to do her foundation when she was fifteen.'

I feel like I should be taking notes. Joe squirms and moans in discomfort.

'Go to your fridge, do you have anything cold?'

'Beer?'

'Food wise.' My fridge is a strange entity these days that consists of a top shelf dedicated to sauces and old pickles. The middle shelf is currently an altar of ready meals that should serve two people but regularly feed one. There's milk, a pot of mouldy yoghurt and some blueberries for the health.

'I have carrots?'

'Bingo. Give him a carrot stick to gnaw on, a bit of resistance on the gums will help.'

'What? Do I just let him suck it?'

'Yep. Suck on that bastard; he can get his teeth into it too. Sorry, Tim.'

'Who's Tim?'

'Work friend.'

I love how she's giving me this advice from her work desk. I force the carrot in his mouth and watch as he gets his chops around it. *This is new. It's not a breast. Or a bottle. Where are its nipples?* His shock alone means the noise disappears for which I exhale slowly.

'You're a bloody miracle worker.'

'I've just had practice. What's going on there? Are you alone? Are you still in your pyjamas?'

'Yeah? It was a tough night,' I mutter, defensively.

'Oh, I'm not judging you. I'm jealous. I miss those early baby days of heavenly slovenliness. If you wear the right pyjama bottoms, you can just slip on a coat and Uggs, go out and people just think they're fancy harem pants.'

Why aren't you here, Meggers? We could have done parts of our pre- and post-pregnancy together over desserts and daytime TV. It would have been the next stage of our adventures from bar-hopping and over-drinking.

'I used to spend my mornings eating Doritos, napping with my boobs out,' she says. 'Anyways, what's new? You OK? Are the sisters looking after you?'

This seems to be the case of late. I'm getting a lot more phone calls to check up on me and invites to random sister events. I even got a call from Emma asking me if I wanted to go food shopping with her the other day, like I needed airing.

'Yeah, the collective huddle is tight,' I reply.

'It's what we do. We did it for Emma, for Gracie. And Gracie is back soon which will be good. I'll drag my lot down for Christmas then we can huddle super tight.'

I can't work out if that's a good or bad thing. Will it be a reminder of all these things that are missing from my life? Or will the company from all angles be warming and protective?

'Oh, and Lucy told me you're working with Yasmin King on your shoots? She still a bitch?'

'You knew her at school?'

'If memory serves, she was the one who gave someone a hand job in the phone box near the Esso garage. I think we also did a magazine spread with her once about the perfect eyebrow. I didn't engage but she had an air, you know?'

'She still has the air. It's a bit aloof. I'm not sure if she likes me or not.'

'She always seemed very lonely. I think I felt sorry for her. Obviously quite a troubled girl at school – super pretty, sexualised way too young.'

'So what you're saying is it pays to be kind of mundane and plain-looking like us?'

'Speak for yourself. I'm bloody gorgeous, me.'

Meg does this sometimes – she slips into Northern which just makes me realise how far away she really is from us.

'And when can I ask about Will?'

I exhale deeply. Meg has not said much when it's come to Will but maybe that's the beauty of her; the judgement is more subtle compared to my mother or Lucy.

'He made me a mix CD,' I say, almost as if I'm trying to defend what's he's done.

She pauses. 'When did he regress to his fifteen-year-old self? Did he send it with a pack of Love Hearts and then inscribe your name on his locker?'

I see it doesn't impress her much. It didn't me, but Lucy made me play said CD in the car. He'd thought about every song on there so deeply. It had everything from our favourite Britpop to gigs we'd been to, referencing the concert where he first told me he loved me, and finished with 'Hey Joe'. That nearly made me cry. It made me think of how we came up with Joe's name. We'd liked the idea of celebrating his male midwife, the simplicity of it, but we needed to check the musical connections, naturally. Joe

Strummer, Joe Cocker, Joey Ramone and a classic by Hendrix. It all fell into place so easily.

'I'm just letting us have a moment.'

She pauses. I know what she's thinking. A moment by definition doesn't really last a fortnight.

'Did I ever tell you about what happened when Tess was first born? What happened with Danny?'

'No.'

'Well, you didn't hear this from me but she was born and when we got down to the maternity wards, the man broke down.'

This is a strange image of someone we all thought was a tad surly and non-emotional.

'And it didn't stop there. He cried a lot. I used to find him crying folding the laundry, blubbing at how little she was and how he was scared she'd break.'

'That's really… sweet.'

'It was annoying as fuck. There I was sitting in a rubber ring on the sofa with piles the size of dates and there he was crying about how beautiful the baby was…'

I laugh. Mainly because at least I didn't have the piles.

'The way I always see it is that we carry the babies, we grow them inside us, we feel everything when they're born, like *everything*. But men don't have that run-up; suddenly, BOOM, this is your baby. You're a father. Own it. People deal with it in different ways.'

'Like running away?'

'Where does Peter live? Battersea? It's hardly the other end of the world.'

'And what if I said looking after Joe was too much, what if I wanted my time out and I just walked out on him?'

'You'd never do that. Which makes you immediately better than Will but then, you are my sister. You're a good mum. And a good person.'

Oh, Meg. That's why she crafts words for a living. Would I walk out on this one? I look down at him in my arms, still trying to work out what the deal is with the carrot. Days like this can be a struggle, but it really would suck not to have him around. I pat him on his nappy and realise that it's possibly full. That's probably not helping his woes.

'I have to go and change this one. Thanks for the carrot advice.'

'It's all I'm good for really. Love you, B.'

I hang up, imagining if Meg had been at that party a few weeks back. She'd have chased Will down the street and dragged him back by his collar, made us get over ourselves – and then probably slapped some sense into the sisters in the kitchen too.

I lay Joe down on the change mat I have permanently parked next to the sofa, opening up his nappy, and study his sad baby eyes. *You're hurting, aren't you, bubs? You're growing teeth. Next it will be puberty. Then you'll move out and I'll only see you when you want loans or Sunday lunch.* Maybe a shallow bath might help instead. I clean him up and hook him over my arm. Filling the bath, I dunk him in. Is this the right thing to do? Who knows anymore? Just don't pee in there, please. My phone suddenly starts vibrating on the floor so I scoop Joe out with a towel and answer it by placing the handset under my chin.

'Hello?'

'Beth?'

I pause for a moment to work out whose voice that is on the end of the line. 'Yasmin?'

This is a surprise. Why is she calling me? Shit, should I be at a shoot or something?

'Are you busy?' she asks.

I'm not sure how to answer. I'm about to baste my son's baby butt in cream and scramble to get a nappy on him but apart from that…

'I'm just with Joe.'

The sound which greets us next is a breathless sobbing, like she can't quite catch her words.

'Are you OK?' I ask.

'I'm just… I'm bleeding. I don't know anyone else with a baby. I don't think this should be happening.'

I stand here, silent. Mainly in shock that she's called me but also sad that out of what I assume to be a large circle of friends and family, I am her first port of call. How scared and desperate must you be to call someone you hardly know when you're hurting?

'Are you cramping?' I ask her. 'Is there pain? I'm not a doctor but I can call my sister?'

'Don't do that,' she says abruptly. 'I have an appointment lined up with the antenatal clinic in an hour. I just can't do this… what if…'

As strange as it feels, I think I know what she's hinting at. *What if I've lost a baby and I'm just sitting there, having to cope with that information on my own?* I would never have coped. And I had sisters, my mother. There was Will.

'Tell me what hospital and we'll meet you there.'

*

'Everything is fine. Can you hear the heartbeat? Healthy baby.'

A kindly sonographer and a midwife have a Doppler over Yasmin's stomach as she lies back on the bed, the echo of the heartbeat skipping in time with the clock in the room. I've not been in a hospital since Joe was born so it's bizarre to be back. The crackle of the paper sheets draws me back to my first scan. Will cried when he saw what he thought was the baby. Turns out it was just a random part of my innards. But he squeezed my hand so tight, inhaled sharply to hear we were having a boy. We still have that scan on the fridge.

'All looks good to me. The baby is well. How is your morning sickness?' asks the midwife.

'Pretty bad. And not just confined to the mornings,' replies Yasmin.

'OK. Well, some women get spotting as their bodies adjust to the pregnancy. If the bleeding gets heavier or you get any cramping then call us again but your baby looks fine to me. The morning sickness should subside as your body gets used to all the extra hormones. Your blood sugar is low. Do you eat enough?'

I want to say that as a model, food is an alien concept.

'I've had trouble keeping anything down. Beth told me to eat Tangfastics.'

The medical professionals look at me in disgust. I wasn't telling her to eat those solely; as part of a balanced diet of course. If she's just eating them, that baby will come out with some angry soured expression.

'Well, just make sure you're eating other things too. Did this happen with your other pregnancy?' she asks, looking at Joe. He looks up from his stroller, big eyes like a lemur penetrating the gloom of the room.

'Joe's mine,' I mutter.

'Are you her partner then? Sister?' she asks me, trying to work out our relationship. Shit. She thinks we're either married or related. Talk about a total mismatch in terms of genes or coupling.

'She's my friend,' Yasmin says.

Friend: an interesting definition of our relationship. I don't know whether to correct her and just say we used to take the same number bus home when we were sixteen.

'Well, you must be a very good friend to be here. Look after her. Lots of liquids and make sure she's taking antenatal vitamins. Folic acid, in particular.'

I feel the need to salute this instruction as it dawns on me that I have been assigned follow-up 'friend' duties. They both leave, pulling the curtain behind them while Yasmin rubs the ultrasound jelly off her still enviably flat stomach.

'I'm glad you're OK,' I say.

Silence. She seems a bit sheepish, at a loss for words.

'I don't know how to thank you,' she says finally. 'No one's ever, I mean… I'm sorry you came all this way for nothing.'

'Well, it wasn't nothing. You were scared, emotional.'

She runs her tongue along the top of her teeth, almost like I'm shaming her for feeling something about this incident, this pregnancy.

'Is Jethro on tour?' I ask her, curious why he isn't here instead of me.

Her nostrils flare and her face quivers with emotion.

'Jethro moved out. With Dicky. About a fortnight ago now.'

'Oh.'

Simple maths tells me that was around the time of the shoot. Has she been carrying this on her own since then?

'What about… your family?'

'I… I haven't told my family yet. And all my friends are' – she pauses to find a word – 'they wouldn't be interested.'

'I think if you were sick or hurt, they might want to know.'

She shakes her head sternly. 'No one needs to know.'

That puts me in my place. Is this her way of telling me that I'm supposed to remain tight-lipped?

'I haven't told anyone, if that's what you're implying.'

'No. I meant my friends are different to you. They wouldn't care,' she says, ruefully. 'To be fair, I don't have many friends. Real friends.'

'What about Kelly Taylor from school? You went out for lunch with her the other day.'

I realise that's evidence I've been stalking her on social media.

'Kels is just some social hanger-on. She likes the freebies. I think she's leaked stories about Jethro to the press before.'

'Oh.' Surely you shouldn't have lunch with people like that then? But now doesn't feel like the time for a lecture.

'Are *we* friends then?' I ask her. It feels ridiculous to ask this, like I'm seven years old and confirming that we might get to play together in the playground.

'Well, yeah?'

'I mean you have peed in front of me,' I joke.

She looks at me strangely. 'I pee in front of everyone. I'm a model. I have no inhibitions, I have to strip in front of strangers.'

'Oh, well… It's not what I usually do.'

It feels good to lay down the peeing boundaries now if we are going to proceed with this relationship.

'Does Jethro not want the baby then?' I ask.

Her eyes glaze over and she exhales, almost laughing. 'It's not Jethro's.'

'Oh.'

My eyes scan the room on receiving that information. That sucks. For Jethro. And for her. But it makes me piece together what I know, what I've seen.

'Harry?' I whisper.

She nods, staring into her lap. 'We've been seeing each other for about eighteen months. I brought him to your party. He was Boba Fett.'

I pause to take that information in. Lucy said you did the fandango in Emma's downstairs bathroom. We can officially put that party down as the worst party in the history of birthday celebrations.

'So Jethro found out?'

She nods. 'To be fair, we'd both been doing our own thing for a while. He'd been shagging some music exec on tour but the pregnancy was the final nail in the coffin.'

Momentarily, I think about how Instagram has always painted a very different picture. If you were to follow their feeds you'd see they were still taking pictures of their non-dairy low-fat coffees and happy faces in paid promotion work, and there was no mention of a separation, not even a cryptic meme referring to heartbreak.

'Does Harry know?' I ask.

'I called him before you. I've been calling for a lifetime. Today, he told me I was making this up to get his attention. Told me not to ring him anymore. Or talk to him. And told me it was my responsibility to do the right thing and get rid of this baby,' she says in a whisper.

The emotion, the raw fragility in Yasmin's voice, destroys me.

'And then I could only think to call you.' She sits on the edge of the bed, cradling her head. 'I just don't know what he's thinking. All that time we've been dating, he's been telling me he's going to leave his wife, that he loves me, and then as soon as this happens, he fucks off and tells me it's over. He tells me he has a family, that I would be breaking it up.'

I'm doing a whole series of mental calculations in my head. This was not a one-off snog in a corridor or a rando shag at my least favourite birthday party ever. This was a whole affair. And I think about what Giles told me about Harry, about how he was a social climber, someone vying for work and attention and my heart twinges that Yasmin fell into that trap. Because her heart aches; she entered into that relationship with the intention of something greater. I am conflicted, too. Shouldn't I be feeling angry with her for conducting an affair with a married man? Weirdly, I'm not. This girl, who I thought to be devoid of emotion, is revealing herself to me, peeling back the wrapper slowly. Before, I thought her barely human, some caricature of a girl I used to go to school with. But now, I've seen a baby growing inside her, its tiny heart beating. All the emotion that comes with this life-changing moment flows out of her. You can read it all over her perfect face. And I just want to hug her. I want to tell her it will all be alright. I've done this, I've been there, it's not completely awful.

Joe gurgles in the corner and we both look down at him. That plum-sized baby in your stomach could one day grow into that. It's amazing, if terrifying. Yasmin stares at Joe for a moment too long then gets her phone out, scanning numbers.

'I'll book an Uber. How are you and Joe getting home?' she asks me, dabbing at her tears with her sleeves. I hand her a tissue. Oh God, me and my bleeding heart. Because I think of her returning to that empty house now, how it's devoid of company and warmth and her tiny whizzing dog. I recall how I felt when Will first left and the crushing loneliness of him not being there. At least in that moment, I had a Joe. That feeling I know she'll carry forces the words out of my mouth.

'I'm driving. Come, I'll give you a lift and you can come back to mine for a bit.'

Track Nineteen

'Parklife' – Blur (1994)

'Yasmin King is living with you?' asks Lucy, her words slow and enunciated. 'You really are some stupid but very special saint, aren't you?'

'Not living, really. She kinda just pops by with food and coffees. Like nice food, too. Bento boxes, frittata and actual chimichangas from posh food places.'

Lucy doesn't seem too sure about this type of recompense but when someone is bringing you miso salmon bento and you know they're pregnant and alone, you don't turn them away. The afternoon I brought her home, she curled up on my sofa and we binge-watched *Gossip Girl* and we debated about how Penn Badgley has got better-looking over the years like a young George Clooney. I fed her crisps and made her tea, grateful that I hadn't thrown away the camomile shite my mother had gifted me. She stayed the night on my sofa and left the next morning. She started coming back on random days, usually without warning. She'd look at Joe, watch me change his nappies and hand me wipes. We'd occasionally sit in silence on our phones or have debates over noodles (apparently I should be going brown rice soba. Like that's going to happen) and about whether it was normal to lust over Zac Efron. The answer is yes since he did *Baywatch*. When she asked about Will, I panicked and lied, telling her he'd gone away on a trip. Where to? Baku, I blurted out. All sorts of architectural shit happens in Baku, apparently. To have told her the truth would just be too complicated, too sad. And on bad days, she'd stalk Harry on social media. She'd look up his wife and gawp at their family pictures and we'd both do next-level detective work to work out his plan, his agenda. He would post family pictures with pointed comments almost directed at Yasmin talking about family, love, his wife and they would floor her. She'd hold onto her stomach and sob and I'd hand her tissues and not know what to say or do except stuff her with Haribo and let her soak through my sofa cushions.

'She really is desperate for company then,' says Lucy.

'Charming.'

'Not what I mean. Like, what about her family? Do they not like her?'

Lucy is pushing our niece, Violet, on a swing while she talks to me. Our other niece, Iris, walks precariously over a climbing frame. I don't think that's safe. Is that safe? It's making me very nervous.

'It's the pregnancy thing. The shame. Her dad is quite traditional. So I think she's just attached herself to someone with a child who won't pass judgement. She remembers you though, she liked you at school,' I say.

'Who wouldn't? I'm a fricking dream. Come on, Vee, let's see if we can swing you so high you go over the bars.' Violet's face reads horror and delight. 'And so some bloke called Harry is the father and there's a whole shitstorm there because he's married? That's juicy gossip. So she left the rock star? How do we know he's not the dad?'

'Because of the dates. He was on tour. And he's taken custody of the dog.'

'The one that pissed on you?'

'Yes. And you can't tell anyone. Keep that trap shut.' I realise I may have disclosed all the details to the wrong sister here. 'I want to make sure she's OK. She's given me no clue as to whether she's keeping the baby or not, but you can tell she just needs someone.'

'Beth, if she takes advantage of your good nature, I will track her down and beat her.'

She would but to be fair, I think all that Yasmin is seeking out is a warm body to ensure she's not on her own. What also confuses me is how she doesn't disclose any of this on her social media. On Instagram, it's as if nothing has happened. She isn't letting on that the boyfriend isn't around anymore. She posts pictures of her cross-legged on her concrete floor and yoga mat looking serene and poised and aligning her chakras. I don't get it. Mainly because at that early stage of pregnancy when my body was adjusting to those extremes of hormones, I constantly looked like I'd been on a bender and dragged home by my hair.

'Aunty Lucy, my eyes have gone fuzzy. I'm going to throw up,' Violet squeals.

'Get her down, Lucy,' says a voice from behind us. 'She's on my watch.'

Dad appears, Joe in his buggy fast asleep; he's done the gallant thing of walking Joe around the park a few times so he'll nod off.

After this park visit, Dad is taking charge of the little ones as Lucy and I have plans for a long overdue night out, though I do hope I can stay awake long enough to actually survive it. Lucy catches Violet and allows her to run off to find a bouncy seahorse.

'I love him so much, Beth. He really is so lovely,' my dad says to me as he half hugs me. In Joe he has his first grandson – my little one broke the Callaghan girl curse. He treats them all the same regardless – he loves taking Meg's kids to football matches, he taught Iris how to mend her bike – but he likes to joke that he finally has an ally for when it all gets a bit too screechy. I have no idea what he means.

He is also the kindest, gentlest person I know. He's a world away from my mother in so many ways – an antidote to her perhaps. Will thinks he always looks a bit shocked. Like all these women appeared around him out of nowhere and he's still learning how to deal with it. He knows about Will now, even though we tried to keep it from him, and I can see he's been trying to work out the best way to give advice. Lucy comes over and drapes herself off his shoulders.

'Not as cute as me when I was a baby though, eh?'

'He may have you beat, Luce. You looked just like a Pre-Raphaelite cherub, but the noises you made – it could have caused seismic shifts,' he replies.

I laugh as she pouts. I was five when she was born. It was my earliest memory, my mum introducing us to this mass of platinum-blonde curls. *We're calling her Lucy. That rhymes with juicy,* said Meg. We all laughed and she responded by grabbing a handful of Meg's hair and pulling, hard.

'AUNTY LUCY! I'M STUCK!'

Our three heads swing around immediately to Iris and then back at Lucy. She's the only one who's going to fit up there. She rushes to the rescue and Dad and I take a seat on a nearby bench.

'It's all she's good for these days, eh?' he says, watching her as she extracts Iris from the top of a ladder. 'That and keeping your mother on her toes.'

'Don't we all do that?'

'Lucy seems to have a talent for it.'

We sit quietly and he studies me staring into space, picking at some errant spot on my forehead.

'And Will? How's all that?' he asks me.

'Still AWOL.'

'That's a very accurate use of that term.'

'How so?'

'Without leave. I am sorry that he's having this moment. I like Will. Have you been chatting more?'

'We've been trying. I think. Actually I try not to think about it too much.'

He pushes the buggy back and forth to keep Joe asleep. Mum bundled him up with a sleepsuit, hat and two blankets before we left to shield him from the early winter air and I am immediately jealous. While I love my parka, it was bought on the cheap and without insulation. I snuggle up closer to Dad.

'Your mum and I used to book in leave when you lot were growing up.'

'Leave?'

'Beth, we had four daughters under the age of ten at one point. It was necessary.'

'I don't remember…'

'Your mother made us both a rota.'

'That seems a bit drastic.'

'Have you not met your mother? It wasn't all smooth going though. I walked out on you girls one summer.' He says this thoughtfully, obviously with some regret.

I sit up, curious, as I have no recollection of this ever happening. 'You did?'

'I won't lie. It wasn't my proudest moment. I think it had hit peak hormones and in-fighting. They'd changed all the exam marking systems on us, it was the summer the car broke down on the South Circular and your mother made me buy that stupid van.'

I remember that bit. The police had to tow us away after we caused two-mile tailbacks, and then came the van. Mum thought it was cost efficient but by the time we'd all piled out of it, we looked like some musical tribute act, with Dad the leader.

'I remember that summer. Mum said you went on a DofE trip with your school.'

'I went walking in the Peak District with my friend, Johnny.'

'You were gone for weeks,' I reply, confused, slightly hurt.

'I did a lot of walking.'

I can just picture him now. It's Dad's thing. He'd have worn knee-high socks and a compass around his neck. He'd have drunk a lot of tea, quietly, pensive. He'd have eaten his beloved corned beef which my mother refused to have in the house because it looks like dog food.

'Oh… But you came back?'

'Naturally. Your mother didn't speak to me for a month after. She was glad I'd "got it out of my system" but she was fuming. I was on washing-up duty for six months after that.'

'And Mum? Did she ever do similar?'

'Never. Which is why she's much better than me, always has been. We just don't say that to her face.'

We both smile. Lucy is still on that climbing frame and other parents look on in dismay. Someone reminds her that the equipment is for people aged twelve and under and she tells them to wind their necks in.

'I just needed space to see things a bit more clearly. Parenthood has quite a sharp, intense spotlight; it's stressful. You forget to look after yourself sometimes, to breathe. You're not a bad person if you need to work out your feelings sometimes, if you don't do it right all of the time.'

'You think that's what Will's done?'

'I don't know, love. You, Ems, Megs and Gracie picked such different partners. All very different to each other and me, I reckon. I am sorry I can't help more. Lucy told me he wrote you a letter though.'

'He did but I didn't read it.'

He goes silent for a moment. 'Lucy may have taped it back and sent us all a photo of it.'

I swing my head around to hear this. 'Us?' I glare over at Lucy, trying to work out ways I could kill her on a slide.

'Everyone else in the family. It's a very sincere note. He is very sorry. It explained that he thought there was a way this all should be. Family life, parenthood. How your sisters made it look so easy and how hard he was finding it. He apologised for being selfish and callous with your feelings.'

I pause. I know why I didn't read it. I didn't want to be disappointed. I didn't want my pride to get in the way. And he's still not here.

'Do you think it's enough?' I ask my dad.

'I think parenthood isn't a perfect thing. He's working that out for himself now.'

I hug him and rest my head on his shoulder. It is my favourite shoulder. He's helping more than he knows by not judging Will. We watch as Lucy storms over, pushing her sleeves up as she does so.

'Did you see that mingebag over there trying to pick a fight?'

'Handled so classily too, Lucy,' our dad says.

I scowl at her for what she did with that letter. I'll tackle that later.

'I learned that from Mum. Anyway, squidge up…'

We move up so she can have Dad's other shoulder.

'Did you see me climb that climbing frame, Dad? Did you? Wasn't I great?'

He rolls his eyes at her. 'Very good. Do you remember that time you scaled the shed and tried to jump into that paddling pool in the garden?'

'Didn't I break my fibula?'

'Three days in hospital and a visit from social services.'

I understand now why Dad may have taken that long walk that summer. I remember Lucy's accident well. We thought she was faking until she got up and her leg turned into spaghetti. Emma saw it and threw up which is a wonder, Mum says, that she ever made it into medicine.

'They've done this park up nicely,' Dad says, looking around at the crowds of children squealing and doing rounds of the monkey bars. Nearby, a dad is spinning the roundabout, then puts his hands to his thighs, looking like he might pass out. 'It was a dump when I used to bring you here. Mum and I had to do the rounds first to check for needles and used condoms.'

'Nice, Dad,' I say.

'Your mum used to come here with nail polish remover and take off all the tags and bad words on that climbing frame before she'd let you on it.'

'She did?' Lucy says. 'Obviously worked on me.'

Dad shakes his head. We look over to see Violet and Iris playing on a see-saw.

'So I have news,' Lucy suddenly announces. 'It's very important news but I need to tell just the two of you for now. Don't tell Emma because she has all that ex-husband gubbins going on.'

Dad furrows his brow. Why can't we tell Emma? Have you shagged her new boyfriend?

'And don't tell Mum because she'll stress and fly out there and make a fuss.'

Dad's whole body tenses up next to me. 'Grace, what's wrong with Grace?'

My mind also goes into freefall. Dad's eyes glaze over. Lucy met up with Grace for a weekend in Amsterdam a couple of weeks ago. It was fun, debauched, but Gracie had sounded fine. We just all hope and pray that the universe is looking after her and showing her some kindness. She is owed.

'Grace is coming back next week,' she says slowly. We all know that, we're excited about her returning.

'She's coming back with some babies.'

Dad and I sit here, trying to take this information in. I do the calculations in my head. She wasn't pregnant when she left; did she get pregnant out there? Does she have a boyfriend? Or did she have a fling? I can see Dad asking himself the same questions.

'When she was in Vietnam she met these two little girls out there and she's adopted them.'

Grace? Grace is a mother? I look over and tears start to trail down Dad's cheeks. He hits Lucy on the arm.

'You've had this information for an age, why didn't you tell us? Why hasn't Grace told us? Does Meg know?'

I hug him and hand him one of Joe's muslins to wipe his face. These muslins are *really* useful.

A whole new identity, a brand new life, just like that. Our Gracie, with daughters.

'She wanted to be sure. I found out in Amsterdam. Their names are Maya and Cleo, they're three and one, and man, they are cute as hell.' She gets out her phone and shows me a picture of them sitting on Grace's lap. It's the best picture I've ever seen. The girls are laughing, pure joy on their faces, and Grace looks relaxed, happy.

Dad studies it for ages, his bottom lip trembling. 'I'm going to have eight grandchildren,' he says, confused. 'How?'

'She'll tell you the story when she gets back. It's lovely.'

'Does she need anything?' Dad asks.

'She just wants to do things on her own for the moment. I offered, but she said to just tell you two so you can help prepare Mum. This will be a shock and Grace doesn't want drama, so you have to help, Dad. Rein her in a bit.'

Dad looks like it might be an unfathomable task.

Lucy turns to me. 'And she wanted you to know because you're chill. Plus she needs baby things and you have all the baby stuff.'

'I have a shop's worth,' I say, smiling broadly. 'Oh, Luce. She's a mum?' Tears roll down my cheeks too. She's going to be an amazing mother. I have new nieces. And for a split second the first person I want to tell is Will. He loved Grace and her husband, Tom. When Tom passed away it broke his heart. The news would mean the world to him.

'Why are you all crying?' asks Violet, skipping over. She instinctively goes to Dad first and hugs him, embedding herself in his fluffy beard.

'I've just heard some really lovely news, that's all.'

'But Pops, you never cry.'

She's right. However stressed, angry or sad he may have been while we were growing up, I never saw tears. I wonder if he shed them elsewhere. This makes me cry even more. Violet gives me a strange look, probably because I'm an ugly crier. I snot like a SodaStream.

'I thought you were crying because that woman over there told Lucy to stick something up her bum?' Violet says.

We look over at the woman glaring at us from the sandpit. It's not the face of a happy woman.

'I hope you gave her what for, Luce,' Dad says.

'Of course. I told her to stick it up her own arse, she might like it.'

Dad closes his eyes. 'Another phrase you learned from your mother?'

Lucy roars with laughter. 'I didn't think you and Mum were into that?'

'Only on Wednesdays,' Dad replies.

I crease over in laughter as Lucy sits there and, for once, has no words. Nothing.

Track Twenty

'Songbird' – Oasis (2002)

'Is that a bra? Or an actual top?' I ask Lucy. I scan her outfit from the giant puffer coat to the skinny ripped jeans. 'I swear we used to have crop tops like that when we were little. Mum bought them in multipacks and we all shared.'

'And I stuffed mine with socks. Remember that kid who lived down our road, Mitchell? I kissed him in his garden when I was twelve. He felt my boobs, one of the socks fell out and he cried. He'd thought he'd squeezed too hard.'

I sit on the Tube in hysterics as a man opposite us watches closely. *How are these two people related?* he seems to be thinking.

'It's Calvin Klein. There's an overlay thing,' Lucy replies.

'That's completely see-through.'

'Prudey Judy.'

'Slaggy Maggie.'

The man opposite is even more confused now. It really does look like I've taken this reprobate under my wing as part of some community project. I peer over Lucy's shoulder as she trawls through lengths of Snapchat messages, where she appears to be chatting to someone called D'Shaun.

Lucy and I used to go out a lot, pre-Joe. She was the sort whose evening would start at eleven and Will and I, like sheep, would get sucked in. Eight hours later, we'd be eating bagels and watching the sun come up over Stoke Newington. I want to say I miss those days, but really I think all I might miss are the bagels. With salt beef, pickles, dripping in mustard. I could totally be down with that tonight.

'Hey. After we're done, I could get us into a club in Mayfair?' she says.

'Posh.'

'I mean there's a bit of an S&M vibe but you don't have to partake.'

I give Lucy a strange look. So we go to a bar in trainers, sit and have a G&T while we watch rich people get teased, blindfolded and shagged? 'I'm good. How do you know about this club?' I reply.

'I worked there for a bit.'

I raise my eyebrows at her.

'I expect that sort of response from Emma but not from you,' she says. 'It was bar work, you mucky thing. I saw some stuff though. It's a lot of fun watching old men show up in their stained Y-fronts sitting in cages with their leather masks.'

I'm pretty sure if I wanted to do that, I could just log onto Pornhub and drink from the comfort of my own sofa.

'Speaking of which… Have you had a ménage à moi yet?'

I love how Lucy says this so casually as we sit on the District Line. If I didn't know what that meant, she also does a strange action like she's mixing at imaginary decks.

'Ummm…'

'I'll take that as a no.' She looks unimpressed with me. 'I'm disappointed with you, Beth. I thought sexually, you and me had something in common. We had to literally push Emma into having sex again. You used to be quite open about these things.'

'Are you calling me frigid?'

'I'm saying that when I'm feeling shit about life, I have a wank and I feel better. It's finding joy in small things.'

'I don't reckon your bits are that small anymore.'

She pushes me in my seat. 'Ha. Ha. Ha. I haven't had a baby come through mine yet. Yours must be a like a wizard's sleeve.' The insult comes with more actions. 'At least you haven't lost your sense of humour. You are all awful to me, it's because you're so jealous.'

I'll admit there are shades of truth there in her words. We'd all like to be a little more Lucy.

'It's because you're perfect.'

She hooks her arm into mine, sensing no sarcasm in my tone.

'There's no such thing, you know that, right? Even I have my things.'

'What? A scar on your leg from when you fell off the shed?' I joke.

'I'm coarse, flighty, desperate for attention, immature and I've worn so many wigs for work that I have really bad scalp psoriasis.'

To prove a point, she takes off her beanie and shows me lines of red patches and flakes on her head. A couple on a date next to us look at us strangely.

'Luce. That looks sore. What are you putting on that?'

'Olive oil. Emma keeps telling me it's scalp herpes and I keep telling her she's a bitch.' She puts her hat back on and then cups her hands around my face.

'Perfect is boring. Now do I need to get you a vibrator for Christmas?'

I laugh and shake my head. I have one of those somewhere but I may need to dust it off and replace the batteries.

'I just want to see you happy, B.'

I shrug. Am I happy? Who knows? In these situations, I tend to compare my happiness to the lowest alternatives and by that measure, I am OK. I love Lucy checking in to see how these levels can be topped up though. My phone beeps with a message from Giles.

QR codes and VIP passes attached for the after-party too. Looking forward to seeing you xx

It's not just any night out tonight. We're off to see Special K do a guest segment alongside one of the biggest rappers in the country. I was in two minds about accepting the invitation as I'm not sure I have the energy for a full riotous rap gig, but Lucy persuaded me otherwise.

Lucy peers over my shoulder.

'VIP drinks, bitch. It is going to kick off, you know, right?'

'Just make sure the socks don't fall out of your bra.'

'Cow.'

*

By the time we get to the venue, there's still a queue outside the large white building but we manage to flash our codes around and the security guard ushers us in kindly even when faced with an excitable Lucy, who grips on tightly to my shoulders.

'You've missed this, eh?' she whispers into my ear over the roar of the music, the intensity of the crowd.

Missed is an understatement. Gigs were my thing. Actually, they were mine and Will's thing and with a jolt, I think about how it should be his arm hooked into mine, not Lucy's. He would love this. From large stadiums to small jazz venues, we used to hunt down listings and camp in queues. We were experts in balancing pints, knowing where to stand for the best sound quality and how to navigate the trek to the toilets. As we walk into the hall, hundreds of flashbacks hit me, from the touch of his hand around my midriff (Ben Howard) to Will starting sing-offs (Stevie Wonder, Hyde Park) to trying to get to the front of the mosh pit (Red Hot Chili Peppers; it was a mistake, I got kicked in the face). Rap concerts are always a different crowd though, everyone looks younger and much cooler in a sea of black sportswear, midriffs or the waistbands of their underwear showing.

Lucy manages to drag us around to the VIP area and another bouncer looks at me suspiciously. I know my jeggings sag a bit around the crotch. 'Do you know who she is?' Lucy asks.

I cringe as she says it. The security guard doesn't look too impressed.

'Her baby is on the album and stars in the video. This is his mum.'

He doesn't look totally convinced. Lucy gets her phone out and shows him a photo, meaning this is the second time I've shown a security guard baby pictures in an attempt to prove a point. He smiles but still looks at us like we're mad. That said, the passes I have on my phone help matters and he lets us through a roped area where everyone stops to look at us. I use Lucy as a shield and she struts in with all the confidence I'm lacking. It's a small bar area but the crowd is naturally trendy – music people and press here for the freebies, sipping at champagne. To my relief, it's not overly rammed so we weave our way through the crowd to find the alcohol.

'Beth?'

Giles. Thank hell for that. I launch myself at him in an awkward fashion. 'So glad we bumped into you. This is Lucy, my sister.'

'Oliver, my husband.' There's a trade in greetings and air kissing. Oliver is lean, and towers over me with designer glasses and a trendy undercut going on. And they're both in matching black; so they got the memo about the dress code.

'We're glad you came,' replied Giles. 'Kimmie was keen to have you on the list, to say thank you. Joe was a big part of the covers, the video.'

'Was I supposed to bring him?'

'To a rap gig, maybe not.' He and Oliver laugh at me in what I hope is an affectionate way.

'Are you both British rap fans then?' I ask, trying to break the silence.

They both give me a strange look. 'Not our usual genre of choice. We're not sure if we're supposed to be dancing?' Oliver whispers.

'I wouldn't,' I reply. 'Rap concerts can be quite intense. Like good intense. It's mainly jumping and the young ones will take their shirts off and run in circles at the front.' I point to the main stage where the crowd throbs in time to the music. 'I'd stand there, firm head nod…'

'Or a co-ordinated shoulder move, one hand in the air, it's all in the pout,' Lucy says as we both demonstrate. Both Oliver and Giles look at us curiously. It's a sister thing. But give Lucy an hour and a few beers and she'll have choreographed a routine. Oliver and Lucy seem to start some sort of strange dance-off as Giles comes over to stand next to me.

'Do you know those two?' he asks. I laugh. Our attention is suddenly turned to the screen as in amongst some strobe lighting and dry ice, Special K emerges.

'Look at our girl, eh?' Giles whispers.

She strolls up and down the stage. The crowd bay with immense volume and her face is projected over dozens of screens, the lyrics pouring out of her double time and thousands of people spitting out the chorus with her. It's a young crowd – they look like they belong in my school. The girl commands the space, her star quality shining through. Why do I feel like a proud parent?

'Can I ask what the lioness means in the video? What does it signify?'

'It was just based off a conversation I had with her. She likes nature shows and in the wild, lionesses do all the work. They own the pride, they're the real stars of the show. So we threw that in as a nod. And all the other symbols reflected that: youth, birth, female power. I knew the spotlight was going to be intense so I wanted people to look at the right things.'

'It's clever.'

We fall silent watching her as she pauses to let the crowd chant a line back at her. Lucy did this on a girls' holiday once. She stood on a bar. No one repeated the line back and I think she tripped over a beer tap and split her lip open.

'Look at all that spotlight though, I hope she has good people looking after her,' he whispers.

I like how Giles shows genuine concern for Kimmie. At seventeen, I was sitting on park greens drinking cider and sneaking around Cineworld trying to watch 18-rated films.

'How are you, anyway?' He looks at me reassuringly. I can tell he's different to most in his industry, that he looks out for people.

'Getting there.'

'I sensed some issues with Will when I dropped you off that time. Are you OK? You can tell me if it's none of my business.'

I glance over at his husband, Lucy hanging off his shoulder and laughing.

'How long have you and Oliver been together?' I ask.

'Wow. Sixteen years. Married for five.'

'Then you'll get how there are sometimes glitches in the system?'

'I'd be more surprised if there weren't glitches. Sometimes you need those moments for clarity. I get it. I hope you work things out.'

I'm grateful for his concern.

'Also, interestingly, we had a call from Yasmin's agent last week. It turns out she's pregnant.'

I blush intensely and look out into the concert knowing I'm probably giving myself away.

'You knew?' he asks.

'I didn't say anything. It's her business and I didn't want her to be judged unfairly for it.'

'Is she OK?' Giles asks.

I've been sworn to secrecy but I feel Giles has her best interests at heart. The secret is out and I don't think he'll swing it about like gossip.

'She's on her own; Jethro left her. She's just working some stuff out. I'd go easy if you have any work lined up with her.'

He nods. 'I thought you two weren't friends?'

I laugh. Would she be the first person I called in an emergency? Are we going out on the razz next weekend? We're not even mates on Facebook but I care about what happens to her now, and that's what matters, I guess.

'I'm glad she's got you on her side.'

Giles links arms with me as we watch Kimmie take a bow. A group to the left of us have got more animated and one gentleman in head-to-toe Armani and who's partaken in quite a fair bit of alcohol bumps into me, spilling some of that alcohol down my front. It's cold. It's very cold and I shriek as it runs down my cleavage.

'So coooooollllllddddd…'

I pull at my T-shirt as the man looks absolutely horrified. It's ice cubes and liquor and it's sticky, slick and frigging arctic. I dance around fishing it out of my front, in what looks like some badly timed interpretative dance move. Lucy stares at me strangely, wondering if this is alcohol-induced, but as ice flies about, she realises what's happened.

'Oi, mate. What the hell are you doing…?' she says, striding over, her hands up in the air.

Our small bar area goes quiet. Where did this girl get her front? Giles rushes around to grab at napkins while Oliver stands there, reluctant to get into a fight right now.

'I am sorry. I am so so sorry,' the man mumbles, his eyes transfixed on my chest quite awkwardly.

'It's fine. It was an accident. No harm done, seriously,' I say, smiling.

Lucy's not quite done with him though. 'Well, you owe us drinks now. Our whole group. And that T-shirt, the coat will need to be dry-cleaned, you know?'

Oh, Lucy, don't create a scene. I'll fling this T-shirt in the wash at thirty degrees. It's got baby puke stains on it that, embarrassingly, look like another sort of bodily fluid. The man looks me up and down, squinting to understand why I'm in the room. I know, mate, I know.

'You're that baby's mum, innit?' He embraces me tightly, his six-foot-something frame enveloping mine. 'I'm Kimmie's dad. Look at our babies together. It's a beautiful thing.'

I can't help grinning. 'My boy is just the icing. It's mainly your girl and her talent. You should be proud.'

'You too, mama. She loves that boy, he's her lucky charm. Champagne? I owe you. I'm a clumsy bastard at the best of times. We should toast these bloody brilliant babies of ours.'

I nod. Yeah, we should.

I'm standing backstage in a Christmas T-shirt with a dancing elf on it. Express Your Elf. It was this or a reindeer. Naturally, I didn't pack a change of clothes so despite Lucy's suggestion of turning a scarf into a boob tube, I borrowed this men's size top from one of the bar staff instead.

Giles looks across at me and chortles. 'You look so festive.'

'Ho ho ho!'

The concert over, he's guiding us through the venue. I realise this is a behind-the-scenes part of gigs I've not seen before. Normally, I'm out front just digging the music and drinking the alcohol but there are people in radio mics running about with ropes and clipboards; for them it's a job, it's their everyday. We head over to lines of doors and Giles knocks on one. It opens to a man eyeing us suspiciously. There's a real party atmosphere inside, alcohol flying, music turned up and because my senses are so finely attuned to these things, I smell chips, meat, possibly a burger. Yes, I smell burgers. If you want to talk about superpowers I've acquired post-partum, this is one. It contains onions and barbeque sauce.

'Yeah?' says the man at the door.

'Gillllles! I know him, Kyle, let him in!' screams a voice from the back of the room. We see Kimmie, sitting down sipping from a tin of cherry Coke. She waves us in and we head over. I get the looks. The room is buzzing with what's just happened on that stage, people singing and chanting her name. I have no experience that's comparable to this, I really don't.

'God, it's— Too loud— here…' Kimmie shouts at us.

Giles and I nod, pretending that we know exactly what she's said and she laughs and beckons us out of the room into the corridor.

'I am so sorry. It is madness in there. I don't know half the people either…'

Giles puts an arm to her. 'You OK?'

'I literally just shared the stage with the biggest rapper, like ever.'

It's a lot to take in, I get it. Giles takes her hand, kissing it. I'm taken back to the moment I first saw these two sitting with their calamari sharing platter in a pub in my suburban neck of the woods. How are we suddenly here? The door of the room re-opens.

'Giles, mate. You should come in. We've got plans for the next video.' He's dragged into the room by some music executive in a suit and I'm left there with Kimmie. Instinctively, I bring her in for a hug and she wraps her arms around me. She's in just a cropped top, leggings and military boots in winter – have some of my body heat or you'll catch a death. Her body is almost shaking under mine.

'I met your dad earlier? He's a joy,' I tell her.

'Oh my days, he is wasted. Was he completely embarrassing?'

'He was a proud dad. And rightly so, you looked pretty amazing out there,' I tell her.

'You're too kind. How did it sound though?'

'Loud?'

She laughs. 'I'm just glad Giles is here. I've got this whole section of my team in there who feel I should be taking what I do in a different direction. Like put me on a stage in my bra and a thong and have me thrust about, but that's not what I want, you know? I want people to hear the words. I'm more than my body, right?'

'You are.'

'And if I have people spitting my lyrics back at me then this is about responsibility; it's about telling girls my age to love and respect what's in here.' She taps at her skull as she says that, adrenalin carrying her rant. I'm in awe. When I was her age, all I had to worry about was the number of friends I had on Myspace (I had ninety-three).

'One of your lyrics… it's something about only a coward would spend their life in the hamlets. That's Charlotte Brontë, yes?'

She looks up at me and smiles broadly. 'You know Brontë?'

'That's my English-teacher brain talking.'

'Not enough people know about *Villette*,' she replies. 'Usually it's all Jane Eyre and Heathcliff with the Brontës but that book is all about independence, growth, loneliness. I get it.'

Oh, how I love this girl. Half my career is trying to get kids to be as enthusiastic about books as this, rather than them staring blankly at the walls or texting someone under a desk while I'm trying to teach them about Chaucer. But now, I'm having a literary conversation in the corridors of the Hammersmith Apollo.

Her eyes light up, maybe even more than when she's on a set with a stuffed lion in the background. 'Thanks for that Zadie Smith recommendation too, I loved it,' she adds.

'I'm glad. So you write all your own lyrics then?' I ask her.

'Yeah… I performed them as poetry to start and then I don't know, I guess you could say it snowballed. My brother put it on YouTube and then people got in touch.' She sips quietly from her can of soft drink.

'So this was never the dream?'

'It's… something. I've had to put university plans on hold. It's all been a bit of a surprise. One moment, I'm Kimmie from Tower Hamlets and now I'm the voice of black female youth in Britain. We had Beyoncé on the phone the other day.'

I laugh. I see that's a big weight for such small shoulders, so I urge her to sit on the floor with me and relax for a moment. I don't know what I'd do if Beyoncé called me. I'd sing her songs back at her including any Jay Z raps and attempt all the high notes in between, which would probably do the opposite of impress.

'What were you going to study?' I ask.

'English literature I think, maybe creative writing.'

I smile and put on my professional cap for a second. 'You know there's still time for that, right? This here doesn't define you. I have students do all sorts of gap years. I have some who have to stop school to work and earn money and they do their studies part-time or much later.'

'Really?'

'I'm going to assume you don't rap 24/7. You have gaps in between to keep reading and you can go back to it when you're ready.'

'That's true. I guess I'm just not sure if this is for me, forever. I'm still trying to figure out who I am.'

Her words ring so very true to me. I don't think that ever changes. But I don't want to freak her out by saying you can get to thirty and still not have a bloody clue what you're doing with your life. The door suddenly flies open again and the tall gentleman who was guarding the door stands there, glaring at us.

'Kimmie, you should be in here,' he tells her. I'm not overly fond of the aggression in his voice.

'She's just having a breather,' I tell him.

'And who are you?' he asks.

'She's my friend, Kyle. Piss off.'

He slams the door shut and I worry for a moment about poor Giles as the music gets turned up.

'That's my brother. He thinks he's a hard man but really he manages a phone shop and still lives at home,' she says with the attitude only one can have when talking about a sibling. I study her face. I can't quite tell if she's happy or not. I'd imagine this is overwhelming, being yanked out of your everyday and then landing in something that you're not one hundred per cent prepared for. I put a hand to hers.

'I'll give you my number later. We can start a book club,' I joke.

'I'd like that. Follow me on Insta? I want to see pictures of Joe, he really is so cute.'

'I will.' She'll be the coolest person out of my followers, bar none. I'm mainly friends with people like my uncle Jack, who posts pictures of his allotments and boasts about the girth of his marrows. 'And you know, thank you. I've told some of my students that Joe was in your video and now they think I'm marginally cooler than I was before.'

'Excuse me, you're totally Gucci,' she says, defiantly.

I assume that's some sort of slang because I'm totally high street. 'Kimmie, your dad spilt a drink on me. I had to change into an elf T-shirt, at a rap gig. The elf is actually flossing.'

'I just thought you were being ironic. Harry Styles is in there and he's wearing pearls.'

We both laugh. Harry Styles is in there? Don't tell Lucy.

'You're rocking it, Beth. You're one of the few people in this game that I trust. You talk *to* me, not at me, not down at me. You're just trill.'

'Is that a good thing?'

'True and real.'

'I'll take that.'

'Will you sit with me for a bit longer?' she asks. 'I just want a timeout, is that OK?'

I nod. A timeout. I think about those words and take my parka, draping it on her shoulders.

'A gentleman also said something before,' I say. 'Could you translate it for me? He said I've "got cake".'

She giggles uncontrollably. 'It means you've got a good arse. You have booty.'

'Oh! I thought he was asking me for drugs. I apologised.'

She starts to howl. 'You've got a good rack too.'

I blush at the observation. 'We'll thank Joe for that.'

'I guess without Joe, you and I wouldn't have met either, eh?'

So very true. We'll thank Joe for everything. She sits next to me and pops her head on my shoulder as we allow the noise around us to melt away. Without Joe, where would I be? I'd be out the front enjoying this gig, paying for the privilege. And for a moment, I think about Joe's tiny wonderful face, this little mash-up of myself and Will, a backstage pass to another life. And even though the next chapter is uncertain and this T-shirt is bloody ridiculous, I have cake, I have a Joe. And that is everything.

Track Twenty-One

'Learn to Fly' – Foo Fighters (1999)

I am sitting in a pub in Kingston, staring at a blackboard notice telling me it's ten more days until Christmas. Why do they do this to us now? When you were little, it was exciting – the thrill that Santa was fattening up his reindeer; the worry if you had been good enough to get what you wished for; the looking forward to Christmas movies. Now, it's like a sand timer counting down what remains of the year, reminding you of everything you haven't done. You'd better lose some weight, write some cards, get on Amazon to buy everything and pray a DPD man doesn't leave it outside the wrong door. Behind the bar, Mariah Carey sings at me. I don't think that all she wants for Christmas is me but I appreciate the sentiment and those banger high notes at the end. I remember Will sang that song at karaoke once. It was a summer in Brighton and he thought he was being ironic. Oh, Will. How on earth is it Christmas and we're still in limbo? This is going to be Joe's first Christmas. Surely the dream is us buying him his first bike (or whatever you give a baby for its first Christmas) and sitting in matching pyjamas in front of a log fire. Isn't that what Christmas should be?

'They're out of Corona so I bought you a Bud,' says Sean. I nod and watch as he mouths the words to the next Christmas song that comes up on the playlist. He knows all the words to Cliff Richard? You think you know a person. I'm here tonight, in this pub in Kingston, gatecrashing the school Christmas knees-up. It's supposed to be a way for me to reconnect with everyone. There's a set menu dinner later (soup, dry turkey dinner, woeful slice of Christmas pudding) and a Secret Santa too. I've just got mine. It twists the knife in my heartbroken back a little more, but it's a pocket book of how to say 'I love you' in different languages and a Toblerone. I won't lie, I think this book has been regifted because there's an inscription in the front to Keith. *Happy Birthday Keith, love D.* This means Keith from modern foreign languages (he flits between French and Spanish) has palmed me off with a gift his wife gave him once. That's not good, Keith. Poor D. I thought a repurposed gift card was bad. But the Toblerone helps.

Christmas is always the time that the faculty let loose and you see personality start to shine through. Nick from maths will don a comedy antler and Jonathan, who works the science labs, will be the first to drag the staff from the office onto the dance floor.

'Oh my God. Hi!'

Connie from the PE department (previously known as Beyoncé) comes to sit next to me on our bench. She looks stunning in a red bodycon dress and holly earrings. How does she get her legs so smooth? Why isn't she wearing tights? The joy of winter is not having to upkeep legs, no?

'I just wanted to say thank you for inviting me to your birthday party. It was so much fun. Actually I met someone there who gave me his number. He was dressed as Boba Fett?'

As soon as she says that, my nostrils flare. Yasmin's Boba Fett. Harry was dressed as Boba Fett. My silence is slightly too prolonged while I process it all. 'Just someone my sister works with. He's married,' I finally reply.

'Oh,' she says, both shocked and disappointed.

'I'd avoid him like the plague. Man whore, riddled, complete dick.' She senses I'm trying a little too hard to throw her off his scent. 'Just you deserve better than him.'

'Thank you,' she says, surprised at the compliment.

I look over her shoulder to see Sean approaching.

'Sean is single…' I say.

'I did debate that. He's funny and all but his mum still packs him Fruit Winders in his lunchbox,' she mumbles to me.

'But if you can get past that… He's pretty cool?'

She's not sure how to respond as he's currently wearing an actual elf hat with ears and a bell.

He approaches the table. 'Ladies…'

'I'm just going to chat to the drama lot,' Connie says, standing up to leave and Sean takes her seat.

'Something I said?' he gestures.

'I was trying to matchmake you.'

'And obviously underselling the assets.'

The hat flattens out his fringe so he looks like he has a bowl haircut underneath. I'm not sure how I'd sell that asset. Sean has been busy organising everyone's drinks, sorting the gin from the dark ales.

'Soooo…' I say.

'Grace is back. I saw that on Facebook. Don't think your mum took enough photos,' he says.

'Two days ago. It's everything. She looks amazing.'

'Tell her I said hello.'

'I will.'

'And what about Alicia?' I ask. We've spoken briefly about that whole ordeal at my party. I mainly told him off for going at it with the head teacher on my sister's bed but I never got all the details. Like how did you woo her in that burger costume? Did you ladder your tights? He swings his head around to check she's not in the vicinity.

'Yeah. File under anecdotes to tell in the pub one day.'

'Good. I won't tell you who to date but I don't think you two are meant to be.'

He nods in agreement. 'She's a proper wild one though. She wanted me to call her names and stuff.'

'Like?' I whisper.

'You don't want to know. The burger costume added layers to the conversation. A lot of talk about meat and special sauce.'

'Ewwwww!' I cup my hands over my ears but can still see Alicia standing at the bar. She always comes straight from work so she's in her usual shift dress and sensible heels. It's always the quiet ones.

'That was quite a party though, eh?' Sean adds.

I nod. I've almost blocked it out of mind given it was the event that triggered Will's leaving. I haven't told Sean anything either. In fact, I've purposely kept all of it pretty quiet from him and from social media.

'Also, I have news. It's been coming and I should have told you, but I'm off soon,' he tells me.

'Off?'

'This was before your party, but Alicia entered me into some exchange programme with a school in Toronto. I'll be there for six months.'

'Sean! That's pretty epic, mate. From when?'

'After Christmas.'

I'm still grinning from cheek to cheek at such an exciting opportunity for him, but I'll admit, knowing that he won't be there when I return to Griffin Road makes my heart twinge.

'Please tell me you're not taking your mum with you,' I joke.

'She's currently teaching me how to iron. It's painful.'

'It's good. You need this.'

'I know. I think you having a baby made me re-think what I should be doing with my life too. Live a little, eh?'

I lean over and hug him. God, I'll miss him. Who will make my crap coffee now and help me joke about the art department shouting at us for stealing all their pencils? He's my work husband. This now feels like some temporary separation of sorts and I immediately think of the other separation in my life. Of Will. With Sean and Will gone, Joe will be the only man in my life.

'So, you, me and Will need to go out. My mum's doing a farewell dinner first week of January.'

I nod, reluctantly.

'Or not?' he replies, reading my face.

I take a deep breath. 'Will's not living with me at the moment. He moved out.'

He widens his eyes at me, speechless, and gestures we go outside for a bit. We head for the heated patio area, clutching our drinks. Christmas fairy lights sparkle in the fruity thick mist left by a trio of vapers. We head for some railings overlooking the Thames, both of us probably wondering in this moment why we ever gave up smoking.

'Beth? What happened? You didn't say anything...' he says, slightly hurt.

I shrug my shoulders. 'It's just been a shit time. Not stuff you want to share with people.'

'But I'm Sean. Not people. Has he gone for good?'

'He's with his brother. He was stressed and overwhelmed is the official line, but he kissed someone else on a night out. It's just all a giant shitstorm. It's been a while now – since my party...'

He pauses, working out how long that's been, then comes over and gives me a hug.

'Oh, mate. You really should have said something.'

'Yeah, sure... *Come over, let's get a takeaway and talk about how my life's falling apart?*'

'You idiot.'

I don't cry because I'm not sure what's left to talk about when it comes to Will. He's still not here. He's missing out on the important moments with Joe when he smiles or cuts a tooth or babbles away at me in the bath, but then he's also missing out on the nappy rash, the early morning feeds and the intense exhaustion. I'm resentful that he's having a break, that he's abandoned us when we need him most, but I also ache with how much I miss him.

'So much has changed, Sean. Good stuff, like Joe. But I don't even recognise myself these days…'

'How?'

'I used to be fun. Now fun feels tiring. I was fun, right?'

'You're still fun,' he says, a little unconvincingly. 'You have that rapper girl in your life? She's cool.'

'The unlikeliest friendship in the world. But in reality, everything's a reminder of how different I look and feel.'

'You look great, shut up.'

It's a sweet compliment but the three times he's seen me now have been the only times in the last year where I've been forced to brush and wash my hair.

'I feel bad going to Canada now.'

'Why?'

'You need me.'

'I'll survive.'

'What if Canadian teachers are weird, don't drink in their lunch hours or understand my humour?'

'Then you can FaceTime me from your staff room. Make sure you send me Canadian stuff, won't you?'

'Like a moose?'

'Yep, one of them.'

A biting breeze swoops across the river, picking up plumes of foam and I stand that bit closer to Sean, clinking bottles. It's too bloody cold to be out here, even with my very classy parka over my maxi dress, but I'm glad for the chance to chat. To chat to a friend.

'I'm really going to miss you,' Sean says.

He puts a hand over mine on the railings. We're close; maybe too close. And for a moment, something overtakes my good sense. We can blame Christmas, the arctic outdoor setting or the fact that someone of the opposite sex has expressed an outpouring of emotion to me, to my sad lonely face. But there's something that draws us together and suddenly we're kissing, on the lips. His lips melt into mine and part slightly. Shit. I am snogging Sean. Then he backs away.

'Woah there, sailor,' I say, shocked, wide-eyed. We don't do that. That's not what we do. I don't know how to react. I shouldn't have done it and I know why I did it. Revenge snog? Tit for tat? He was there, he said something nice.

'I'm sorry,' he says, snapping out of the moment.

'That was…'

'Nice but you're Beth. It's like kissing…'

'A cousin?'

'I was thinking more a sister.' His body shudders and we both erupt into laughter. 'You're confused about Will. Figure that all out. I'd kiss you any day of the week if you weren't Beth. I love you to bits, you know that, right?'

And I get it completely. I love him too. I'd show up for him. I'd defend him, visit him in hospital, write him the best character reference ever, but even in this semi-romantic setting with The Pogues on in the background and the fairy lights on high twinkle, I don't love him. Not like that.

'You're getting emosh on me now,' I say.

'I'm leaving, I'm allowed. Few more drinks and I'll love everyone in there.'

'I feel really special now.'

He brings me in for a hug and kisses me on the forehead. You're not supposed to do that either, that's Will's move.

'I hope things work out with Will. I really do,' he says, holding me back and looking into my eyes. 'You and Joe deserve the world.'

I never know what people mean when they say that. It sounds greedy, like I deserve it *all*. Every pound, penny, mansion, holiday, comfort; everything your heart desires and needs. But in reality my world is so small, and yet it is all I need. My world is Joe. It's someone else who isn't here who I love. More than all the world. That would be everything.

'I deserve another beer,' I say instead.

'Smooth, but not very subtle. Such a cheapskate.'

'And just like that, we've found the wording for your Tinder profile.'

He laughs, the sound echoing in that empty patio area, his breath fogging the air as he heads back to the bar.

I make my escape after dessert that evening, to get back to Joe at Mum and Dad's. I left Sean in a circle dancing with the 'technology lads' – all of their shirts untucked, the movements ungainly and jumpy even though they were dancing to 'Rockin' Around the Christmas Tree'. Sean hugged me deeply as I left. I hope I see you again before you go, I wanted to say. I hope you make it home safely and don't shag Alicia again.

'You're early?' a familiar face says as she opens the door. Grace. She's been back from her epic travels for two days now, with the two sweetest little girls you could ever wish to meet – an expansion to our family that fills us all with joy. I enter the house and embrace her closely. It's all I've done since I've seen her. That and beam like the frigging sun. My Gracie is back. I missed the feel of her, the sound of her voice. And so every time I'm near, I launch my body at her, demanding she be as close to me as possible. At the moment, she's camped out at Mum and Dad's doing something called cocooning which involves keeping her lovely girls close and introducing all of us Callaghans slowly but surely so as not to overwhelm them.

'Did I wake you?' I whisper.

'I don't keep time anymore. I really hope those are cheesy chips in your hand.' She stands there in jersey pyjamas and a duvet worn around her shoulders like a cape. The look is worn and sleepy but I know it well: it's the look of first-time motherhood. I open up the polystyrene container and see her eyes light up at the smell of melted cheese and deep-fried potato goodness.

As predicted, the portions at the Christmas party tonight were small and flooded with gravy and limp vegetables. Chips will save the day. She ushers me in to keep the winter air flooding through the front door, grabbing at my crispy chips and leading us through into the front room. I enter to see both of her daughters asleep on the sofa, limbs intertwined, the glare of cartoons filling the room.

'Don't mind us. It seems they only can sleep to the sounds of *Sesame Street*,' she mumbles, turning down the volume on the television.

'Is Joe OK?'

'Asleep upstairs, snug as a bug.'

I sigh with relief and take a seat on an armchair, kicking off my ankle boots, watching as Grace nestles in with her daughters. I rest the chips on the arm of the sofa so she can help herself.

'How was it?' she asks.

'Standard. And a bit weird. Me and Sean had a kiss.'

Grace's eyes open widely. 'Your mate, Sean? The one with the ears?'

'All my friends have ears.'

'His are a little like trophy handles though. Tongues?'

'No.' I try and shrug off the memory.

'You don't fancy Sean, do you?' she says, grimacing.

'He's alright, Sean. But no, I don't fancy him. And I know why it happened.'

'To get back at Will?' Grace says it calmly, not with the anger and judgement that would have radiated off Emma and Lucy. And what she says is true. I was desperate for the affection. It was a reaction. Maybe I needed to know what kissing someone else felt like too.

'Heck, that's what good friends are for, to snog in stressful situations,' she says.

'You have a friend you snog in stressful situations? Actually, Lucy tells me you did a lot on your travels that you need to tell us about.'

'Lucy got me very drunk in Amsterdam and I divulged far too much. I snogged a friend in New York on my travels. I went to a rave. I wore a fishnet jumpsuit thing.'

I laugh a little too loudly and she gives me evils. Grace usually only wears monochrome but there's a flash of colour now, a yellow bracelet on her hand, and a smile she's not worn for the longest time.

'Was he a good kisser?' she asks.

'Bit fishy?'

'What? His breath?'

I snigger. 'No, the lip action. It didn't last long.'

She shrugs. By that measure, it's basically a non-event then and she's right. Cleo wriggles in her sleep and comes to rest her head on Grace's lap. I watch as my sister strokes her head to settle her down again.

'Sean also looks like the sort of man who wears bad shorts in summer. Am I right?'

'Cargo, knee-length. Sometimes the ones with the zips so he can add some length if the weather gets cooler.'

'If you married that, I'd voice my objections at your wedding, just so you know.'

I chuckle through mouthfuls of potato but she can read me like a book. She knows that it made me realise I was in love with someone else. I don't need to say that out loud so focus on the chips. I should have got a kebab.

'The things you miss when you travel. No other country in the world does cheesy chips,' she says.

'The Americans have chips.'

'Nope, they have French fries and the melted cheese is moussey and bright yellow. If you ask for mayo with your chips too, they think you're posh and continental like that's a bad thing.'

'I hoped you missed me as much as you missed chips.'

'I missed you the most,' she says.

'Do you say that to everyone?'

'Of course.'

It is an absolute joy to have her back here in the family fold, to see a new side to her, renewed and accepting of a future without her Tom. The old Grace was always sensible, cautious, guarded even. We never knew how everything would change her. But I see a sister scoffing chips and dangling stringy bits of Cheddar over her mouth and realise the bits I loved about her are still there.

'You're stopping here tonight, yeah? Mum bought the mini Kellogg's selection boxes so you must,' she says.

'Of course, I'll wrestle you for the Coco Pops.'

'Bring it.'

Maya and Cleo seem to be in a deep slumber so Grace rests her head back on the sofa, resigned to her fate. 'Excellent, when you're ready Mum's made a bed for you upstairs. Can you bring me down some pillows?'

'Of course. Can I ask you a favour too?'

'Sure.'

'There was a letter that Will wrote to me. Dad said Lucy sent it to everyone. Did you have a copy?'

'I do.'

'Can I read it?' I ask.

'It's a good letter,' replies Grace. 'Good penmanship. I'll warn you though, he may have also spoken about the kiss.'

'Oh.'

'Everyone's been quiet about it to your face but in a group chat, Mum said next time he was here she was going to piss in his tea.'

'Like drop her pants in the kitchen and pee in a mug?'

'I didn't question the mechanics of how she was going to do it,' she says, laughing. 'I'll forward the screen shot, or do you want me to add you to the group?'

'There's a family group chatting about my relationship?'

'Yeah?' she says calmly. We once had a group chat because Meg's kids had nits and gave them all to us one Christmas. We shared scalp pictures and compared horrors.

'Send me the screenshot. And anything from the group that's tasty.'

She salutes me in return.

'What do you think I should do, Gracie?'

She pauses for a moment. She is qualified now to comment about love, life and all its sharp turns and bends. She has lost, she has gained and her heart has experienced much more than mine. I await her words of wisdom.

'Tea. Make me tea.'

'Is that the answer to everything?'

'Yes.'

BONUS TRACK

'Love's Theme' – Barry White's Love Unlimited
Orchestra (1973)

Dear B,

*You know me well enough now to know that I don't write letters.
I write postcards and texts and Post-it notes that I leave on the
fridge telling you to buy more milk. So I must really need to tell
you something or must really bloody love you to put pen to actual
paper and tell you what's been going on in my head.*

*Firstly, I need to say sorry. I'm so unbelievably sorry. I've been
a complete arsehole. Pete tells me this every day, so does Kat but
in more subtle ways like when she stands over me checking I've
done the washing-up properly. I've run away from the best thing
that's ever happened to me. There's no other way of saying it and
that was an awful thing to do, both on your birthday and just
because it was you. My best friend. The mother of our child. I
kissed someone else and totally betrayed your trust. The lies, the
cover-up that followed were unacceptable and I totally get that.
Please believe me when I say I don't want anyone else. Only you.*

After your party, I sat on the platform at Richmond and I cried. I cried so hard that they called staff on me because they thought I was going to jump onto the tracks. I wasn't, but I got a free cup of tea out of it. I told a woman called Caroline in a hi-vis vest that I was just overwhelmed because I had a new baby and she told me this story about how her son had acid reflux and she couldn't lay him down for the first four months of his life. She hugged me. She told me to hang on in there because babies can sometimes be dicks.

The problem is, I think everything is just hanging on in there by the thinnest of threads.

Joe is amazing. I can't believe we made that. I could just look at him for days. But it's more than just the three of us now, coasting through life, winging it. Taking this job with Sam's studio was all for me. I didn't want to be some architect in a local office designing identikit boxes on housing developments. I wanted to still feel young and relevant and bring home better money, but it was all a mistake. Sam is a car crash. She rattles with the amount of pills in her and she's an awful human being. I need to figure out work. I need to think about being closer to where we are. Not getting the promotion floored me. I felt rubbish after that. Like I'd let you down for nothing.

And I'd got to the stage where all the pressures of everything got to me. It was work but it was also Jason, teasing me with how settled and how dull I'd got, it was knowing that every day I needed to come back to you and help and be part of our family. It was exhausting. And then thinking about the mortgage, money, flat. And just being a dad. God, Beth… I'm a dad. Dads are older and they know what to do in every situation. My dad did. He fixed bikes and knew how to fish and change filters. He was present. He was so on it. So I panicked. I took all that panic on myself as well because I didn't want to burden you with it. I should have just told you. You'd have understood everything because you're Beth.

And then last week. Last week was awful. I still couldn't tell you what I wanted to and then we tried to have sex and it all went so wrong. Not because of you – never think that – but because my mind was going over everything. I worry you think I'm less of a man because I've done this. And so this was in my head, this was all I could think about. How I'd failed and fucked up and didn't deserve you and those thoughts obviously travelled down to my balls. I do love you, I fucking adore you. I'd shag you any day of the week and you know that. Upside down and hanging off a wardrobe, hairy pits and everything.

I don't know what to do now. I want to graft and work through this. Hand on heart, I know I've made mistakes and I just want to do better. What we have is a bit messy and all over the place but I want to make us work. I want a future with you, by my side. I'd marry you in a heartbeat. We both know that's not a proposal, but it is something I have to say, something you need to know. Next time I ask you, I'll do it properly. I promise.

I've put a CD in here. Hopefully, the songs make sense. It was the birthday present I should have made for you. I even included Barry White's 'Love's Theme' because I'm a soppy bastard really. And it's OK if you put it back in the wrong case, because that is all you. And I love you.

All my love,
Will xx

Track Twenty-Two

'Scar Tissue' – Red Hot Chili Peppers (1999)

I don't stick around the next morning. It's still a strange feeling to wake up from an evening out stone-cold sober and ready to take on the day, so I think about what Joe and I might get up to. I might wash my hair during one of Joe's naps. Oh, the excitement. I think about what food is in the house and I realise I have Super Noodles and so I suddenly fantasise about being in my favourite hoodie and pyjama bottoms, slurping them out of my favourite orange bowl. I can watch re-runs of *Grey's Anatomy* (I do this a lot now). I'll put some laundry on. I'll mooch. I may also read Will's letter again. Lucy and Dad were right, it was an important read and maybe something I shouldn't have dismissed so quickly. I read it last night through misty eyes but it deserves to be read and considered again. He just wants to be sure he gets parenthood right. He is sorry. He loves me.

As we get home, I trundle along with Joe in his car seat and hear noises through the front door and I pause, wondering who it might be. It's either burglars or Will and I'm not sure I'm ready to take on either. I put my keys in the door hesitantly and open it.

Oh.

Of all the people it could be, I see Yasmin asleep on our sofa. She's covered in one of our posher fleece blankets, her shoes next to the sofa. A head pops out from the kitchen. Will. This is not strange. Not strange at all.

'Where have you been?' he whispers.

I could ask him the same question. But I don't. Instead I put sleeping Joe down next to our coffee table and Will pulls me into the bedroom.

'What on earth is going on?' I ask.

'Why isn't your phone on?'

'It ran out of battery.' This is my default thing. I always carry about twenty-five per cent on a good day and then am surprised when it dies on me. 'Why is Yasmin King asleep on our sofa?' I ask. 'Why are you here?'

There's also a part of me that wants to tell him I read the letter. I loved the letter.

'I needed to see you yesterday. It was our nine-year anniversary, did you know that?' he replies.

I shake my head.

'Facebook told me. Some picture of that gig came up. And it kinda broke me. So I came round with an Indian at around nine-ish and instead of you being here, there was a model sitting outside our flat.'

'Yasmin.'

He nods, concerned.

'I lied and said you were away for the night with your sisters and invited her in. I think she must have thought I was a right pig too. I bought quite a lot of food for just one person. She ate all my tarka dhal.'

'She would. She's into lentils.'

I poke my head around the door. She's lying there in one of Will's old sweatshirts and leggings, her expression strained even in sleep. I guess I should be worried that my boyfriend was home alone with a model but strangely that doesn't enter my brain. I plug my phone in to charge in our bedroom and my WhatsApp notifications ping like a fruit machine.

'And she told me everything,' he carries on. 'About that Harry bloke, her pregnancy, how he's not leaving his wife. How her fella has thrown her out and won't let her see their dog and yeah…'

I nod. 'She does this now. She comes round, we hang out. Do you know why she was crying?'

A voice suddenly trails in from the doorway, where Yasmin's resting a sleepy Joe on her hip. The little man's eyes light up to see his dad.

'Harry's tried to pay me off. He booked an appointment in some fancy clinic for me to get rid of our baby.'

Yasmin hands Joe over to Will and he nestles into his father's chest, as he hugs him tightly. I watch them for a moment, together. 'You two should talk,' says Will. 'I'll get Joe changed.'

I nod and lead Yasmin back to the sofa where she was sleeping, urging her to take a seat while I take my shoes off.

'Yasmin, that's bloody awful. How?' I say.

'He came round with a cheque,' she says, the tears welling up in her eyes. I lean over to the coffee table and pass her a tissue, shaking my head in disgust.

'We fought. I threw him out. I was scared so I came here. I'm sorry.'

'Don't be. I'm glad Will was here.'

'He's really nice. He's a bit of a closet feminist, eh?'

'How so?'

'He told me it was my body, my choice.'

He's always been like that, a liberal, an advocate for choice and kinder politics.

'He was sweet, we spoke for a long time and I drank lots of your tea. I think he talked me off the ledge.'

I realise how very fragile she is. I am glad Will was here and decent enough to catch her.

'Will can be good like that. I'm glad he was here for you.'

It pains me to say it out loud when he's not done the same for me but I don't want to shatter her illusions of men completely. We hear Joe giggling next door.

'Is he a good dad?'

I pause. 'He has his moments.'

'He's really cute, you know?'

'Joe or Will?'

She laughs. 'Joe, of course. How do you make the whole mum thing look so easy?'

As is the way with Yasmin, it's difficult to know if she's being sarcastic or not.

'Are you joking?' I ask her.

'No. You have a good thing here. It's cosy, the three of you together.'

I stare back at her, wondering what it is she sees here. She's never once mentioned my dodgy carpet or the fact that when she is here hanging out with me, I mainly wear men's trackies. She sees some other picture, some perfect little family. I don't have the heart to tell her otherwise.

'Do you think I could do it?' she asks me.

'Motherhood? On your own?'

She nods.

Girl, you'd have to eat something.

'My sister recently adopted two little girls. She's planning on raising them on her own. Well, not in a complete bubble. Do you remember Grace?'

'Vaguely? You Callaghans all merged into one for me. Did she get dumped too?'

I pause. 'Her husband died of cancer.'

She looks alarmed, dropping the spikiness of her tone. 'Shit.'

'Babies... all of this is pretty relentless. I change a lot of nappies. It's the hardest thing I've done in my life for no other reason than it's not just me anymore. I have a Joe.' I could barely take care of my own needs most days, it was miracle to ask me to do that for another person. 'Look, I won't tell you what to do but if you have this baby then find friends, family... people to support you?'

She looks at me, pensive, like she wants me to fill that role. I'm hesitant. I'm not sure what to tell her. I'm not sure what we have in common. She puts her hand to her belly. We do have that, I guess. Maybe this starts with more tea.

'I'm making myself a brew. You want one?' I say, getting up.

She nods and I head to the kitchen. Inside, leftover takeaway boxes litter the worktops. There's a trail of raita. Will remembered raita – and from the looks of it, my onion bhajis, despite the fact I'd destroy a tray of them and then complain about them repeating on me afterwards.

And Will came back. With an Indian meal. To apologise? Or as some sort of romantic gesture? But he's now here, with our baby. And yet I don't know what to think about that.

I want to lie on our bed in the room next door with him. Just that. I don't want to be naked. I want to tell him Grace is back. I have new nieces with matching bob haircuts. Emma's life is still complicated. Joe has teeth. But I don't know how to pretend the last few months didn't happen.

'Will, did you want tea?' I shout.

There's no reply. I hear the front door shut firmly and pop my head around the door again. Inside the living room, Joe sits next to Yasmin, looking a tad confused.

'Where did Will go?'

'He kinda left?' Yasmin replies.

How has he vanished? Again? I head into the bedroom and look around, sifting through some more drawers and wardrobes to see if he took any more things. His passport is still in the drawer of my dressing table so he didn't come here on some ruse to feed me takeaway and then flee the country. I suddenly see my phone nestled in the duvet and pick it up. Wasn't that charging?

Urgh, so hungover. But mega night. I'll stand by what I said. I'd snog you any day of the week. Love you xxx

Oh God. Oh no. Oh shitballs. I run out of the bedroom.

'Look after Joe for a minute. Will forgot something,' I mutter.

I don't have any shoes on. Or have keys. But Will needs to know. Crap, it's freezing fucking cold and icy earth bites at the soles of my feet. I run up and down our communal drive manically, trying to decide which way to go. He could have gone in five different directions. How are they so good at running after people in films?

It was just a kiss. Not even a kiss. Like a peck. It's Sean. He knows Sean. He's got drunk with Sean. We mock him because his dad cuts his hair and he supports West Ham. Why am I so worryingly breathless? Why does the ground feel like I'm walking on pins? This was a mistake. It was all a mistake. Why does Will keep doing this? It's like we're magnets, the forces which draw us together keep holding us back too. And for a moment, I just stand here. How is this fair?

'Beth?' Yasmin suddenly appears with Joe wrapped in a blanket, a pair of slipper boots in her hand.

'Put these on. Are you OK?'

I can't seem to answer her. *I think Will's left again.*

'Was he angry when he left?' I ask. 'Did he have a bag with him?'

She studies the desperate, panicked expression on my face.

'He looked sad, maybe. He was crying. Muttered something about being replaced?'

My breathing becomes shallow and I rub at my forehead. He's not angry. He thinks I've just moved on, with Sean. That he has become some sort of disposable father figure.

'Are you alright?' she asks me.

'He's gone again…'

'Will? You told me he went to Baku?'

I did. It was such an awful lie. I couldn't even tell you where Baku is on a map.

'He's not been in Baku. He's been in Battersea, living with his brother. We're going through something. I can't quite explain it. He kissed someone, I kissed someone. We're both getting to grips with life and Joe and we just can't seem to make our lives slot together.'

The words pour out of me, double time. Is that pity or shock in her eyes? Please, be kind. Say something.

'I went to Baku on a shoot once. I had to pose with a goat,' she says.

I laugh in surprise but she can already see the tears collecting in the creases of my eyes. Joe looks up at her. *We're leading with that?*

'Can I tell you about it? Maybe then you can tell me about Will. Over some tea? I'll get some food in.'

I nod. 'Was it a big goat?'

'No. But he was an angry bastard. And you thought I was a diva.'

I try to summon up a smile. She stands there looking so natural with Joe. He shuttles looks between the two of us. Real mum, fake mum. In some strange world, this would be an awesome eighties sitcom. We could all live together and share trainers. She puts a hand to my back, Joe in her other arm, and draws me into her shoulder. Was that a hug? Let's walk back to the flat. I'll tell you about Will. Every sad last detail. You can tell me about that goat too.

Track Twenty-Three

'Please, Please, Please Let Me Get What I Want' –
The Smiths (1984)

'THEY HAVE FUCKING LEBKUCHEN!' Lucy shouts out in excitement. Only Lucy would get that excited about an iced German cake, but then only Lucy would swear in a crowded forecourt in front of children. A woman tuts and Emma looks across, apologetic, rolling her eyes.

'GRACIE, YOU LOVE THIS SHIT!'

I look over and Grace studies her phone intently. I tap her on the shoulder and she nods, confused. Christmas will be all the more special this year because she's here, but it means she has to participate in the great British Christmas shopping frenzy. Presently, we stand in the middle of a high street that they've tried to turn into a cosy European winter market. Except it's not. It's all fake lederhosen and garden sheds decorated with cheap tinsel. Hangry people queue for fragrant hog roasts with a side of Diet Coke, and there's a stall with a man selling phone covers and Tibetan-style coats and rugs.

'Stop checking your phone,' I tell Grace.

'I shouldn't be here.' She stares at her screen, terrified, almost waiting for emergency calls about her girls. I notice that her screen-saver is still a picture of Tom that makes my heart hurt.

'No, I shouldn't be here.' I point to Joe swaddled into me while I drink mulled wine over his head like any responsible parent would be. She looks over at him and strokes his cheek, puts a head to my shoulder and exhales loudly. She wears the same fatigue as I do, but differently. Hers is physical – I think the girls are still a touch unsettled so she sleeps with them, sometimes on the sofa, sometimes on the floor with them wrapped around her, triggering her sciatica.

My fatigue is emotional. Will still keeps his distance, guessing from that one text that Sean and I are now an item. When I got back in from trying to chase him through the streets, I sobbed on Yasmin's shoulder and then I texted Will to let him know the truth. I was clear and explained that Sean and I were not a thing. For him to have even presumed that was borderline insulting. Will didn't reply. He didn't get it. I ache with how ridiculous this is all starting to feel. Grace hears a phone ring and gets hers out again to double-check.

'Gracie, Mum will know what to do if there's a problem,' I tell her.

'I just can't relax. Ems, is it like this all the time now? Is this what motherhood is about? Just a constant state of worry?' she asks.

'Yes,' Emma replies, as she watches Lucy buy her girls marshmallows on sticks without her say-so, 'a never-ending circle of self-doubt and paralytic fear that something's going to happen to them… But fun bits in between. You wait until the hormones kick in.'

Everyone's experience of parenthood is just one big cautionary tale. Lucy returns to the table stuffing her face full of cake and offering it to us. Emma recoils in horror at having to share something covered in Lucy's spittle.

'We all came out of the same vagina, dear sister,' Lucy announces, putting on a wise scholarly accent.

'Charming,' says Emma.

But Grace doesn't refuse. Lucy's right, Gracie does love lebkuchen and one of my favourite memories is when I found both of them under our dining room table one Christmas scoffing a whole box my mother had put aside for an elderly aunt. She stuffs one into her face and gets out a list on her phone. I smile. I miss Gracie's lists.

'So I need to find this Baby Annabell thing for Cleo, she saw the commercial and her eyes lit up.'

Emma salutes. She looks like she's been through the doll adventure before.

'And what do you girls want? Seriously? I have nothing for you,' Grace says.

I shrug. I'm still bagging on getting my Premier Inn night away.

'We got new nieces this year, we don't need anything,' Emma says.

'I mean I could do with a NutriBullet,' Lucy says. Emma elbows her for giving Grace more gift stress. 'Or a gift card I suppose.'

Do I need another gift card? Probably not. They're tainted to me now.

Grace types away furiously on her keyboard. 'And Violet, Iris?'

'Pyjamas. Any. They grow like grass so buy big.'

Lucy rolls her eyes. 'Or if you want them to be excited on Christmas day and not think you're boring, they also go shit crazy for glitter gel pens.'

Violet's eyes light up when she hears that and she bundles herself into Lucy's arms. 'Aunty Lucy, when can we have our surprise too?' she asks.

Emma looks at Lucy suspiciously. The marshmallows were more than enough in her eyes.

'I may have booked us into the grotto over the way in ten minutes.'

'But Luce – shopping. I have to get back to the girls,' Grace says.

'Come on, for the little ones? Joe's never met Santa. He won't know who he is, how will he know to add him to his list?' Lucy replies, dramatically.

Violet looks horrified at the thought. 'Please, Aunty Gracie?'

Grace looks as thrilled as I do but nods reluctantly.

Lucy points over to the shopping centre and we start weaving our way around people armed with bags like it's a competition to see who can fit as many as they can in one hand, they march and queue, and I see a grown man who looks like he's sobbing outside a GAP. Inside the shopping centre, it's all Christmas themed and every conceivable spare space is lined with a bauble or fairy light. It'd be magical were it not for the kid in front of me on the floor throwing some sort of tantrum. A father scoops him up and fireman lifts him out of there. *I'm going to ring Santa when I get home and tell him what a little twat you've been.* Grace and I look at each other in horror.

'MISS C!' I swing my head around. A group of youths approach Emma, Grace and me.

I have no idea what passes for fashion these days but they're in a selection of trackpants, leggings and puffa coats accessorised with chains, AirPods and bum bags worn on their shoulders. I smile broadly. 'Harvey, Imogen…' There's a whole gaggle of them so I don't introduce them, but Emma and Grace look terrified. Imogen and Harvey still look to be an item with the way her hand seems to be wrapped around his waist and I'm glad they've upgraded their dates to the local shopping centre – it's a step up from the school toilets. I really hope these two are behaving themselves.

'Oh my days, that baby is still like the cutest. Lads, it's the Special K baby, innit? This is the baby. We saw him in that video too. That's so mental,' Imogen announces to the crowd.

Some of the children in the group who haven't met Joe before are falling about in shock, snapping their fingers in response to the information. As if on cue, the little man's eyes spring open. Some of the kids clap.

'These are my sisters, Emma and Grace – and these are some of my kids from school. Christmas shopping, are we? I like milk chocolate, no candles or crappy signs saying, "World's Best Teacher", please.'

They all laugh. It comes as a surprise to my sisters, who've not seen me in a classroom before. I guess to the outside world, a group of fourteen-year-olds has become something to fear, some loud brazen, attention-seeking group of know-it-alls out to cause trouble. I can vouch for this lot though. Fifteen years ago this was me too, without all the chains and with an iPod Mini and a wine-coloured velour tracksuit.

'I've got you after Christmas, Miss. I think some of us are in your class,' Harvey mentions, grinning. I nod at him. 'Can we take a selfie, Miss? Can we Snapchat you?'

'Only if you use good filters,' I joke.

Grace stands there laughing while they all gather around me, girls pouting and boys trying their best to look double hard. Joe is completely unbothered as the crowd descends upon us.

'YEAH, MISS C!' one of them shouts.

Emma holds the top of her handbag close.

'Be good, kids. Have an excellent Christmas.'

They all laugh and move on, chanting my name as they walk through the shopping centre. Grace and Beth give me strange looks.

'Miss C?' Grace mimics in their strong London tones. 'That was not the sort of teaching I thought you were doing?'

'What do you mean?'

'Look at you, Miss C with all the cool lingo, getting the teenagers to listen,' Emma says. 'Just, you know, guiding the next generation to greatness. And you were worried about being a mum.'

I digest that for a moment. The great thing about teaching is that I get to hand them back to the parents. Hell, if all I had to do was crack jokes and take selfies, the last months would have been a cinch.

We head for the super sparkly floor to the top of the centre where Lucy and the girls wait for us by some animatronic bears baking cookies to high-pitched chipmunk voices singing Christmas music. Grace looks at me in alarm while Emma laughs, almost cackling.

'Welcome to my world, girls,' Emma says, drily. 'It's not Christmas anymore. It's working how to get your kids to believe in Santa, and Christmas Eve rituals whereby I have to skip through my garden and sprinkle glittered oats on my lawn for the reindeer.'

She almost looks pleased that she has more people to now share in this trauma. Before you thought Christmas was a cute couples' activity with alcohol and *Love Actually*. Now it's this fresh hell.

'Lucy,' Emma whispers, 'their dad is taking them to Harrods in a couple of days. This might be really embarrassing.'

'No, it won't,' she says, shimmering with as much excitement as the little people. 'You just tell them that Santa has lots of representatives. It's what Mum told me for years and I believed her.' We all did, and were mercilessly teased about it at secondary school.

'Hello, welcome! I am Elfie the Elf.'

Grace tries hard to hold in her laughter. Elfie, mate… you could have chosen a better name. But I also vaguely recognise Elfie as one of Lucy's drama friends who was possibly dressed as Britney Spears at my party, confirmed when Lucy goes to hug him.

'You know Elfie!' cries Violet, in wonderment.

'We go way back,' Lucy says, pushing them in. 'What sort of shite name is Elfie?' she mutters.

'We're all called Elfie. Have fun!' he says through gritted teeth, obviously overtaken by the spirit of Christmas. I put my thumb up at him and we're led through a strange grotto of gifts and more animatronic bears, a hideously lit Christmas version of a house of horrors.

A curtain is suddenly drawn back. 'HO! HO! HO!' the voice rings through the room.

Oh dear. It's budget Santa. I see Emma shake her head at Lucy, and Grace and I try to hold in our laughter. I mean, there are enough old men in the world to try and at least hire someone of age. He looks like he's in his thirties, wearing modern framed glasses and I can see dark chest hair under his suit, and a beard that looks like it's made of an old sheepskin rug. He's also in black Nike Air Force 1 trainers. Violet, being Violet, doesn't seem to care and runs into his arms but Iris studies him intently. He's not even fat. I'm carrying more weight than shopping centre Santa. I am wondering whether it's the right choice to taint Joe with this.

'Please can I have some glitter gel pens, a Hatchimal if that's OK and maybe a cuddly Dalmatian?' says Violet.

Lucy looks over at Emma to confirm that she was right about the glitter pens but the Dalmatian seems like new information.

'And how are your reindeer? How many do you have again?'

'Eight?'

'NINE!' Emma shouts, coughing.

'Oh yes, I forget Rudolph sometimes.'

'How can you forget your own reindeer?' asks Violet.

'In the same way that Pops sometimes forgets our names,' Lucy says, glaring at him. 'Beth, Joe's turn.'

I nod, Grace helping me unbuckle him from his carrier so I can put the baby on Santa's knee. Joe sits there but turns to look up at Santa and I see his expression immediately. *Who in the holy titbags is that, Mum?* Up close, he smells like cheese and onion crisps. Grace stands there dancing, trying to get Joe's attention while Lucy tries to take a picture. He's not convinced. *I don't trust this man.* Joe's bottom lip is out. I've never seen him so scared so I grab him before he goes full wail. He wraps himself around me. *Don't ever make me do that again.*

'I don't think I want to, Mummy,' Iris says. I don't blame her, but then Lucy heads to Santa's side and urges us over.

'Come on, girls, one picture. Please. We can get it put on a mug for Mum for Christmas. Iris, could you hold Joe for five seconds?'

She loves Joe so it's no-brainer and another 'Elfie' in the room takes Lucy's phone. Lucy is brazen so goes for the lap, which takes Santa by surprise. She'd better behave herself because no one likes a Santa with a boner.

'So I hope you've all been good girls?' Santa asks jokingly.

'No, Santa, no,' Emma replies, sternly. I look over at Grace, who cackles and I smile, hoping that's the look the picture caught.

'Thank you, Santa,' Lucy says, getting up. I think he winks at her. He's very generous and gives us all a free gift that feels like crayons. I will use mine well. Joe looks at Santa again as he waves goodbye. *Nope. Get your crap beard away from me, freak.*

The next stage of this experience is gingerbread icing and we're led to a large room with folding tables, posters of snowy scenes and blow-up reindeer. It's just how I imagined the North Pole to look. We let Iris and Violet loose with all the other kids, armed with tube icing and sprinkles, and take stock for a moment to trade photos and digest what we've just seen.

'How much did you pay for this?' asks Emma, rolling her eyes.

'But look at this picture,' Lucy says. 'I know Meggsy's not in it but look how happy we all look.' We peer over her phone and she's got a leg in the air like a showgirl. She shares all the photos with us and my fingers hover over the picture of Joe looking bewildered, but still trademark cute. I forward the picture to Will. It's Christmas, after all. And this is our son. Even after all that's happened, look at this mega baby we made together. The image pops up in our

WhatsApp chat and I notice an old message featuring a lemon. Don't tear up now, Beth. Not now.

'Did Beth tell you about Yasmin King from school?' Lucy says, munching through a gingerbread snowman. 'They're besties now.'

I roll my eyes. 'We are not.'

All the sisters wait for the story to distract us from the wail of children. Yasmin ended up staying after Will left. She heard my stories about Will, I showed her the letter and a photo of Sean, and she made me tea. Proper tea with caffeine. She let me cry, held Joe and observed. I wasn't sure if it was because she cared or whether both of us had some innate understanding that we both needed each other at that moment but she stayed for another night. She ordered us rice and dumplings and she stared at Joe a lot, obviously hoping that looking into his eyes might help her locate the sense of motherhood she was desperate to find. I've since texted her to check in and she does the same, but I also text our aunt Melanie for the same reason and I don't think she'd call me a bestie.

'You know I think we all had the wrong measure of her. She may have grown up, even changed. She's actually quite lonely, and generally defensive because she doesn't know who her real friends are. I also reckon half of what we heard about her was rumour,' I say.

'Like what?' Emma asks.

'Remember the sanitary pad on the locker incident?' Everyone nods. That horrific story hung around school for years. 'That wasn't her. That was Amy Laslov who orchestrated it and pinned it on Yasmin. She also didn't sleep with Mr Baker though she says he did flash her in a store cupboard and she threw a tenon saw at him and that's why he walked for a term on crutches.'

The sisters listen intently.

'I spoke to Deena about her, my old school mate,' Grace says. 'What about the rumour that she's got some condition where she has no body hair?'

I look at Grace bizarrely. 'She has hair on her head?'

'No, I mean she's got no hair anywhere else. Like all the boys said she was as bald as a Barbie.'

'She stayed at my flat. Why would I know if she has body hair? I wasn't exactly looking.'

'Maybe she's always waxed down there?' Lucy adds.

Emma looks horrified. 'Who waxes down there at such a young age?'

'I don't even wax, I shave. And I didn't even do that until my twenties,' Grace adds.

'With the orange Bic, right?' Lucy says. 'The one that was in the bathroom on the shelf.'

'*My* orange Bic?' I say.

'I always thought that was Meg's?' Emma adds.

My sisters and I descend into giggles as we realise what we all used the orange Bic for, hoping our own dear Dad never used that thing on his face. Lucy escapes for a moment to stop Violet eating the sprinkles via spoon like cereal.

'But she's keeping that other bloke's baby?' asks Grace.

'Looks like it. His name's Harry Banstead. Complete shit.'

'And we'll assume the wife doesn't know?' Emma adds.

I shake my head. Emma looks deep in thought. Recently, she's also had to disentangle all the lies her husband told her over the years and we've seen how painful that's been for her. I pull her in for a hug.

'Secrets come out eventually,' she says. 'Just look after you, B. You've got enough going on with Will without having to take that on too.'

I shrug. She may be right. But however Yasmin conducted this affair, I still feel some sympathy for her. She's alone in all of this and I know how that feels.

'No, Jago... not like that. Come on, we have to go.' I suddenly hear a voice next to me in raised angry tones. I turn around to see another mum. Her light brown hair is pulled back from her face and she's wearing well-fitting jeans with gold Converse. She's better styled than me but I see the frustration that comes from wrangling two children alone on a shopping trip. Her baby girl cries in her buggy. I peer over to sympathise but the girl faces us and looks familiar to me. I know you. I've met you. Your name is Delilah. Oh... Noooo. Oh fuck-a-doodle-do. Her mum looks up at me and realises I've clocked who she is. I've stalked her on social media with Yasmin. Harry's wife. Standing right here. Did she hear any of that? She did. I am pretty sure she did judging by the way she's looking at me.

'You OK, B?' asks Grace, watching my reaction. How do I tell the sisters everything with the power of my eyes?

Harry's wife stuffs everything into her buggy and drags her children away, out of here. I need to explain; I need to do something. I follow her sheepishly.

'Hi... I'm sorry. This is Delilah, right?'

She looks up at me cautiously. 'Yes. Who are you?'

'I'm Beth. Delilah and Joe did a music video together. I've met Harry.'

'So I gather,' she responds sarcastically.

My face floods red with embarrassment, mainly because I was standing around gossiping about her family, her life.

'I… what you just heard there…'

She comes over to me so that she's unfeasibly close to my face, standing away from her kids. Oh my days, I'm going to have a stand-off in a low-rent Christmas grotto. 'I pretty much knew already. Thanks for the confirmation though, Beth.'

Shit. I can see tears glass her eyes and I put a hand to her arm. 'Are you OK?' I ask her.

'How far gone is Yasmin?' she whispers.

And then, just like magic from behind a curtain, Harry appears. 'They won't give us a refund but I got the photo for free at least. Scammers.'

He holds a Christmas family photo in a cardboard frame and I realise they're all matching in Fair Isle jumpers. He scans my face, trying to work out who I am; when the moment drops so does his expression.

'You're the Special K baby,' he says.

'Well, I'm not. He is.' I point a finger down to Joe. 'I'm Beth. I'm a friend of Yasmin's.'

Harry glares at me. He's aware I know about the kiss but not much else. Well, I know you didn't go to the hospital when Yasmin was scared, that you used her for sex, and dealt a million promises which you never followed through on. The power I have here is ridiculously nerve-wracking – it's life-changing – but I read Harry's wife's face. It says, *Don't say anything more. Not here, not now. My kids are here.*

'Oh yeah, Yasmin. How is she?' he asks casually.

'Pregnant. She's nearly into the second trimester so I hope the pregnancy will go more smoothly for her now,' I say calmly, looking into his wife's eyes.

She nods. Harry pauses, his neck rippling, having to swallow that information. I assume he thought the cheque paying Yasmin off to get rid of the baby would have worked. Harry's wife looks at me, her eyes still and pensive, trying to piece all of this together.

'I didn't realise you and her were friends?' he says, looking me up and down.

'Well, she's single now so I'm just helping her out. She was abandoned by the baby's father.'

Harry's complexion gets paler.

'Well, you know models. They get about, it's a wonder she knows who the father is,' he adds.

We're in a corridor pasted with bin liners and fairy lights to represent the winter night sky and at this present moment, I want to disrupt this silent night and karate kick his head with my baby attached to my front. My physical limitations curb this desire for the moment but God, what a complete and utter shitbag. Harry's wife appears to still be processing everything, and I try to make eye contact with her again. She deserves my respect in all of this, no one else.

'Well, we have a table reserved for 1 p.m. We should go.' Harry doesn't even say goodbye as he meanders off with their son, his wife lingering with the buggy. She takes a deep breath.

'Well, Beth and Joe. I hope you have a lovely Christmas. It was nice to meet you,' she says.

'Likewise.'

Her reaction is totally mellow, calm. *I will not break down here, in front of a virtual stranger.* She looks up and around this corridor we find ourselves in. 'This was really quite awful, wasn't it?'

I nod.

'This was Harry's job but he left it too late to book anywhere decent so here we are,' she says. 'Bye, Beth. If you see Yasmin, wish her a good Christmas from me too.' Then she heads off. I stand there slightly stunned, only flinching when I feel Grace's hand to my shoulder.

'Where did you go?'

I'm not really sure, if I'm honest.

'That was Harry and his wife.'

Her eyes open widely realising what must have unfolded. We, the sisters, really need to do quieter work.

'Are you OK? Was it weird? Shit…'

'I think she already knew?' I tell Grace.

'Double shit. Did she confront you?'

'No. But that was really random. Can we go now?' I ask. I'm suddenly exhausted, overwhelmed, and my mind running over whether to tell Yasmin and how.

'We might have to skedaddle anyway. Emma's complaining to the management about crap Santa and Lucy drew an icing penis on a cookie.'

The fairy lights in the corridor suddenly crackle and Grace and I bend down to take cover. Children emerge from a corridor in floods of tears, rowing over candy canes. Through a crack in a door, I see crap Santa on his break, downing a can of Red Bull and rearranging his balls. He looks at me and puts a thumb up. Really, Santa?

Track Twenty-Four

'Home Again' – Michael Kiwanuka (2012)

Christmas Day. I've been up since 2.23 a.m. I'd like to say it was because I heard Santa coming down our chimney and we had a drink and some festive chat but no, it was all Joe. He didn't even cry. He was doing his usual thing of just lying there gabbling at me, wanting a snackette of milk. I am now sitting in the living room and in the twilight, I pull up Will's letter on my phone. I do this a lot; I mull over its contents and then I stare at my phone, wondering whether to message him or not. *I love you too, Will. I didn't know how to do this either. I'm sorry.* But I don't message him. I just look at those words and think about what they mean.

I think about the mornings we used to have when we'd come back from a night out, collapse on each other, end up kissing, undress each other and have slow morning sex, with all the bloody time in the world. God, I miss him. I put my fingers over the elastic in my knickers. Now? Well, it is Christmas. I try to remember what it used to feel like, all of it. Claim ownership, remember what those bits were once used for. I slip a finger over myself thinking about all the things we were good at. He was good at waking me up by spooning me and whispering things into my ear and then using his hands to feel my breasts, to kiss the back of my neck. It's still there. I have a feeling it's still working. I think. A warm fuzzy feeling overwhelms me.

But then I hear a gurgle. Saved or denied, I can't quite work it out. I get up off the sofa in my hoodie and pyjamas and find Joe in our bedroom, eyes wide open staring at the ceiling. *Hey there, little guy. Merry Christmas.* I was unsure how to celebrate the season for him. Do I put a stocking up? I bought a fake tree but because the flat was so small, I put it flush against the wall with half the branches missing. I decorated it with tacky coloured fairy lights that hypnotise his little baby eyes. What I really want to give him is a father. I had secretly hoped that Will would be wrapped complete with a bow under my crappy tree, delivered via some Christmas miracle by Santa himself. But nothing. Just piles of gifts I mostly wrapped myself. Pyjamas, books, garish musical toy, hat, selection pack of chocolate for me. Random gifts from Paddy next door and others who've posted things on.

Am I allowed to feel angry? It's Christmas, right? He should be here despite everything. Even though the concept of days means nothing to me anymore, this one is special. This state of limbo is just heartbreaking; for me, for Joe. He sits here in my arms looking up at me in his sleepsuit with snowflakes. I'm not completely beyond getting into the spirit. But I am deeply sorry that I can't give him more.

I sit down on the floor with him and teach him how to rip paper. *You only rip this sort of paper though. Not other paper. Like I'll come home in a few weeks with coursework, definitely don't rip that.* I get to Paddy's present and open it to find a T-shirt that says *My*

Mummy Is The Best. You bloody old charmer, you. There's also a pack of custard creams and a teapot with a note saying *Tea's Up!* It makes a tear run down my face. I open up an unlabelled package too and find some books, both from Kimmie. She must have got mine then. I smile to see one dedicated to one of the coolest mums she knows. She's also given Joe a little stuffed lion toy. I log on to social media to see people from different time zones already bestowing their greetings upon the world. An old uni mate who is now living in Sydney is living the shrimp-on-the-barbie dream and another who's in Singapore seems to be seeing in the season with an all-you-can-eat buffet. I scroll through people's memes and musings and wonder whether to add in a selfie. Except Will won't be in it and I'll have to admit to the virtual world that I've failed and am alone this Christmas. Instead, I take a picture of Joe, illuminated by coloured lights and my mixed box of bargain baubles, and I post it on Instagram.

What A Cracker #JoesFirstChristmas

I kiss the top of his head gently. I then have a scroll checking my notifications:

@TheMrsBanstead started following you.

Banstead. That's Harry's wife. I click on her most recent post, which is a photo of her and her kids in front of an impressive Christmas tree, decorations all matchy-matchy to the outfits. I read the comment:

♥ 871 likes

Good news to report on no other day than Christmas Day. I've thrown @TheMrBanstead out. This is his Christmas present: this post and a nice new suitcase to put his belongings in. I hope wherever he is, he's choking on his sprouts. You see, Harry got another woman pregnant. I've known this for a while because he used to book their hotel dates on my company credit card but I was just waiting for the perfect moment to tell the world. He's a cheat but he's also a stupid cheat. I won't mention the other woman here because I am pretty sure he's lied to you too and I feel for you deeply. I could be dignified about this all but this is also the most fun I'll have all year so au revoir, Harry Banstead. Though that technically means 'until we meet again' so I guess what I really mean is 'until I see you again in my lawyer's office making sure you get none of my money'. P.S. Changing my username in a few hours #HarryChristmas #twat

I sit there slightly slack-jawed, watching the like count get higher and higher. She knew. I knew she knew. But she knows everything. From Yasmin to pregnancy to Harry being a complete and utter shit. I sit up in awe at her bravado to not speak in shame about anything; this was not her doing, this was Harry and she has destroyed him on her chosen platform. I go to Yasmin's Instagram page, where she's still doing her yoga and sharing recipes involving chicory which, I will admit, I always thought was something you added to coffee. Maybe she's not seen it yet. It is early. I hope she's alright. My phone suddenly rings.

'Shiiiiit. Did you see what the wife put on Instagram?' says Grace when I answer.

'Merry Christmas to you too.'

'Yeah, that too.'

'How do you know?'

'Hun, the moment you told us sisters and after what happened at that grotto, we've all been following that drama, I think mostly out of guilt. Nothing better than a real-life soap opera. What do you think Harry's going to do?'

I put her on speaker and then go to his Instagram page. There is nothing there but squares and squares of selfies of himself, his kids and the occasional well-made salad.

'It's a pretty searing damnation. I'd drink, a lot. Hang my head in shame over a tin of Celebrations.'

'She's sassy. She will not let him win this fight.'

'How do you know this?'

'I've done my research on her. I've been at home with the girls. I've been bored.'

'How are they? Are they enjoying their first Christmas?'

'Mum's spoiling them rotten downstairs while I get changed. They've been up since five.'

She doesn't sound tired though; she sounds like this might be the first time she gets to enjoy Christmas in the last couple of years. And I'll be there soon and we'll get to play Battleship and we can drink sherry on the big sofa until one of us passes out. That might be something to look forward to.

'You're changing the subject though. Do you think Yasmin and Harry will end up together?' Grace says.

'No, no… he was vile to her…'

'Get some gossip, that can be your present to me.'

'I got you soap.'

'Keep the soap.' I hear a little girl run into the room, singing.

'I'll see you later.'

She hangs up and I lie down on the floor. Joe rests his head on my belly which if anything makes for a good pillow. Stroking his head, I look at the lights blinking on and off and I pick up my phone.

Merry Christmas, Yasmin. Love from me and Joe. I know you're with family today but if you need us then just give us a bell x

I press send and see Joe looking up at the underside of my phone. I put it down. How do I make this more Christmassy for you? Should I sing? There is a light knock on the door. Joe and I both stare at it.

'What do you think, fella?'

It could be Santa. Hopefully, not budget Santa. Or it could be your dad. Maybe he's brought coffee. But nothing will be open so it'll have come from the petrol station machine.

I feel my heart race as I walk towards it, Joe in my arms. Maybe this is the Christmas miracle I need. I open the door.

'Hello.'

'Mrs Siddiqui.'

It's the lady from the flat upstairs. The corridors of this place are always quite chilly so over her light, patterned dress is a heavy-duty winter coat.

'I'm sorry, did I disturb you? I know it's early,' I say, apologetically.

'No, I thought you might be up. I just wanted to bring you this before you headed out for the day.'

She takes a gift out of a shopping bag.

'I saw this for your boy in the shops a long time ago and I never knew how to give it to you. I thought Christmas might be a good time.'

I stand back from her, shocked. 'That's so sweet, thank you.' I take the impeccably wrapped package.

'And I am sorry, I walk with a cane now. Up and down, up and down all night sometimes. I must make a lot of noise. I am sorry if I wake the baby?'

I smile, thinking about that banging noise we used to hear, assuming it was her voicing her complaints.

'Oh no, not at all. We're always worried we wake you? The baby crying and up all hours.'

'My love, I'm deaf. I can't hear a thing.'

We both laugh.

'Can I offer you anything? A cup of tea?'

She shakes her head but grabs a good wedge of Joe's cheeks.

'Beautiful like your mama. Can I hold him? I don't meet a lot of babies.'

I smile and nod. 'Of course you can. Come in, it's cold out there. This is Joe.'

By the time I get to Mum and Dad's, all the clan have already descended on the house and I hear a symphony of high-pitched squeals when I ring the doorbell.

'IT'S AUNTY BETH! IT'S AUNTY BETH!'

There's a clamour of tiny footsteps coming down the stairs and the fuzzy outlines of red, pink and purple in the frosted window as it opens and four little faces preened to velveteen perfection look up to greet me.

'Hello, girls! Merry Christmas! Say hello, Joe.'

The Callaghan family home has been the same house in East Sheen for the last thirty-seven years. A terraced house with giant bay windows, slap bang in the middle of one of those busy narrow streets where the need to parallel park and label your bins correctly is imperative. The house grew with the family – more daughters saw my parents knock space into the roof and out into the back. I always remember bare walls that slowly filled up with photos and prints, piles of Mum's psychology books that now exist as part of the foundations, and Dad's shabby old piano that he only uses to belt out Billy Joel covers and Christmas songs. Since we've all flown the nest and created our new homes, it's always been a place to regroup, to eat, to Christmas.

That said, Callaghan festive times have lost some meaning in recent years. Once upon a time, turkey, togetherness and tinsel (royal blue, circa 1975) was the tradition, whereas now growing families and rival in-laws mean it has become a more mixed affair, much to my mother's consternation. Two years ago, Christmas was effectively taken over by Mother breaking Emma's husband's nose and last year we lost Tom and then Grace to her travels. So now is the year where we bring some element of nostalgia and celebration back into proceedings. Callaghans, assemble. Mother has spoken; never mind Will not being here or these poor new nieces that we're going to bombard with people and mince pies. Meg and her troop have come down from the Lakes and all of Mum's girls will be in the same house. This doesn't happen very often; the world may well implode from excitement.

Now, as I get through the front door, the troop of kids that have bombarded me with hugs and kisses disperse to make way for the big guns. Mum emerges from the kitchen with oven gloves on her hands, directing the big show.

'Tess, be a love and put Aunty Beth's presents under the tree. Take that snowsuit off the boy, he'll be way too warm.'

Just through the door, Mum. Give me a moment.

Heads pop out from the kitchen to wave hello: Dad and Lucy, who unsurprisingly looks like she's already cracked into the drink. I wave my arms around at them as Meg and her husband, Danny, emerge from the lounge with glasses of what looks like Baileys. They both look different for some reason. Happier? Or are they already drunk?

'Merry Christmas, middle sister,' she says. Definitely drunk, with the way she's slurring.

'Ditto, biggest sister. Have you met the new little ones?' I ask her.

'I cried, quite openly. They now think I'm Crazy Aunt Meg.'

'We all cried.'

I see she's dying to ask me about Will but she knows now's not the time.

'Right, give me a cuddle with my only nephew.' She hands her Baileys to Dan then takes Joe from me, heading back into the lounge.

'Drink for you? Or I could put brew on?' Danny asks me. His tone is always broad and lacking in articles. I channel him whenever I'm monologuing Mr Rochester from *Jane Eyre* to my GSCE lot.

'Aye, will take that off your hands,' I say, stealing the Baileys from him. Hearing Polly's wails from next door, he excuses himself and I'm left standing there in the hallway alone. I take off my coat and then look up to see a set of eyes peering down at me through the banisters. I wave. It's little Cleo. I climb the stairs and go and sit next to her. I've only met her a few times since she's joined the family. Grace wanted to do things by the book and not barrage them. Cleo's English is limited but her eyes always study everything in such detail, like she's looking deep through the colour of my irises, trying to read my soul. Downstairs is a hive of noise and frenetic activity. It's safer here, eh? I've spent a lot of time here on these steps myself. It was a good place to eavesdrop, but also to slide down on my belly. Cleo pulls my palm out, runs circles in it and nods at me.

'Oh, this one. Round and round the garden, like a teddy bear…'

She smiles and laughs, poising her fingers, ready to bounce.

'One step, two step, tickle me under there.'

I pretend to collapse into giggles and her face broadens into laughter. I can't help but be won over. I don't know your whole story yet, but I know your mum and she is so going to take such amazing care of you.

'What are you two doing there?' Grace appears from the bedroom, carrying bright-eyed and adorable Maya, who looks freshly changed and napped, ready to take on the day.

'We're doing the teddy bear in the garden.'

'I did that fifty-six times this morning.'

Ah, the joyful rituals of motherhood.

Grace sits next to me and starts stroking Cleo's jet-black hair as she clings onto her new mum. 'Is it madness down there?' she asks.

'When is it not?'

She looks over at my sense of caution then puts a hand in mine. Maybe the Christmas spirit, the one in the air as opposed to the one in my glass, will buoy me. I really need it to.

'It'll all be good. Come and see the "back massager" that Mum put in Dad's stocking.'

'Do I want to?'

'I don't want to know where she got it from, but Lucy will show you how it *actually* works.'

Oh my days. It's a vibrator, isn't it? I've warned Mum about buying stuff randomly on Amazon. We stand up and Cleo puts her arms out to me to carry her. Alright then, little one. She wraps her legs around my hips and rests her head on my shoulder. It's the best present anyone could give me.

'I remember Pops got drunk after a night out once, came home and peed on our Christmas tree and Granny Fi chased him around the house and he had to hide under Aunty Beth's bed.'

Lucy has all the nieces gathered around her for the Callaghan tales of legend session. The youngest sister does have a titanic memory and a flair for vivid storytelling, digging deep into our dramas of old. The nieces all cover their mouths and Emma sits there shaking her head. Every year, they get a new story, from the time Meg tried to pierce her belly button with a stapler to when Lucy decided she wanted to live alone in her room in protest against the new washing-up rota and survived off bottled water, Kit Kats and did all her business in a bucket.

'Did he really hide under your bed?' Eve asks me.

'I think he actually slept under there in the end,' I say.

Naturally, Mum and Dad aren't here to defend themselves but are in the kitchen beavering away and arguing about oven temperatures. Meg and Danny, meanwhile, have been assigned table-laying duties. There's sixteen of us here today so it's a bumper, supersized Christmas with enough gravy to fill the Thames. I watch as they do bad dinner party maths around the table while we entertain this crew of children we seem to have acquired. Danny looks confused.

'If littl'uns are going in highchairs then what's that extra space for?' He points to Meg.

'Count again, addition was never your strong point,' Meg tells him.

I smell turkey but also quite a fair bit of bacon, as Meg accused Mum of a dry turkey a few Christmases ago and so Mum now douses the bird in fatty substance like sun cream on a baby to prove a point. I glance over at Joe in his nest of cousins, trying to work out who they all are. *It's all girls, Mum. I can't work out if that's a good thing or not.*

Our attention is soon diverted by the doorbell and Emma goes to answer it. I don't even question who it may be as the old folks have all sorts of neighbours and friends nearby. As the figure appears though, I look up and the room goes quiet.

'Uncle Will!' Eve shouts in excitement.

Emma follows, looking a bit sullen, obviously not knowing what the right call is to make. He holds bags of gifts in his hands and wears his parka, a checked red shirt (Christmassy) and his standard Converse. Grace, who is sitting on the sofa with Cleo, Maya and Violet, looks over to me, concerned. Lucy refuses to even turn around and look at him. Meg and Danny freeze, still cradling armfuls of crackers.

'Merry Christmas, everyone,' he says.

Someone needs to say something, fast, because at the moment all I can hear is my own heartbeat and the sound of Michael Bublé telling me to have a 'Holly Jolly Christmas'.

Danny goes over to shake his hand. 'Alright there, Will?'

Meg glares at him. Please, someone say something.

'Are you here to do magic then?' asks Eve.

Will bends down to her level. 'Not sure I know any magic, Eve.'

'Yeah, you do. Because when we were driving up here, Daddy said you did a disappearing act on Aunty Beth. Show me what you did.'

'EVE!' barks Danny.

Lucy can barely contain her giggles.

'But I like magic. You're rubbish at magic,' she says to her dad. He widens his eyes, ordering her over.

The Callaghan sisters all smile smugly, knowing a six-year-old just shamed him on their behalf. Extra roast potatoes for that one.

Will turns and suddenly sees Grace. 'Oh my God, you're back!'

Grace isn't so stony-hearted to not reply and stands up to give Will a warm hug, as he studies the new children on the sofa. He doesn't even ask who they are but bends down and shakes their hands, introducing himself. Cleo giggles. Violet comes over and nestles into me. A strange silence still hangs in the air like static.

'Why are you here?' I suddenly say.

He looks at me, almost hurt.

'Because I invited him,' says a voice emerging from the kitchen. Dad. 'Will, I'm glad you could make it.'

'Thanks for the invitation, David.'

Lucy stares daggers at Dad, knowing she can't unleash her trademark rapier wit as she's surrounded by little people. I look at Emma and Meg, their faces both reading concern. My mother suddenly enters, still wearing oven gloves. That's not a happy face.

'Oh. It's you. Is that why everyone went so quiet? What are you doing here?'

Will stands there, rubbing his forehead awkwardly. So Mum wasn't expecting him either? You're a brave man, Dad. You didn't consult the chef? I scan over the table. Is that why there was also an extra place set out?

'Fiona, I invited him.'

'Why?' she enquires.

'Look, if it's weird. I don't want to cause a stressful situation. I can leave,' Will says.

'No, stay,' Dad replies, calmly.

'Did you think about Beth in all of this?' Meg says.

Mum, for once, agrees with Meg and folds her arms, which is no mean feat in her oven gloves.

'Well, I was actually thinking of Joe.'

Joe looks up at everyone. *I was fine, Pops. I was just nibbling away at the edge of this tissue box.* The whole room goes silent; even the Christmas music has clicked off.

'It was actually Joe who told me to get both Will and Beth in the same room to see if they could try and work things out.'

'Joe told you…? Have you been drinking, David?' my mother exclaims.

'Hand on heart, that's what Joe told me to do.'

All the nieces giggle.

'You see, Joe told me about two people he cares about, the most important people in his life, stuck in some first-year-of-parenting rut. He wanted them to see that despite falling out of love with life, with themselves, he didn't think they'd fallen out of love with each other.'

That's the thing about Dad, he can come out with things occasionally which are undeniably super cute, that radiate with such heart that it makes it impossible for us to get angry with him. Joe looks up at all of us, wondering when it went quiet. And why Meg might be crying.

'You really are a bloody idiot, David,' my mother whispers.

His face is all ruddy and blushed. He probably has been drinking – Pernod would be my bet – but his words spill into this Christmas air with such clarity.

'And to be fair, it's getting quite boring you two not getting your acts together. Sort it out.'

Will blushes. Dad might just be right. We're stuck this side of a wall, and we need to get over the other side, wherever that is.

'So, Will. I'd like you to stay for turkey. I'd like you to talk to my daughter and spend time with your son and us. If you want to, of course...'

Will nods. 'I'd like that a lot.'

Will then digs into a gift bag and pulls out a box. Oh no. No no no. Not here, not now. Emma looks absolutely horrified at the cheesiness of it all. *Don't do that here.* I open the box. Meg exhales with relief. Inside is a small keyring with a lemon on the end. Lemons. A tear slides down my face. No one else gets it. No one else would.

'Did Uncle Will buy that because he's been a complete and utter lemon?' asks little Violet.

'Yes,' says Lucy. 'But really they've both been lemons. Biggest lemons I know.'

Track Twenty-Five

'I See You Baby' – Groove Armada (1999)

We leave my parents' house that night at nine. All the nieces were starting to tire and as is the way with Meg and Mum, the tension was starting to build after a competitive game of charades where they fought over the appropriate way to act out the Tube station Angel. *I've got one right in front of us on my bloody Christmas tree, Meg, and there you are flapping your arms around. Of course I'm going to think you're a bird.*

It was a day littered with gifts, hugs, laughs, chocolate coins – and Will was there. It was a strange day because there was no peace, no time to sit down and really talk things out. Instead, my family bombed him with distractions and food and noise. Mum, naturally, ignored him and made him sit at the kids' end of the table. Lucy made it clear to him that he'd have to pay some sort of penance for the kiss at least. But there was a lovely moment too where we were all opening presents and I found out my lot had all chipped in some money to get me some new flooring for my flat. The card read PLEASE GET RID OF YOUR CRAP CARPET. And I cried. I mean, I was pretty tired at that point but it really was the best thing they could have given me. Lucy also got me a three-month free trial at my local gym. *But it's a free trial?* Emma asked. *You got it for free. How is that a gift?* And we all laughed. Especially when we found out that Lucy had got Emma the very same thing.

It's always bone-shatteringly exhausting coming home at the end of a day of celebration, especially a Callaghan Christmas, so it's strange that this is now our moment of quiet to finally talk: sitting in the car stuck in some bizarre roadworks that have appeared on the A316. We're too tired to say much, too shocked to go over what's happening here. I stare over at Will in the passenger seat. He slips his fingers over mine on the gearstick.

'Do you think your mum will ever forgive me?' Will asks.

'Well, you're not Emma's Simon. And she's always disliked Danny for taking Meg away, so there's hope.'

'She made me a cup of tea.'

Did it smell of wee? I'll keep that to myself. There's a pause as I negotiate a roundabout.

'I feel like there's so much to tell you,' I tell him.

'Grace is back. That's amazing.'

'That too, but also I want to ask you about work. And I want to explain that kiss with Sean.'

'There's no need. Sean rang me up to explain. He wanted to meet up for a drink and apologise. He was really good actually. He bollocked me for doing what I did. No one had really done that yet. No one had taken me to task on it and I deserved that. I know I was a hypocrite about Sean but I panicked. You were such good friends. I seriously thought I'd lost you for a minute, for good. I'm sorry, B.'

'Yeah, you kind of were… Sean did that?'

'He's a better mate than you'll ever know. I'm sorry I thought there was something going on there. I guess I had such a low opinion of myself, I thought maybe you'd chosen to be with someone better.'

'Never even crossed my mind. All I ever wanted was just the band back together again.'

That much was true. The car stops and we appear to be gridlocked on this bloody road. Who puts five-way temporary traffic lights on during Christmas?

'I now realise I just dug a bigger and bigger hole for myself the longer I left not coming back. I just assumed you'd be angry, that you wouldn't want me around.'

'There were times when I didn't. I told you to leave when…'

'My knob wouldn't work?'

'Well, yeah…'

We both smile. We tried to cement us back together with awkward sex. It was a mistake all round.

'That time I was hurt, I felt completely rejected. But I did need you around. I needed you here to help me with Joe. No matter how you were feeling, we needed to work out our problems together, as a family.'

'I was selfish. I get that now. After Sean's rant, your dad told me that much. He was the only one from your side who rang me to have a chat.'

'What did he say?' I enquire, curiously.

'He called me a chuffing idiot and that I'm missing out on the best thing, a family, a life with you. He called you his favourite daughter.'

'He says that about all of us...' But my heart glows to think of Dad behind the scenes, the quiet director of this crazy multi-act play, gifting us all with his love and wisdom.

'I think he also wanted a big Christmas reunion to wind up your mother.' I laugh. He looks at me intently. 'I missed you so, so much. I just didn't know how to communicate any of it. I was rehearsing big, romantic speeches to photos of you on my phone before I went to bed. Kat found me one night and told Pete he needed to call a doctor. But still, I didn't do anything and I'll always be sorry for that. I'll always regret giving you months of pain. For letting you and Joe down.'

We glance at each for a moment. The apology, the clarity of thought from him is a start but this isn't over. He has many nappies to change as penance.

'I quit my job. I start at some new set-up in Clapham after the New Year. No more standing desks and commutes.'

'Is that what you want?' I ask, knowing I never wanted us to interfere with his love for his career.

'No more ego-driven, unpredictable Sam and her ridiculous demands so it's the right decision for now. I'll have to start wearing chinos but it saves my sanity, brings me closer to you guys.'

'Chinos will work if you wear them with a monocle.'

He laughs and just to hear that noise makes me sit back, relieved. Will fiddles with the stereo. He plays the CD in there and starts to smile as Liam Gallagher's voice booms out.

'You did listen to it then.'

'Maybe. I put it on occasionally. "Songbird" is a bad choice though. I'd have gone with "She's Electric" or "Champagne Supernova".'

'I like the lyrics of "Songbird" more.'

'But I have a family full of eccentrics. It makes perfect sense. If you're going with "Songbird" then you go Fleetwood Mac. But then "Landslide"... You also put in "Shallow".'

When *A Star is Born* first came out, we watched it together at the cinema and sobbed. We then came home and drank in the characters' honour, learning the parts of that duet and singing it (badly) while we heated up oven chips, still crying and raving about what a revelation Lady Gaga was. I can tell we're both thinking back to that memory. I hear our clutch making weird squeaky sounds and Will mumbles away at lyrics. He never gets them quite right but it's part of his charm.

'I read your letter too,' I tell him. 'Thank you.'

'I couldn't think what else to do to win you back. I wanted you to know I was serious about everything.'

'The sisters liked the penmanship.'

He turns his head, sharply. 'Everyone read the letter?'

I nod. To be fair, that is probably all the punishment he deserves.

'You wrote something... about becoming a dad? Being a good dad. I got that, I felt that.' He looks worried that this is me commenting on the quality of his fatherhood skills. I go on, 'What I mean is I haven't got the hang of this parenthood thing either... I've got a new body, a new role in life, a new human. I want to love it all so much, but nothing is immediate, nothing is perfect. The flaws, the things we get wrong, the mistakes we make...they're all part of the process – and Joe needs to see that. I'd rather he sees us as two people trying our bloody best, but not always getting it right. And most of all, he needs to see us doing it together.'

Will nods, looking out into the glowing red brake lights that line the road for what seems like miles. Nine years together and they've been the best ones of my life but as the adventure moves on, the challenges have changed, we need each other more than ever.

'Don't walk out like that on me ever again, or next time I won't let you back in,' I say in serious tones.

'Noted.'

'And thank you for not asking me to marry you in my parents' front room too.'

'Did I scare you for a moment?' he asks.

'Maybe. Did you see Mum's face?'

We both laugh.

'I don't want to marry you, Will.'

He looks over. Even though we've already discussed this, I can't tell if he's crestfallen or relieved.

'I like us. I want to work at us and that's all. I have no idea what that is supposed to look like. But it's not a white wedding and being married… and it's not as anything else. And I think that's OK. Does that make any sense at all?'

He nods. 'Just you and me and Joe.'

'Just hanging out forever?'

'I can do that.'

You'd better. The song changes on the CD and skips a little. It's the car, it does this occasionally. It also has a tendency to stall and the windows fog up far too much. I see Will trying to catch my eye from the passenger seat, trying to work out it if I've forgiven him or not.

'I missed this,' he says.

'This?'

He nods. I know exactly what he means.

'Can I kiss you, Beth?'

I reply by leaning over and initiating the act myself. There is a flash of light as our lips meet. Then a car beeps its horn. We smile, our faces millimetres away from each other. The lights have changed colour, the traffic is moving again. They can wait.

By the time we get in and through the door, Joe has passed out and we enter our building to find a face sitting outside our front door, having a drink with Paddy. Yasmin. I have a feeling that Paddy might be drunk – I know he's spent the day with his sons, enjoying Christmas and plenty of whisky. They both sit on camping chairs, laughing hysterically.

'Hello?' I say.

'Oh my God, Beth. I'm moving in with Paddy. I'm having my baby with him!'

Paddy does his best not to blush. 'Can you imagine? I'll call my sons and tell them I'm moving in with a supermodel who's a fraction of my age.'

'And he thinks I'm a supermodel, so I love him even more now.'

They continue to laugh while Will and I look on, confused. Paddy suddenly realises what's happening and points at Will.

'You're back!'

'I am,' says Will.

Yasmin looks at me, her eyes sparkling. She's never doubted that this would be the case. I guess in comparison to her own woes, she felt this was just two people ironing out creases, as opposed to the red sock in the ruined white-wash mess that was her own life. Plus, she always saw our threesome through other eyes, like it was something she coveted.

'Good to have you back on the block, young man,' Paddy replies. He comes over and gives Will a forceful hug, ending with patting him quite hard on the back. They disappear into our flats to retrieve glasses and such so we can partake in this mini Christmas piss-up in the corridor.

'You're here?' I ask Yasmin.

'I actually came with presents. I got something for my "fake son" and also for you as a thank you for everything. You sent me a text this morning. I should have replied.' She hands over a gift bag.

'And you're OK? You've seen the wife's Insta post?' I ask.

'It wasn't what I thought I'd be waking up to on Christmas day, but it certainly led to an epiphany. I've been waiting a whole year for him to leave her. And all that time, it wasn't just me. There were other people involved. He's done poorly by us all and that's not the sort of man I want fathering my child.'

'I met his wife the other day, locally and quite by chance. I may have pushed that along…'

'Geez, for a quiet one in school, you're quite some social butterfly now.'

I shrug jokingly.

'I'm moving back with my parents for a bit, but yeah, I'm going to have a baby. And none of my mates have babies so you're kind of stuck with me now.'

We make an unlikely pair. I'm about a foot shorter than her and I feel a foot wider but hell, let's see if this works. Though if she does one of those naked pregnant photo shoots where it looks like she's swallowed a basketball then the deal is off.

'Your present is inside. It's a tub of Tangfastics,' I say. 'It was that or a parenting manual.'

'They come with manuals?'

'Apparently. I didn't read a single one. You can also just wing it and they still come out half normal.'

We glance over at Joe, hoping he didn't hear that in his sleep. Paddy emerges with some more mugs and Will with a wireless speaker blasting out some Dean Martin, doing that clicky finger move that anyone does when swing music starts playing.

'Would the lady like a dance?' Paddy asks Yasmin. As she's so tall, Yasmin gives Paddy an underarm twirl like she's taking the lead. Joe's eyes spring open and Will unbuckles him from his car seat and picks him up. We prop him up between us and he wipes a drooly hand on Will's cheek. I'm not sure either of us expected we'd be ending our first Christmas like this but here we are, huddling in our corridor, swaying gently to keep us warm.

'I had a thought over lunch. Do you think you could batter a Christmas pudding?' Will says suddenly.

'And deep fry it?'

'Well, yeah?'

'*This* was all you thought about at my parents' house?'

'I also thought about how many times I've seen you in that maxi dress now and I've not even seen you that much in the last few months.'

'Says he, king of the checked shirt.'

'I'll give you that. Are those trainers new?'

'Courtesy of my bezzie mate.' I look over at Yasmin. In all of this, she also provided distraction, companionship, some way to perceive everything differently.

'Is she OK?'

'I think so.'

Will twirls Joe around a few times and he giggles and kicks his legs in the air.

'We should get a picture of us. Of our first Christmas together,' Will suggests.

'Here?'

'Good a place as any?'

He whips out his phone, pulling a surprised face which makes Joe and I laugh, and he snaps the picture. He shows it to me. I look drunk, all teeth. Old shoes and a buggy are in the background against the peeling paint on the walls and the holly wreath that Paddy hangs on his door. Errant hairs sprout out from my hairline and I think that might be a bogey stuck up one of Will's nostrils.

'That's awful,' I say. 'Delete.'

'Never,' he says, kissing me on the forehead. 'It's perfect.'

Epilogue

Six months later

'Hey Joe' – The Jimi Hendrix Experience (1967)

Motherhood. So everyone tells you to buy a crap load of muslins, how your boobs grow to the shape of generous honeydews, the teething, the nappy rash, the wind, but they never tell you about other mothers. Christ alive, they are bloody everywhere. People pop babies out like Pringles and you know what, no one is getting it right. If anyone says they are, then they are lying to you because I will bet you that there are times when they've been standing in a dark room at three in the morning, pondering what day it is, asking whether they're the only people in the world who are awake, and questioning whether that smell is them or the baby.

Will and I are currently standing in a hospital ward, taken back to that time when I pushed Joe out. I was awful. I'm told there was a lot of next-level swearing and I had to buy chocolate for everyone on the ward by way of apology. This is not the same ward but there's everyone from the pregnants who tread the corridors clutching toiletry bags, to fresh mums who sit in beds with their bras on show, drooling into pillows, their complexions flushed, hair pulled back, wearing new pyjama bottoms that cover up all horror of paper knickers, giant sanitary wear and freshly carved C-section wounds.

'I want all the drugs, Richard. My boobs feel like they're on fucking fire.'

I don't know where that voice comes from but, Richard, give the lady what she wants. Give all these ladies everything they want. They all deserve medals, respect, lots of chocolate and to watch as much crap TV as their soon-to-be tired hearts will require. A couple toddle past trying to get a baby moving out of its cosy womb-home.

'I remember doing that,' Will says, like I may have forgotten.

'All you did was buy the Magnums.'

'And look how well they worked? That's why Joe is so sweet,' he says, squidging his cheeks.

'Or nuts.'

Will wrestles Joe in his arms. He walks now and no one warned us about this either. That suddenly, he's fleeing us in all directions, grabbing stuff, claiming his independence and freedom. He's a bloody unpredictable dynamo of a child, nothing is safe. I mean, still edible but just like a constantly moving escape artist. Will puts him down on the floor and he punches his dad in the nuts and then runs off. To where, who knows?

'She's ready now,' a midwife says, approaching us. Will scoops up Joe as we go through to the ward we need. It's visiting hours so there are many a grandparent and helium balloon in the vicinity. They all stand around Perspex cots housing tiny babies that look like well-wrapped shawarma. We get to a closed curtain and I peek my head around.

'Hey.'

Yasmin doesn't say a word. Her baby lies there in her arms and she sits there cross-legged in jersey joggers and a vest, her hair tied into a perfect plait.

'You cow. You're not supposed to look so well.'

I remember that first day in the hospital. Photos confirm that I looked hungover and extremely bloated. I go over to hug her and inspect the newborn. She has a little rosebud mouth and lashings of caramel-coloured hair.

'Oh, she's beautiful, Yas.'

'That she is,' adds Will. 'Congrats.'

Yasmin waves at Joe, who pulls a face back at her. '"Well" might be an overstatement. Underneath it all, it's a bit of a car crash.'

Will's eyes scan the room wondering if he needs to hear any more detail.

'And feeding is weird. We've had to move on to bottles. I don't know if it's the right thing. Does it feel like my milk's coming in?'

I reach over and press my hand to one of her breasts. 'It'll come. Don't worry, there's no right answer. Do whatever gives you greater peace of mind.' I pull a present out of my bag. It's muslins. I'm passing on that wisdom, at least.

She smiles. 'Thank you. And I didn't forget – I posted Joe's present before I came in here. Happy birthday, little man.'

If meeting Yasmin King again after all these years was weird and coincidental enough, she goes and has a baby induced today, of all days. Yes, one year apart, we are in possession of kids with the exact same birthday.

'Does she have a name yet?' Will asks.

'Jo.'

Will and I look at each other. I mean, we like you and everything but be original, no?

She cackles to see our faces. 'Of course it's not Jo. My last name is King. She'd be Jo King.'

This makes Will howl. Meanwhile, I'm still trying to work out how Yasmin is laughing. I sneezed post-labour and thought my bladder had fallen out.

'Posey. This is Posey.'

I like that. Goes with the cheeks, her pursed little lips and the fact that's what her mum does for a living. Yasmin looks down at her and I'm just glad she's got to this point. Harry is not in the picture, but she has family support, us and the right people who've shown up when it matters. I can't describe the next part of this journey for her but that glow in her face, the calm she exudes, tells me she's well equipped to take it all on. Will and Joe go over to inspect. That was you once, Joe.

'Posey and Joe. Do you think they'll be mates as they grow up? What if they get married?' she asks.

'Then I'm not standing next to you in the wedding photos,' I say.

A midwife enters the space.

'Oh wow! Is this big brother and Daddy?' she asks.

We all stare at each other, grinning. Who am I then? The hired help? The sister?

The friend.

'Not quite, this is my fake son,' Yasmin says to confuse matters further. She pulls a face at Joe.

'I'm his mum,' I say.

The midwife looks confused, obviously checking to see if we match. Joe wrinkles his nose at her. *No, I definitely came out of her. I was there, I should know.*

HAPPY BIRTHDAY, JOE! BIG LOVE FROM ALL OF US! EAT LOTS OF CAKE! WELL DONE, B&W, FOR GROWING A BABY FOR A WHOLE YEAR!

The excitable text message is accompanied by a ridiculous family selfie that involves Tango in a wine glass, a cat wearing streamers and long lines of emojis. Well played Meg et al. I smile at my phone and reply with a heart.

It's been a quiet day so far for one so momentous. We woke up together in bed, grateful it was a weekend, and spent a good half hour staring at and hugging Joe, wondering where this year has gone. One minute, pop, a baby had come out of me; the next, a year has flown by, filled with emotions and 365 days of doing everything and nothing. I've changed thousands of nappies, I've milked enough milk to fill several bathtubs, I've been awake all the hours, and I've spent an absurd amount of time in leisurewear and big knickers. I could slay you at daytime TV quiz shows now and also show you how well I can fall asleep, pretty much within the same breath. Will had a moment. He left us, he came back. I gained two extraordinary new nieces. Joe was slightly famous for five minutes and I hope that will make him an answer in a music trivia-based quiz one day. I still chat to Kimmie. We tell each other what to read and she sent Joe expensive designer Gucci stuff I've seen on Kardashian children for his milestone first year. We are pondering whether to flog it on eBay. My social circle these days includes the sisters (goes without saying), a model I went to school with, a pensioner who lives opposite me and a wonderful couple in Giles and Oliver, who have taught us where all the best baby-friendly brunches are. Joe gave up the modelling for a quieter life of obscurity, but Giles still tries to lure us back occasionally with tales of projectile vomit and diva babies who aren't Joe. I'm also back working again. I feel all the guilt, especially as I was rubbish at sorting childcare so am leaning on Mum and Dad, but I went back into classrooms to do my bit for the youth. Imogen and Harvey are still together. I miss Sean in the staff room but he's doing alright in Toronto revelling in the fact that you can pretty much order anything on a Canadian menu and chances are it'll come with maple-cured bacon. Another highlight is the new floor in our flat, the Callaghan clan's Christmas present to me. Engineered wood floorboards: game changer.

Will and I are not the same people we were when this year started and this is most likely down to our little person. Will is happier, less frantic about what parenthood all means, completely at ease, as if he no longer worries about fatherhood like a series of problems that need fixing. He's begun to love this. He doesn't look awful in chinos. I don't wear chinos but I am eighty per cent midi wrap/ smock dress and the other twenty per cent is still sugar, carbs and stretch marks and that suits me just fine. Two months ago, I did listen to Lucy, who said a fringe would suit me. It doesn't. I now have to wait another year to grow that fucker out.

I look over at Will now, Joe on his shoulders. This birthday is not quite over, not yet.

'Has he thrown up in my hair?' Will asks as we traverse a pelican crossing. I go on my tiptoes to inspect. Joe grabs at handfuls of Will's hair.

'I think that's just drool.'

'That is lovely, Joe.'

'Cooling on such a warm summer's day, no?' I say.

'Oh no, it's all counteracted by the very warm feeling around my neck.'

Joe doesn't care. Let's just hope his nappy doesn't leak. When we arrive at our destination, a bouncer inspects our tickets and gives us the once over. Are we cool enough to enter? I mean these two are in matching Converse hi-tops (a parenting goal realised, by the way). We're way cooler than the dad behind us in Birkenstocks, that's for sure. Yet for once, the presence of a baby and a sensible rucksack filled with breast pads is actually a pre-requisite to enter this Brixton venue. *Big Fish, Little Fish*. Yes, we opted against a round of pass-the-parcel in our flat and have brought Joe to his first rave to celebrate a whole year of being alive. Let's party properly, young man. It's a family-friendly rave, Lucy told me, and two to four hours long, as opposed to twenty-four hours. One of her mates works here. He'll be the one on stilts with the hula hoop apparently. Lucy couldn't tell me much more but I suspect there will be big Capri Sun energy and glowsticks for miles.

Will looks genuinely excited as we enter the premises. 'Do we know if they'll play the classics?' he asks. 'It has to be full on rave music. If they play "The Grease Megamix"…'

'Then we will leave,' I reassure him.

There's the sea of people that I've come to expect at gigs and club nights but the demographic has changed for sure. There are still face paints, fairy wings and foam but the ladies now also come armed with sippy bottles and jeans with a hint of stretch, and the men herd children away from sharp edges and staircases, weighed down with Bugaboos. *No more sweets. Don't hit your brother. Why have you taken off your jumper? Where is your jumper? Why is your tongue blue? Stay together. Don't run off. Who's having fun? I told you to have a wee before you left the house.*

We weave through the crowds and suddenly enter the main room. Oh my days, that bass is pleasing to the heart and I notice the large grin plastered across Will's face too. Joe, still on Will's shoulders, looks like he may be in shock. Or maybe he's confused? *Didn't you get the memo, parents? I was hoping for jelly, maybe a clown.* But we put him down on the floor. He pauses for a moment and then he starts bopping away, bending his knees at the music. He is most definitely ours. Tentatively, we join in. I guess this is a rave. There is an actual DJ in a shell suit but you have to dodge toddlers as opposed to people off their tits on drugs. It also feels bizarre not to have any alcohol in my veins. And we're not the embarrassing ones for once. There are people in tie-dye and a lady next to us in fluorescent fur boots and a cowboy hat. She has fully embraced some party persona from her youth, punching the air while her children look on, bewildered. Still. That music. My shoulders decide to join in. Will comes over and slips a hand around my waist.

'It's very loud,' he says, looking concerned for our son's ears.

'Alright, old man.' He shakes his head at me, laughing. 'There's a man making balloon swords over there if you want.'

'And a confetti machine.'

We jest but both of us are standing here dancing away, Will's fingers twitching to go full happy raver, a thin veil of sweat already covering both our faces. It's like we're home. Except we'll have to change a nappy in the breaks. I reach into my rucksack and pull out some accessories: a whistle for Will, a hat for the birthday boy. I kneel down to put it on Joe and he reaches out to hug me, small hands reaching around my neck. Don't mind if I do, young man. He smiles his big toothy grin, dons the cardboard hat without fuss then breaks into a strange dance move like he's doing the running man. I look over at Will doing the exact same thing.

How did we get here, Joe? I'll tell you how. You want to know something about this venue? Your dad and I met here. Over by that cloakroom where they're now selling slushies and sherbet. You want to know something else? We both still have the coats we were wearing that night we met. We're thrifty like that. Joe looks at me in the way that he does, like he knows everything but is just waiting for me to figure it all out. I bundle him into my arms and stand up. Hi, little baby of mine. Welcome to my world. The beat suddenly changes and an overexcited Will, with whistle in his mouth, suddenly has both arms in the air. Will knows, his eyes connect to mine. We have both danced hard to this tune. He comes bounding over as we both engage in the best jumping spaghetti arm moves this room will ever see, co-ordinated shoulders and everything. Sod the consequences to my pelvic floor.

'Mama,' Joe squeals. That word. I hold him tightly to me and inhale him.

'Happy birthday, kiddo,' I whisper into his ear, kissing him on the cheek. One whole year of Joe. Thank you for being here, for letting me be your mother. He looks up at the ceiling as the confetti rains down on us, flashes of pastel light scattered across his face, reflecting in his big brown chocolate eyes as the three of us jump in and out of time to the music. God, I love this song.

A Letter from Kristen

Dear lovely reader,

Hello again! Or maybe you're new? Either way, thank you so much for reading – you are a superstar! I really hope you enjoyed Beth's story and were able to laugh, cry and relate to all her tales of first-time motherhood. I know many will ask: do babies really poo that much? And the answer is yes. I remember those days well; the nappies, the mega voms, my boobs aching so hard I wanted to punch them, and being so tired I once fell asleep sitting on the toilet. God, I really hope it was like that for everyone else.

If you enjoyed Beth's story, you'll be glad to know that her sisters all have their own books. *Has Anyone Seen My Sex Life?* is about Meg and *Can I Give My Husband Back?* is Emma's tale so please go and spend some time with the other Callaghans. And look out for Grace and Lucy's stories coming out in the very near future. If you want to keep up to date with details of my writing, just sign up at the following link. Your email address will never be shared and you can unsubscribe at any time.

www.bookouture.com/kristen-bailey

So as you may have guessed, I am a mother and I have four little squirrels at home. Motherhood has been amazingly generous to me, so this book was always going to be a love letter to my kids and my experiences as a mum. Fact fans might like to know that this was the first book I ever tried to write, back when my eldest was a baby – he's now fourteen and has facial hair. But those memories of early motherhood – the joy, the fatigue, the despair and the complete mania that underpinned those first years – are still vivid in my mind. They changed me for life – and for the better – but they became the reason I first sat at a computer and wrote anything down. I thought those stories, those experiences were too good, too hilarious not to share. And yes, I did birth my first baby that quickly, I did swear like a marine, and I did get completely bladdered on the gas and air. The only thing missing from the prologue is the fact I bruised my husband's neck from having him in a headlock. (Sorry about that, love… but a baby was coming out of my vagina…) As much as this book is a celebration of motherhood, I hope it's also a tribute to love, sisterhood, friendship and quality music. I do recommend the chapter headings as a playlist: it's pretty kick-ass.

A note that this book was also part-written in 2020 when the world was not in the best of places. I've decided to skim over the worst parts of that year because I do believe and hope that things will get better. We will be able to go to concerts again, have Christmas with those we love, and hug the hell out of everyone we know. And a special tribute to anyone who's had a baby during this time. Motherhood is hard enough when the world isn't going to pot so to be experiencing it in the circumstances of 2020 is an ever-greater achievement. I am in awe.

I'd be thrilled to hear from any of my readers, whether it be with reviews, questions or just to say hello. If you like retweets of videos of dancing pandas then follow me on Twitter. Have a gander at Instagram, my Facebook author page and website too for updates, ramblings and to learn more about me. Like, share and follow away – it'd be much appreciated.

And if you enjoyed *Did My Love Life Shrink in the Wash?* then I would be overjoyed if you could leave me a review on either Amazon or Goodreads to let people know. It's a brilliant way to reach out to new readers. And don't just stop there, tell everyone you know, send to all on your contacts list. Especially to anyone just about to have a baby; this is more honest reading than any manual – perfect if accompanied by a jumbo pack of muslins too.

With much love and gratitude,
Kristen xx

kristenbaileywrites

kristenbaileywrites

@mrsbaileywrites

www.kristenbaileywrites.com

Acknowledgements

CHRISTINA! I really do have the most brilliant editor in the whole entire world and I owe her everything and more. This book was part written in lockdown and it was *tough* to attempt to write funny, but she drew it out of me like an editing magician. She's a cheerleader, a critic, a caregiver – and I am so grateful for her support. Behind the scenes at Bookouture, a huge thanks also to Sarah Hardy, Kim Nash, Lauren Finger, Natasha Hodgson, Kelsie Marsden and all the team, who work tirelessly behind the scenes to make my books happen.

From the very start, the theme of this book has been about the transformative effects of being a mother, so I have my kids to thank most of all. At the time of writing, they are 14, 11, 9 and 6. Naturally, they love TikTok, their father, and a triple pack of Jaffa Cakes more than me but I hope they realise they gave me the greatest gift in being their mum. Love, always.

The person who gave me the biological tools to help make the babies is the long-suffering Nick, who is *still* here, people, despite the book titles Bookouture give me, which never really cast husbands in the best light. He still makes the tea and tells me on a daily basis that I am as funny as toothache. Thank you for shouting at me for not backing up my work. Thanks for all them babies. Thanks for all the architecture references too. You work too hard.

Like the Callaghans, I also went to an all-girls' school and I believe getting out of there alive still remains one of my greatest life achievements. I want to thank Mr Kelsted for being my first ever English teacher and instilling a love of literature and writing in me. To all the lovely people I met at Tiffin Girls', many of whom I still call friends, I hope *Sapere Aude* rings in your ears, daily.

When I talk about the transformative effects of motherhood, this book also explores Beth's journey to love and respect her body after childbirth. This was difficult to write as it made me realise what a poor relationship I have with my own body image. To gain different perspectives on this, I sought out Instagrammers, music, books and TV shows. I marvelled at the number of people out there who focus on promoting the message of self-care and body positivity and who help re-define how we see beauty. Their songs, posts and activism helped this author on many different levels. So thank you for the important work you do. And thank you, Lizzo, because you're bloody marvellous. 'Juice' became this book's anthem and dancing around to it (badly) became my thing when I was writing. Thank you for reminding me that the juice ain't worth a squeeze, if the juice don't look like this.

And here's a list of names of brilliant people who provided me with answers, support, inspiration, laughs, chats and memes over writing, lockdown and beyond: Sara Hafeez, Joe Rigby, Graham Price, Drew Davies, Dan Turkington, Leanne Paul, Gabi Code, Gloria Long, Gavin Dimmock, Chris Hooley and Chris and Sarah Aggett. I also have a wonderful neighbour known as Patsy aka Paddy. He regularly flirts with me in his crazy Irish tones and tells me on a regular basis that I'm doing an amazing job with my kids. He drops that in every time I see him. He'll never know how much this means to me. Next time you see a mum, tell her just that.

Printed in Great Britain
by Amazon

'That better?' Will asks.

'I mean it'd be better if someone attached their mouth to it and drained it properly.'

'That's kinky. Are we ready for that?'

I laugh a little too loudly and Will hushes me as we hear the shuffle of feet waiting by the door. He pushes some hair away from my face as I re-adjust myself in the mirror. I smooth down the hair frizz and reapply Vaseline to my lips and the dry patch of skin that has formed on my chin like some hormonal soul patch. As I do so, Will opens the door and as joy and luck would dictate it, Sam stands there, beaming like she's had too much of the organic wine. That doesn't look suspicious, us hogging the loos together and me re-applying my lip balm. I wonder how much she may have heard of our conversation too.

'Oh.' I can't tell if she's disgusted or impressed. 'How are you both enjoying the evening?'

'It's a really lovely pub. The food is great,' I say, my face rising to an ever deeper blush.

'What did you have? she asks.

'I had the chicken,' Will mumbles.

'I had the burrata and the risotto, it was all a delight,' she replies. 'So fresh.'

I pause. Burrata is a food trend I've not caught up with in the past year. I think it's cheese. It's not a burrito. But I can't look uncultured and ask. She grabs my hand which takes me by surprise.

'It's so nice to finally meet you. I'm totally in love with your boy.'

With Joe? Oh. Will? Like literally? If she is then we need to have a fight in these loos, right now.

This is a perfect date night activity. It's what all new parents do. I can do this. I can milk my tits into a sink. I have to lean forward slightly, angling the nipple over the basin and squeeze. As is the case with my milk supply, the first squeezes are a relief and shoot out across the porcelain before they peter out into a dribble. This must sound like I have an extraordinarily unpredictable bladder to anyone outside. Will can't stop laughing.

'If you get your phone out, I will smother you with these things,' I say.

'Can I have a go?' he asks, half drunk but half trying to help me preserve some sense of dignity. I shrug. These boobs don't belong to me anymore. Have a squeeze. I place my hand over his to provide instruction.

'Like, fingers there and there and squeeze.'

A stream of milk trickles over his fingers.

He giggles. 'It's warm.'

'It's not come out of a fridge,' I tell him.

We're both in hysterics. This is the first time he's been near my breast for a while, so there's relief he's not completely fearful of them. It feels like he's dipping his toe in the waters again to check it's safe.

'You want me to milk you next?' I ask.

He raises his eyebrows at me but we both keel over laughing. I remember a time when I gave him a blowie at a concert. We're so far removed from that point. I poke at my breast, now softer to the touch and grab his hand, kissing the fingers. It's not remotely sexual in any way but it's a comfort. I wouldn't want to be milked by anyone else. I want to ask if we can just stay in this cubicle for the rest of the evening, away from the rest of the world.